unhuman

Also by Wilkie Martin
Razor
Relative Disasters

As A. C. Caplet
Hobbes's Choice Recipes

Children's books as Wilkie J. Martin
All in the Same Boat
The Lazy Rabbit

Inspector Hobbes

and the Gold Diggers

unhuman III

Wilkie Martin

The Witcherley Book Company
United Kingdom

Published in the United Kingdom
by The Witcherley Book Company

First published in paperback and ebook (Kindle, ePub)
by The Witcherley Book Company in 2014

British Library Cataloguing in Publication Data.
A catalogue record for this book is available from the British Library.

ISBN 9780957635142 (paperback)
ISBN 9780957635159 (kindle)
ISBN 9780957635180 (epub)
ISBN 9781910302071 (hardback)
ISBN 9781912348534 (large print paperback)
ISBN 9781912348046 (audio)

LIC Library Subject Headings: Character., Cotswold Hills (England)--Fiction., Cotswold
Hills (England)--Humor., Crime fiction, Crime and the press—Fiction., Crime—Fiction.,
Crime--Great Britain--Fiction., Detective and mystery fiction., Detective and mystery
stories, English--Fiction., England--Fiction., English wit and humor--21st century.,
English wit and humor--England--West Country., English wit and humor--Great
Britain., Fantastic fiction., Fantasy fiction, English., FICTION / Crime., FICTION /
Humorous., FICTION / Mystery & Detective / General., Humorous fiction., Humorous
stories., Humorous stories, English., Journalists--England--Fiction., Mystery and
detective stories--Fiction., Police--England--Cotswold Hills--Fiction., Police--England--
Gloucestershire--Fiction. Vampires—Fiction., Vampires—England-Fiction., Vampires
Humor.

'This evening,' said the newsreader, just as my head was starting to nod, 'the quiet Cotswold town of Sorenchester was rocked by an explosion and small arms fire when a gang attempted to snatch gold with an estimated value in excess of one million pounds. Jeremy Pratt reports from the scene.'

I sat up agog as the familiar buildings of The Shambles appeared on television, with Jeremy Pratt, tall, thin and solemn, standing with a microphone in his hand. He was outside Grossman's Bank, which was enwrapped in police tape. In the background a van was smoking, while a fireman coiled up a hose as thick as an anaconda.

'Good evening,' said Jeremy, smiling with maximum condescension and minimum humour. 'At nine-thirty this evening, a gang, who were armed and wearing balaclavas, made a daring raid on the armoured security van behind me, which, a spokesman has confirmed, was being used to transfer a large consignment of gold sovereigns to the vault of Grossman's Bank. I have with me Mr Percival Longfellow, the driver.'

Jeremy turned to a tubby, balding man at his side, a man who looked utterly bewildered. 'Tell me, Mr Longfellow: is it true the robbers used explosives to break into the van?'

'Eh?' said Mr Longfellow, cupping his already prominent ears in his hands.

'Did the robbers use explosives to break into the van?'

'I can't hear very well since they blew the bloody doors off.'

'I see. Was anybody injured?'

'What?'

'Did the explosion hurt anybody?' asked Jeremy, articulating every syllable.

'You need to learn not to mumble so much, mate. I'm a little deaf since the explosion. They blew the doors off, you know.'

Jeremy raised his voice. 'And then what happened?'

'You what?'

'What happened after they blew the doors off?' Jeremy shouted, red faced and exasperated.

'No. What happened was they blew the bloody doors off and stole the money.'

'Amazing,' said Jeremy, looking baffled. 'Thank you very much, Mr Longfellow.' He shoved him out of shot.

'What?'

'Anyway,' Jeremy continued, 'it would seem that, after the gang had blown the van's doors off, they threatened a guard with firearms and there are unconfirmed reports of several shots having been fired. Then, having overpowered the guard, they seized the contents of the van, which, I have been led to believe, included a substantial quantity of gold sovereigns. They loaded them into the back of a get-away vehicle and made off with their ill-gotten gains. However, it appears they were thwarted by the local police, who have arrested three members of the gang and retrieved all of the gold.

'A police spokesman has, however, confirmed that two of the gang managed to escape and that the police are now looking for a white van with a large hole in its roof.'

The picture returned to the studio. 'Thank you, Jeremy,' said the newsreader. 'We'll come back to that story as soon as further details emerge. Now, over to Penny for the latest weather forecast.'

Once I was over the initial surprise, I was disappointed that I was missing all the excitement, for, much to my amazement, I'd become something of an adrenalin junkie since coming to know Inspector Hobbes of the Sorenchester Police. Anyone spending time with him needed to adjust, and quickly, to living with high intensity excitement: and fear. It had struck me just how often I'd been terrified since our first meeting and, although sometimes I wished I'd never set eyes on his huge, ugly frame, I'd survived and come to realise I wouldn't have wished to miss any of it. Life with Hobbes in it was interesting.

As I lounged in my chair, a number of thoughts kept resurfacing in my head. The first was why would anyone be taking gold to a bank at night? The second was how did the robbers know it was going to be there? The third was that if the robbers had been inside the getaway van, then how had the police retrieved the gold and arrested three of them? It all sounded weird to me, and since that was the case, I suspected Hobbes had been on the scene.

I was frustrated I wasn't there. A case of extreme bad timing had meant that I happened to be overnighting at my parents. Trying to get a good night's sleep on their ancient camp bed – uncomfortable, unstable and creaking with every breath – had proved a colossal failure and, giving up, I'd crept back into their lounge, switched on the television and slumped into an armchair, hoping the twenty-four hour news would be showing the usual boring stuff, and that I'd soon be lulled to sleep. Instead, I ended up sitting in front of the news for another two or three hours before, getting cold and there being no further developments, I returned to bed, where I supposed I must have dozed in between long intervals of tortured wakefulness.

I'd finally dropped into a deep slumber when there was a knock on the door and Mother walked in with a mug of tea.

'Good morning,' she said in a loud, cheerful voice. 'Rise and shine!'

She meant well, so, suppressing a groan, forcing a smile, I sat up and reached for the mug, muttering my thanks.

I should have taken more care, should have remembered how unstable the camp bed was. I didn't and it collapsed in a sequence of awkward stages, propelling my head backwards, flinging my feet upwards and resulting in a wave of hot tea breaking over my face as the mug caught me a mighty wallop on the bridge of the nose. As I thrashed about in the wreckage trying to break free, my big toe struck a bookcase at my side, but I had no time to fully appreciate that particularly exquisite agony, because I'd dislodged an old-fashioned alarm clock that dropped, with a merry jingle, into my right eye socket. Groaning, one hand reaching for my toe, the other clutching my face, I curled up, believing the worst was over. A foolish mistake. A deluge of books, all of them hardbacks, rained down, heavy wooden shelves battered me, and finally everything went dark. The bookcase had crashed down, like a coffin lid.

As I lay there, stunned and in pain, I heard the muffled voice of my father: 'What on earth is the idiot doing this time?'

'He's had an accident,' said Mother.

'He is an accident.'

'It wasn't his fault, really. It was the camp bed.'

'Pah! The boy's a fool. He takes after your brother.'

'You leave Harold out of this. He can't help it.'

I was unable to move, and interesting though my parents' discussion was, I wanted air. 'Help me,' I cried.

'Help me, what?' said Father.

'Help me, please.'

'That's better.' With a grunt, he lifted the bookcase, allowing me to roll free.

'Well, what do you say?' asked Father, as I got to my feet, shedding books like a moulting dog sheds hair.

'Ouch?'

'Bah!' Turning, he walked away, shaking his head and muttering.

Mother handed me a wad of tissues to staunch my bloodied nose and fetched a cold flannel for my eye, which was already swelling. Then Father insisted that I cleared up the mess I'd made, which took a surprising time, since all the books had to be replaced in alphabetical order.

Some good came of the accident, for my nose was so stuffed with blood clots I could barely taste the breakfast kippers. I'm not keen on them at the best of times, but the blackened, chewy relics Mother favoured were appalling. As a guest at Hobbes's, where I was fed daily by Mrs Goodfellow, his housekeeper, I now recognised and appreciated excellent food and knew just how terrible a cook Mother was. I could barely believe that, once upon a time, I'd thought she wasn't too bad.

Yet it was, indirectly, her cooking that had brought me to stay with them. The previous afternoon, she'd phoned in a panic, telling me Father was ill; dying, she'd suggested. Although we'd never got on, mostly because he'd always treated me as an imbecile, I'd felt compelled to do my filial duty. Arriving after a forty minute bus ride from Sorenchester and a long walk, and fearing the worst, I'd pressed the doorbell of *Dunfillin,* their new bungalow.

I'd been astonished when Father opened the door. He was not dying, but had merely been suffering extreme indigestion after overindulging on Mother's lasagne. Since it was late, I'd had little choice other than to pass the evening with them and to spend the night. Mother was, as ever, too clingy, while Father's sarcastic streak had broadened since he'd retired from dentistry and had no one to torture. Besides, now he ate all his meals at home, his chronic dyspepsia had not improved his temper.

Despite a slight nausea, fatigue, and being well battered, I volunteered to wash up after breakfast. I should have known better. It turned out that a kipper had exploded in the microwave and it took me over an hour before I was able to chip off the last few chunks. At least it gave me time to think about the robbery, though having no more information than I'd had last night, I had no idea what had really happened.

Eventually, having finished my chores and eager for further news, I went through to the lounge, where Mother was ironing socks, while Father read the newspaper, providing a running commentary on whatsoever caught his attention. Having learned in my youth not to disturb them when they were thus engrossed, I sat down, kept quiet and fretted. I thought of ringing Mrs Goodfellow and finding out what was happening but, having bought a bus ticket, I was short of cash and feared Father's acerbic comments should I not drop a substantial donation into the tin they kept by the hall phone. I wished I had a mobile. I'd had one once, when I, Andy Caplet, had been the worst-paid reporter on the *Sorenchester and District Bugle*, the *Sad B*, as it was affectionately known, but it had perished with the rest of my belongings when my flat had burnt down. Since then, having lost my job, I'd never had the money to buy a new one, or, to be honest, much need of one.

For the next half hour or more, I struggled to keep still, forcing myself not to wriggle, scratch or sigh. Instead, I stared at the deep, brown carpets, the heavy plush furniture, and the porcelain figurines that had to be dusted twice a day. It seemed like an aeon had passed when Father went to the bathroom, leaving the paper behind. I grabbed it, flicked rapidly through and was disappointed there was nothing about the robbery. I guessed the story had broken too late. Wishing the bungalow had thicker internal walls, I tried to ignore Father's rumblings.

'Did you know there was a gold robbery in Sorenchester last night,' I asked when he returned, still doing up his trousers.

'When are you going back there?' he asked. 'The sooner the better, I say, before you demolish the bungalow.'

'Oh, no,' said Mother. 'He's no trouble, really. He's going to stay with us for a few days, aren't you, Andy? I counted four changes of clothes in his bag and I can always wash them if he needs more. It'll be no bother. He's lost weight and looks like he could do with some good home cooking.'

'That would be really nice,' I said, 'but, since Father's better, I think I really must go back today. Hobbes might require my assistance.'

'God help him if he does,' said Father.

'Sorry,' I said, trying to ignore Mother's look of disappointment, 'but I'd better get there as soon as possible.'

2

My departure was hastened by the sight of the lump Mother disinterred from the freezer, intending to warm up for our lunch. Too polite to ask what it was, convinced nothing edible should be such a mottled grey, and certain it should not have such a peculiar, rainbow sheen, I made my excuses. Grabbing my bag, saying my farewells and promising to keep in touch, I set off for Sorenchester. It was approaching midday, and I was hoping to be back in time for dinner, as Hobbes habitually called lunch. Not that I was overly concerned about being late, because I was confident Mrs Goodfellow would rustle up something delicious, should I look hungry enough, and I had a talent for looking hungry. Just as importantly, I was desperate to find out about the attempted gold robbery, straight from the Hobbes's mouth.

My first problem arose on reaching the bus stop, when an increasingly frantic search through my pockets revealed a horrible truth: I'd lost my return ticket. In desperation, I counted out all the money on me, a scanty collection of silver and copper coins, my heart sinking as I realised it totalled less than one pound. Although I could have returned to *Dunfillin* and begged, I did have a modicum of pride, and besides, the bus was approaching. As it stopped, I made up my mind. I was nothing if not decisive.

The doors opened and I stepped aboard, where the driver, a spotty young man with short, greasy hair, smirked at me as if he'd never seen anything so funny.

'How far can I get for ninety-eight pee?' I asked, clutching my change in a sweaty grasp.

With a shrug and a long-suffering sigh, he consulted a dog-eared scrap of paper. 'Ninety pence will get you to the Deerstone stop.'

'Will I be over the hill, then?'

'Looks like you're already over the hill, mate,' said the driver, displaying an irregular set of teeth with a greenish tinge.

'I mean,' I said, 'will that take me past the top of Nobby Hill?'

'That it will, mate.'

'I'll do it!' Counting out ninety pence, I dropped it into the slot and picked up my ticket.

The bus was three quarters empty, with an ingrained residue of sweat mingled with diesel fumes. I took a seat by the window, reasonably pleased, because, after Nobby Hill, which was renowned both for height and steepness, the road to Sorenchester was relatively flat and I thought it would be a moderately easy walk from there. Certainly, it was going to be a long one, fifteen miles I'd guess, but it was a nice day and I hoped to thumb a lift. Even if I couldn't, I reckoned I'd make it to Sorenchester in four hours or thereabouts.

As we chugged though town, although glad to be going home, my mind was ticking over and barely aware of anything happening in the dusty streets, until we pulled up at a stop.

'All aboard,' said the driver, as the doors opened. 'Hurry up!'

'I am hurrying,' said a woman. 'I just need a moment to put my clothes on.'

Instinctively my head turned towards a pretty young student, dressed in tight jeans and t-shirt. She was shoving a large laundry bag aboard. I settled back down, amused, but disappointed.

It wasn't long before we reached Nobby Hill, where the bus, slowing to little more than jogging pace, strained to reach the summit. Massive trees flanked the sides of the road, glowing green under a sun that was still fierce for the time of year, although here and there a dash of tawny and the reddening of rowans hinted at the changing season. A pair of puce-faced hikers toiling up the hill made me even gladder I was riding the bus. Yet, all too soon, having reached the summit, we dipped towards the Deerstone stop.

'It's the end of the road for you, mate,' said the driver, as if I was thinking of staying put.

We stopped and I disembarked, pleased I'd remembered my bag. I watched the bus drive away, took a deep breath, slung my bag over my shoulder and began walking with my thumb stuck out in the time-honoured signal. Half a dozen cars and a lorry passed by almost immediately, all of them ignoring me, and then there was nothing: absolutely nothing. After about twenty minutes, I began to wonder if hitching a lift had been a fanciful idea, although it had seemed reasonable enough on a road that was normally busy. There was nothing I could do but shrug, keep walking, and wonder what had happened to the traffic.

The sun was making the road ahead shimmer. I guessed I'd been walking for an hour with nothing passing in either direction, and home felt a weary distance away, when, at last, I heard a car's engine. A muddy green Land Rover drove towards me along a rutted side road. Hoping it was heading for Sorenchester, I stopped, waggling my hitcher's thumb and trying to look like a perfect passenger. To my delight, the Land Rover slowed down and stopped.

The driver's window opened and I stepped forward, leaning in, seeing my benefactor, a young man in a checked shirt, corduroy trousers and a baseball cap, was looking at me expectantly.

'Can I help you?' he asked.

'Where are you going?'

'Home.' He pointed along the road to Sorenchester.

'Me too,' I said, nodding. 'Can I have a lift?'

'Yes, but, I'm going home ...'

'That's fine. Just take me as far as you're going.'

'OK.' He shrugged. 'Suit yourself. Hop in.'

I hopped, shut the door and belted myself in. 'Thank you. It's very kind of you.'

'It's nothing.'

He was right. Setting off towards Sorenchester, he turned almost immediately into a dusty lane and came to a stop by the side of an old red-brick farm house.

'Home,' he said, grinning. 'I tried to tell you.'

'Thanks very much,' I said, gritting my teeth, getting out and trudging back the way we'd just come. At least it was downhill.

That was the only vehicle I laid eyes on, apart from a distant glimpse of a tractor in a field. The cylinder of hay it was carrying reminded me of a giant Swiss roll, an unfortunate analogy, as I was already starting to feel ravenous and guessed it was lunchtime. No doubt that was why the farmer had been heading home. The sun was at its zenith, sweat was sticking my shirt to my back and I had to keep moving my bag from shoulder to shoulder, aware they were starting to chafe, and, as if to distract me from that particular woe, a blister was coming up on my heel. Licking dry lips with a dry tongue, I wished I'd had the foresight to bring a drink and my thirst wasn't helped by seeing a sign to the Red Dragon Inn. I wondered how much ice-cold lager they'd let me have for eight pence. None whatsoever, I suspected. I trudged on.

The road really was remarkably empty. Nothing, besides the occasional bird, was moving, and I could almost believe I was the only human left in the world. I guessed there'd been a major accident or something that had meant the road was closed, and it now seemed a very long road, a very hot road, and one that was increasingly hard on my feet. Eventually, a most welcome downhill section took me to the tiny village of Northsorn, about half way to Sorenchester, where I beheld the Squire's Arms, a fine, old-fashioned, thatch-roofed pub, just off the road.

On reaching it, I loitered near the front door, which was wedged open, and stared longingly at the rows of beer pumps, considering my chances of begging for a drink. Unfortunately, there was a huge, shaven-headed, scowling man behind the bar. He reminded me, with his dim-witted, ugly, malevolent face, massive, thick arms and general look of belligerence, of 'Featherlight' Binks, the landlord of the Feathers in Sorenchester. He did not look the sympathetic type. Giving up on beer, I considered getting a drink from the tap in the gents' toilet but, since it was on the far side of the bar room and I'd have to walk there under the scrutiny of that scowl, I hesitated. When he glared at me, flexing his biceps, displaying an impressive red rose tattoo and giving an impression of great strength, I gave up. I'd just have to keep walking.

However, my situation wasn't quite as bad as it seemed, for the River Soren appeared out of the fields next to the Squires Arms and ran beside the road for a short distance. Coming across a flat, grassy spot beneath the shade of a fine old cedar tree, I laid down my bag, removed my shoes and socks, rolled up my chinos to my knees and plunged my feet into the stream. Although the initial shock made me gasp, it was soon blissful. I sighed, wiggling my toes as a large rainbow trout rose to inspect them before taking fright and concealing itself within a mass of streaming weeds. When my feet were sufficiently cool, I knelt on the bank, splashed my face and felt much better, despite still being desperate for a drink. Yet, the river, glinting, gleaming, gurgling and burbling, held enough drink for thousands. It was tempting, though I dithered a while, trying not to think of all the bugs it might contain and what the trout did in it. The temptation was too strong. Lying flat on my stomach, leaning over the stream, I opened my mouth and drank greedily. Though a little earthy, the river water was cool, fresh and delightful.

Gulping it down, drinking my fill, I was happy until rough hands grabbed my ankles and lifted them, plunging my head under the surface, causing water to pour up my nose, and explode into my sinuses. Panicking, in pain, desperate for air, flailing, writhing, squirming and kicking, unable to escape, I was certain I was going to drown until I was released to slide into the river. I grazed my hands on the pebbly bottom before, pushing up and kicking, I made it to the surface. Gasping for air, I floundered as the current took me.

'Help!' I screamed.

'We don't like poachers,' said the man from the pub, bending to pick up my bag and hurl it.

It hit the water in front of me and I grabbed it, clinging like the proverbial drowning man clings to a proverbial straw, and with about as much effect.

'I can't swim well!' I cried, raising my hands and sinking.

'Well, stand up, you daft bugger,' said the man. 'Then take your sodden bag and clear off.'

My feet touched bottom and I struggled to stand, finding the river was only waist-deep, though the flow was strong and the pebbles underfoot offered little grip. It was a relief to reach the bank, to drag myself ashore and to lie there panting, while my brutal assailant laughed his ugly head off. I wished Hobbes were there to sort him out.

Then, getting to my feet and drawing myself up to my full height, I turned to face him. 'Can I have my shoes back, please?'

He threw them. I nearly caught the first one. The second caught me on the ear.

'Now get lost,' he yelled, taking one giant step towards me.

Clutching my shoes and bag, I fled down the road until it felt safe to stop and catch my breath. After rubbing my ear, I sat on the verge to pull on my socks, which luckily I'd stuffed into my shoes. Then, to my surprise, I heard a car approaching. Unfortunately, it was heading in the wrong direction and was a police car that turned up the lane beside the Squire's Arms and sped into the hills.

Having put on my shoes, I stood back up and resumed my walk, leaving a trail of drips on the hot asphalt.

I could hardly believe what had just happened. Even Featherlight Binks had to be subjected to some degree of provocation before resorting to violence, and I'd noticed how he usually managed to restrain himself until he'd taken as much of a customer's money as he was likely to get before punching him or throwing him out. Besides, Featherlight had never, to my knowledge, tried to drown anyone in the river, although this might have been because the Soren was a five minute walk from the Feathers and his rage rarely lasted that long. However, according to Hobbes, he had once made an attempt at drowning a complaining customer in a pan of spicy cat stew.

I couldn't understand what I'd done to provoke the man, although I'd have been the first to admit I was not to everyone's taste. There'd been no reason for accusing me of poaching, although I had seen a trout when bathing my feet. I'd never heard of anyone poaching trout with their toes. Hobbes had once told me that he'd been fishing with bears, who'd used their paws to hook in salmon, but I had nothing in common with bears, other than that my bedroom had once been the den of a retired circus bear, called Cuddles, whose mortal remains, now stuffed, occupied the attic of 13 Blackdog Street. That was according to Hobbes; Mrs Goodfellow insisted he'd discovered it in a skip and brought it home as a curio.

Still, the dunking had cooled me, which was no bad thing as I still had a long way to trudge. All the water I'd taken in reached my bladder just as I was entering a lay by. Concealing myself behind a tree, I unbuttoned my flies, aware such bashfulness was silly with the road so empty.

I'd reached full spate when I was shocked by the sudden roar of car engines and a clang. Twisting my neck, I saw a white van had demolished the gate at the bottom of the recently ploughed field below and was being pursued by four police cars, which were tanking after it, spraying great clods of earth as they bounced and twisted over the furrows. The way the van was being driven, it was clear the driver had little regard for safety and was absolutely desperate. A man's torso popped up through a hole in the van's roof. He was holding a shotgun and fired both barrels at the pursuers. One of them, attempting to swerve out of harm's way, bounced high over a furrow, came down on its side, rolled onto its roof and skidded to a standstill. The others continued the chase, wisely hanging back out of range.

The white van seemed to be heading straight towards me and, as I retreated behind the tree, buttoning my flies with panicked haste, another car hurtled into the field, a familiar blue, rusting Ford Fiesta. I could make out Hobbes's vast figure wrestling the wheel, as the tortured engine screamed and the car bucked and bounced, leading a swarm of muddy clods. The van roared closer before veering towards a gap, where the thick hedge had been replaced by a section of wire fence. It smashed straight through, landing with a bone-jarring crash and hurtling off down the road, trailing wire and fence posts. Hobbes, who had already overtaken the police cars, waved as he shot past and, feeling somewhat foolish, I waved back, as his car, leaping suddenly like a startled lamb, plunged through the gap, careered down the road and disappeared around a bend. The other pursuers followed at a less breakneck pace.

Down in the field, two dazed-looking police officers crawled from the overturned car. Neither, so I gathered from their remarks, interspersed with bouts of swearing, was injured, so, since there didn't seem to be anything I could do to help, I continued homewards, mile after aching mile.

Tired of foot, with sore legs and dripping with sweat, I was nearing Fenderton, on the outskirts of Sorenchester, when the traffic started again. I wondered if that meant Hobbes had caught the van, and I hoped he hadn't been hurt, for, despite his strength and toughness, he wasn't immune to guns.

At last I reached town, where people kept staring and grinning. I guessed it was because of my clothes, which, although fully dried by then, were limp and filthy, my sharply creased chinos reduced to saggy bags and my shirt more like a cleaning rag. Then I caught a glimpse of myself in a shop window. My hair had dried into a sort of wild afro frizz and mud was smeared diagonally across my face, making me look like a new romantic who'd fallen on very hard times.

At least the mud concealed my identity, as well as my blushes, for as I turned into Blackdog Street, I was astonished by the crowd milling round the door of number 13. As I approached, a man walked up to the front door and rang the bell. No one answered.

Tapping someone on the shoulder, I asked: 'What's going on?'

He turned to face me, his eyes widening, a chuckle escaping. The camera round his neck and his jacket stuffed with notebooks and pens made it clear to me, a man who'd once worked for the *Bugle,* that he was a reporter, as was everyone else there, unless they were cameramen.

'It's the gold robbery,' he said. 'We want a word with the inspector.'

'He's out chasing the ones that got away.'

'Oh, really?' said the reporter, looking suddenly interested, 'and how would you know that?'

'Because I saw him.'

Taking a small recording device from his jacket pocket, he held it beneath my nose. 'Would you mind telling me who you are, and precisely what you saw?'

'I'm not sure I should say,' I replied, aware of having become an object of interest.

Reporters were jostling, thrusting microphones and cameras, shouting questions, and I wasn't enjoying my moment in the spotlight.

'I won't say anything unless someone tells me why you're all here.'

'After last night,' said the man I'd accosted, 'we want the low-down on this Inspector Hobbes.'

'Why?'

'Isn't it obvious?'

'Not really. What's he done?'

'You should check out the news. He was awesome.'

'I will,' I said, 'if you let me get to the door.'

'Do you live here?' asked a little, fat guy.

'What's your name?' asked a fierce looking young woman.

'What's your relationship with Hobbes?' asked someone I couldn't see.

The crowd was pressing from all sides. 'Look, I know nothing and my name is—'

'What?'

'—not important.'

Getting out my keys, ignoring questions, deflecting cameras, I shoved and dodged through the throng until I was in touching distance of the front door.

'Why are you so muddy?' asked a particularly pushy man, who looked vaguely familiar, and was trying not to let me pass. 'How old is Hobbes?'

It was Jeremy Pratt off the news. I shook my head. 'Sorry, I know nothing. No speakee English. Leave me alone.'

Managing at last to angle past him, to get up the steps and to stick my key in the lock, I opened the door, hoping I'd be able to stop them following me inside.

I needn't have worried. Out of the house, big, black and bristling, burst Hobbes's dog, Dregs. Brushing me aside, making the reporters scatter, he seized Jeremy Pratt firmly by the groin. Jeremy froze, his mouth open in a silent scream.

'Dregs,' I said in my authoritative voice, the one he usually ignored, 'drop!'

To my surprise he dropped, and Jeremy, clutching himself, teetered on the top step and stumbled back down to the street, moaning. I doubted Dregs had done any serious damage, for, beneath his ferocious exterior, he was quite benevolent. As I shut the door he leapt on me, delighted to see me again, and not happy until he'd given me a thorough licking.

'Get off!' I said, my authoritative voice having no effect until he'd finished.

16

'What on earth is going on out there?' I asked.

Dregs didn't know. At any rate, he wasn't telling. More to the point, there was no sign of Mrs Goodfellow, and worse, no smell of cooking. Heading to the kitchen, I helped myself to a flagon of cool ginger beer, gulping it all down in record time and burping freely. I washed my hands and face, put the kettle on and had a search around for food.

The result wasn't at all bad. I found a fresh, crusty loaf in the bread bin, a little butter, and some Sorenchester cheese in the pantry, and a selection of Mrs Goodfellow's home-made pickles in a cupboard. Although my attempts at slicing the bread wavered between slab thick and wafer thin, the sandwiches I put together tasted just fine. Sitting at the kitchen table, Dregs by my side, I tried not to stuff myself and to appreciate the delicate home-baked aroma of the bread and the wonderful, crumbly cheese with its sweet, tangy, almost nutty flavour. And then there were the pickles, which she made on wet autumn days and were, quite simply, the best I'd ever tasted. Hobbes had once remarked that she'd won the Parish Pungent Pickle Prize twenty-seven years in succession before stepping aside to let lesser cooks have a chance. Dregs watched every mouthful and drooled, though he knew I considered Sorenchester cheese was far too good for dogs and he didn't much like pickles anyway. When I'd finished, I made a pot of tea, rested my weary feet on a chair, and drank the lot.

Relaxed and fed, my leg muscles aching, my feet sore, I wondered where the old girl was, and why Hobbes had apparently not returned for lunch; even when busy, he usually made it.

A glance through the letterbox showed the reporters were still out there, so, turning on the television, finding a news channel, I sat back in the threadbare old sofa.

I didn't have long to wait. After a rather dull piece about a financial probe, the topic turned to the attempted gold raid. To start with, there was little more than an extended version of

17

what I'd heard last night, plus something about the police closing the main road as they chased the remaining robbers, who had, unfortunately, escaped. I was a little surprised, for Hobbes, on the hunt, rarely came back empty-handed.

The matter-of-fact tone of the newsreader's voice changed: 'Last night, the gang had just finished loading the gold into their getaway vehicle when a plain clothes police officer arrived on the scene. A guest in a nearby hotel took this remarkable footage.'

There followed a rather wobbly video clip of the events. Black smoke was pouring from the back of the security van as four men appeared, their faces concealed in balaclavas. As they strutted, showing off a selection of guns, a white van, the one I'd seen earlier, roared into the picture and stopped to let three of the gang transfer a number of heavy-looking bags, while a fourth, a large man, holding a shotgun, covered the guard and two guys in business suits, who were lying face down on the pavement.

As soon as the last bag was loaded, the gang leapt into the back of the van, slamming the door behind them as they began to pull away up The Shambles towards the Parish Church. Hobbes came into view, sprinting, hunched up, his knuckles nearly scraping the road. He leapt at the van, holding on with one great hand and tearing at the loading doors with the other. Despite the van swerving from side to side, he somehow managed to open the doors and to swing inside. Unfortunately, as the van sped up the road, it went out of shot temporarily as the photographer changed his position.

The video continued, showing bags of gold rolling out and bursting in the road before, one after another, in rapid succession, three of the gang flew out the back and skidded along the tarmac. The final clip, just as the van disappeared from view around the corner, showed Hobbes swinging onto the roof.

The newsreader continued. 'The police officer, identified by witnesses as Inspector Hobbes, incredibly managed to knock a hole through the top of the van, despite coming under small arms fire. His amazing attempt at apprehending the entire gang only ended when the van crashed into a hedge and he was brushed off. Fortunately, he was reportedly unhurt and is already back on duty.

'Now, we're going over to Jeremy Pratt in Sorenchester for an update.'

The hapless reporter, dishevelled, and paler than usual, appeared on screen, with our house behind him. It was strange how different it looked on the television.

'Good afternoon, Jeremy' said the newsreader, 'is there any further news of Inspector Hobbes?'

'Good afternoon. Not much. However, a witness claims to have seen the remarkable inspector in hot pursuit of the fleeing villains.' He grimaced.

'Are you alright, Jeremy?'

'No, I am not. I have recently been indecently assaulted by a vicious dog, which bit me on the ...'

'Thank you, Jeremy! We'll be back for more, later.'

It seemed Hobbes was hot news, which was hardly a surprise, for his heroics must have looked truly stunning to anyone who hadn't previously seen him in action. For me, who'd watched him playing leapfrog with rhinoceroses and arresting a rogue elephant, his behaviour had been, more or less, par for the course. I knew, though, how much he would detest all the publicity. It wasn't that he was shy – quite the contrary – it was just that he was naturally reticent about his own achievements, which, as soon as they were completed, belonged to the past. He preferred living in the present and looking forward to whatever came next.

There was, of course, another, huge reason why he never courted publicity; Hobbes wasn't exactly human. Although I'd never actually worked out quite what he was, I'd accepted his 'unhumanity' long ago and it rarely bothered me. When it did, on those, thankfully rare, occasions when he reverted to a wild and savage state, I was still not bothered. I was terrified, and, although he'd never attacked me during one of his little turns, part of me couldn't help feeling like a lamb in a lion's den, fearing that one day he'd have me. Most people failed to see past his veneer, the thin layer of policeman. He was a damn good one, even if he did not necessarily adhere too closely to the letter of the law. Furthermore, he was by no means the only non-human in town, for Sorenchester was a weird place and I'd never quite worked out whether he was the source of the weirdness or just a symptom of it.

I changed channels, switching to a local news programme, which, to my horror, was showing my arrival at 13 Blackdog Street. With my filthy, crumpled clothes, wild hair, muddied face, and the wounds from my battle with the alarm clock and bookcase, I, too, gave off an aura of weirdness, which was quite depressing. However, the look on Jeremy's face when Dregs nipped him in the bud quickly cheered me up. The clip was repeated in slow motion, before the grinning newsreader joked that the dog had been rushed to the vet with food poisoning. Turning off the television, I headed upstairs for a bath.

Sometime later, thoroughly soaked and deep cleansed, I went into my room and started putting on clean clothing. The street outside was still packed with reporters and cameramen, as well as a host of sightseers. At least the Black Dog Café down the road was doing extremely well, to judge by the number of cups and cakes I could see.

Feeling a little warm, I opened the window to let in some fresh air, and was thinking about combing my hair when a huge, horrible figure, wearing well-polished black boots, baggy brown trousers and a scruffy jacket, swung in through the window, and landed on the rug with barely a sound.

'Afternoon,' said Hobbes. 'Put the kettle on. I'm parched.'

3

Hobbes's unexpected arrival set my heart pounding, caused instant jelly legs and made me slump onto the bed, where I lay quivering, trying to control my breathing. It took a few moments before I felt able to get up and find my comb. I stared into the mirror, thinking that, despite my usually wispy short brown hair looking relatively neat, my face was not at its best, for although it had lost much of its pastiness and puffiness, my nose was swollen, a tender red split across the bridge merging into the bruise around my eye.

Before knowing him, I would, no doubt, have been feeling sorry for myself, and would most likely have stayed in bed to mope, but I'd grown accustomed to injury, because, in the same way as Hobbes attracted weirdness, I was a magnet for accidents and minor disasters. Although it would have been a lie to have claimed I took them in my stride, I could usually manage to stumble through.

At last, I went downstairs to the kitchen, put the kettle on and made tea. When it was nicely brewed, I handed a mugful to Hobbes, who was sitting at the table, with his hand on Dregs's head.

'I wasn't expecting you back today,' he remarked, stirring his steaming tea with a great, hairy finger. 'How is your father?'

'He's fine.'

'The lass told me he was at death's door.'

'That's what I thought, but it turned out there was nothing wrong with him, or at least, nothing a sensible diet wouldn't cure.'

'I'm happy to hear he's well.'

'Thank you. I was going to stay there for a couple of days, but I had a little accident ...'

Hobbes chuckled.

'... and after seeing the news, I wanted to get back here.'

'Why? What's happened?' He looked puzzled.

'The gold robbery, of course.'

'Oh, that. It was nothing.'

'That's not what the press think, and they've been showing a film of you in action.'

He frowned. 'I was filmed?'

'By someone staying at the Golden Fleece,' I said, 'and it's been all over the news and it seems to have made everyone excited.'

'So, that's why all those people were loitering outside. I did wonder.'

'If you knew nothing about it, why did you come in through the window?'

'It was open,' said Hobbes, 'so I thought I'd take a shortcut.'

'Umm ... wouldn't it have been quicker to park outside and come through the door?'

'It would, had I anything to park.'

'Why? What's happened to the car?'

'I broke it.' He grinned. 'It turns out it wasn't up to jumping walls, or, rather, it couldn't cope with landing afterwards. All the wheels came off – even the steering wheel. They don't make them like they used to. I'll have to buy another.'

'Won't the police buy you one?'

'No, we have an arrangement. I get what I want and they don't tell me how to drive it. It saves Superintendent Cooper a lot of stress.'

'That doesn't seem fair when you were on police business.'

He shrugged. 'Well, I was, it's true, but I was enjoying myself, too. I could have left the pursuit to the other lads, but why should they have all the fun?'

'Fun? Yeah, OK. But the robbers still got away.'

'For the time being.'

'You might have been hurt. I saw that police car crash.'

'I wasn't and nor was anyone else. As for the lads who

crashed, it'll teach them to drive better next time.'

'Fair enough, but someone was hurt last night. There was the poor driver of the security van who got deafened.'

Hobbes scratched his head, sounding like someone brushing their feet on a coconut doormat. 'The driver wasn't deafened. I spoke to him.'

'Yes, he was, I saw it on the news. Some guy called Percival.'

'Are you referring to Percival Longfellow? He is most certainly hard of hearing, but he's been like it ever since getting too close to an explosion years ago in London.'

'But,' I said, 'didn't that happen last night? And wasn't he driving the van?'

'I think you are getting confused. The gang did indeed blow the doors off the security van last night, but Percival wasn't the driver. He hasn't worked in security for twenty years or more; not since a gang of jewel robbers blew open a bank vault he was guarding. He received a substantial amount of compensation for his deafness, which he invested in a nice flat in town. Nowadays, he manages a boy band.'

'I don't get it,' I said. 'A reporter spoke to him about the robbery.'

'Reporters have been known to get things wrong. You should know.'

I nodded, wondering if he'd made a dig at me. For far too many years, I'd been a cub reporter for the *Sorenchester and District Bugle*, and my failure to move up the pecking order in that time might have been down to the sackful of mistakes I'd made.

'What concerns me now,' said Hobbes, 'is how long those reporters are going to stay outside.'

'Probably until you give them a story.'

'In which case, they'll be there a long time.'

'Actually,' I said, thinking rapidly, 'it might be better to give them what they want now, because if you don't, they'll just stick around and make something up. That's what I used to do.'

I didn't mention that most of my fictions had been discovered, sooner or later, resulting in embarrassing exposures to the Editorsaurus's sarcasm.

'No,' said Hobbes. 'It sounds like I've already got more than enough publicity and I don't intend to give them any more.'

'What if they make up something bad? And there's another thing to be considered: if they can't get to you, they'll try pumping anyone who might know you.'

Hobbes shook his head. 'I've got nothing to say. I was just doing my job.'

'They'll hang around and hassle people, at least until the next big story pops up. Think what it'll be like for Mrs Goodfellow when she goes shopping. By the way, where is she?'

'She's gone to Skegness for a long weekend.'

'She didn't say anything to me.'

'Because you weren't here. The lass thought she'd take the opportunity to visit her cousin Ethel, who runs a guesthouse. They normally only see each other once a year.'

'Oh no!' I said, stricken with a horrible realisation. 'What are we going to do for supper?'

'We'll manage.'

I groaned, remembering past culinary disasters when the old girl had been away, most of which had been my fault, or to be more truthful, all of which had been my fault.

'Tonight, for instance,' said Hobbes, 'I have been invited to dine by my friend Sid. Have you met him? Sid Sharples? He came to see me after I'd been shot the last time.'

'Umm … I might have done … I think. Well, I guess you'll be alright, but … umm …what about me?'

'That will not be a problem. Sid won't mind an extra body at the table and he's always glad of new blood in his circle. However, he's an old-fashioned sort of gentleman and likes his guests dressed for dinner.'

'If you're sure he won't mind, that'll be great. I think there's a dinner jacket and bow tie at the back of my wardrobe.'

One of the advantages of living at Hobbes's was that I'd acquired a whole new wardrobe and, more to the point, the clothes to fill it. They had once belonged to Mrs Goodfellow's husband, Robin, who, so far as anyone knew, was in Tahiti, attempting to found a naturist colony. Although most of his stuff might have been considered a trifle old-fashioned, I liked to believe it was classic tailoring, and was sure it gave me an air of distinction. I hoped so, anyway. Nonetheless, I still found it spooky that everything fitted as if made to measure.

'Excellent,' said Hobbes. 'He expects us at eight.'

'Does he?'

He nodded and poured himself more tea. 'There is,' he said casually – a little too casually – 'something I ought to tell you about him.'

'Go on.'

'Sid is a vampire.'

'Oh, is that all?' I said, trying not to look like a victim, my muscles turning to mush.

'But, don't worry, he won't hurt you, or harm you in any way, and he's a good cook and a generous host.'

Despite my best efforts, and Hobbes's reassurance, my hands shook. I was going to dinner with a real vampire; it had been bad enough meeting a wannabe vampire, in the form of my former editor's deranged wife, who had bitten me, leaving her false teeth sticking in my neck. If I looked under bright lights, I fancied I could still make out the scar.

When I felt able, I got up, walked calmly to the sink, picked up a cloth, returned to the table and wiped up the pool of tea I'd spilt when he told me. He watched, smiling wickedly, as I rinsed out the cloth, hung it over a tap, and returned to my seat.

'Sid,' he said, 'is quite harmless.'

'So, he won't want to drink my blood?'

'No. As is well documented, vampires only drink the blood

of virgins.'

'That's alright then.' I forced a smile as if reassured.

Hobbes laughed. 'You have a very expressive face. I should tease you more often.'

'Is he really a vampire?' I asked, recalling numerous occasions when he'd made me fall for tall stories, although in fairness, some of the tallest had turned out to be true.

'He really is, though there's nothing to worry about, because although of the vampire race, he can't stomach the taste of blood.'

'So, what does he eat?'

'He particularly likes soup.'

'Soup?'

'Correct. He's getting on a bit, and finds it easy to digest and much more palatable than blood. No doubt he'll cook one for us tonight.'

'Umm ...' I said, 'what sort of soup?'

'He usually goes for the meatier varieties, such as oxtail.'

'Good,' I said, slightly reassured, having had a horrific vision of him serving up a large bowl of something warm, red and frothy and passing it off as cream of tomato soup.

Although I did have a vague memory of Sid's visit, I couldn't picture him, yet my mind insisted that he was tall and slim, with slicked back hair, sharp teeth and a strange accent. Still, I told myself, he was only a vampire, so why worry? After all, I knew a family pack of werewolves quite well and, although they occasionally made me nervous, especially at night, particularly around full moon, they'd never hurt me, or, so far as I was aware, anybody else. They hadn't even bitten the postman. The worst I could say about them was that they had once given me fleas, and I'd still not completely recovered from the ignominy of being tricked by Mrs Goodfellow into sharing a flea bath with Dregs, who'd also been infested. Besides them, I'd eaten crumpets with the Olde Troll and was slowly learning not to give in to prejudice and to take people, of no matter what persuasion, on their individual merits.

Hobbes, finishing his tea, downed his mug, loped from the kitchen and returned a few moments later. 'Those reporters are still out there and showing no signs of moving on, so we'll need to get past them.'

'How?'

'I'll think about it, but not now. I'm going to take forty winks. It's been a long night and day.'

As he left, Dregs approached, sat by my side and tried to persuade me to take him for a walk. My attempts to ignore his hypnotic gaze soon crumbled.

'Oh, alright then,' I said.

Jumping up, thrashing his tail, he fetched his lead from the hook, waited for me to clip it to his collar and dragged me to the front door. In my naivety, I hadn't expected to spark much excitement, since I obviously wasn't Hobbes and looked relatively normal. I was wrong. As soon as I opened the door, we were confronted by cameras, flashing lights and thrusting microphones. However, Dregs's earlier actions had earned him a right of passage, and he only had to growl for the crowd to part, leaving a clear route. A nervous-looking Jeremy Pratt, dried slobber on his trousers the only evidence of his canine encounter, lurked towards the back of the mob as, ignoring the questions and the cameras, I let Dregs lead me to Ride Park.

Thankfully, no one followed us far and Dregs and I were able to pass an enjoyable hour or so. He chased squirrels, without ever getting near one. For him, all the fun was in running free and barking up the wrong tree. I mooched along, feet sore from the long trek, my leg muscles still aching, and appreciated the late afternoon sunshine, the buzz of insects and the changing tints of the trees, trying not to think about later, but wishing I'd asked Hobbes more about the robbery. I also wondered if I'd be on television again. I hoped not.

Despite my best intentions, one question kept buzzing round my head, as annoying as a wasp at a picnic: could a vampire really be as safe as Hobbes had suggested? I tried to believe him, to convince myself he wouldn't really put me into a dangerous situation, at least not on purpose. I knew, of course, that if I ever got into danger, he was the best person to get me out of it, but I was far from comfortable with the idea of visiting a vampire, even one with a preference for soup. Despite recognising my fear was based entirely on prejudice, my knowledge gleaned only from horror films, it was, nonetheless, genuine.

At length, all the squirrels having been treed, the evening approaching, and the temperature dropping, I called Dregs, clipped him to his lead and returned home, running the gauntlet of reporters. Again he proved invaluable and we got back inside without too much hassle.

Hobbes was already up and dressed. Having never seen him in his dinner jacket before, I was impressed. He looked almost smart and quite respectable, despite wearing a bow tie, a relic of the sixties I assumed, that looked as if a large velvet bat had seized him by the throat. Dregs apparently thought the same and growled and bristled until Hobbes let him sniff it. Then, relaxing, he waited for his dinner. While Hobbes was feeding him, I took a bulb of garlic from Mrs G's pot and secreted it in my pocket; I had an idea it might be useful.

'You'd better get ready,' said Hobbes.

'OK. Umm … have you worked out how to get past that lot outside?'

'Yes, though I suspect you might not like it.'

'Why not?'

'You'll see.'

He refused to elaborate and I went upstairs in a state of extreme trepidation. I'd already been shaky and his manner had really set me on edge. On reaching my room, I turned on the light and ferreted around in the wardrobe, finding a pair of black, sharply creased trousers, a crisply pressed dress shirt, and a dinner jacket. I laid them on the bed, and started to dress, popping the garlic bulb into my jacket pocket, finding its pungent aroma strangely reassuring.

I was doing just fine until the bow tie, a conundrum way beyond my abilities. Having made a right pig's ear of the whole rigmarole, frustration got the better of me and I punched the wall, a method that worked surprisingly well, since my yelp of pain and subsequent swearing brought Hobbes up to see what was the matter. He found me collapsed on the bed, clutching my hand and groaning.

Summing up the situation at a glance, he said: 'Bow ties can be tricky blighters. Stand up, shut up, and I'll tie it for you.'

Taking me by the throat, he set to work, his massive hairy fingers tying the black rag into a beautifully neat bow. It was a little tight: a little too tight. Clutching at it, I struggled to breathe, until, recognising my antics as signs of distress, he loosened it with a deft twist.

'Thank you,' I croaked.

'Don't mention it. Now put on your jacket, and quickly. It's time to go.'

'So, how are you going to get past those reporters?' I asked, combing my hair and admiring myself in the mirror.

'By distracting them and going over the roof tops.'

'That's all very well for you,' I said, not liking the way this was developing, 'but what about me? Shall I take Dregs?'

'No, you're coming with me.'

'I can't. I'll fall off. No, it's impossible.'

'It is possible. I have a plan and you'll probably be fine. You'll see. First, however, I need something from the attic. While I'm getting it, open your window and turn off the light.'

'OK,' I said, my insides churning, but as usual, I realised I was going to let him do his stuff, and I was going to hope for the best. Turning off the light, I opened the window and looked down. Even from there, the street seemed a bowel-loosening long way below.

Hobbes returned, carrying an ancient canvas rucksack that

looked just about big enough for a human body. Surely not, I thought, as he put it down.

'Get inside,' he said, grinning benignly.

'Do I have to?'

'Yes, and quickly.'

I stepped into it and made myself small, discovering my initial assessment of its size had been a little wrong, as my head and shoulders poked out the top. However, before I could object, Hobbes grabbed the straps, lifted me and swung me onto his back.

'Keep your head down,' he said.

'I can't keep it any more down and how are you going to distract that lot outside? They are bound to look up.'

'I'm not going to do anything.'

'Do I have to do anything?' I asked, peering over his shoulder, feeling precarious enough already.

'No. Just relax and keep quiet. It's time.'

A tremendous cacophony broke out in the street, as if a tone deaf brass band on steroids was performing.

'Here we go,' said Hobbes, springing lightly out the window.

Had my mouth not been dry, as if coated in peanut butter, I might have screamed. Twisting my neck, I stared down at the street, which was glittering under silvery streetlights and already looking much further away. The rucksack swung as Hobbes, twisting in mid-air, reaching out with one great, muscular arm, grabbed the top of the window frame, and hauled us up and onto the roof. As he scrambled on all fours to the summit, the tuneless braying ceased.

'Alright, Andy?'

'Umm ... I suppose.'

'Good. Hold on tight.'

'Hold on to what?'

There was no reply.

Blackdog Street consisted of two parallel rows of tall, terraced houses and shops. Hobbes, as agile as a monkey, despite me swinging and bumping on his back, ran along the ridge towards the end of the street next to the Parish Church. Even in my terrified state, I was struck by how magnificent and strange the church looked from such an unusual vantage point. I tried to think about its architecture and not about what would happen should Hobbes slip, or should the frayed old straps on the rucksack snap.

He stopped and stood upright.

'Where does Sid live exactly?' I asked.

'Number one, Doubtful Street.'

'That's to the left, isn't it?' Below was the gentle curve of Pound Street. Doubtful Street, one of the oldest in town, led onto it.

'Yes.'

'How do we get down?'

'Getting down from a roof is easy, although getting down safely may be less so. Do you see that wall over there, the one around the big garden?'

I grunted an acknowledgment, fearing the worst.

'Well, once we're on that, it's an easy drop into Pound Street.'

'But, it's miles away! How can we possibly reach it? It's impossible.' I wished I'd decided to stay home and make do with toast.

'It's not impossible. I don't think so, anyway.'

'You're not going to ... oh, God!'

Hobbes, having taken a few paces back, sprinted along the ridge until, when there was no roof left, he leapt. I didn't scream, the acceleration having squeezed all the air from my lungs, but I did manage a pathetic whimper that was instantly carried away in the wind rushing past my face. There was a sensation of weightlessness, a long moment when my heart seemed to have stopped and a thud that nearly bounced me from the rucksack. Within a few steps, we came to a halt.

We were on the wall.

Hobbes clapped his hands. 'I thought we'd make it.'

'You didn't know for sure?'

'Not for sure. I've never carried anyone before. It was fun.'

'We could have been killed.'

'But we weren't. Now, let's get down before somebody sees us and calls the police.'

The jump down seemed trivial, and I was suddenly safe, or as safe as anyone could be who was on their way to meet a vampire.

'You might as well walk from here,' said Hobbes, setting the rucksack down on the pavement.

Getting out wasn't as easy as getting in; my legs wobbled like those of a punched out boxer.

'Come along,' he said, swinging the rucksack onto one shoulder. 'We don't want to keep Sid waiting.'

'OK,' I said, struggling to keep up, trying not to think of how we'd get home, 'but can you explain something?'

'I can explain many things.'

'I know, but what made that awful racket?'

He laughed. 'That was Billy testing his new car horn. I phoned and asked him to put in an appearance. It worked rather well, don't you think?'

I nodded. Billy Shawcroft, a good friend of Hobbes, was a dwarf of no small ability, who had shown himself a very useful man in a crisis, and the reconditioned hearse he drove had proved its worth on several occasions.

Turning into Doubtful Street, we stopped outside number 1, a high, narrow, old house of dusty, lichen-encrusted stone, with a shiny black front door. Leaning forward, Hobbes gave the old-fashioned bell-pull a sharp downward tug and from within came the deep tones of bell. So far, so Gothic, I thought, closing my hand around my garlic bulb.

A moment later, there came a sound of shuffling feet and the door opened with a satisfyingly spooky creak. Inside, all was dark, except for the flickering light of a single candle held in a pale hand.

'Enter,' said a soft voice.

Nervously, I followed Hobbes inside, going down a corridor in which the candlelight cast grotesque flickering shadows onto dark, heavy-looking furniture. The front door closed behind us.

'Welcome to my humble abode,' said the soft voice. 'I'm dreadfully sorry it's so dark, but the bulb's just blown. Please, go into the kitchen.'

Hobbes, opening a door, led us into a large, comfortable, well-lit, modern kitchen, where he introduced me to Sid, who was not as I'd imagined. He was shorter than I and rather paunchy, with a balding head and plump, florid cheeks. Yet what surprised me most was his welcoming, white-toothed smile and friendly dark brown eyes.

'Delighted to make your acquaintance, young fellow,' he said, taking my hand in his soft pudgy one and shaking it vigorously.

'Pleased to meet you,' I said, wondering again whether Hobbes was playing a trick on me.

Sid nodded and then looked distressed. 'I'm afraid I'm having a bad day. First the bulb goes and then I discover I've completely run out of garlic.'

Reaching into my pocket, I held out my hand.

'Thank you,' said Sid. 'I don't suppose you brought any dill?'

4

The kitchen was mostly white, with every surface gleaming, and, above a sharp hint of bleach and a faint scent of apples, there was a beautiful, rich, delicious smell rising from a large copper pot bubbling on a vast wood-fired range. Sid, smiling at us over a bow tie that was nearly as large as Hobbes's, gestured towards the table and Hobbes and I sat down on cushioned pinewood chairs.

'It was lucky you had garlic with you,' said Sid, 'because the soup is not the same without it.'

'Umm … yes, it was. I don't usually carry it.'

'Was it anything to do with me being what I am?'

'Umm … well, yes, I suppose it was,' I said, more embarrassed than afraid.

'I expect,' said Sid, with a glance at Hobbes, 'that Wilber told you part of the story, just enough to get you worried.'

'Would I do anything like that?' said Hobbes, trying to look innocent.

'Yes,' I said, nodding, 'you would. Umm … Wilber?'

'It's short for Wilberforce,' said Sid.

'Wilberforce?' I said, staring. 'Is that his name?' I'd never dared ask, though I had noticed the signature on his paintings was W.M. Hobbes.

Sid nodded.

'In that case,' I asked, 'what does the M stand for?'

'His second name,' said Sid. 'is—'

'A secret,' said Hobbes, shaking his head and looking embarrassed.

'—is Makepeace.' Sid, breaking the garlic into cloves, sniffed them and nodded his approval.

Hobbes, putting his head in his hands, groaned. 'My awful secret is out. It was bound to happen one day.'

'Wilberforce Makepeace Hobbes?' I chuckled.

'Apparently both Wilberforce and Makepeace were popular names when I was a lad,' said Hobbes. 'I'm quite proud of them ... really.'

'Anyway,' said Sid, 'before I was interrupted, I was trying to say that I love a bit of garlic and, furthermore, I have no adverse reaction to crosses, or holy water, or any of that nonsense.'

'I guess everything I think I know about vampires is wrong,' I said, feeling more at ease. 'Umm ... what about stakes, though? Would a stake through the heart kill you?'

'Andy,' said Hobbes, 'that's not nice.'

Sid held up his hand. 'No, it's a fair question, if a little daft. So far as I'm aware, a stake through the heart would kill anyone and, before you ask, so would decapitation.' With a chuckle, he turned towards a chopping board, and selected a broad bladed knife.

'I'm sorry,' said Hobbes. 'He's not normally so forward. He's probably tired.'

'Don't worry, old boy,' said Sid. 'Most humans take a while to adjust. You can't blame them, really. There's so much piffle out there. Just try googling the word *vampire* and you'll find there are millions of hits and hardly any of them come even close to the truth.'

'I did tell him,' said Hobbes, 'that you would not dream of drinking his blood.'

'He did.' I agreed.

'That's alright then,' said Sid, examining the edge of the knife. 'Did he also mention that I prefer to dine on human brains?'

I shook my head, my mouth dropping open.

'I'm surprised,' said Sid. 'He usually does.'

Having crushed and chopped the garlic, he threw it into a small pot on the range, along with a knob of butter. The fragrance cut through everything else and made me even hungrier.

Hobbes was grinning and, I thought, looking somewhat sheepish.

'When the garlic is nicely browned,' said Sid, 'I'll add it to the soup and then we can have a good chat while it finishes. Help yourselves to wine while you're waiting.'

'Thanks,' said Hobbes, reaching for a bottle in the middle of the table. Pulling off the foil capsule, he gave three sharp smacks to the bottom of the bottle, making the cork rise up. Pulling it out with a gentle pop, sniffing it with a nod of approval, he flicked it across the kitchen, straight into a flip top bin.

'Would you care for a little, Andy?' he asked.

'Yes, please.'

Having filled three glasses with the dark red, almost purple liquid, he pushed one towards me and took one for himself. 'Cheers.'

'Cheers,' I said, sniffing, satisfying myself that it really was wine, and taking a sip. It was rich and fruity, with a warm velvety feel and was more than acceptable. Since living at Hobbes's I'd developed a rudimentary palate and considered I now knew enough to avoid anything likely to dissolve my teeth or blind me.

We sat in silence for a few moments, sipping, enjoying the flavour, relaxing as the sizzling garlic, combined with the other cooking aromas, set my mouth watering.

'Is he really a vampire?' I whispered.

'I really am,' said Sid, who was suddenly standing right behind me.

Jerking with shock, I knocked over my glass. Sid caught it and handed it back without a drop spilling.

'We have sharp ears as well as sharp teeth,' he said.

'Not to mention sharp reflexes,' said Hobbes.

'Hardly, old boy, I've slowed down with age.'

'Age?' said Hobbes, looking severe. 'More like your drunken life style.'

'Drunken? I haven't touched a drop since 1950.'

'Since it's only ten-past eight, now,' said Hobbes, 'you've lasted all of twenty minutes.' He handed a glass to the old vampire.

'Much obliged,' said Sid, raising it to his lips. 'Good health!'

If he was a vampire, and I had few doubts anymore, he was a cheerful one.

'The soup will be ready in just a few minutes,' he said, taking a seat at the head of the table.

'What is it?' I asked, raising my voice over the rumbling of my stomach.

'It's borscht, my own recipe and I hope you like it.'

'It smells great,' I said, unsure what borscht was, but unwilling to expose my ignorance.

'It does indeed,' said Hobbes and refilled his glass. 'It's very good of you to have us.'

'Not at all.'

'Your invitation was most opportune. You see, my house is currently under siege, and getting out is a trifle tricky.' Hobbes took a gulp of wine and stretched out his legs.

'Ah, yes,' said Sid, 'the barbarians at the gates. I've been keeping an eye on the news. I'm always a little nervous with crowds, because they are, in my experience, only one step removed from turning into mobs and taking up flaming brands and pitchforks.'

'You've had no more trouble of that sort since moving here, have you?' said Hobbes.

'No, and for that I give you thanks, old boy.'

'I'm just doing my job.'

'Like you were last night,' said Sid. 'It's regrettable someone caught your antics on camera, but otherwise you did well. I don't like losing our money.'

'Your money?' I said, surprised, for the news had suggested the gang was trying to steal over a million pounds in gold sovereigns and, although Sid's house suggested he was comfortably off, he didn't strike me as a millionaire.

'In a manner of speaking. The gold actually belongs to Colonel Squire, but since he was depositing it in my bank, I have a stake in it.'

Colonel Squire, the owner of Sorenchester Manor and several estates, was reputed to be very rich indeed.

'That's right,' said Hobbes. 'The colonel said he was diversifying his investments.'

'But why was he doing it at night?' I asked. 'Why not during normal banking hours?'

'There are two good reasons,' said Sid. 'Firstly, the colonel is rich enough to make the bank jump to his command. Secondly, he wanted me to accept the deposit personally and, if I have to go out, I prefer to do it at night. Now, if you'll excuse me, I'll serve the soup.'

Rising, he strolled across to the stove, very light on his feet for one so portly, and, returning with a vast tureen, ladled out generous portions into three large, white bowls. The soup was red and frothy.

I looked at it, then at Hobbes. He smiled.

'What is this?' I asked, trying to sound calm, trying to dispel a rising horror.

'Borscht,' said Sid, fetching a basket of thickly sliced, crusty bread and a butter dish. As if that explained everything.

'Yes, but what's actually in it, besides garlic.'

'I'll bet,' said Sid with a chuckle, 'that the colour is worrying you.'

I nodded, feeling sick.

'It's made with beetroot, and don't worry, there's no blood in it.'

'Oh, good,' I said, relieved. 'I didn't really think there would be.'

'Of course not,' said Sid, looking solemn.

I felt no fear. Whatever he was, he was no threat.

'Please, help yourself to bread,' said Sid, 'and eat. I hope you enjoy it.'

After Hobbes had said his customary grace, I did eat. The borscht had a robust, almost earthy flavour with a hint of sweetness, not to mention a satisfying nuttiness and a strong meaty flavour, with just a hint of sourness that piqued my taste buds. In fact, it was so good I even entertained the possibility that it might equal one of Mrs G's soups, though it felt disloyal to think so. Maybe it was because of my extreme hunger, or the contrast to Mother's well-meaning horrors.

I tucked in, listening with half an ear to Hobbes and Sid talking about Rocky, the Olde Troll, who'd apparently fallen asleep while out standing in his field, and had woken up covered in graffiti. Although the brisk application of a wire brush had restored him to pristine condition, Rocky had complained bitterly about the loss of his lichen patina. Then, when I might have expected more talk of old times and old acquaintances, the conversation turned to gold and banking. I was surprised to learn that Hobbes kept a deposit box in Grossman's Bank, a box he hadn't touched since 1922.

'Help yourselves to more borscht,' said Sid as I finished the bowl. 'There's plenty.'

'I don't mind if I do,' I said. 'It's delicious.'

'Delicious? I should jolly well think so. I've had plenty of practice since my wife died.'

'I'm sorry to hear that.'

'Don't be, young fellow. She had a good life. Until she married me, of course.'

Hobbes, with a laugh, helped himself to more and said: 'Your Queenie was a good woman; she was like a mother to the lass.'

Once again, I experienced the strange sense of dislocation that struck whenever I was confronted with the age of Hobbes and some of his associates. Although I'd never plucked up the courage to ask how old he was, I had ascertained that, despite appearances, he was old enough to have been a policeman for some years before joining up as a soldier in the Great War. Mrs Goodfellow, 'the lass' as Hobbes called her, had been orphaned during the Blitz in the next war, and yet still ran Kung Fu classes in the church hall. It was no great step to accept Sid as older, far older, than his smooth, plump skin suggested.

When we'd finished the borscht, Sid gathered up our bowls, stacked them in the dishwasher and returned to the table with three sundae dishes filled with another dark red, frothy substance. 'Raspberry mousse,' he said, before I could embarrass myself. 'I hope you like it.'

It was sweet and tart and fruity and smooth and utterly delicious. Hobbes didn't say another word until he'd scraped the dish clean. Then he said four words: 'Is there any more?'

Sid, looking well pleased, fetched him another dish, which went the same way. Although I would have loved to indulge my taste buds, I couldn't, for my belly was so tight I didn't dare and it was all I could do to find room for my wine.

Afterwards, Sid took us through to the lounge, painted a cosy, bright orange, dominated by an enormous book case, and containing a pair of magnificent green leather chesterfield sofas. A capacious armchair was positioned where its occupant might watch the vast television on the wall in total comfort, while benefiting from the fire that was dispelling any hint of autumnal chill and imbuing the air with the soft, soothing scent of warm, ripe apples. Hobbes and I, sprawling, replete, took a sofa each, while our host, having returned to the kitchen, brought in a steaming jug, whence arose the wonderful aroma of fresh coffee, adding to my feeling of comfort and ease. Having filled three translucent white porcelain cups and passed them to us, Sid approached a large, beautifully polished drinks cabinet.

'Could I interest either of you in a snifter of brandy?' he asked. 'I fancy one myself.'

Hobbes nodded.

'I'll stick to coffee,' I said. 'Brandy is a bit strong for me these days.'

'No problem,' said Sid, pulling out a pair of brandy glasses, filling them and handing one to Hobbes. 'Perhaps you'd like something else?'

'Umm … I don't know … I …'

'How about a cocktail? I suggest one the youngsters used to drink in the Old Country.'

'Maybe. Which old country? You don't really come from Transylvania, do you?'

He laughed. 'No, I come from a small village in Norfolk. The Old Country was a wine bar I used to own.'

'You wouldn't know it,' said Hobbes. 'It was way before your time. After he sold it, it became the Black Dog Café.'

'I'll tell you what,' said Sid, 'I'll make you one and see if you like it.'

With a sinister chuckle, he set to work with three bottles and a crystal glass.

'This,' he said, handing me the results of his alchemy, 'is a Brain Haemorrhage.'

It was an apt name. Floating in a colourless fluid was what appeared to be a small clump of brain with great bloody streaks running through.

Although I tried to act cool, I failed to suppress a shudder and a grimace. 'What is it?'

'Two parts peach schnapps, topped with a measure of Irish cream and drizzled with grenadine. It's normally drunk in a single quaff. I'm sure you'll like it. Enjoy.'

Though my brain said 'no' and my stomach said 'no room', I felt, for the sake of my honour, that I should give it a try. Taking a deep breath, I gulped it down, finding it wasn't nearly as bad as I'd feared. In fact, it was rather pleasant, with a sweet, fruity taste. Overcome with a sudden fatigue, I slumped in the chesterfield, resting my eyes, while Hobbes and Sid enjoyed a heated discussion on the subject of sticklebacks.

Having exhausted the topic, Sid asked about the

investigation.

'It's too early to tell yet,' said Hobbes, 'but we have several lines of inquiry. Firstly, how did the gang know the gold would be delivered to the bank at that time?'

'Someone must have told them,' said Sid.

'That would seem likely, so we are working on the theory that it was an insider job. I'd be obliged if you'd let me have a list of anyone who knew, but it may not have been malicious; it may have been carelessness.

'Secondly, we're holding three of the gang in the nick, and I may persuade them to talk. Unfortunately, my first impression is that we caught the foot soldiers, who know very little and that the boss got away.

'Thirdly, there's the van. When we find it, it's likely to provide some clues – and it shouldn't be hard to find, as it's quite distinctive, having a hole in its roof and a huge dent where it hit a tree. I'd have caught them this afternoon, had my car not broken.'

'But, surely, old boy, they'll burn the van to get rid of any clues? That's if they haven't done so already.'

'I fear you may be right.' Hobbes sighed. 'Still, I do have one further line of inquiry, because I got a good view of the driver and I'd recognise him anywhere. In fact, I thought for a moment that I did recognise him. Unfortunately, I didn't get much of an impression of the other man, except that he was tall and wearing a tweed suit. I suspect that one was the boss.'

'What are you going to do next?' asked Sid. 'Won't all the reporters get in your way?'

'Maybe, but I don't really know what they want from me. Andy reckons they'll hang around until they've got a story, or they'll make one up.'

'He's probably right. They can be extraordinarily persistent until the next big news breaks. Do you remember what they were like that Walpurgis Night when Skeleton Bob Nibblet got stuck up the chimney? That could have become a very sticky situation. Another brandy?'

'Yes, please,' said Hobbes.

Sid got to his feet. 'Another Brain Haemorrhage, Andy?'

Although I could easily have dropped off in the warmth of the crackling fire, and my head, already fuzzy, felt as if it were spinning, I opened my eyes and sat up. 'Don't mind if I do,' I said, ignoring a sober portion of my brain whispering that I'd already had too much.

Sid fetched the drinks. 'Here's to solving crime ... Cheers.'

'Cheers.'

Having taken a gulp of neat brandy, Sid, looking thoughtful, said: 'What I'd suggest is that you get away for a few days, until things quieten down. After all, you've already done enough. You saved the money and the bank's reputation and arrested three of the gang.'

'But at least two others are still free,' said Hobbes, 'and one of them is the brains and he might be planning something else.'

'Possibly, old boy, but he's more likely to be in hiding, afraid he's going to be arrested. Your police colleagues should be able to find him.'

'I don't like to leave a job half done.'

'Surely you don't want to take all the glory?' said Sid. 'Give someone else a chance. It was only an attempted robbery after all.'

Hobbes stared deep into his brandy as I gulped down my Brain Haemorrhage. They were moreish, so I didn't object when Sid fixed me another.

'Maybe you're right,' said Hobbes, after a long pause.

'I'm sure I am,' said Sid. 'Take a few days leave. I'll bet you've got a few accrued.'

Hobbes grinned. 'Superintendent Cooper reckoned I'd built up over four years and that was ages ago, so I dare say there's a few more now.'

'When did you last take a holiday?'

'Last week.'

'For how long?'

'All of Sunday morning.'

'What about a proper holiday?'

'I took a few days off last year, soon after I met Andy.'

Admittedly, my head was stupid with drink, but I couldn't think what he meant. 'The only time I remember you not going into work was after you got shot.'

'That's when I was thinking of,' said Hobbes. 'I spent a couple of days in bed.'

'That doesn't count as holiday,' I said. 'You're supposed to enjoy them.'

'He's right, old boy. You deserve a break.'

'But,' said Hobbes, a little peevishly, 'policing is so much fun. Why would I want a break?'

'It won't be so much fun with those vultures outside your door,' said Sid. 'You'll get a lot of attention. Remember back in '53 when they ran the story of you breaking the four-minute mile? They were after you for days, and it would probably have been much worse had it not been for the coronation.'

'I thought,' I said, 'the four-minute mile was broken in 1954.'

'Officially,' said Sid, 'but Wilber got there first.'

'I wasn't first,' said Hobbes, 'and it wasn't in a race and, I'm glad to say, never made the record books.'

'What happened?'

'I was in pursuit of a suspect,' said Hobbes.

'Who was on horseback,' said Sid. 'It was at Hedbury Races and Wilber was timed between mileposts before he made the arrest. According to the course clock, he'd covered the distance in well under four minutes '

'It wasn't a very good clock,' said Hobbes.

'But,' said Sid, 'the point is, it caught the press's attention and they swarmed around you like mosquitos, until the events in London distracted them.'

'True,' said Hobbes. 'It made my job a little difficult.'

'It'll be worse now. There are more of them, they've got telephoto lenses, they'll buy stories off people, and they'll use all sorts of unscrupulous methods.'

'Perhaps you're right,' said Hobbes, nodding. 'I suppose a few days off wouldn't hurt.'

'Quite right,' said Sid. 'You'll need to do something about the lass and Andy, or they'll be subjected to unwelcome scrutiny. More drinks?'

When they arrived, Hobbes was looking thoughtful and, maybe, a little wistful.

'Thanks,' he said, accepting another large brandy. 'I've decided to head up to Straddlingate. I don't know why, because I haven't been there for years, but it just popped into my head. I'll let the lass know what's happening and I'll mention it to the superintendent as well.'

'Good idea,' said Sid. 'Now that's settled, did you hear about Daft Abel?'

'Abel Clutterbuck? Not since he saw the headline in the *Bugle* saying man wanted for burglary and he went in and applied for the job,' said Hobbes.

'Well,' said Sid, 'Tom Pollack told me he'd had a postcard from him. He was on Easter Island and it seems there was this shark …'

And I think that must have been when the final drink hit me.

5

I awoke, sorely afflicted by a raging thirst, a thumping headache and a bursting bladder, the latter of which was demanding urgent attention, despite my trying to wish it away and fall back into sleep. From the scent of apples and the absence of the underlying taint of Hobbes or Dregs, I knew I wasn't in my own bed and, since I was comfortable, with soft blankets pulled up to my chin, I wasn't at my parents'. Even after I'd prised open bleary eyes, I was still confused and lost, as the cold, grey light of early morning showed I was in a strange room, albeit one I felt I should recognise. I was lying on a chesterfield sofa. I sat up and realised I was still dressed, except for my jacket, bowtie and shoes. My head throbbed as I forced myself to stand, and I was panicking because I had no idea where the bathroom was and my need to reach it was rapidly approaching critical. As I staggered to the door, weak and shaky, my head was spinning and I came close to being sick.

I went into a gloomy hallway, where the scent of stale borscht made me understand that I was still at Sid's. The house was as quiet as the grave and, unable to see any stairs, my panic grew. A pair of large, matching china vases stood by the front door and I was seriously contemplating using one of them as an emergency pisspot, when I spotted a gap in the dark wooden panelling in front of me. Closer examination revealed a sliding door and, behind it, the stairs.

I would have run up them, had I dared. Instead I climbed steadily, concentrating on bladder control. At the top, faced with five closed doors, I came close to disaster, until my eyes adjusted to the gloom and I noticed the small china plaques on each door. Starting on the left, I read them: Bram's Room, Stephanie's Room, Sid's Room, Airing Cupboard, and finally, Batroom.

I opened the door and, seeing it was, indeed a bathroom, rushed inside, burst forth and stayed there for some time until the relief of Andy had reached its natural conclusion. As I tottered out, my headache more massive, my nausea barely under control, and my body shivering and weak, a small, ball-of-fluff cat hissed at me, put its ears back and fled downstairs. Taken aback, I stumbled, putting out a hand against a door to steady myself. The door flew open and I lurched inside.

Sid was staring at me, but he wasn't in bed. He was hanging by his ankles from a steel frame beside the wardrobe.

'I'm sorry,' I said, regaining my balance, 'the cat got in my way'.

'That's quite alright, young fellow. She's often in my way, too. My word, you do look rough, though it's hard to tell from this angle. Excuse me one moment.'

Grasping the side of the frame, he pulled himself upright, released his feet, stepped out of the contraption and slicked back his hair. For a moment, I almost forgot my hangover, paralysed by ancient preconceptions of vampires.

'Did I scare you?' he asked.

'Umm ... no ... yes.'

'I suppose you think I always sleep upside down, like a bat?'

'Don't you?' I asked unhappily.

'No,' he said, 'but, a few minutes inversion therapy does wonders for my stiff old back.'

'When my old editor had a bad back,' I said, grasping for normality, 'he swore by acupuncture. You could try it.'

'It's a little too close to being staked for my liking.'

'I see,' I said, and nodded, causing another wave of headache to break inside my skull.

'Hangover?'

I nodded again: a bad mistake.

'I'll fix you something that should help.'

'I don't want to be any bother.' I was desperate to lie down, to cover up, and to not move for hours.

'It'll be no bother.'

'What are you going to fix me?'

'A Bloody Mary.'

I might have guessed.

'It's my own recipe. It'll do you good, and I think you'll like it.'

Leading me back to the lounge, he propped me up on the sofa with cushions and headed for the drinks cabinet. With a laugh, like a mad scientist creating a monster, he selected a number of bottles and prepared his concoction.

'Get this down you,' he said, handing me a glass, 'and you'll soon be feeling more chipper.'

Grunting my thanks, I took it, mesmerised by the red, frothing contents and trying to think nice thoughts. Bracing myself, I took a sip. It was spicy and peppery and salty and thick. I wasn't sure I liked it but, before I'd come to a final conclusion, I'd finished it. Though I thought I felt a little better, less likely to throw up, my head was spinning again. Pulling the blankets to my chin, turning onto my side, I slept.

It must have been a couple of hours later, when I awoke again to full daylight, this time feeling like I might live, with the scent of roasting coffee making me want to. As I sat up, the door opened, the small, ball-of-fluff cat swaggered in, hissed, and scarpered, and then Sid was there with a steaming mug of coffee.

'Drink this,' he said, 'and your cure should be nearly complete.'

'Thank you.' I said. 'Is Hobbes here?'

'No, he's arranging a few days' leave.'

'That's probably a good idea. Did he stay last night?'

'No, he went home. He had some things to pick up and a dog to walk.'

'Why didn't he take me?'

'You were dead to the world, young fellow,' said Sid with a

toothy smile, 'and it would have been cruel to wake you. Wilber was all for it, but I convinced him you needed plenty of beauty sleep. Drink your coffee. Then, take a shower if you wish; I've laid out towels and stuff in the batroom. When you're ready, come through to the kitchen and I'll fix you some breakfast.'

'That's very kind.'

'Nonsense,' said Sid with a pleasant smile that made me decide I liked the old vampire. I was rather pleased with how cosmopolitan my outlook had become.

He left me to my drink. When it started to hit my stomach, and was infusing my body with a rosy glow of well-being, I was able to get up and look around the room and to examine the contents of Sid's enormous bookcase. Mostly it was filled with handsome, leather-bound volumes with titles, so far as I could make out, in Latin. The exception was the middle shelf, full of lurid paperback detective novels. They were so tightly packed I didn't dare remove any, fearing I'd never be able to get them back.

Then, heading upstairs, I enjoyed a long, hot shower, a rare luxury, as the one at Hobbes's, which he'd installed for himself, put lesser users in mortal peril. The last time I'd used it, I might have drowned had Mrs Goodfellow not come to my rescue.

Glowing and clean, I dressed and headed for the kitchen, where Sid prepared a full English breakfast for me to devour. That, washed down with more coffee, left me buoyant and ready to face anything. I'd just finished when the doorbell rang and he went to answer.

A moment later he walked in with Hobbes, who was sporting a bushy beard, a matching moustache and sunglasses.

'Good morning, how are you?' said Hobbes.

'Quite well. Sid's been looking after me.'

'Good,' said Hobbes. 'Do you fancy going camping?'

'I don't know. When?'

'Now.'

'Umm … where to?'

'Straddlingate.'

'Where's that?'

'It's in the Blacker Mountains,' said Hobbes. 'I haven't been back there for ages and it should be splendid this time of year.'

I could think of no reason why I shouldn't go. Perhaps I should have tried harder. 'OK then,' I said.

'Excellent,' said Hobbes. 'I've packed a tent and rations and clothes for both of us.'

'Umm … how do we get there? You broke the car.'

'Billy's agreed to take us until the road runs out. After that, we're on our own.'

'Alright.'

'I've brought you some fresh clothes,' said Hobbes, handing me a small bag.

I took it, hurried upstairs and got changed. A tweed suit was not quite what I'd envisaged, but it was, at least, an improvement on evening wear. I went back down.

'Let's go,' said Hobbes, turning to shake Sid's hand. 'Thank you for supper last night, and for looking after Andy and for your advice'

'Always a pleasure,' said Sid. 'Take care.'

'Goodbye. I'll be in touch soon,' said Hobbes, bundling me from the house into the street.

Billy Shawcroft was leaning against his old hearse, which was glinting in the sunlight.

'Wotcha,' he said, looking up.

'Hi,' I said and was knocked onto my back.

Dregs, who'd been preparing for the journey against a lamppost, had leapt at me, greeting my return to his world as if I'd been away for a month. As his great, pink tongue snaked towards my face, I rolled to the side and pushed him off, alarmed by the white flecks around his jaws.

'Stop messing about,' said Hobbes, 'and let's get away

before any reporters show up.'

Although there was plenty of room in the front of the hearse, I had to go in the back because Dregs insisted on riding there in case he wanted to stick his big, black head out the window. I wasn't much bothered for, despite having to share my space with a bagged tent and two bulging rucksacks, I could stretch out and relax. Billy, having strapped the wooden blocks to his feet that allowed him to reach the pedals, adjusted a pile of cushions and, when able to see over the steering wheel, drove away.

'I take it the reporters are still there,' I said.

'Yes,' said Hobbes. 'Even more than yesterday.'

'How did you get out of there with Dregs?' I asked, unable to imagine even Hobbes persuading him into a rucksack.

'I squirted shaving foam around his chops, opened the front door and shoved him out. As soon as the reporters saw him, they scattered like leaves in the wind, and I ran round the corner to meet Billy. I don't think anyone saw me.'

I laughed, impressed and amused by the brilliant simplicity of the plan. 'So how long will it take to get to wherever we're going?'

'About two hours,' said Billy. 'I've filled up, so we won't have to stop.'

He drove at a good speed, nowhere near as fast as Hobbes went, yet considerably faster than was normal, or decorous, for hearses. Fenderton passed in a blur and in no time we were heading upwards through lush green hills towards the dual carriageway. As soon as we were out of town, Hobbes peeled off his facial hair. He had a touching faith in his disguises, though his sheer size and enormous presence made him stick out like a panda in a poodle parlour.

When we reached the motorway, we headed north, maintaining a steady seventy miles per hour. Billy hummed along to the radio, switching stations whenever a tune failed to reach his standard. Hobbes was relaxed, his patience surprising for one more used to breakneck speed. Billy was just about the only other driver he trusted.

When the news came on, the attempted gold robbery had been relegated to third place, but Hobbes sat up when Jeremy Pratt reported a fresh development.

'Within the last few minutes,' said Jeremy, sounding both excited and pompous, 'a police spokesman informed me that a white van suspected of having been used in the attempted robbery was discovered burnt out on waste ground close to where it was last spotted. Although a forensic team is on the scene, it seems unlikely that any evidence will have survived the blaze.

'Of Inspector Hobbes, who, you will remember, heroically battled the gang, there has been no sign. There is speculation that he is actively pursuing the remaining gang members.'

Hobbes shrugged. 'Sid was right about the van, more's the pity. I'm glad to be taking a break. He was right about that, too.'

The journey continued peacefully, until Billy, running out of acceptable radio stations began singing. His high-pitched voice was strangely musical and soon I joined in, as did Dregs, who assisted on the high notes with howls, while supplying percussive barking and tail thumping where appropriate. Hobbes, despite claiming not to like this modern rubbish, sang along when the fancy took him and, fortunately, kept the volume down.

At last we left the motorway, heading west through fertile, undulating countryside, intersected with small rivers and streams. It was new territory to me, and the black and white cottages with their neatly thatched roofs, the fields and the orchards appealed, yet we quickly passed by, the road rising and narrowing as we headed towards the blue-grey of distant hills. A motorbike overtook at reckless speed.

'I'd have had him,' said Hobbes, 'if I was on duty. It's his lucky day.'

But it wasn't. A few miles further on, as we entered a village called Much Wetfoot, we stopped at a T-junction, something the biker had apparently failed to do, having ploughed straight ahead, demolishing a road sign, hitting a wall, flying over it and coming to rest amid the shattered glass of a greenhouse. A small crowd of local yokels had gathered to watch.

We stopped to help, but the biker was unhurt, seemingly more upset by the damage to the front forks of his bike than by his near death and the mess he'd caused, until Hobbes took him aside for a quiet word. As Dregs relieved himself on the bike's back wheel, a tall man in a battered jacket, his dark eyes strangely unfocussed, stared at Billy and me. His breath reeked of cider.

'Good day, sir' said Billy. 'What's the quickest way to get from here to Blackcastle?'

'Drive there,' said the man.

'But which way?' said Billy, with a glance at the demolished sign.

The man laughed and sat on the wall. 'Only joking, lads. Take the left fork.'

'How can we ever thank you?' I said.

'A drink wouldn't be a bad idea,' said the man, oblivious to my sarcasm.

'I'll sort it,' said Billy, taking something that rustled from his trousers, reaching up and stuffing it into the man's top pocket. 'Have one on us.'

'Cheers, lads,' said the man, with a grin and a cidery burp.

When we piled back into the hearse, I noticed our helpful friend was looking glum.

'What did you give him?' I asked.

'A sachet of drinking chocolate,' said Billy, chuckling. 'We were given free samples at the Feathers, only Featherlight won't do drinks like that. He says they're for wimps.'

A few miles on, the ground ever steeper, Billy asked where to turn.

'Soon,' said Hobbes. 'You see up there?' He pointed. 'That's the start of the Black Mountains.' He moved his finger a little to the left. 'That steeper ridge over there is the Blacker Mountains.'

'I hadn't even heard of them,' I admitted.

'I'm not surprised,' said Hobbes. 'No one lives there since the tenants were evicted and they can be dangerous. Even hill walkers give them a miss.'

'Dangerous?' I said. 'What d'you mean?'

'There are many perils up there for the unwary, but don't worry, I'm not unwary.'

I could feel the usual flocks of butterflies testing their wings in my stomach.

'What sort of perils?'

'Let me think. There are cliffs, caves, canyons, crevasses, screes, streams, gullies, rockslides, pitfalls, overhangs, marshes, icy waters, trackless wastes, mine workings and uncovered wells ...'

'Oh, great.' The butterflies, having taken wing, were flapping madly.

'... but probably the biggest danger is the weather, which can change within minutes and there's precious little shelter, unless you know where to look.'

'So, why are we going there?'

'Because it seems like a good idea.'

'Why?'

'I'm not sure really. It's wild, beautiful in its way, and exciting. I used to wander there when I was a child.'

'Wasn't it dangerous?'

'Not for me.' He glanced towards Billy. 'See that milepost? Turn immediately after it.'

We turned into an overgrown lane, finding it blocked by two enormous boulders.

'Well,' said, Billy, braking, 'I guess that's about as far as I can take you.'

'Nonsense,' said Hobbes, getting out. 'I'll shift them.'

Dregs went with him to lend moral support.

Putting his shoulder to the smaller of the two rocks, Hobbes heaved. For a moment, nothing happened, except that his face grew redder and the veins in his neck bulged like hose pipes. Then a dandelion toppled, and the boulder rolled aside, leaving a deep hollow. As he turned to the other one, he removed his raincoat, and hung it on a bush.

'Do you want a hand?' asked Billy, freeing his feet from his wooden blocks.

Hobbes, smiling, nodded. Billy joined him and, though he only came up to Hobbes's waist, his expression was determined.

'On three,' said Hobbes. 'Three!'

They pushed and grunted. For a few seconds, I thought Hobbes had met his match and even considered offering my help. The boulder moved a fraction.

'Heave!' cried Hobbes and the boulder, ploughing a furrow through the stinging nettles, rolled to one side.

'That's far enough,' said Billy, his round face puce like a plum. 'I can squeeze through now.'

'That,' said Hobbes, wiping his brow on his handkerchief, 'was fun. We need to go about five miles down the lane. That will take us to an abandoned manor.'

Although I'd witnessed some incredible feats from him, this one took some beating, for the boulder was as tall as him and even broader, but, as he retrieved his coat, he frowned and dropped to his knees. I had a sudden fear he'd suffered a heart attack and jumped out to help, but he was crawling forward like a monstrous toad, sniffing the grass, and examining the track. He stood up, brushing dust from his knees, and looking puzzled.

'It appears,' he said, 'that a heavy vehicle passed this way, sometime after last week's rain. I can't tell which way it was heading, but, whichever way, someone would have had to roll the boulders aside and then put them back. Why would anyone want to drive up here?'

'I don't know,' I said, 'but we're going to.'

'Very true,' he said, as we got back into the car.

The next couple of hundred metres took us over rutted, bumpy land but, just as I feared my brains would be shaken out, the going became much easier, the lane smooth and covered with short grass. I suspected the abundance of rabbits kept the vegetation down. They certainly kept Dregs interested. He made several frantic attempts to squeeze out of the window as white bobtails bounded away.

The track ended at the manor, a long, single-storey building of grey rock, still showing traces of whitewash, though the roof had long since fallen in.

'This is the end of the road,' said Hobbes, as we stopped. 'Thanks for the lift. Do you fancy a coffee or anything before you go? I can have the kettle on in no time.'

'No,' said Billy. 'I'd better get back. I'm working this evening and Featherlight doesn't like me being late.'

We unpacked our gear and piled it by a wall. Billy turned the hearse about.

'Have a great time, guys,' he said, 'and, when you need picking up, you've got my number. See you.'

He drove away, leaving me with feelings of abandonment and panic. I wasn't used to the wild and the mountains and moors seemed to be gathering around, threatening me with their vastness.

'This old house belonged to the dowager Lady Payne,' said Hobbes, chewing on a blade of grass. 'I knew her well.'

'What was she like?'

'I don't know,' he said. 'I never met her.'

'Then how did you know her well?'

'I used to draw water from it. I could do with a nice hot cup of tea and this dog will need a drink before we set off, so I'd better find it. It was over there, I think. The kettle and the mugs are in the black rucksack and the stove is in the grey one, if you wouldn't mind getting them out.'

Taking a jerry can and a length of rope from the pile, he strolled towards the old barn, shoved a heap of rusting, crumbling, corrugated iron out of the way and uncovered a round, flat stone, about the size of a dustbin lid. As I dug through the rucksacks, he slid the stone aside, peered into the hole, gave me a thumbs up and returned with the can full of water. Within a few minutes, we had tea to drink. Afterwards, while I rinsed the tin mugs and Dregs's bowl, Hobbes sorted out the gear.

'Right,' he said, picking up the larger rucksack, 'let's get into the mountains.'

6

Within minutes, with the straps of the smaller rucksack digging into my shoulders that were still tender from the previous day's hike, I was struggling to keep up as Hobbes led me into a pathless waste of rank grass, bracken and heather. The odd sparse, stunted gorse bush appeared to cower in the occasional dips and hollows, though what they were hiding from I couldn't imagine. The sun was bright and I might even have been too warm, were it not for a gentle breeze whispering through the grass. Hobbes, striding along, was almost hidden beneath his massive grey rucksack and our supplies. He either didn't believe in modern, lightweight tents, or hadn't heard of them, for, bundled on top of his rucksack was a great, folded sheet of faded green canvas, a couple of heavy wooden poles, and a ball of tangled, thumb-thick ropes. At least he didn't need to carry a mallet, for I'd seen how he could drive tent pegs into the stoniest ground with a few blows from his great, hairy fist. Although Dregs, much to his annoyance, had been saddled with panniers full of tins, he soon got used to them and bounded ahead, making barking forays in the general direction of rabbits. A tapestry of muddy brown, green and khaki, interspersed with startling yellow swathes of gorse, stretched before us and, away to our right, a tiny waterfall, splashing over a low black cliff, filled the air with rainbows.

It wasn't long before our path grew steeper and rougher. Now and again there were patches of bare, black rock, corrugated with deep cracks that Hobbes and Dregs took in their respective strides, while I had to scramble on hands and knees. Despite the breeze, I was soon sweating like a wrestler, and, despite having filled up with tea, my mouth was as dry as custard powder. My stomach began grumbling that it was way past lunchtime and I hoped Hobbes had brought something good to eat that wouldn't take too long to prepare and that he'd stop soon – very soon. I had a horrible suspicion that Dregs's panniers contained only dog food, which he would eat if sufficiently hungry, but which had little appeal to me.

'Did you see that?' asked Hobbes, pausing by a deformed and stunted thorn bush.

'What?'

'The fox.'

'No.'

I trudged after him, beginning to feel light headed with hunger as we reached the top of a ridge, with a narrow valley stretching below us, hemmed in by moorland and sheer cliffs, broken up by massive boulders. As we began the descent, I made up my mind to not get lost, for, although Hobbes might be able to find his way around this horrible wilderness, I was certain I couldn't. A low-grade panic was building, forcing me forward, ensuring he never got too far ahead and, when he finally stopped and I caught up, I was panting and dripping. Apart from his load, he looked as if he'd just stepped from the office after a morning's paperwork.

'Did you see that?' he asked.

'What?'

'The red kite.'

'No,' I said, frustrated, but determined to keep my eyes skinned and to point something interesting out to him.

'Never mind. We'll stop here for lunch.' He swung his kit to the ground.

I wriggled free from my rucksack, enjoying the breeze, feeling my shirt sticking to my back. The day was somewhat cooler than it had been and the valley, to my eyes, was uninviting; bare, broken rock with now and again a whiff of stagnant water from a nasty, green bog at the bottom.

'Is there a reason for stopping here?' I asked, rummaging in my rucksack for my cagoule, already having had enough of the wind.

'There's fresh water.'

'I can't see any,' I said, peevish with hunger, wrinkling my nose, 'unless you mean that stinking stuff down there.'

'No.' He laughed, and said, 'There's a spring.'

'Where?'

'In the cave.'

'What cave?' I asked.

'This one,' he said, dropping to his knees and crawling into what I'd taken to be a hummock, where there was a fissure just big enough for him to squeeze through.

'Pass me the jerry can,' he said, disappearing, leaving only his hand remaining in the light.

I passed it, and can and Hobbes were gone. Although Dregs found the procedure most entertaining, he showed no inclination to follow and nor did I, for I'd had too many bad frights in dark places. Instead, I dug out the kettle, the stove, and a box of matches and waited, hoping Hobbes did not get himself lost or stuck. If my worst fears were realised, I would have to attempt a rescue, as I had no mobile phone and would undoubtedly get lost should I go looking for help. After a few minutes of silence, my stomach tightening with nerves, I dropped to my knees and stuck my head into the dark, narrow cave.

'Are you alright?' I yelled.

There was no response, so, I crawled inside.

'Hello!' I cried, my voice muffled.

'Are you shouting to me?'

I jumped, headbutted the low ceiling and groaned. Puzzled, but relieved, I reversed into the daylight.

'Umm … how did you get here?'

'It's like a labyrinth in there,' said Hobbes. 'I came out another way.'

As I stood up, I considered punching him, and might have, had I believed it would hurt him more than it hurt me. Instead, I put the kettle on and, with a flourish like a stage magician pulling a rabbit from a hat, he produced a large, brown paper parcel from the rucksack. Inside was bread, cheese, pickles and salad, and two of Mrs Goodfellow's best china plates. I couldn't help thinking that he'd really catch it if we broke one.

I could barely restrain myself until it was time to eat and, as Hobbes passed me a plate, I fell to eating, like a wolf on the fold. Hobbes was more restrained, and Dregs was disappointed to get only water. The bread was fresh, crusty and fragrant, the Sorenchester cheese sweet and tangy, and the pickle pungent and perfect.

Hobbes, having filled two mugs with tea and given me one, took a slurp from the other. 'You'd better make the most of it. There's a meat pie for supper and after that we'll have to rely on what we can find or catch.'

'What,' I asked, staring at the desolate, empty landscape, 'is there to eat around here?'

'There are rabbits, hares, hedgehogs, stoats, fish, ducks and all sorts of roots and things. And there may still be wild strawberries, if we're really lucky.'

'But, how will we, umm ... you catch them?'

'Strawberries don't usually require much catching,' he said, smiling. 'As for the others I will use stealth, cunning, and possibly a rock. If we're unlucky, there are emergency rations in Dregs's pannier.'

'What are the chances we'll need them?'

'We'll see.'

Although his answer failed to reassure me, I experienced the sudden realisation that I didn't *not* want to be there and that I would have hated giving up on the life adventurous. Sometimes, I doubted my own sanity, because when things became dark, dangerous and uncomfortable, as was frequent when Hobbes was around, I still wanted to be there. I had sometimes cursed myself for not sticking to safe, familiar ways, but not often.

Having rested and eaten my fill, I was in a fairly cheerful

mood as we set off again, finding the going far easier on my feet than yesterday's road had been. It was hard to believe that had only been a day ago.

'Where, exactly, are we heading?' I asked breathlessly, having caught up.

'Straddlingate.'

'I know, but what is it? A camp site? Or a village?'

'It's a valley with an old quarry and some mine workings. It's said there was gold in these here hills, long ago.'

'Why are we going there in particular?'

'Something, I'm not sure what, is drawing me back. Possibly, it's because I always felt comfortable there, even though it can be a fearful place.'

'Fearful? What d'you mean?'

'I don't know exactly. Careful where you tread; that's a bog asphodel and it's quite rare.'

Looking down, I avoided crushing a plant with small orangey capsules and smooth stems, but only by stepping into a patch of thick, stinking, bubbling mud.

'Well done,' said Hobbes, as I extricated myself. 'Let's get a move on.'

As we strode deeper into the bleakness, he occasionally stooped to throw a stick for Dregs. Where Dregs had found a stick in such a desolate landscape was a mystery, but he was really in his element, his long legs making light work of the rough terrain.

It was a lot later when I realised that Hobbes had distracted me from questioning him about Straddlingate. Still, I reasoned that the company I was in would keep me fairly safe.

Hobbes stopped and pointed. 'Did you see them?'

'What?'

'The stoats.'

'No.'

He shrugged and carried on. I was annoyed with myself and feared he'd perceive me as a hopelessly unobservant clod.

The land remained bleak and lonely until we crested another ridge and started heading into a valley, where the air was fresh and clean, scented with gorse and some sweet herb. At the far end was a small pool, fringed by broken reeds, its dark waters backed up by a rugged cliff. I was feeling strangely euphoric, as if I'd cast off all the cares of the world, even though I'd never felt so far from the comforts and security of civilization, and even the tiredness of my leg muscles seemed pleasurable. I speculated that perhaps I was, at heart, a mountain man. Still, I was grateful when Hobbes said we'd arrived, for even Dregs had run out of bounds by then.

'Did you see that?' he asked as I stopped.

'Yes,' I lied.

'Then why did you step in it?'

My right foot was in the rotting, maggoty carcass of a crow or something. Its stench was such that even Dregs fled before it. I used a rock to prise it loose and finished the clean up on a tuft of heather.

'We'll camp down there,' said Hobbes, pointing towards a spring, bubbling from the side of the valley and forming a small stream that trickled and twisted down to the pool, where a grey heron, hunched on the far side, ignored us.

'This,' he said, still appearing as fresh as he'd been at the start, 'is Stradlingate. Let's get the tent up.'

Dropping my rucksack, I sprawled on a flat, sun-warmed rock and let him get on with it, for he knew what he was doing, and I would only have been in his way and got tangled up in all the lines. I did, however, pick up the bag of pegs, ready to hand to him, while Dregs, who believed Hobbes was being attacked by a vast canvas monster, growled encouragement and attacked any flapping edges. Yet, even with Dregs's contribution, it was not long before the tent was secure in the shelter of a gorse bush and Hobbes was punching in the final peg.

Although I couldn't stand up straight in it, there was plenty of room for all three of us. I just hoped the musty, dusty smell would go away. Dregs, accepting the transformation from monster to shelter with equanimity, lay down and went to sleep as soon as his blanket had been unrolled. I wasn't surprised that, instead of modern lightweight, micro-fibre sleeping bags, Hobbes had brought woollen rugs, which we piled on a pair of rubber-backed canvass groundsheets.

'That's yours,' he said, pointing to the left, 'and this is mine.'

'Will it be warm enough?' I asked. 'It must get pretty nippy at night.'

'We'll be fine ... probably,' said Hobbes. 'I doubt the weather will turn bad for a day or two.

'I fancy a bit of a run up the Beacon. D'you want to come?'

'I think I've had quite enough exercise today,' I said, yawning. 'Where is the Beacon?'

Taking me outside, he pointed to a distant peak that rose high above the ridges. It was conical, covered with browning bracken on the steep sides, with bare rock as it reached the domed top, reminding me of Friar Tuck's tonsure. The sun, still bright and hot, was over the summit.

'It looks a long way off,' I said, glad I'd chickened out.

'Not really,' said Hobbes. 'I'll be back by dusk.'

'When's that?'

'When it starts to get dark.'

He left, his great loping strides taking him along the valley and then, via a cleft, towards the peak. I watched until he was out of sight and joined Dregs, who was snoring gently and twitching on his blanket. With a yawn, I lay down on top of my rugs, it being too warm inside to cover up, and rested my eyes for a few moments.

I awoke to Dregs's low growling, though that wasn't what had woken me. He was outside, bristling and ill at ease, and I understood, for something felt wrong, though I couldn't put my finger on quite what. I got up, surprised how gloomy the day had grown, and shivered, wishing Hobbes was back. Then I felt it, a weird sensation, an odd vibration, passing through my feet, up my body into my head. Though I couldn't have explained why, I decided it was coming from some distance, but as I left the tent, it stopped. In the distance, I could see Hobbes jogging towards us. Dregs rushed to greet him.

'Did you feel that?' I asked when they were back.

Hobbes nodded.

'What was it?'

'I don't know, but I remember something like it when I was a boy.'

I had never envisaged Hobbes as a boy. He gave the impression of having arrived fully formed, although he had made occasional remarks about his childhood, particularly about Auntie Elsie and Uncle Jack, who'd adopted him and guided him through his troubled youth. From what I'd gathered, he'd caused much of the trouble.

'It felt,' he said, 'like machinery in the mines.'

'Does that mean someone's mining?'

'Possibly,' he said, 'but I'd expect to see some signs.'

'Back when we left the road, you reckoned a heavy vehicle had been along before us.'

'That is true,' he said, 'but it seems unlikely they'd restart mining. They were all closed in the nineteenth century.'

'Then it's a mystery,' I said, with masterful insight.

'It is,' said Hobbes with a laugh, 'but it's nothing to do with us. All the land round here is private and what the owner does on it is his business.'

'What do you mean private land? We're not trespassing are we?'

'Only in the legal sense,' said Hobbes.

'What other sense is there?'

'Moral, or ethical. This whole area used to be common land, land that many families depended on. Then Sir Rodney Payne enclosed it and took it for himself, but his right to do so is debatable. What is not debatable is that Sir Rodney used considerable force and the enclosure was, in effect, robbery with violence.'

'How do you know all this?'

'Uncle Jack told me. His father used to have a small farm, grazing sheep on Blacker Knob, until Sir Rodney threw him and his family out.'

'So, if he hadn't, would the farm have come to you eventually?'

'No. Uncle Jack was a younger son and, back then, inherited property went to the eldest.'

'When was that?'

'Late in the eighteenth century. Sir Rodney was widely regarded as the most odious man in the county and the same family still owns it. Most of them are no better than Sir Rodney, if the stories are to be believed. The point is, I have no compunction in being here. The Payne family may have the law on its side, but it does not have justice and, besides, we won't be doing any harm; there's nothing we could damage. Furthermore, we have the legal right to roam these days.'

'Good,' I said. 'Umm ... when is supper?'

He laughed. 'You have a talent for getting back to what is really important. Supper's ready as soon as you've made tea and I've got the pie out.'

I filled the kettle and set it to heat on the stove, worried that there only appeared to be one gas cylinder, but hoping he had a plan for when it was used up; although he might not have had a problem with raw stoat, I certainly did and even Dregs preferred cooked meals. Still, that was a worry for later and the sight of the huge meat pie set my mouth watering. I made tea, Hobbes said grace and sliced the pie into generous chunks. We sat at a long, smooth rock that made a useful table, stuffing ourselves. Afterwards, he produced a bag of apples and, munching one, I began to feel comfortable and confident. The sun had long ago dipped beneath the Beacon, the temperature was dropping and night was falling fast. Hobbes lit a candle lantern, our only light.

'What are we going to do tonight?' I asked, hoping there'd be a cosy pub within easy walking distance, but fearing the appearance of being in the middle of nowhere was no illusion.

'We're going to wash up,' said Hobbes, 'and then I'm going to turn in. You can do what you like.'

'I hoped we might grab a beer or something.'

'The nearest pub is in Blackcastle. It's about eight miles due east of here. You can't miss it.'

'OK … Which way is east?'

'Over there.' He pointed. 'Roughly opposite to where the sun went down. Of course, to get there you'll have to cross Dead Man's Bluff.'

'I might give it a miss tonight.'

'Suit yourself.'

As soon as we'd washed up in cold water and stacked the plates to drip dry, he retired into the tent.

Wrapping my jacket around me, I lay on the flat rock, gazing at the stars. I'd never seen such abundance. Hobbes had once tried to teach me about them, displaying a vast theoretical and practical knowledge, but astronomy was way over my head. I could, at least, recognise the moon, half of which was rising, making the mountains shine with a pale, silvery light. Once or twice I noticed the flickering silhouettes of bats and, faraway, an owl screeched, emphasising the quietness and the isolation and filling me with a sense of melancholy and loneliness that was almost exhilarating. Sprawled, relaxed, contemplating the cosmos, I thought deep thoughts and pondered much on the meaning of life, until Dregs started licking himself. The mood shattered, I relieved myself in a gorse bush and decided to turn in. Anyway, I was starting to feel cold.

Hobbes, fast asleep, didn't stir as I snuggled into my pile of rugs. I was sure the ground was too hard and rocky and the rugs nowhere near thick enough to allow me to sleep, especially as Dregs had decided to lie on my feet.

When I awoke it was morning, and Hobbes and Dregs were already up. It took me a while to join them, because my back was rigid and my neck stiff and besides, it was warm where I was. Yet I had to move sometime, so, with a sigh, I crawled out into bright daylight and got to my feet, grunting good morning, stretching and yawning. Hobbes, having made a fire from old bits of gorse, was filleting several large trout.

'Where did you get those from?' I asked.

'Over there.' He pointed down the valley to the pool.

'Great. How did you catch them?'

'With difficulty, because they didn't want to be caught. I think they were nervous of the heron.'

When he started frying them, along with a handful of green leaves he'd found, the air was filled with delicious scents; they tasted even better. Fresh fish cooked and eaten in fresh air really piqued the appetite.

'I could get used to this,' I said, stuffing the last bit into my mouth.

'Yes. This is good living. There's plenty to eat around here and I doubt I'll have much trouble at this time of year. It's not so good in the depths of winter, though.'

'We won't be here that long, will we?'

'No. At least, I hope not, but it is October and the weather up here can change within minutes. Still, it should stay warm and sunny for the next few days. After that, I'm not so sure.' He sniffed the air and glanced at the sky. 'We'll see.'

'Do you think bad weather's on the way?'

'Maybe, but let's enjoy the good stuff while we can.'

Having never gone camping in really bad weather before, I wasn't much looking forward to the prospect, but Hobbes didn't concern himself with future problems that might not even arise. It struck me as a good way of living, one that I wished I could follow. Unfortunately, I had a tendency to worry, despite having learned that the worrying about a dreaded event was often far worse than the event itself. This wasn't always the case, for I had another tendency to drop myself into messes far deeper than I'd anticipated.

After we'd eaten and I'd scrubbed the dishes, I asked a foolish question.

'What do we do about washing ourselves?'

The pool was cool and clear and, once the shock of being thrown into it had passed, refreshing.

The next two days were glorious. We'd turn in as the light faded and wake early. I made it to the top of Beacon Peak, where I sat stunned by the vastness of the landscape as the morning mist dispersed. The hills looked pristine, as if human kind had never intruded, and it felt like we'd awoken into the first dawn of a clean, new world. When we got back down, Hobbes, naked and as hairy as a bear, his beard grown shaggy already, would plunge headfirst into the lake, often emerging with an eel or a trout between his jaws. Later, he would gut them, clean them and fry them for breakfast. The rest of the day, we would walk over the ridges and, despite Dregs's attentions, Hobbes would hunt for rabbits and hares, or scratch around for herbs and roots. He discovered a hunched, arthritic old apple tree, a remnant, so he said, of an ancient farmhouse, and roasted some of the ripe fruit on a sheet of corrugated iron that he unearthed in a cave. We ate like lords and never had to eat a stoat or open our emergency rations, though we had to drink our tea without milk.

By my reckoning, it was on the third day when our morning walk took us to Blacker Knob, a tall peak, where near the top, a pile of rocks might long ago have been a cottage. That was where our camping trip took a dark turn.

7

Hobbes was chasing a hare and, since he appeared to be enjoying his workout, I found myself somewhere sheltered to sit and watch. Dregs, for once not bounding after him, started barking, and something in the tone suggested urgency. I stood up, the wind blustering and raising goose pimples, and went to see what was bothering him. Bristling, excited and ill at ease, he was sniffing round a pile of small rocks and pawing at something.

'What is it?' I asked.

A smooth, round, white object, a bit like a child's ball, rolled towards me. Bending, I picked it up and was nearly sick. I had a human skull in my hand and, although my first instinct was to drop it, I couldn't let go. I stared into the empty eye sockets.

'Alas, poor Yorick!' I said, a long-forgotten incident popping unbidden into my head. 'I knew him, Dregs.'

It was a conditioned response and I was as unable to restrain myself as Pavlov's dogs could have stopped drooling at the sound of a bell. It all went back to when my class was studying the graveyard scene in Hamlet and I still remembered the malicious expression of Psycho Simms, our English teacher, who, book in hand, called me and 'Bill' Bailey to the front.

'Caplet,' said Psycho, 'although you are, perhaps, the most unlikely prince, you will recite Hamlet's part. Bailey, you play Horatio. Take it from where Hamlet picks up the skull.'

'Yes sir,' I said, my mind instantly going as blank as the freshly-wiped whiteboard. 'Alas ... umm ... alas ... alas ... alas ... umm.'

'Poor,' said Psycho.

'I'm sorry, sir. Oh, I see: that's what comes next.' I turned towards Bailey 'Alas, poor ... umm ...' I stared at his round, pimply face, struggling to recall the stupid name, growing ever more desperate, my mind empty of everything but embarrassment. As Psycho and the class waited and waited, someone sniggered and the blood burned my cheeks as my dramatic pause seemed to stretch towards infinity.

Bailey, taking pity, was mouthing the name.

I nodded, confidence flooding back, and, raising my hand dramatically, staring at an imaginary skull, I came out with the immortal words: 'Alas, poor Yogi!'

I never finished the speech. My role ended with a stunning rap on the head from the complete works of Shakespeare, mocking laughter from my classmates and having to write out the scene one hundred times.

Hobbes appeared with a brace of hares dangling limply from his belt.

'Hello, 'ello, 'ello,' he said. 'I take my eye off you for one minute and find you engaged in all sorts of skulduggery.'

I grimaced.

'I always knew you'd get ahead one day.'

'How can you joke about it?' I asked, trembling and hoping I'd only picked up a prehistoric relic, not a recently dead skull.

'Sorry,' he said, 'but humour soothes the sting of horror. Give it to me, please.'

I handed it over, nearly losing my breakfast when he sniffed it. He frowned, turning it over and round, running his hand over it, holding it up and examining it from all angles.

'It's only a few years old at the most and, judging by the size and the brow ridge, I'd say it belonged to an adult male human. It has received a severe blow to the top which caused a penetrating fracture. Of course, that might have occurred post mortem. I'm not an expert.'

Carefully, he put it down and began sifting through the rock pile, pushing aside a number of slabs to reveal a skeleton, still partially covered in ragged, faded scraps of clothing and with a pair of boots on the feet. I grabbed for Dregs's collar, but he made no attempt to go for the bones.

'Again,' said Hobbes, frowning and thoughtful, 'the hips suggest an adult male and, to judge from the long bones, quite a tall one.' He pointed to an arm. 'The upper bone plate and radius have fused, suggesting he was out of his teens, while the collarbone development indicates he was probably older than his late twenties.'

Squatting, he peered at the torso, where it was exposed beneath what might have once been a red-checked shirt. 'There is a little degeneration of the spine and that, together with the wear and tear on his teeth, leads me to speculate that our man was in his mid-forties.'

His calm assessments felt like soothing balm on my raw nerves and my brain started functioning again.

'How long has he been here?' I asked. 'And how did he get here?'

'It's not easy to be accurate,' he said, 'and as I said, I'm no expert, but I'll take a stab at it. The rocks and slates have protected the body from larger scavengers, so the skeleton is mostly intact and, although small animals have disturbed them to some extent, the bones are in reasonably good condition. The clothing and the boots are modern and appear to be of a type suitable for hill walking. I'd guess the cloth has made many a mouse nest cosier.

'I'd say he's probably been dead for two, maybe three years, and that someone killed him and carried him here to conceal the body.'

'It was murder then?' I said, my sick feelings returning.

'It seems likely. Clearly he didn't bury himself and the skull fracture suggests a violent attack. Assuming that's what killed him, the wound would have bled considerably, but there's no sign it bled round here, although that might be down to time and rain. I would also have expected a hill walker to have some sort of backpack and, at least, basic survival gear.'

'So,' I said, 'the poor guy was probably killed elsewhere and the murderer hid the body here. He didn't do a very good job.'

'No,' said Hobbes, 'but he wouldn't expect anyone to be up here.'

I shivered and it wasn't because of the cold wind.

'I suppose,' he said, scratching his chin, 'we should tell the authorities.'

'I suppose so.'

'The trouble is that I came here to escape publicity and, although I expect things have quietened down by now, I would rather not draw attention to myself again. You'll have to go into Blackcastle and tell the police. You could say you were out walking your dog and came across the skeleton on Blacker Knob, which is essentially the truth.'

'OK,' I said, reluctantly, 'but how do I … umm … get to Blackcastle?'

'I'll guide you to the outskirts. It's not far.'

'You said it was eight miles away!'

'Exactly.'

'Fine. How will I find my way back? I don't know where here is.'

'That's a good point,' he said. 'I'll lay a trail.'

We set off straight away, despite my hints that it was nearly lunchtime. He led Dregs and me to the outskirts of the little grey town, and handed me some money for a bite to eat and to buy a newspaper, asking me to check if interest in him had yet waned. Then he left us.

Dregs and I followed a potholed track into Blackcastle, walking past a row of seedy terraced houses that might have been transformed into something reasonably attractive had anyone been bothered. A slab pivoted, its front end going down, its back end rising and catching my foot, making me stumble and put my hand on a sturdy-looking garden gate. Giving a sad sigh, it crumbled into dust, falling onto a garden path that was ankle deep in dandelions and grass. As I hurried on, pretending it had been nothing to do with me, a terrier in the next garden along woofed once before relapsing into apathy and going back to chewing what appeared to be a flat cap. Dregs, knowing he was on a mission, ignored him and we turned onto a narrow street, hemmed in by squat, concrete buildings that I imagined estate agents might have referred to as bijou maisonettes. Their grey walls were stained and cracked, the paintwork bubbled and peeled and the doors and window frames were rotten.

Although some areas of Pigton, the nearest big town to Sorenchester, were rather rundown, I'd never before been anywhere as spirit draining as that godforsaken place. Even Dregs's normal bounding enthusiasm was dampened and he walked obediently to heel. As we reached the last house of the terrace, an old woman in a shabby brown cardigan appeared to be scavenging from a dustbin and, despite my friendly smile, she flinched and scurried inside, slamming the front door behind her. I blamed Dregs for alarming her, though I found his presence comforting.

We turned onto what appeared to be the main street, which took us towards an unexpectedly broad market square with a war memorial and a drinking fountain in the middle. The Badger's Rest, an old-fashioned and tatty pub, filled the nearest corner, while the police station, relatively modern, yet possibly even tattier, occupied the opposite one. A glance into the pub showed it was full of morose, down-at-heel drinkers. I led Dregs towards the police station, passing one small, dejected shop, allegedly a mini-supermarket, with its pathetic display of wrinkled, yellowing vegetables in a rack outside. The other buildings in the square appeared to be houses, one or two of them apparently derelict and covered in ragged posters for the approaching autumn fair. Near the police station, one place really stood out, looking clean, freshly painted in bright pink, with baskets bright with flowers hanging from brackets. A sign printed in large, frilly letters declared it was Pinky's Tearoom.

I took the most direct line towards the police station, striding there with due urgency, only to find it was locked. A faded sign pinned to the door said: 'back in 5 minuets'. I couldn't stop myself looking around for a dance hall.

'Are you after the cops, love?' asked a soft female voice.

I turned to see a plump, pretty, blonde woman, dressed in a trouser suit in the same shocking pink as the tea room.

'Yes,' I said, trying not to stare.

'They'll be down the Badger's. I'd look in there if I were you.'

'Thank you.'

'Don't mention it, love.'

'Umm ... are you Pinky?'

Her big blue eyes widened in surprise. 'I am. How did you know?'

'Just a hunch.'

'Are you a detective?'

'No ... not really ... it's sort of a complicated story.'

'Well, come in for a cup of tea and tell me.'

Although I did fancy a drink and had money in my pocket, duty called. 'Maybe later, but I must tell the police something: something important.'

'Alright then. See you, love,' She turned and headed towards her tearoom in a cloud of perfume.

Leaving Dregs by the drinking fountain, I walked into the pub, its door opening with a horrible creak and the murmur of conversation immediately dying. The silence was broken only by the door creaking back and somebody coughing. As my eyes accustomed themselves to the gloom, I felt something zip past the tip of my nose and heard a clunk.

'Three!' said a male voice.

'That wanker put me off,' said a deeper, angry male voice.

I jerked backwards as the next dart flew past my face, wondering what sort of idiot would throw when someone was almost in the firing line, and what sort of idiot would position a dartboard between the door and the bar. It wasn't exactly welcoming, but then, as I looked around, nor was the rest of the pub. Dingy was the first word that came to mind, followed by dirty, dismal, disgusting, and smelly. As the third dart hit the board, I took my chance and scuttled towards the bar and, I hoped, safety. I couldn't see any policemen, just a bunch of drunken, scruffy men hunched on plastic covered stools, glasses in their hands, watching me. One man, flat on his back on the worn, sticky lino, began emitting blood-curdling snores.

The barman, a tall, skinny old man, whose cardigan was so riddled with holes it might have made a passable fishing net, nodded. 'You're not from around here, are you? I know that 'cos we don't get many strangers in here.'

'I can't understand why not,' I said, smiling, trying to establish friendly relations.

'Are you trying to be funny?'

'No... umm ... it's quite quaint, really.'

'It's a total shit hole,' said the man. 'Are you blind?'

'I nearly was,' I said. 'Isn't it dangerous having the dartboard there?'

The barman shrugged. 'I didn't put it there. What's your poison?'

Although I hadn't intended buying a drink, I thought doing so might endear me. 'A half of lager, please.'

Someone sniggered.

'We don't serve poncey drinks in here, mate,' said the barman. 'We've got bitter or scrumpy.'

'OK ... umm ... I'll have a half of scrumpy.'

'We don't sell halves, except if it's for a lady.'

'I'll have a pint then.'

Turning, he sauntered towards a plastic barrel and poured my drink into a glass that was so chipped and greasy I feared it might be harbouring bubonic plague at the very least. He returned and placed it in front of me. I took a sip, surprised to find it wasn't bad.

'I went to the police station,' I said, adopting my most ingratiating expression and leaning on the bar, 'but it was closed. A lady said I might find a policeman in here.'

'You might,' said the barman, 'but that's none of my business.'

'Isn't it?' For a moment, I was stumped. Then I had an idea and addressed the drinkers: 'Is there a policeman in here?'

There was silence, apart from a thud from the dartboard, a very rude word and the deeper, angry male voice complaining that I'd put him off again.

'A policeman?' said a youngish man with a thin moustache and a plastic cigarette balanced on his lip. 'In that case, I reckon you'll be wanting Sam,'

'Who's Sam?'

'Sam,' said the man, grinning, 'is a police officer.'

'I gathered that, but where is he.'

'In here.'

'I see … umm … are you Sam?'

'No, but I, too, am a police officer.'

'Well, perhaps you could help me?'

'Perhaps I could, but you'll be wanting Sam.'

I addressed the pub again: 'Which one of you is Sam?'

Though there was no reply, everyone, except for the two playing darts, was watching me, as if I was a strange curio. Rare inspiration struck.

'It's him, isn't it?' I said, pointing at the man lying on the floor, who had stopped snoring, but had started drooling.

'Yep,' said the other police officer and, as if suddenly realising what he was supposed to do, rose to his feet, a trifle unsteadily, holding out his hand. 'I'm Constable Jones. Sergeant Beer is, regrettably, indisposed at the present time. How may I help?'

I shook his hand. 'My name is Andy Caplet and I have something to report.'

'Go on, then.'

'Umm … it might be better at the police station.'

'He's come to make a confession,' said the barman with a grin that was as lacking in teeth as the bar was in comfort. 'I reckon he's run over a sheep.'

'I haven't run over a sheep. I don't have a car.'

'Has it been stolen?' asked Constable Jones, pulling a notebook from the pocket of his trousers.

'No, I've never had one.'

'Then, how did you get here?'

'I walked.'

'I believe you, sir. What brings you to these parts?'

'I'm on holiday.'

This provoked a general guffaw from the onlookers. It seemed I was the best entertainment they'd had for weeks. With the exception of Sergeant Beer, I was the focus of everybody's attention and even the darts had stopped flying.

Constable Jones was shaking his head and grinning. 'No, really, what are you doing here?'

'I'm really on holiday.'

'Escaped from some sort of institution, have you, sir? We don't get tourists round these parts, and walkers don't usually wear tweed.'

'I haven't escaped from anywhere, I am on holiday and what I choose to wear is my own business. I really have got something terribly important to report.'

'Important, eh? Why didn't you say so?'

'I haven't had the chance.' I said, starting to get flustered. 'I've found a skeleton. Well, my dog did.'

The levels of public amusement increased.

Constable Jones made a pantomime of looking about him. 'Your dog, sir?'

'He's outside. He found a man's skeleton on Blacker Knob. It's been there for about three years.'

That stopped the laughter and Constable Jones's expression

switched to serious. 'You'd better come with me, sir.'

Taking my arm, he led me outside, where Dregs introduced himself by thrusting his nose into the constable's groin before jumping up and licking his face. Jones, pushing him down, led us to the police station and unlocked the door.

'Come in, sir,' he said, 'and bring your dog. I'll open Interview Room number one and then I'd be obliged if you'd tell me your story.'

Blackcastle police station, its shoebox entrance hall painted a blotched khaki, the front desk chipped and covered in scrawls, wasn't much to write home about. The place stank of damp and feet, with an underlying aroma of urine. Jones, unlocking a battered door to the side of the desk, ushered me through a grim, open plan office, with three empty desks, towards Interview Room number 1, which was, so far as I could see, the only interview room.

'Take a seat, sir. Not the wooden one: that's mine. Would you like a cup of tea? Or would you prefer to finish your scrumpy?'

I sat down on the cheap, white, plastic chair, behind a manky, old wooden table and, realising I was still carrying my drink, gulped it down and asked for tea. Jones left us for a few minutes, giving me time to adjust. Besides the background stink, the room retained a residual pong of stale coffee and vomit. If I'd stretched out my arms, I could have touched two walls at the same time, had they not been blackened by mould. There was a tiny square of frayed, brown carpet beneath the table and Dregs, having sniffed it with evident interest, rubbed his bottom on it. I tried to ignore him.

'Right sir,' said Jones, returning with a chipped mug, containing industrial-strength tea, and setting it on the table in front of me, 'I'll need to take down a few details.'

Sitting down, taking out a notebook and a pencil, he prepared himself. I gave my name and address and, despite my concern that he'd react at the mention of Sorenchester, he did not appear to recognise it. Then I explained why I was in the area, avoiding any mention of Hobbes, and how Dregs and I had come across the skeleton.

'That, sir,' said Jones, pleasantly, 'is an interesting account, but I wonder if you could enlighten me on one point before we move on? When we were in the Badger's, you said the skeleton had been there for about three years. What makes you think that?'

'Umm ... it was just a guess really. I've never seen a skeleton before, but there was no flesh on him and his clothes, or what was left of them, looked modern.'

'Him, sir? What leads you to suppose it was a male skeleton?'

'Well, I don't know really. It was quite big and the skull had brow ridges, but I'm just guessing.'

'You had no idea there'd be a body there?'

'None at all. I'd never been there before.'

'Could you point out the location on your map?'

'Umm ... I'm not sure ... I don't have a map.'

'I find it interesting that someone who has never been around here before manages to walk straight from Blacker Knob to Blackcastle without a map. How did you manage it?'

'I reckoned that, if I headed ... umm ... east, I'd find the town. I left a trail so I can take you back.'

'How did you know you were on Blacker Knob?'

'I didn't know,' I said, surprised at the acuity of Jones's questioning and getting agitated, '... I think someone must have told me.'

'Who? When?'

'I can't remember.' As I floundered, I wished I'd paid more attention to Hobbes when he was giving me a cover story.

'I'm forming the opinion,' said Jones, 'that you are withholding information. I wouldn't advise you to do that, sir.'

A small flare of anger erupted. 'Look,' I said, 'the important thing is that I've found a skeleton. The man may have been murdered and ...'

'Murdered, sir? That's a new one. What makes you think he might have been murdered?'

'I don't know ... it looked like he'd had a bump on the head.'

'Did you bump him off, sir?' Constable Jones's gaze held me in a tight grasp.

'No ... no. It wasn't me,' I said, squirming, but unable to break his stare.

An electric bell rang, making me jump.

'Wait here,' said Jones.

When he left, I tried to reassure myself that I hadn't done anything wrong and, consequently, had nothing to fear. Unfortunately, I was still worried about what was going to happen, even though I had, essentially, told the truth and had held nothing important back. All I had omitted was Hobbes; admittedly that was a rather large omission and I wished he'd turn up and explain. I finished my mug of tea, which wasn't as bad as it looked, and burped as the scrumpy bubbled back, with a sharp overtone of onion, or was it garlic? Dregs seemed to be taking my discomfiture in his stride, or rather his sleep.

Jones was talking. I assumed he was on the phone, until I heard a woman speaking. The voices faded and I sat in silence for a few minutes until Constable Jones returned, wearing hill walking gear.

'Sorry about the wait, but I had to brief Mrs Duckworth about your information.' He said the name as if he expected me to recognise it.

'Who,' I asked, 'is Mrs Duckworth?'

'Councillor Hugh Duckworth's wife.'

I shrugged and looked blank.

'Councillor Duckworth,' said Jones, 'vanished in mysterious circumstances, just over three years ago.'

'I see. Umm ... do you think it's him?'

'Quite probably and so does Mrs Duckworth. She insists on accompanying us. It's against regulations, but I have no intention of stopping her.'

'But what about your sergeant? Shouldn't he come too?'

'He may not be capable.'

'Of course I'm capable,' said the booming voice of Sergeant Sam Beer. He walked in, tall, fat, red in the face, stinking of beer and sweat and wearing dirty khaki shorts, a faded Black Sabbath T-shirt and a pair of flip-flops. 'Since it's the first interesting thing to happen in this godforsaken town in the last three years, I'm not going to miss it. Let's get a move on.'

'Shouldn't you change your clothes, sir?' asked Constable Jones.

'Nonsense. I'll be fine.'

The two police officers escorted me from the station and into the market square, where Sergeant Beer thrust his head under the drinking fountain for so long I feared he'd drown himself. Then, standing up, shaking himself like a dog, he smoothed back his greying hair and stood upright, relatively alert and ready to go. After a few moments, Mrs Duckworth, a small woman about my age or possibly a little younger, joined us and, with her dark eyes, soft brown hair and neat figure, was, in my opinion, highly attractive. Having such thoughts in the circumstances filled me with guilt, for I was going to take her to see what were probably the mortal remains of her husband.

'What are we waiting for?' asked Sergeant Beer.

'For Mr Caplet to stop staring at Mrs Duckworth and show us the way,' said Constable Jones.

'Oh,' I said, 'I'm awfully sorry. It's this way.'

As I turned away, I thought I glimpsed a moving shadow on the rooftop opposite and wondered whether Hobbes was keeping an eye on me.

8

I led my posse through the deserted streets, rarely seeing anything move, besides an occasional pigeon or sparrow. As we were leaving town, an old tom cat, big, ginger and fierce looking, swaggered by, giving us a disdainful glance. Dregs made a point of not noticing him.

On leaving Blackcastle, I came to the conclusion that it was the most depressing place I'd ever visited, which was saying something for one who'd endured so many Caplet family holidays. Father, never having been one for spending more than he had to, was drawn to any apparent bargain, no matter how unsuitable. We'd once spent a week in the middle of an industrial estate, staying in a dingy flat above a derelict abattoir. It had rained nearly every day and petrol was, according to Father, too expensive to take us anywhere, without good reason. Merely enjoying ourselves was not good enough. Effectively marooned, I'd had to make my own entertainment, playing with the rats that lived downstairs and even thinking I'd made friends with one, until it bit me on the lip. The trip to hospital for a tetanus jab and a stitch was the highlight of the holiday.

My spirits lifted as we headed back into the wilderness, following Hobbes's trail, which he'd made by breaking off gorse branches, chewing off the spines and the bark, gnawing one end into a spike and driving them into the ground at regular intervals. I had no idea why he'd used his teeth, since he had a perfectly serviceable pocket knife. The pale stakes, standing out against the green and brown, were easy to follow and we made good progress. Anyway, Dregs seemed to know where he was going.

We walked silently in Indian file until Mrs Duckworth caught up with me.

'Mr Caplet,' she said, 'I understand you are here on holiday?'

'Yes.'

'It's a funny place to choose.'

'Umm ... yes, I suppose so, but he ... umm ... I mean ... I wanted somewhere quiet and off the beaten track.' I hoped she'd not noticed my little slip.

'He?' she said.

'What?' I replied.

'You mentioned a *he*.'

'Did I? I meant Dregs.'

'Are you saying you came here because your dog wanted to?'

There was a hint of suspicion in her voice, which otherwise, was soft and rather pleasant. I tried to allay her worries. 'I'm sorry, I didn't mean to say he. It's just that I've been a bit distracted since I found the bones. He reckons ... I reckon it might have been murder.'

'There's that *he* again. Are you here with someone?'

'Just my dog,' I said, putting on a spurt, trying to avoid catching her eye, and attempting to project an aura of honesty and reliability. I suspected I'd only made myself look shifty.

Mrs Duckworth caught up again, frowning. 'Don't take me for a fool, Mr Caplet. Your story doesn't ring true.'

I was aware the two policemen were listening in and couldn't stop myself blushing and biting my lip, making it look as if I really did have something to hide, something to be ashamed of. I tried to be firm.

'Look, the truth is that I've never been anyway near here before and just happened to come across the bones while out on a walk with Dregs. As soon as I found them, I immediately went to Blackcastle to inform the police.'

'For which we thank you,' said Constable Jones. 'It was very clever of you to find your way to us, without a compass or map and it's puzzling that, having managed so well, you had to mark the path.'

'Umm ... I didn't ... or rather, I sort of did. I ... umm ...

thought the sun might dazzle me on the way back.'

It wasn't a very convincing response, but I was getting in a flap. The constable was obviously no fool and I feared I was going to drop myself into some serious trouble, unless I mentioned Hobbes. Instead, feigning deafness, I strode on, as fast as I could go.

We made good progress, climbing steadily, and had reached what might once have been a lane, when I found myself on the horns of a dilemma for, although I was merely a little out of breath and sweaty, Sergeant Beer's face was as red as a raspberry and he was panting like an old steam train. I was worried I'd have another body on my hands if I didn't call a halt, but if I did, they'd start questioning me again. I had not yet come to a decision when I heard something.

'What's that?' I asked, though it was obviously a car's engine revving hard.

Sergeant Beer, slumping against a rock, sighed. 'Trouble. How did he hear about it?'

The engine noise grew louder and a gleaming, white Land Rover with mirrored windows rounded the bend, heading straight at us, not bothering to brake until the last possible moment. If the driver was trying to intimidate us, and I thought he was, then he only partially succeeded, as I was the only one who dived for cover. At least I amused Dregs and, by the time I'd pushed him off and got to my feet, a tall, dapper man, sporting a clipped moustache, was stepping from the Land Rover.

'Ah,' he said in a posh drawl, 'it's Sergeant Beer and his mob. Would you explain what you're doing on my land?'

Sergeant Beer, standing straight, mopping his brow with a grim, grubby handkerchief, said: 'Some say it is common land, Sir Gerald.'

Sir Gerald laughed. 'Not according to the law, which you are, are you not, paid to uphold?'

'Yes, of course, sir, but that's neither here nor there.'

'I'm astonished to hear a police officer speak so lightly of the law of the land. Now, would you mind escorting these ... people ... off my land?'

'Let me explain, Sir Gerald.'

'I wish you would.'

Sergeant Beer took a deep breath. 'We are here to investigate a report that a body has been discovered.'

'Nonsense. No one comes here, so how could anyone discover a body?'

'This gentleman,' Sergeant Beer pointed at me, 'claims to have discovered a human skeleton on Blacker Knob.'

'Preposterous! What was he doing on Blacker Knob?'

'He says he's on holiday.'

'He must be an idiot.' Sir Gerald spared me a glance. 'He certainly looks like one, doesn't he?'

'That's not for me to say, sir,' answered Sergeant Beer, 'but we must investigate.'

Sir Gerald shrugged. 'It sounds like a wild goose chase to me. I'd arrest the blighter for trespass and wasting police time, if I were you.'

'I can't do that yet, sir.'

'We have to check,' said Mrs Duckworth.

Sir Gerald peered at her, as if noticing her for the first time. 'Oh, it's you,' he said. 'I might have known you'd be at the bottom of this. I suppose you think the bones belong to that waster of a husband of yours. What was his name? Pugh?'

'Hugh.'

'Well, don't go raising your hopes. It's most likely your old man left town with some floozy. You're wasting your time. This fellow's probably just stumbled across a dead sheep.'

I didn't much like being referred to as *this fellow*. 'It wasn't a sheep.'

Sir Gerald, giving me a most condescending smile, turned back to the sergeant. 'Well,' he said, 'your time is evidently not as valuable as mine and, since I'm obviously not going to stop you, I'd be obliged if you'd let me know what happens. Then I can say I told you so.'

Nodding dismissively, he got back into the Land Rover, allowing me a glimpse of the driver, a bald, thickset man, whose bare arms were plastered in tattoos. The Land Rover drove away.

'Who was that?' I asked.

'That,' said Mrs Duckworth, 'was Sir Gerald Payne.'

'He's a big landowner round these parts,' added Sergeant Beer.

'Does he really own this land?'

'So he claims, sir, and he's got a court order to prove it.'

'But Hob … but I was told it's really common land.'

'So some say,' said Constable Jones. 'Mr Duckworth was one of them.'

'That's right,' said Mrs Duckworth. 'He spent a lot of time trying to prove this was all common land. But we need to get a move on.'

As the way steepened, we carried on without further talking, other than Sergeant Beer muttering that his flip-flops were giving him gyp. I had time to think about Mrs Duckworth. Her softly accented voice was melodious and pleasant, her pretty face suggested a friendly nature, but I was glad our conversation had been interrupted; I'd had enough interrogation for one day.

When, at last, we reached Blacker Knob, I pointed out the position of the skeleton and sat down out of the way with Dregs. The wispy morning clouds had congealed into a heavy grey mass, and the afternoon was as dark as early evening. I pulled my jacket tight to keep off a wind that kept thrusting chilly fingers everywhere it could reach and realised I hadn't yet had any lunch. My stomach was grumbling so much that Dregs was staring, as if he expected an alien to burst forth.

The voices of Mrs Duckworth and Sergeant Beer were

carried on the wind.

'Those boots certainly look like Hugh's,' she said, 'and he used to wear a shirt like that.'

'Are you sure it's him?' asked Sergeant Beer, still breathless.

'Of course not, but I think it's likely.'

She spoke clearly and firmly, without any sign of the tears I'd been expecting. I admired her courage. Constable Jones, talking on his mobile, drowned out the rest of their conversation as he called for a forensics team. I heard him mention a helicopter. When he'd finished, putting his mobile back into his pocket, he sat beside me and shivered.

'It's a lonely place to die,' he said.

I nodded.

'It's not somewhere I'd choose to go for a walk,' he said, 'and I wouldn't want to come round here for my holidays.'

'I don't think I'll come back,' I said, 'but it seemed a good idea at the time.'

'I prefer Spain, or Greece, somewhere warm with a bit of nightlife.' The constable stretched out his legs. 'Where are you staying?'

'We're ... umm ... camping.'

'We?'

'Me and Dregs,' I said, covering my slip brilliantly.

'Where's your tent?'

'Umm ... it's over there somewhere,' I said, waving a hand in what I hoped was the right general direction.

'If you don't mind me saying, you don't much look like a hill walker.'

'I'm not normally much of one.'

He sighed. 'Mr Caplet, I'm sorry if I'm bugging you with these questions, but I get the feeling you're hiding something.'

'I've told you the truth,' I said.

'But not the whole truth, eh?'

'I've told you everything that's important.'

He laughed and patted Dregs. 'I'm inclined to believe you

about finding the skeleton, but, come on, you're not this dog's master, are you?'

'What do you mean?'

'I can see he knows you well enough, but I've had experience with dogs and it's obvious you're not his master. Plus, it's clear that someone else marked the path and that you haven't got a clue where we are and what's up here.'

'Umm ...'

'Don't worry. I won't press. I think you are honest and, no doubt, you have your reasons.'

I nodded. The constable was much sharper than his sergeant, who was standing on a tussock, adjusting his shorts and complaining about his poor feet, while staring blankly at the bones.

Mrs Duckworth joined us and although her face showed strain, she was still in control. I just wished she wouldn't look at me with such deep suspicion. Still, I was used to similar reactions in women who didn't know me and even in some who did. Only once had I really believed I'd got lucky. Her name was Violet, and I'd nearly been sure she loved me, as I thought I loved her. Unfortunately, love's course had failed to run true since the girl of my dreams wasn't quite as she appeared and had bloody murder on her conscience, if, indeed, she had a conscience. I might have let myself feel sorry for myself again, had it not been for Mrs Duckworth's example.

'I'm sorry,' said Constable Jones.

'I suppose I already knew he was dead,' she said. 'He wasn't the type who'd run away when he had a cause to fight and he was convinced all of this,' she waved her hand to encompass the Blacker Mountains, 'is common land, whatever Sir Gerald Payne might claim.'

'Still,' said the constable, 'it must be a shock to find him. Assuming it is him.'

'I'm almost sure it is. It's those boots. He got them in Peru. As for a shock, I guess it is, though I've already done my grieving. In any case, we'd grown apart, because he was too interested in his good causes to waste much time on anything else.'

Constable Jones pulled a sympathetic face. 'That was a shame.'

'Maybe,' said Mrs Duckworth. 'Although, if he hadn't left me to my own devices so often, I'd never have had time to study.'

'What are you studying,' I asked, feeling left out.

'That's none of your business.'

'No, of course it isn't. Sorry.'

'I'm sorry, too. I wasn't fair. I studied archaeology, something that's always fascinated me, and I have a degree now. Recently, I've been conserving some amazing Viking pieces.'

'I suppose,' said Sergeant Beer, approaching, 'archaeology is a bit like police work. We also dig things up and make deductions from the evidence. In this case, though, I don't think there's much to be investigated. It looks like he got caught in a storm and tried to build himself some sort of shelter. I'd guess he died of exposure. That's what does for a lot of hill walkers.'

'But,' I said, 'what about his fractured skull?'

'Your dog probably did that when he dug it out.'

'He barely touched it,' I said with a glance at Dregs, who was innocently sitting by Mrs Duckworth, wagging his tail.

Sergeant Beer shrugged. 'Bones become fragile with exposure to the elements and there are a lot of elements up here. Aren't I right, constable?'

'Well, yes, Sarge. Blacker Knob is reputed to have some of the worst weather in the country. That's one of the reasons no one comes up here. It's dangerous.'

'It doesn't seem so bad,' I said.

'Well, sir,' said Sergeant Beer, 'I don't suppose you've been here when the winds come up sudden, like, from the south-west. It can be terrible and there are many tales of people dying in the old days. Old Walt, who runs the Badger's, told me that when he was a child, he was up the Beacon. The wind was really strong and he saw this little fluffy cloud blowing towards him. It knocked him down. It turned out to be a waterlogged sheep. Not sure I believe him. Old Walt's not quite right in the head since then.'

He glanced towards the bones. 'The thing is, it's still dangerous up here, so I'd take care if I were you, Mr Caplet, because my feet reckon the weather's turning. I hope the chopper gets here soon, because I want to be getting back before it starts. I'd strongly advise you to get out of here.'

'I'll be fine,' I said, trying to look resolute and intrepid while my insides quaked.

Still, I'd have Hobbes with me and was confident he'd know what to do, though I had some concern that his concept of bad weather might differ from mine. I wondered where he was, for although I'd kept an eye out, I'd seen no further sign of him. That was probably unsurprising, but I was puzzled that Dregs, who had curled up at Mrs Duckworth's feet, had shown no indication that he was anywhere near.

I got to my feet, looking around casually as if admiring the view and, to be fair to Blacker Knob, it was picturesque in a rugged and bleak sort of way and it was difficult to see why it had such a bad reputation. It appeared to my, admittedly inexperienced, eyes to be excellent walking country, for any who liked such exercise. I wasn't yet convinced I was one of them, for although I did appreciate fresh air and scenic views, I wasn't so keen on the actual walking bit. My legs were already tired and I had a horrible suspicion I'd have to go back to Blackcastle to make a statement or something, and I'd bet there would be no room for me in the helicopter. Turning up my collar, I sat back down. The wind was strengthening and I was sure I felt a spot of rain on my cheek.

I shivered. 'How long will we have to wait?'

Sergeant Beer shrugged. 'As long as we must.'

'They said it'd be here within the hour,' said Constable Jones.

'As long as it's here before the rain,' said Mrs Duckworth.

I prepared for a long wait that never happened. The helicopter arrived within minutes, its downdraught showering us with debris and dust. I held my hands to my ears and half closed my eyes until it landed and the rotors had slowed to a standstill. A door opened and a man and a woman in white coveralls emerged. Sergeant Beer stepped forward to greet them.

'You two had better stay here,' said Constable Jones, joining the newcomers.

I nodded, having grown accustomed to keeping out of the way when Hobbes was investigating. Mrs Duckworth, on the other hand, was not so experienced and, fearing she'd get up and interfere, I thought I should try to take her mind off what was about to happen.

'Umm …' I said by way of a start, 'what do you do?'

She turned towards me, frowning. 'I beg your pardon?'

'What do you do for a living?'

'I work. How about you?'

That was a poser. 'I used to be a reporter for a newspaper, but I'm sort of freelance now.'

'I had some experience of reporters when Hugh went missing. They didn't strike me as very nice and I couldn't get rid of them.'

'I know what you mean,' I said, nodding.

'I very much doubt it.'

'I really do. We had loads of reporters outside when … I mean … umm … What I mean is, I've seen them in action.' Again, I'd nearly let slip too much and it was just lucky I'd still got my wits about me and could cover it up. I continued. 'I never got the hang of pestering people. That's probably why they sacked me. Umm … one of the reasons anyway. I wasn't very good.'

She laughed. 'I can believe that.'

Her response, better than I'd expected, came across as only slightly hostile and I ventured another question: 'Have you lived round here all your life?'

'No, I only came to Blackcastle because of Hugh.'

'Because of me?'

'Not you, Hugh!' She laughed again, this time genuinely amused. 'Yes, his family were originally from these parts and we moved here when he found a job. Things were fine until he discovered some documents linking his family to sheep farming and quarrying and got obsessed by researching them. I must say that I'll be glad to leave. I've never liked the place.'

'You're moving then?'

'I've got myself a job in a museum miles away from here.'

'Where?'

'That really isn't your business.'

'No, I suppose not. Sorry.'

'I intend to put all of this behind me,' she said. 'I see it as moving on mentally as well as physically and I do not intend to allow what's happened to spoil my future. That's why I'm only telling family and friends where I'm going. You are not the only one who can withhold information, Mr Caplet.'

After this exchange, we sat in near silence, watching what little of the action we could see, which wasn't much.

After no more than an hour, the two white-clad people loaded a black plastic bag into the helicopter and, following a brief discussion with Sergeant Beer and Constable Jones, climbed inside. As soon as the policemen retreated, the helicopter took off, turned slowly, and departed into the darkening sky.

Sergeant Beer walked back, looking glum. 'They're off,' he said, 'and they wouldn't take me. We'd better start moving before this storm hits.'

As if to reinforce his words, a spatter of rain propelled by a squally wind struck.

'Do you need me to go with you?' I asked, hoping the answer would be 'no'.

I was pleasantly surprised when that turned out to be the response.

'There's no need, sir,' said Sergeant Beer. 'We have your details and can contact you should we require anything further. I doubt we will though. This looks to me like an unfortunate accident and Forensics agreed. But, thanks for your help, sir. It's much appreciated. We don't get too many cases out here, but it's still satisfying to tick one off the list. Enjoy the rest of your holiday, but seriously, I would advise you to get off the tops soon. These hills really can be dangerous and besides, you are technically trespassing. Good day, sir.'

With that they left me. I watched them go, disappointed Mrs Duckworth hadn't acknowledged me, other than by a single, cold nod. I didn't blame her, for it's not every day a woman has to identify her husband's skeleton and I imagined she'd found it somewhat distracting. Maybe as distracting as I'd found her.

'Well,' I told Dregs, 'we're on our own now. I suppose we should find Hobbes.'

Dregs put his head to one side.

Then, remembering that I'd promised to buy a newspaper, I groaned and decided to return to Blackcastle anyway. Dregs, refusing to come, trotted away, heading back to the tent, I supposed.

9

Drizzle stung the back of my neck and made me shiver, but at least there was shelter in the lee of Blacker Knob as I descended. Despite my leg weariness, I was making good time, though the sky had darkened to the colour of the slates on the roofs in Blackcastle.

It wasn't long before punching rain took over from the drizzle and my tweed jacket and trousers, so good at keeping out the wind, proved to have the absorbency claimed by the manufacturers of certain brands of kitchen towel. Before long I was drenched, weighed down, as if in a suit of armour, and with icy trickles running down my legs and back. It was like being under a waterfall, except the rain seemed to be falling parallel to the ground. I could barely see and my feet slipped several times. Twice I was nearly blown over. I needed shelter, and quickly, and could have kicked myself for not heeding the warnings. The Blacker Mountains were, indeed, dangerous.

Giving up on any idea of fetching the newspaper, I turned around, heading back to Blacker Knob, hoping I'd be able to find the tent from there. I hadn't gone far when a white stick slalomed past on the torrent. I tried to convince myself that even I couldn't get lost between stakes.

It turned out that I could, and after perhaps five minutes I turned to retrace my steps, hoping to find where I'd been, but very soon, unable to see much of anything, I had to accept that I was utterly lost and in dead trouble. Failing to think of a brilliant plan, I turned again, heading upwards, hoping to stumble upon Blacker Knob, because from there I would, no doubt, be able to find the tent. I hoped so. I really hoped so.

Walking against the flow of water, I kept losing my footing on the sparse grass, which might just as well have been oiled for all the grip it offered. Reaching a rocky area which was a little less slippery, I followed it, moving with renewed confidence until it became suddenly steeper, forcing me to crawl on hands and knees. If anything the storm was intensifying, and it felt like marbles were being hurled into my eyes, making them feel bruised and sore. Blinking, I groped forward, because I didn't know what else to do, having lost all chance of finding Blacker Knob, but hoping still to chance upon some sort of shelter.

From somewhere, I found the strength to keep going, clinging onto hope, trying to believe Hobbes would find me and trying to choke off the insidious growth of despair. Then, I was no longer climbing, but sliding, horribly aware there was nothing in front of me.

A roaring wind, blowing full in my face, swallowed my cries and, although I scrabbled, grabbing at anything that might be solid, I plunged into nothingness. Yet even as I dropped, my left hand, by no conscious action, seized a sturdy root or something and I was left swinging by one arm. This was the moment, so experience told me, when Hobbes would put in an appearance. He didn't.

Sometimes I'd been able to make quick decisions and I made one then; I was not going to let go. Still, the weight of my sodden suit, plus the slipperiness of my hands, conspired against my decision and I began to slide, until somehow I managed to get a grip with my other hand. For a moment I was euphoric, a bizarre sense of relief flooding my nervous system, before my predicament struck home. I was dangling over what I assumed was a precipice, and my situation was not helped by a gush of water that seemed determined to sluice out my mouth. I had to act and, fuelled by adrenalin, using sheer muscle power, something I'd never believed I possessed, I hauled myself up, hand over hand, my shoulders agonising, until, just before my strength failed, with one final, valiant effort, I dragged myself over a lip of rock and lay face down, gasping like a landed fish and just as wet.

After a while, the heat my efforts had generated leaking

away, my teeth began chattering, reminding me of the wind-up ones sold in joke shops, and making me laugh like a madman. As the hysteria subsided and I pulled myself together, congratulating myself on a lucky escape, I got wearily to my feet and tried to get my bearings.

A sudden, huge blast of wind caught me off guard, blowing me over the edge.

Too surprised to react, even to scream, I plummeted, fearing and expecting a bone-shattering encounter with sharp rocks, but, instead, I squelched into soft mud up to the waist. Although for a few moments, despite the bad-egg stink I'd let loose, I considered myself fortunate, it wasn't long before I had to reconsider. I was stuck and struggling to get free only seemed to drive me deeper into the mire. The storm showed no signs of abating and I was getting colder. The only good thing was that I didn't sink any further if I stayed still. It wasn't much of a good thing.

'Help!' I yelled as loudly as I'd ever shouted, realising my chances of being heard in that wilderness, in that wind, were infinitesimal.

Nevertheless, I wasn't going anywhere, so, every few minutes, I unleashed a lung-busting bellow in the hope that Hobbes, or anybody, might hear me, pull me out and take me somewhere warm and dry, somewhere I could have a hot drink and something to eat. I still hadn't had my lunch. At the back of my mind a terrifying thought was growing; no one was going to hear me. I was going to die of hypothermia, unless I struggled and drowned first.

As time passed, my cries became weaker and less frequent, while the invading cold overcame all resistance. My throat was sore, even though, by tilting my head, I could swallow rain, and I was exhausted and hopeless. Although I desperately wanted to lie down and rest, I was stuck in a standing position, but even so, my head lolled, my chin rested on my chest, and I fell into an odd sort of semi-conscious doze.

'Hello, dear.'

I raised my head. A small, yellow wigwam was addressing me, in Mrs Goodfellow's voice. Could hypothermia cause hallucinations, I wondered?

'Are you having a nice paddle?'

'No,' I said, wondering why I was in conversation with a wigwam, 'I'm stuck.'

'Then I suppose we ought to pull you out.'

At least the hallucination was talking sense, but I could see a problem: 'I'm stuck fast,' I said, 'and you're too small a wigwam to do much good.'

'Nonsense, dear. Billy will help me.'

'He's a good man, that Billy, but he's in Sorenchester.'

'No, mate. I'm here.' The wigwam had swapped to Billy's voice.

'Clever wigwam,' I murmured, which was difficult as my teeth were chattering again and my eyelids were too heavy to keep open.

Both of the wigwam's voices spoke, there was a racking pain in my shoulders, a pop, and a sudden sense of release.

'It is very strange,' I said to myself, 'that I feel warm and the rain has stopped.'

I still couldn't move and thought the bog still had me until, realising I was lying down, I opened my eyes. For reasons I was unable to fathom, I was on my back, swaddled in blankets, as immobile as an Egyptian mummy. The rock ceiling above me was flickering red. Something smelt good, making my mouth water.

'Where am I?' I asked of no one in particular.

'In one of the old mine workings,' said Mrs Goodfellow. 'How are you feeling?'

'Stiff ... and hungry,' I said, turning my head to see her. 'What happened?'

'Billy and I pulled you out. You were stuck fast and getting dozy.'

'Thank you. I ... umm ... seem to remember a yellow wigwam talking to me in your voice.'

She laughed. 'I was wearing Mr Goodfellow's old cycle cape. It came in very handy on such a wild night. It kept the rain off both of us.'

'Both of you? Oh, yes, I remember, Billy was there. That's why the wigwam had two voices.'

'That's right, dear. He drove me here.'

'But why? I mean ... what are you doing here?'

'We came to let the old fellow know the press has moved on and that he can come home when he wishes.'

'How did you know where to find us?'

'You'd better have something to eat and drink before we talk any more. Sit up.'

'I can't. The blankets are too tight.'

Leaning across, she tugged a corner, freeing me. I sat up, dislodging a hot water bottle in the shape of a deformed hippopotamus, and looked around. A brisk fire was burning in the entrance and there was a pile of twisted, dark logs by the far wall. Outside it was pitch black, the wind still blustering and howling, the rain still pounding the rocks. There was no sign of Hobbes, or Billy, or Dregs, but I was far more interested in the pot bubbling on the fire, which was sending out tendrils of steam and, more to the point, enticing, savoury, warm smells.

Mrs Goodfellow ladled out a bowl of what turned out to be stew, stuck a spoon in it and handed it to me. I stuffed myself until there was nowhere left to be stuffed, almost crying with delight, and it was only when I was on to my second bowl that I could really appreciate the flavours: vegetables, stock and a variety of meats expertly blended into one delightful whole. My ordeal almost began to feel worth enduring for such a reward. It was another of the old girl's masterpieces.

When I finished, she took the bowl away and handed me a

mug of tea and, by the time I'd drained it, my spirits were quite restored, though my arms and legs were heavy and aching.

'That was wonderful. Thank you ... and thanks for getting me out of that horrible bog.'

'You're welcome, though I might have struggled without Billy's help. He crawled over the top and prised you out with an old pit prop, while I pulled on a rope. You came out with a slurp and a cloud of stinky marsh gas. At least that's what he said it was.'

'Well,' I said, 'I'll thank him when I see him. Where is he?'

'He's with the old fellow and Dregs. They've gone for a walk.'

'Out there?' I said, with a glance at the storm. 'But, it's horrible.'

'No, in here.'

'I don't understand'

'They've gone into the mine.'

'Isn't that dangerous?'

'That's how the old fellow likes it.'

'I suppose, but ... umm ... why does he want to go for a walk in a mine?'

'He's interested in mining.'

'Is he? He's never mentioned it.'

'He's interested in many things that he never mentions, unless he has a reason.'

'I thought he was only interested in crime and art ... and music ... and films ... and ... and aubergines.'

'Oh, no, dear. He likes zoology and astronomy and gastronomy and history and politics and economics and geology and rheology and theology and agriculture and oceanography and sport and ...'

'Enough!' I said. 'I get the point.'

'That's why he's so interesting.'

'I'm not sure that's why. But, tell me, how did you find me?'

'We were looking for your campsite when we heard

shouting.'

'I was lucky. These hills are huge and you might not have come anywhere near.'

'Well, dear,' she said, 'I expected he'd stay somewhere around Stradlingate, because that's what he usually did when he came up here. I think it comforts him.'

'I'm not comfortable,' I said, shivering as a blast of wind howled outside and made the fire spark.

'Shall I adjust your blanket, dear?'

'No, I don't mean that. I mean this place ... this whole area ... there's something wrong with it. It spooks me, if you know what I mean.'

'Not really, dear. It is wild and lonely, but it's beautiful in its own way.'

'Perhaps,' I said, doubtfully, 'but Blackcastle is the pits.'

'It was quite prosperous long ago, but it's fallen on hard times since the Paynes stole the land.'

'The Paynes? I saw a bloke called Payne today ... Sir Gerald. I didn't like him.'

'There aren't many round here have a good word for the Paynes, especially the current crop.'

'I guess,' I said, 'it's the old story of the aristocracy trampling the peasants underfoot.'

'Not really. It's odder than that, according to Roger Jolly's Pirate Miscellany.'

'What's that? I've never heard of it.'

'It's a very old book and very rare, because the Paynes tried to destroy all the copies. A few have survived and the old fellow has one. I imagine it's valuable.'

'I've never seen it.'

'No, dear, he keeps it in a strongbox in the attic.'

'Tell me about the Paynes,' I said, stretching out my legs.

'Once upon a time,' said Mrs Goodfellow, 'late in the seventeenth century, a child was born to a small farmer who scratched a bare living on Blacker Beacon. Such a life was not for Greville, who ran away when he was twelve and joined the navy. Being a bright, active lad, he did well, until he was wounded during the Wars of the Spanish Succession.'

I nodded wisely, pretending I was familiar with the history.

'He lost an eye,' she continued, 'and while recuperating met Edward Teach.'

I must have looked blank, because she explained.

'Better known as Blackbeard the pirate?'

'I've heard of him,' I said.

'When Greville met him, he was still a privateer, but, when the war ended, he took up piracy. Greville became mate of his ship, the *Queen Anne's Revenge*, and prospered, until Blackbeard shot him during a dispute about dried peas. Greville, however, was made of tough stuff and survived.

'He came home with enough wealth to buy a small farm, but was not a success, until he discovered gold and began mining.'

'So, the Paynes' money came from piracy and gold mining.'

'In part, dear, but his fortune bought power and influence and after he performed some small service for King George the Second, he was made a baronet. He was generally well liked, or at least tolerated, by local folk.'

'When did people turn against the Paynes?'

'His son, Sir Rodney, was a greedy and devious man, who inherited the estate and made use of the Inclosure Act to acquire land over which he had no rights. Ever since, the Paynes have been a blight on local people, although Gerald's father did try to make some sort of amends. Unfortunately, Sir Gerald reversed most of his father's improvements.'

'A bad family.'

'On the whole, dear.'

'I wonder,' I said, 'how long the others will be.'

Mrs Goodfellow shrugged. 'I doubt they'll be long. I'll put the kettle on again.'

As the wind outside howled with increased volume, I snuggled into my blankets and looked forward to a fresh cup of tea. It had been a long and trying day and I'd been incredibly lucky to survive. I wondered whether Sergeant Beer might have been correct about Hugh Duckworth's death; a storm such as the one raging outside could kill a man so easily, and perhaps he had just been caught out by its suddenness. It could have been that he'd just run out of luck, and I couldn't help feeling he must have used up a fair amount in attracting such a fine woman as Mrs Duckworth. Though she'd, perhaps unsurprisingly, been cool and distant, she'd still displayed flashes of compassion and passion that made her very appealing. Besides, she wasn't at all bad looking and her soft brown eyes were lovely. I couldn't deny having been attracted to her, which was a bit off in the circumstances. Not that it mattered, for I wouldn't see her again.

Something, beside the wind, was howling, something becoming louder, something coming from inside. It was an echoing, confusing, almost musical sound, rising and falling, with voices in it.

'What's that?' I asked, trying not to sound too nervous.

Mrs Goodfellow poured steaming water into a teapot and stood upright. 'It's the lads coming back.'

As the eerie noise drew nearer, it became apparent that Dregs was making the howling as he backed up the rich, if raucous, baritone of Hobbes and Billy's reedy treble. The echoes distorted everything, producing a weird, twisted, pulsing beat and it was a long time before I could make out the words: 'Heigh-ho, heigh ho'.

Standing up to greet them, discovering I was naked, I clutched at the blankets and wrapped them around me like a toga. Yet I was deceived by the acoustics, for it must have been five minutes before they appeared round a bend.

Dregs, abandoning his backing vocals, charged, nearly knocking me down in his eagerness to say 'hello'. I could only think that he was trying to make amends for his earlier desertion, though I had to admit, he'd shown far more sense than I had.

'Hiya,' said Billy.

Hobbes nodded. 'How are you feeling?'

'I'm fine, now,' I said. 'Thank you.'

'I expect you boys will be wanting a cup of tea and a bite to eat,' said Mrs Goodfellow.

About half an hour later, Hobbes wiped his lips and rose from the rock on which he'd been sitting down to eat. 'That was delicious, thanks, lass,' he said, throwing another log on the fire and staring out into the dripping darkness. 'This weather is set for the night, so we'd better make the most of it and get some sleep. It'll be better in the morning.'

'It's a good job you brought everything in here.' said Billy. 'I wouldn't fancy going out in it.'

'There'd be nothing left,' said Hobbes. 'The tent would have been torn to shreds and the contents scattered over the hillside.'

'Where did you go?' I asked, bursting to know.

'We have been exploring the mine,' said Hobbes.

'I know, but why? And weren't you scared of getting lost? Or of a cave-in, or something?'

Hobbes grinned. 'Which question shall I answer first?'

'The first one.'

'I wanted to see if there was any evidence of renewed mining.'

'Was there?'

'Not as such, but people have been working on the third level. There was some powerful new drilling equipment but nothing for rock crushing or cutting.'

'Perhaps they're just getting ready for mining,' I said.

'Perhaps. As for your other questions, I wasn't afraid of getting lost because I remember these old workings from way back and many of these tunnels have been here for centuries without coming down, so the chances of one falling when we were passing were remote. I'm going to have a lie down.'

Yawning, he stretched himself out by the entrance, his feet towards the fire, his head resting on his hands. Dregs, who'd been allowed to finish the stew and was looking very satisfied, slumped beside him and, within a few minutes, both were snoring gently.

Mrs Goodfellow, perched on a rock, was deep in thought, planning breakfast I hoped. Billy, having washed and stacked our dishes, came and sat next to me, wrapping a blanket around his shoulders.

'Wotcha,' he said. 'It's been puzzling me. How did you end up right in the middle of the bog?'

I told the tale of my ordeal, grateful for his interest, for I'd been a little hurt no one had asked. Although I might have embellished things a little, attempting to present myself in a slightly more heroic, slightly less idiotic light, it didn't seem to work. Billy, having started chuckling near the beginning of my saga, was rolling round on the floor by the end. I hadn't realised how callous he was, and I would have expected more from Mrs G, who I noticed wiping away tears of mirth. I forgave her on account of the stew and Billy on account of getting me out the bog. It was big of me.

Sometime later, I fell asleep.

Cold, clinging, stinking mud was sucking me down, drowning me. I yelled, waking myself up and finding the fire had burned low, though it was still glowing and throwing out heat.

'Bad dream?' asked Hobbes, who was standing in the entrance, staring inwards. Dregs, at his feet, had his head on one side as if listening.

'Umm ... yes,' I said as my senses woke up.

I could make out a throbbing hum on the very edge of hearing.

'What's that?' I said.

'A machine. I'll take a look.'

'Shall I come, too?' I asked, feeling I should show willing, despite my fear of deep, dark tunnels.

He shook his head. 'No, you'd better keep guard here.'

'OK,' I said, as if reluctantly sacrificing adventure on the altar of duty, though, at the time, I would have given my breakfast to avoid going.

He strode off into the darkness, Dregs keeping pace a few steps behind, and they were soon out of sight. For a while, I could hear the faint clicks of the dog's toe nails, but nothing of Hobbes. It still amazed me that he could move more silently than a cat when he wished. Then all I could hear was the distant hum and the occasional crackle from the fire.

Getting up, gripping my blanket against the cool, damp air, I walked over to the fire and threw on a couple of logs. They caught almost immediately and I warmed my hands, looking out into the night, where the storm, as Hobbes had predicted, had blown itself out, leaving only a soft, cool breeze and the occasional spatter of fine drizzle. The nearly-full moon, getting low on the horizon, lit up ragged tails of shredded clouds and an owl yelped in the distance. I shivered and leant against the wall, pulling the blanket over my head and standing guard and, although I wasn't sure what I was guarding against, I intended doing a good job.

I must have fallen asleep where I was standing, sliding down the wall to sprawl on the hard, stony ground, still wrapped in my blanket, because I awoke with bright sunlight flooding in. Outside, I could hear Mrs Goodfellow and Billy making breakfast. Unwrapping myself, I got up, got dressed in my spare clothes and stepped into the morning.

The hills had forgotten their dark rage of the previous night and the sun's gentle warmth fell on my face. I smiled, blinking as my eyes adjusted. Billy was scowling with concentration as he poured boiling water into the teapot and Mrs Goodfellow was heating a frying pan.

'Good morning, dear,' she said as I yawned. 'You have lovely teeth.'

'Thank you,' I said, although they felt in urgent need of a vigorous brushing. 'Where's Hobbes?'

'I expect he's taken the dog for a walk. He was up before us.'

'Ah, yes,' I said, remembering. 'He got up in the night to investigate a funny noise down the mine. I do hope he's alright.'

'I'm sure he will be,' said Mrs Goodfellow.

I nodded, though I couldn't rid myself of a nagging worry. What if he had got lost? Or trapped? Who was going to search for him? Mrs Goodfellow, soothingly, began frying bacon and eggs, as I fretted.

Then Dregs appeared, bounding over Blacker Ridge, running down towards us, with Hobbes loping into view a moment later, a bulging hessian sack bouncing on his shoulder. Dregs greeted us in his usual exuberant fashion and we were still trying to push him off when Hobbes reached us and dropped his sack.

'That smells good, lass,' he said. 'I was worried I'd miss my breakfast.'

10

Sitting lazily in the sunshine after such a traumatic day, eating bacon and eggs prepared with all the old girl's skill, it was not surprising that I over indulged. As a result, I was bloated and lethargic and quite unwilling to offer any objections when Billy volunteered to wash up. Instead, I mooched about, groaning whenever I had to bend over to pick up Dregs's stick that he kept insisting I throw for him. His night-time excursion had not diminished his enthusiasm for running. As Billy dried the dishes and tidied them away into a hamper, the breeze began to strengthen and a curtain of iron-grey clouds appeared on the horizon.

Hobbes, who'd been sitting hunched up, scowling at a lump of rock in his hand, sprang to his feet. 'It's time to get back to Sorenchester. I've been away too long.'

'What?' I said. 'Now? On such a lovely day? Why can't we just enjoy the sun for a while?'

'No,' said Hobbes, shaking his head. 'We need to go ... and quickly. The weather's on the turn.'

'I've packed everything,' said Mrs Goodfellow, emerging from the mine.

Within five minutes we were marching downhill and, although the ground was squelchy and slippery, we made good progress and I soon kicked off my lethargy, managing to keep up despite aching legs. I might even have felt proud of myself, had Mrs Goodfellow and Billy not been carrying more than I was, though admittedly, I was carrying a lot more in my stomach. Hobbes's load, of course, was far greater than any of ours for, in addition to the camping gear and his enormous rucksack, he was also lugging along the heavy sack he'd brought back with him. Dregs, alert like a wolf on a mission, led the way.

It was well we'd started when we did, for the breeze had

developed teeth, turning into a cold, biting wind, a reminder of the approaching autumn, and by the time we reached flatter ground the sky was darkening, though it was not yet midday.

'I wouldn't be surprised,' said Hobbes, looking back, 'to see a foot of snow up there by supper time.'

'Snow in October?' I said. 'It's hardly likely is it?'

'It's not as rare as you might think in these hills. Let's get back to the car while the going's good. And quickly!'

Billy's hearse, parked next to the derelict manor, was already spattered in a slushy, grey sleet when we reached it. Having loaded as quickly as possible, we drove away and, when I glanced back, I noticed the higher peaks were already wearing thin, white caps. I should never have questioned Hobbes's ability to read the weather.

I was delighted to be leaving those wild, barren hills and to be in the comfort and warmth of Billy's car. In the end they had been too much for me, though Hobbes had seemed completely at home, more so even than in Sorenchester.

Although Billy put his foot down as soon as we reached the main road, we soon came across a flood and were forced to make a diversion through Blackcastle. The ancient hearse could reach no great speed but Billy drove sufficiently quickly that people in town stared. The market place was bustling, with a small travelling funfair, stalls, and several hundred people, despite the sleet and the wind. I kept my head down, not wanting anyone to recognise me and think me a liar for having claimed I only had Dregs for company. There was one person in particular I hoped wouldn't notice me and think bad of me, though I kept an eye out, hoping to see her. I didn't.

'What's going on?' I asked. 'It was practically deserted last time.'

'It's the Autumn Fair,' said Hobbes.

'Surely,' I said, suspecting the good folk of Blackcastle of being even dafter than I'd first thought, 'it would make more sense to hold a fair at the weekend?'

'It is the weekend, dear,' said Mrs Goodfellow.

'No, it can't be,' I said. 'We came here on Sunday, didn't we?'

'Yes,' said Billy.

I totted up on my fingers. 'So, we camped for three nights before I found Mr Duckworth's bones. That must have been Wednesday. Therefore, today must be Thursday. Right?'

'Wrong,' said Billy. 'It's Saturday.'

'It can't be.'

'It can,' said Hobbes. 'We'd been camping for five nights before you found the body.'

Although I was at first inclined to argue, a poster, proclaiming Blackcastle Autumn Fair was being held that weekend, took the wind from my sails. Going back over everything we'd done, I just could not make my memory tally with the facts, even when I tried working out what I'd had for breakfast each day. It was as if I'd fallen into a Rip Van Winkle-like sleep and my sense of confusion could hardly have been worse had I really slept for a hundred years.

'I don't understand,' I said. 'I've lost two days.'

'I wouldn't fret, dear,' said Mrs G, patting my arm. 'You probably relaxed so much you just lost track of time.'

Although I nodded, I sat in near silence for the rest of the journey, worrying about losing my mind. It wasn't for the first time since I'd known Hobbes, but at least getting back to Blackdog Street meant that unpacking and lugging our gear inside distracted me. Yet my concern about the lost days remained, becoming just one more item on my worry list whenever I woke in the night and was unable to get back to sleep. Fortunately, such nights were rare, for my list was long and growing, as anyone who has nearly been buried alive by ghouls, has been bitten by a wannabe vampire, has been trailed by a werewolf, and has kissed a werecat might understand.

It felt good to be back home, especially when Mrs Goodfellow fed us a late and extremely welcome lunch, a huge plate piled with cheese and chutney sandwiches, washed down with plenty of fresh tea. Billy ate with us and, afterwards, pulling a chair over to the sink to stand on, washed up. I, feeling extremely virtuous, dried and put the dishes away.

'Thank you for lunch,' said Billy, finishing the last knife and jumping down. 'Now I gotta get to work, because Featherlight doesn't like it if I take time off and I said I'd be back in this afternoon.'

'Thanks for everything,' said Hobbes, who was still at the table and frowning at a rock. 'Mind how you go.'

I went upstairs and lay down. I had a slight headache, with a lot of questions churning in my mind and no answers forthcoming. But, when I heard Hobbes take Dregs out for a walk, I took the opportunity to answer one question: what had he brought back in that sack? It was lying in the corner of the kitchen and, knowing him as I did, I opened it with some trepidation.

I was disappointed to find it contained nothing but rocks, just like the one he'd been frowning at earlier, and that, as rocks went, they weren't at all impressive, looking just like any other in the Blacker Mountains. They were strange souvenirs.

Baffled, I went through to the sitting room, turned on the television and found that watching a rather good black and white gangster film helped take my mind off things. The hero, a hard-bitten cop, reminded me a little of Hobbes until he drew his gun and fired; Hobbes preferred a more hands-on approach to crime fighting. As the hard-bitten hero filled the baddy with lead and ran inside the burning house to rescue the damsel in distress, there was a commotion in the street outside.

A car's engine roared, tyres squealed, and a horn blared. A moment later the front door opened and Dregs bounded in, pinning me to the sofa and licking me in great excitement.

Hobbes followed him in. 'Alright, Andy?'

'Ugh!' I said, curling up into a ball, and clutching myself. Dregs was never careful where he put his feet.

'Good,' said Hobbes, smiling and looking really pleased with himself.

As Dregs galloped after him into the kitchen, I unwound, wondering how he could be chatting with Mrs Goodfellow, because she hadn't been in the kitchen and I was certain only Hobbes and Dregs had gone past. Maybe she'd been in the cellar, dusting the coal, or selecting root vegetables for our suppers.

The phone rang. It was Billy, though it took a while before a lull in the background racket allowed me to hear him clearly.

'Andy,' he said, 'we've got trouble. Ask Hobbesie to come here, pronto.'

'Are you at the Feathers?'

'Of course.'

'Why can't Featherlight sort it out?'

'He's not in. Get Hobbes. Now!'

Glass shattered, someone screamed and the phone went dead.

I raced into the kitchen, where Hobbes was sitting, reading the *Bugle*.

'That was Billy.' I said. 'There's trouble at the Feathers.'

'I'd better sort it out, then,' he said.

'You had, because Featherlight's not there.'

'Let's go,' he said getting up, grabbing his old raincoat and running to open the front door.

Dregs and I followed.

'You better hurry,' I said, the scream having really spooked me. 'Don't worry about me. I'll only hold you up.'

'It's alright' said Hobbes, as he ran into the street, 'we'll take the car.'

I hesitated in the doorway, worry about possible danger competing with a thrill at the prospect of action, until Dregs barged into me and made me lunge down the steps. Before I could object, Hobbes had dragged me into the car and I was fitting my seatbelt. Dregs, for once, accepted the back seat.

The acceleration as he launched us up Blackdog Street seemed to crush me into the seat and I was just getting my head up when we screeched into Pound Street, ignoring the red light and the traffic coming at us. Although The Shambles was packed with Saturday shoppers and tourists, Hobbes was in no mood to slow down, even when a pair of old ladies crossed the road in front of us. It turned out that there was just enough pavement for a car to squeeze past without touching them.

It was only when we'd turned onto Lettuce Lane and the Feathers was already in sight that I realised he shouldn't have a car any more.

'Where did this come from?' I asked, wondering if he'd commandeered it.

'Billy made the arrangements and it arrived this afternoon. Hold on!'

Although I gripped the seat with both hands, the top of my head still whacked the ceiling as we bounced onto the pavement and screeched to a standstill outside the Feathers. A fat man crashed through the pub's window in a shower of glass shards in best western movie tradition, but unlike in westerns, he didn't pick himself up, shake himself down and dive back into the fray. Instead, as we got out of the car, he lay there, groaning and bleeding from a number of cuts. Hobbes stepped over him and strolled inside, with Dregs at his heel. I considered helping the casualty but, since his wounds didn't look severe and he was swearing like my father used to when hauling on an obstinate wisdom tooth, I walked past, intending to take a tentative look inside. Holding the door open, I peeked round it, ducking as a chair smashed into the wall where my head would have been. I was still congratulating myself on my reflexes, when something spinning like a Frisbee struck me full on the forehead with a resounding clang.

As if in slow motion, I sank to my knees and the door, swinging back, struck me on the ear. Although too dazed at first to register pain, I touched my hand to my forehead and wasn't in the least surprised to see blood and, with the realisation of injury, my head began to pulse with a deep, dull throb while the world became distant and muffled.

Crawling forward, I cowered behind an overturned table, pressing my handkerchief to my wound, which felt as if it was on fire, and tried to make sense of what was happening. At least twenty men were brawling, while half a dozen more sprawled unmoving on the filthy, matted floor covering that had, presumably, started life as a carpet.

'Stop this at once,' said Hobbes in a quiet, friendly voice. He was standing just in front of me, watching the action, smiling, with Dregs at his side.

To my surprise, everyone ceased pummelling each other and turned to face him. About half of the brawlers were local tough guys, who were harmless enough, so long as you didn't catch their eye, look at their girlfriends, or spill their beer. The opposition, all of them dressed in a similar smart casual fashion, with their hair cropped short, was unfamiliar.

One of the locals, a large, slow-witted lout, who often frequented the Feathers and liked to be referred to as Hammerfist (though his real name, as I recalled from my brief stint as deputy, temporary, stand-in crime reporter, was Tarquin Sweet), spoke.

'I'm sorry, Mr Hobbes. I didn't come here for no trouble, but these bastards were up for it.'

'That's alright, Tarquin,' said Hobbes. 'Put your stool down and wait for me outside. I'll speak to you later. That goes for the rest of you, too.'

Although the local lads, apologising and carrying three of their unconscious mates with them, hurried outside, the newcomers were not inclined to be cooperative.

A tall, thickset man, with a flat nose and a mouthful of gold teeth, grinned. 'So, you're Hobbes, are you? We've been looking for you.'

'I've been on my holidays,' said Hobbes. 'Why do you wish to see me?'

'We don't exactly want to *see* you.'

'They say you're hard,' said a tattooed oaf, who was nearly as broad as he was tall, 'but we don't think you are.'

'Everyone,' said Hobbes pleasantly, 'is entitled to their opinion. Would you care to discuss the issue, sir?'

'We're not going to discuss anything,' said the first man.

'Fair enough. There's no reason why you should, but since you have contributed to the mess in here, you could start making amends by tidying up.'

'Why don't you make us,' said the second thug.

'I was hoping,' said Hobbes, 'that you'd do it because it's the right thing to do.'

'We're gonna do you,' said the second thug, forming an impressively sized fist with his right hand.

'I really don't think you should,' said Hobbes.

The tattooed oaf, lunging forward, swung a brutal haymaker at Hobbes who, swaying away from harm, raised his hands in a gesture of peace and could not be blamed if the man's wild swing unbalanced him, so he stumbled and his jutting chin struck Hobbes's outstretched palm. Slumping to the floor, he lay peacefully.

'It would be so much pleasanter and easier if we could all be civil,' said Hobbes, opening his arms as two more of the gang charged. It was not his fault that, as he embraced them in a friendly hug, their heads cracked together. As he laid them gently on the bar, out of harm's way, three more of the gang, experiencing unfortunate collisions with Hobbes's knee, foot and elbow, lay down and slept. The others backed away and fled and, to judge from the sounds outside, our locals didn't waste any time in continuing the relationship. Only one man, the tall, thickset one, remained facing Hobbes.

'Very impressive,' he sneered. 'Now, let's see what you're really made of.'

All of a sudden, a long, slim knife appearing in his hand, he lunged only to find Hobbes had swayed to one side. He made a wild slash at Hobbes's face but, unfortunately for him, Hobbes, as fast as a striking snake, displaying the reactions of a well-trained police dog, seized his wrist in his mouth. Although he made an attempt to punch with his free hand, he went limp, crying like a child as Hobbes, growling, increased pressure and Dregs, bristling, butted him in the groin. As the knife dropped, Hobbes kicked it into the dart board that had come off the wall and was lying in a corner. By then, all the fight had drained from the man and, besides his whimpering and the occasional groan from the ranks of the fallen, all was peaceful.

That was when I saw red and my eyes began to sting. Blood was dripping into them. I wiped it away with my handkerchief, which was sopping, and blinked. Looking down, I saw I'd been struck by a battered, rusty beer tray, and got to my feet a little unsteadily. Hobbes released the sobbing thug and sat him on a bar stool.

I leaned against a wall, swaying slightly, and fearing what Hobbes had done to him. After all, someone who I'd seen crunching up raw marrowbones with his teeth was quite capable of biting off a man's hand. I was relieved when everything appeared to be where it ought to have been.

'What did you do to him?' I asked.

'I just gave him a quick nip on a pressure point. It's something the lass showed me and it's remarkably effective, though I have modified the technique slightly. He'll be over it in a few minutes with no harm done.'

'Well done.'

'It was nothing,' said Hobbes. 'A policeman has to be able to deal with high spirits every now and then.

'I see you are bleeding, Andy. Are you alright?'

'It's nothing,' I said bravely.

'Good,' said Hobbes and tossed me a bar towel. 'This will mop it up, until you get it treated.'

Despite many misgivings about what horrible bugs the towel might contain, I pressed it to my forehead.

'Now, sir,' said Hobbes, addressing the weeping man, 'what have you done with the barman?'

He shook his head, looking puzzled. 'Nothing,'

'Then where is he?'

'I don't know. He was here when it all kicked off.'

A Billy-sized groan arose from beneath one of the prone figures. Hobbes ran across and rolled an unconscious troublemaker, one I knew as Sam Jelly Belly, to one side to reveal Billy, who was looking extremely cross.

'The big bully fell on me,' said Billy, and I thought he was going to put the boot in until a glance from Hobbes dissuaded him.

'I don't think he had much say in the matter,' said Hobbes, pointing to an impressive lump on the man's head. 'Are you alright?'

'Apart from my dignity,' said Billy. 'What are you going to do with this lot? Our lads were having a quiet drink when this mob from Pigton burst in looking for trouble.' He glanced around him and grinned. 'It looks like they found it.'

'I am going to have a quiet, friendly chat with these boys,' said Hobbes, 'and then they can help tidy up the mess.'

Billy chuckled. 'Featherlight won't recognise the place.'

'In the meantime,' said Hobbes, 'you'd better call an ambulance. There's some here that need patching up.'

He went over to the dart board, pulled out the knife, which must have been a foot long at the least, and snapped the blade off at the hilt with his bear hands. Handing the hilt back to the thug, who was blowing his nose on his shirt, he slipped the blade into his coat pocket. 'That can go in the recycling,' he said.

Hobbes had such a convincing way with his little chats that within ten minutes seven Pigton penitents were clearing up. The others, plus a couple of local boys, were taken away by ambulance.

When they were all working to his satisfaction, he turned to me. 'You'd better get yourself seen to.'

'I'll be fine,' I said, though I was feeling light headed.

'That cut could do with a couple of stitches and, from the look of that tray, you'll need a tetanus shot.'

'Do I have to? I hate needles.'

'You have to. Billy will take you. On your way. And quickly.'

So, while the great clean-up of the Feathers continued and Hobbes, backed up by Dregs, was organising an impromptu whip-round to pay for the damage, Billy drove me to the hospital, where, I regret to say, too many people recognised me as an old customer. Nearly all my injuries had occurred since I'd known Hobbes.

Two hours later, stitched, heroically bandaged, and shot full of tetanus vaccine, I got back to Blackdog Street, where Mrs Goodfellow enjoyed having a patient to fuss over and I did nothing to spoil her enjoyment, playing the part of a wounded soldier most convincingly until she went to prepare supper.

Hobbes returned and was telling me what a great job his cleaning gang had done, when the doorbell rang and he went to answer it. A woman with orange hair and large, slightly protuberant eyes was standing at the top of the steps, a big red suitcase on wheels at her side.

'Hi,' she said in a soft American accent, 'I'm your daughter.'

11

Since I'd grown accustomed to seeing Hobbes cope with just about any situation, including a pair of rhinos charging at him, without even flinching, it was a shock to hear him gasp and to see him stagger. For a moment, I thought he might collapse, until, pulling himself together with a jerk, he grabbed Dregs, who was attempting to charge the door.

'Could you repeat that, madam?'

'I'm your daughter,' she said, breathing hard, though whether from emotion or the shock at seeing him I couldn't tell.

'But,' said Hobbes, 'I don't have a daughter.'

'Surprise!' Although she looked anxious, she smiled.

'There must be some mistake.'

'I don't think so. Mom recognised you straight away on YouTube.'

'I'm not on YouTube ... am I?'

'You sure are.'

'I don't understand.'

'You were chasing bad guys. Mom recognised you at once. You're famous, Daddy.'

'You'd better come in,' said Hobbes, his face troubled. 'We need to talk. Mrs? Miss?'

'Miss Johnson. Kathleen Johnson,' said the woman, walking into the sitting room as if she owned it.

'Johnson?' said Hobbes. 'That name rings a bell.'

'It should do. It's my mom's name.'

'Shift up, Andy,' said Hobbes. 'Give Miss Johnson some space.'

'Yeah ... Of course,' I said, sliding to the end of the sofa, because she looked as if she'd need most of the rest. 'Can I take your coat, Miss Johnson?'

Ignoring me, she parked her ample rear. Hobbes watched

her, looking bewildered, but keeping a firm grip on Dregs. After a moment of staring and looking nonplussed, he dragged the over-excited dog into the kitchen, came back and pulled up one of the heavy, old oak chairs. As he sat down, facing her, apparently lost for words, I took the opportunity for a good look at the interloper.

My impressions weren't favourable. She was a stout, lumpy woman, a few years older than me, at a guess, with protuberant, dull-brown eyes, puffy, flabby, sallow skin and with short, orange hair (dyed by her own hand, I assumed) that appeared to have been hacked by a hedge trimmer, although for all I knew, it might have been a fashionable and expensive cut where she came from. She was wearing an unbuttoned green coat and a purple dress that was a little too tight and bulged. So far as I could see, her only attractive parts were her even, white teeth.

'This is a nice little house,' she said, looking around.

'Thank you, Miss Johnson,' said Hobbes.

'Please call me Kathy.'

As he nodded, she smiled at him. He was still looking bewildered and I'd rarely seen him at a loss, except the time when my ex-editor's wife shot him, and when he was stricken by acute camel allergy.

'I'm forgetting my manners,' said Hobbes. 'May I offer you a cup of tea?'

'Thank you, Daddy,' she said, 'but I'd prefer a coffee and I'm famished with all the excitement and the travelling, so I wouldn't say no to a few cookies.'

'I'll have the lass see to it,' said Hobbes, standing up and leaving at such a pace I almost suspected him of running away.

'And who might you be?' she asked.

'I'm Andy ... Andy Caplet.' I held out my hand.

After a slightly uncomfortable pause, she shook it.

'So, what's wrong with you?'

'Eh?'

'Your head.'

'It ... umm ... got in the way of a beer tray during a pub brawl.'

'Why were you brawling?' she asked, looking at me with distaste.

'I wasn't. I was with Hobbes, your father that is, when he was stopping it.'

'Oh, I see,' she said, 'so, you're a police officer, too.'

'No, I'm not ... not exactly.'

'So, what are you?'

'I dunno really,' I said, flummoxed and squirming. 'I just help him out now and then.'

'How?'

'In any way I can.'

She frowned, looking suspicious. 'What *do* you do if you're not *exactly* a police officer? What is your job?'

'I don't ... umm ... actually have a job.' I feared my face was turning red.

She shook her head. 'I don't understand. What is your connection with my daddy?'

'He's my friend ... sort of ... and I do try to help him out.'

'I see. Well, Mr Caplet, I need to have a long talk with him. We have a great deal to catch up on and it would be better if we were alone. Do you understand? I think you should go home now.'

'This is my home.'

'You live here? You're a paying guest?'

'Well, I don't exactly pay.'

'So, what exactly is your relationship with my daddy?' she asked, raising her pencilled eyebrows.

I didn't like the way she was thinking, or at least, I didn't like the way I thought she might be thinking. 'I'm his friend. We've just got back from a camping trip, but I normally stay in his spare room.'

'For which you don't pay rent?'

'No.'

'And you don't have a job.'

'No. Your father is a very kind man. So is Mrs Goodfellow ... no ... she's not a man, but she is kind.'

'And who is Mrs Goodfellow?'

'The housekeeper.'

'He has a housekeeper? I guess he must be loaded.'

'I don't really know. He doesn't live like a rich man, but he doesn't seem short of money.'

'I see,' she said, looking thoughtful and, to my mind, greedy and calculating. 'It seems to me he must be wealthy to have a house like this and a housekeeper, and to afford a freeloader – no offence – staying with him. What does he drive?'

'Umm ... a car.'

'No shit. What sort of car?'

'The little red one outside. I don't know what sort it is. He only got it today.'

'That piece of junk? Jeez!'

'The old fellow asked me to bring you this,' said Mrs Goodfellow, appearing with a tray and making Kathy jump. She placed it on the coffee table. 'There's coffee and hobnobs. I haven't had time to bake.'

'You must be the housekeeper,' said Kathy with a nod. 'That will be all for now.'

Mrs Goodfellow stiffened, but returned to the kitchen without another word as Hobbes reappeared, his dark, bristly hair damp around his face.

'Help yourself to biscuits ... or should I say cookies,' he said. 'Sorry, Andy, would you mind leaving us alone for a bit? Miss Johnson ...'

'Kathy, please.'

'... Kathy and I need to talk. The lass is making a pot of tea.'

'Umm ... yes ... of course.' I got to my feet. 'Bye.' I walked away, unwanted.

Going into the kitchen, I closed the door behind me, pulled

up a chair and sat at the table. Mrs Goodfellow was battering a lump of meat with a wooden mallet while Dregs, to judge from the snorting and scratching at the back door, had been confined to the garden.

'Fancy Hobbes having a daughter,' I said. 'Who'd have thought it?'

Mrs Goodfellow, sniffing, continued pounding the innocent meat to a pulp.

'She says,' I continued, 'that her name is Kathleen Johnson. I wonder who her mother is. Well, I expect it might be Mrs Johnson. Why isn't her surname Hobbes?'

'I knew her mother,' said Mrs Goodfellow, the mallet still in her hand. She turned to face me, looking fierce: fierce for Mrs Goodfellow, that is. 'And that woman in there has a definite look of her, a real taint.'

'How did you know her?' I asked, fascinated.

'It was when we were in America, back in 1967. I think you saw the photographs in the attic?'

I nodded, remembering the bizarre snaps of Hobbes hanging out with a bunch of hippies, including a much younger, and confusingly attractive, Mrs Goodfellow. One young woman had always seemed particularly close to Hobbes and it dawned on me that she had looked something like Kathy, particularly about the eyes.

'So,' I said, 'her mother is the one you used to call Froggy, isn't she?'

'Yes,' said Mrs Goodfellow, nodding, brandishing the mallet like a club. 'She used to hang around him like a bad smell and the old fellow couldn't get rid of her until she'd spent all his money. She was off like a shot, taking his car, when it ran out. I knew she was a nasty piece of work all along, but the old fellow wouldn't see it. You know he can't see any bad in a woman until it's too late.'

'That's true,' I said. He'd been completely taken in by Narcisa, my former-editor's wife, until she imprisoned him, starved him and shot him. Not that my record with women was anything to boast about; it had taken me ages to accept that my last girlfriend was a werecat, even after I'd caught cat scratch fever off her.

'What do you make of her in there?' asked Mrs Goodfellow, nodding towards the sitting room.

'Well,' I said, trying to be fair, 'I can't say my first impression is very good, but it's unfair to judge her when she's probably tired and nervous. I'm sure she doesn't think much of me, though. Do you really think she's his daughter?'

'I can't see it,' she said, shaking her head. 'I don't think Froggy and the old fellow were ever … intimate, but it was so long ago and times were very different.'

I shuddered at the mere idea of him being intimate with a woman. It wasn't that I was jealous, or not especially because of that, it was just that I couldn't, or didn't, want to believe it. For one thing, I doubted any human woman was tough enough to survive a night of passion with him. It just didn't bear thinking about. I tried not to.

'What's for supper?' I asked.

'Beef wellington,' said the old girl, who also seemed pleased to change the subject. 'I haven't baked one for years, but the fillet of beef looked so tender and succulent and I had a basket of mushrooms that needed using.'

'If the beef is so tender,' I asked, 'why are you bashing it?'

'That's just a bit of shin for Dregs, dear.' She laughed and then sighed. 'I wonder what's going to happen with that … woman?'

My diversion hadn't worked for long.

'I don't know. Perhaps he'll send her packing.'

'That would probably be best, but what if she tells him a sob story? He's got too soft a heart for his own good.'

I had to agree for, beneath his rough exterior, he was often startlingly kind and, moreover, he tended to treat women with a gentle, old-fashioned courtesy. At least until they started shooting at him, when his feral side could emerge, quite terrifying, even to an innocent bystander such as me. In the quiet that followed, I could hear the murmur of Hobbes and Kathy talking and, although I couldn't make out what they were saying, Hobbes's chuckle suggested they were getting along just fine.

My insides went suddenly cold as I was struck by a horrible fear that something momentous was happening, something that would not be to my advantage. Though my conscious mind couldn't work out why I was so worried, it conceded that my insides might be correct. Somehow, I felt as if a jury was debating my case, that my case was not a strong one and that my future was in someone else's hands. I tried to keep calm by drinking tea.

The old girl, having cut some butter into chunks the size of sugar cubes, was mixing them with flour and salt in a bowl, when the kitchen door opened and Hobbes entered.

'Kathy will be staying for supper,' he said, 'if that's alright?'

Mrs Goodfellow nodded. 'There should be enough beef wellington to go round.'

'Thank you,' said Hobbes, returning to the sitting room.

A few seconds later, he returned, looking a little embarrassed. 'I explained what beef wellington was and she said she didn't think she'd like it. She asked if there was anything else?'

Mrs Goodfellow was silent for a long minute, during which he tried to smile.

'I suppose,' she said, 'I could make hamburgers.'

'Thanks, lass. I'll see if that's alright.'

He turned, walked away and checked. 'That will be fine. She'd like French fries as well.'

'I'll see what I can do,' said Mrs Goodfellow.

Hobbes fled.

'At least it's good news for the dog,' said Mrs Goodfellow.

'Why?' I asked.

'Because he'll get some beef wellington for his supper. I think *he* will appreciate it.'

'I thought you were giving him that bit of old shin you were battering.'

She grinned gummily.

'Oh,' I said, 'I get it.'

I watched her feed the shin through a mincer and then bustle about with pots and pans and meat and vegetables and pastry. Although I tried to pretend that I was thinking deeply, I wasn't. Any intelligence I possessed had been swamped by a flood of vague worries.

At six-thirty, just as the old girl was dishing up, in walked Hobbes and Kathy. He pulled out a chair for her and she sat facing me and nodded. I nodded back and smiled, feeling I ought to appear friendly for the time being. After all, I might be seeing a lot more of her. When she smiled back, a brief smile to be sure, I hoped I'd made a breakthrough, though I feared I might just have come across as gormless.

When Hobbes said grace, as was his wont, Kathy looked a little startled, but went along with it. Then it was time to eat. The fillet, succulent and pink at the centre, burst from its golden crust, filling the world with subtle scents and flavours, helped along by a pungent, breathtaking horseradish sauce. Hobbes and I ate in a reverential rapture while Kathy wolfed her two large burgers and fries, ignoring the salad. She didn't, she said, 'do rabbit food'.

When she'd finished, she leant back in her chair and said: 'That wasn't bad. What's for dessert?'

'I'm sorry,' said Mrs Goodfellow, appearing as if from nowhere, 'but I haven't made one.'

'I see,' said Kathy, raising her eyebrows.

'We don't usually have dessert,' said Hobbes, 'except on Sundays.'

Kathy pouted. 'Do you call that a meal? I heard British meals were insufficient, but … I'm sorry. Thing is I'm still famished.'

My mouth dropped open. Mrs Goodfellow had always struck me as an extremely generous supplier. Certainly I'd never had cause to complain. Nor had Hobbes, even with his colossal appetite.

'I'm sure the lass can rustle up something,' he said.

'Well,' said Mrs Goodfellow, 'there are still some biscuits left, or there's bread and jam.'

'Come on, lady,' said Kathy, 'you must have something in the freezer.'

'We don't have a freezer.'

'Jeez!' She looked shocked. 'No freezer? How do you store things?'

'I make them fresh every day.'

'No kidding? I'll bet you don't have a microwave either?'

Mrs Goodfellow shook her head.

'Fancy that,' said Kathy. 'I had no idea. I guess that means you made the crusty beef thing and my hamburgers … and the fries.'

'Of course,' said Mrs Goodfellow.

'Then,' said Kathy, 'I apologise for putting you to so much trouble. I had no idea what I was asking.'

'It was no trouble,' said Mrs Goodfellow, smiling. 'You weren't to know that the old fellow insists on good home cooking.'

'I do indeed,' said Hobbes, 'and the lass does us proud.'

'She really does,' I said, gushing. 'She's brilliant.'

Mrs Goodfellow blushed, but looked pleased.

'I'm glad to hear my daddy's so well looked after,' said Kathy, reaching out and patting his arm.

'He is,' I said, 'though he can look after himself. We've just been camping up in the hills and he cooked really well. He even caught most of what we ate. Apart from the leaves and roots.'

Kathy nodded. 'Mom said he was kinda practical. And that he loved the outdoors.'

Hobbes grinned and scratched his head and I almost

believed that he, too, blushed.

'I'll tell you what,' said Mrs Goodfellow, 'I can rustle up pancakes in a few minutes. How would that suit you?'

'That would suit me just fine, Mrs Goodfellow.'

The old girl beamed and, having cleared the table, set to with flour, milk and eggs in her massive mixing bowl. Without even being asked, I started on the washing up, trying to prove what a useful addition to the household I was, or at least trying to demonstrate that I wasn't a complete waste of space. When I'd finished, I found a tea towel and not only dried up, but also began to put bits and pieces away, until Mrs Goodfellow stopped me.

'I'll do the rest, dear. I'd like to be able to find them again.' She turned to Kathy: 'I'd normally rest the batter for a few minutes but, since it's urgent, I'll just go ahead.'

Opening a cupboard, she took out a pair of enormous black frying pans that anyone might imagine would snap her bony wrists.

'Would you boys care for a pancake?' she asked.

'No thank you, lass,' said Hobbes. 'I've had an elegant sufficiency already.'

Although not at all hungry, I had too many fond memories of the last time she'd made pancakes to resist. 'I ... umm ... wouldn't mind a small one.'

They turned out so delicious and so fluffy that I overrode the fullness in my stomach and overdid the gluttony. Even so, I utterly failed to keep up with Kathy's unhealthy appetite. When, six pancakes and most of a tin of golden syrup later, she'd finally finished, it was clear how she'd achieved her bulk.

Hobbes led her back to the sitting room, while I helped make coffee, finding, under direction, the correct cups. Kathy had turned her nose up when offered tea.

Mrs Goodfellow allowed Dregs back in and presented him with a plate of beef wellington, which, rather than wolfing down, he ate slowly, with his eyes half closed, savouring every mouthful, like the gourmet he imagined he was. I'd even seen him sniffing the cork from a bottle of Hobbes's good wine, looking every bit the connoisseur.

'What do you think of Kathy now?' I whispered. 'Perhaps she's not all that bad.'

'We'll see, dear' said Mrs Goodfellow. 'I'll make an effort to like her for the old fellow's sake, but she reminds me too much of her mother, and not at all of him.'

'She takes after him in the eating stakes,' I said.

'No, she doesn't. He appreciates good home cooking and he'll have a pudding now and again because he knows I like making them, but he hasn't really got a sweet tooth. Anyway, he's not as fat as … he's not fat.'

Later, while making my way up to my room, I overheard Kathy and Hobbes.

'Yes,' she said, 'I sure would love to stay for a few days.'

'Good,' said Hobbes.

My mind was in turmoil and the dull ache gripping my guts was nothing to do with how much I'd eaten. There were only three bedrooms, so where was she going to sleep? It seemed most likely she'd be offered my room and, although I was supposedly only staying there until I'd found a place of my own, the truth was that I hadn't looked for anywhere else, having found a comfortable berth that was more homelike than anywhere else I'd ever stayed. Even though there had been a time when I would have given anything to get away from Hobbes to find somewhere safe, those days were long gone. I'd developed a quite unexpected regard for him and, besides, there was the old girl's cooking, not to mention her eccentric kindness. Finally, there was Dregs, who'd scared me silly (or sillier, according to Hobbes) when he'd first arrived with his delinquent ways, but I'd grown used to the shaggy beast and liked having him around. He'd become part of the family and it was beginning to look as if I wouldn't be for much longer.

I stretched out on my bed. It wasn't mine, of course: nor was the room. I was merely the occupier, with no more right to stay there than the spider Mrs Goodfellow had evicted earlier in the day. I hadn't felt so insecure for a long time.

I'd grown complacent. I'd not had a job in ages, had no income, nowhere else to live, and was entirely dependent on Hobbes's generosity. That wasn't all, for, in a strange way, I'd become addicted to excitement and got a real buzz from the way things happened when he was around. Yet, like other addicts, part of me suspected it wasn't quite healthy.

It was dark when I crept downstairs, hoping for a cup of tea or cocoa. Hobbes heard me and called me into the sitting room.

I walked in, blinking in the brightness.

Kathy, looking perfectly at home, was sprawling comfortably on the sofa, at the end where I normally sat. Hobbes was on the oak chair.

'Take a seat,' he said, gesturing towards the sofa.

Kathy, shifting fractionally, allowed me to squeeze in.

'I thought you should know,' said Hobbes, 'that Kathy will be staying for a few days.'

'At least,' she said.

Hobbes smiled. 'But, obviously, there aren't enough bedrooms.'

I nodded, guessing what was coming.

'So,' he continued, 'a little reorganisation will be required.'

The cold, heavy feeling in my stomach spread to my legs.

'So, just for tonight, Kathy is going to sleep in my room and I'll sleep on the sofa.'

'No,' I said, grateful that I wasn't going to be kicked out immediately, 'that's not fair. I can sleep on the sofa. Anyway, you won't fit.'

Hobbes shook his head. 'I'll be fine. I've slept in far worse places.'

'But,' I said, reluctantly, knowing I was cutting my own

lifeline, 'it's your house. If Kathy is going to stay, I'll have to move out.'

Kathy nodded. 'He's right, you know, but I don't want anyone to be put out on my account.'

I smiled back and felt rotten. *Put out*: she could hardly have chosen better words. A cat gets put out, evicted from warmth and comfort and forced out into the bleak, cold night, but at least I wasn't going to be put out that particular night. I put on a brave mask.

'That's very good of you to offer,' said Hobbes, 'but you have nowhere else to go, unless you want to go back to your parents.'

I shook my head. 'I'd rather not, but I should be able to find somewhere to stay round here.'

'It won't be easy,' said Hobbes, 'without any money. You'd have to get a job.'

'I know. I've ... umm ... been meaning to.'

'Everyone should have a job,' said Kathy. 'Otherwise, how they gonna live?'

'I don't want you to leave,' said Hobbes. 'I've thought about it and, as you say, it is my house and in matters such as this I will make the decisions. Therefore, as I said, I will sleep on the sofa tonight, and tomorrow I'll clear some space in the attic. The lass has been saying I should. I think she's worried the weight will bring the house down.'

Kathy snorted as she suppressed a laugh.

'There's plenty of room up there for me to make up a bed,' he continued, 'and I will be perfectly comfortable.'

'It doesn't seem fair,' I said, though the relief almost made me dizzy.

'I agree,' said Kathy. 'I don't see why my daddy has to give his bed up.'

Hobbes shrugged. 'Nevertheless, that is my final word.'

His tone of voice indicated that he meant it.

12

I found it difficult to relax that night, being acutely aware of the stranger in the room next door, as well as feeling guilty that Hobbes was downstairs. It wasn't that there was anything wrong with the sofa, besides a little old age fading and scuffing, but it was no place for such a big guy to spend the night and I don't know how he managed, for next morning, after mowing his overnight bristles, taking a shower and dressing in his smart suit, he showed no hint of tiredness or stiffness. Despite the Sunday morning clamour of the church bells and the scent of frying bacon, Kathy was a no-show for breakfast. Although conceding the possibility that she was jet-lagged, I was more inclined to put it down to laziness.

Hobbes had just finished his third huge mug of tea when the phone rang and he went to answer it.

'That was Sid,' he said, on his return. 'There was a break in at the bank overnight.'

'A break in?' I said, always quick on the uptake. 'Was anything stolen?'

'It's unlikely someone broke in to make a deposit. Now I have a slight problem. I was intending to escort the lass to church this morning, so would you mind going with her instead?'

'Of course,' I said, biting back on my objections, hiding my disappointment that I would not be taken to the crime scene and still determined to be on my best behaviour. 'It'll be my pleasure.'

'Thank you, dear,' said Mrs Goodfellow, who'd just reappeared in her Sunday best, a slightly-too-big green frock, patterned with orange flowers. She had inserted her previously-owned false teeth and had topped off the entire creation with a saggy, baggy black hat with artificial daisies. 'Go and put on a suit. A good thick one would be best as it's chilly outside.'

'OK … I'll wear the dark one.'

'And quickly, or you'll be late,' said Hobbes, heading out. 'I'll be off. Dregs, stay.'

Dregs, a connoisseur of crime scenes, slumped under the table as Hobbes left.

Hurrying upstairs, I pulled out the heavy, dark woollen suit that, like my entire wardrobe, had once belonged to Mr Goodfellow and which, like everything else, fitted uncannily well. The last time I'd worn it had been to the funeral of a murdered man, when, although I hadn't realised until later, my then girlfriend had been the killer. In fairness to her, the victim hadn't been nice. Then I tentatively removed the bandage round my head and gazed in the mirror for a moment, impressed by the rainbow colours beneath.

'Very smart, dear,' said Mrs Goodfellow as I came downstairs ready for action. 'Let's go. You can carry this.'

She handed me a large paper bag. To my surprise, it was full of aubergines.

Leaving the house, turning left down Blackdog Street, we headed for the church. The wind was tossing litter and leaves around, ruffling my hair, making me shiver as if it were thrusting icy fingers through my clothes. I wished I'd put on an overcoat, and maybe a trilby, though I doubted it would have stayed on long. A brief shaft of sunlight stabbing through the heavy grey cloud only seemed to make the day colder, and I was pleased when we reached the church door and could leave the wind to its mischief.

Someone was playing a sprightly tune on the organ and the ancient stonework was decorated with flowers, fruits, and sheaves of wheat and barley. Although not a churchgoer, except for the occasional wedding, funeral or christening, it seemed busy to me, with plenty of bums on seats. I recognised a few of them from the Feathers and elsewhere.

'There's always a good congregation for the harvest

festival,' said Mrs Goodfellow, guiding me towards a pew.

After apologising for standing on an old gentleman's gouty foot, and nodding at my friend Les Bashem and his pack of young werewolves, I sat down beside her.

'Is the harvest festival today?'

She nodded.

'Is that why we've brought aubergines?'

She nodded.

'Is that the vicar coming in?'

She nodded a third time, adding a slight frown.

'Should I shut up now?'

She nodded and the service started. Although I made an effort to pay attention, I was itching to find out what had happened at the bank and kept drifting away. It seemed strange that Sid's bank had been targeted twice in such a short time. I wondered why, and what had been taken. After all the publicity last time, I couldn't believe anyone would be so rash, or stupid, to risk the wrath of Hobbes.

Mrs Goodfellow nudged me. I was the only one still seated, apart from a very old chap in a wheelchair. Embarrassed, I rose to my feet and joined in the singing of 'We Plough the Fields and Scatter', rather enjoying myself, until I realised everyone else was singing 'Come Ye Thankful People, Come'. That was probably the highlight for me, and by the time the vicar took to the pulpit for his sermon, my mind had moved on to lunch; in particular, the magnificent fruit pie I'd noticed the old girl had baked. As a result, I couldn't remember much of the vicar's spiel, except for a bit about someone toiling in the vineyard of the Lord, which struck me as odd, since there were no vineyards round Sorenchester. Even so, I made a real effort to fidget as little as possible, lowered my head to conceal my yawns, and tried to look intelligently interested, though my eyes seemed terribly heavy. The thump of my forehead striking the pew in front and the pain it caused made me yelp. I avoided looking towards Mrs Goodfellow, who I feared would be seriously annoyed. Fortunately, my cut didn't reopen.

At least I was awake when the curate, Kevin Godley, known as Kev the Rev because of his motor bike obsession, got up to do a reading from the Bible. Since he was a far better speaker than the vicar, it wasn't difficult to pay attention and a phrase struck me as apposite: 'And having food and raiment let us be therewith content.' I did, I reflected, have food and raiment and was quite content, or would have been had I a little money to call my own.

As if reading my mind, Kev continued: 'For the love of money is the root of all evil'. I shrugged off the attack, for I neither loved, nor needed money, getting on pretty well without it. A warm glow of self-righteousness spread through me, a most welcome sensation in the draughty old church.

'They that will be rich,' said Kev, 'fall into temptation and a snare, and into many foolish and hurtful lusts, which drown men in destruction and perdition.'

Not being rich, or ever likely to be, it was unlikely I'd succumb to that particular temptation and I enjoyed a sudden feeling of righteous superiority over my less fortunate, if much richer, neighbours.

My happy complacency lasted until the vicar resumed control and announced it was time to present harvest gifts. Mrs Goodfellow sent me to the front with the bag of aubergines. As I stood up, I realised I was the only adult, a giant among the children. I was thinking I should sit down again when Mrs Goodfellow gave me the look. Realising the futility of trying to be inconspicuous, aiming for nonchalant good humour, I stepped into the aisle, swinging my bag casually, as a little girl with a wicker basket full of shiny apples rushed past, eager to reach the front. I was on the down swing and my bag smacked her full in the face. She fell, emitting a wail of distress, and my bag split, spilling its bounty in a wide arc. A tubby boy with freckles, the next in line, stepped on a very ripe aubergine, skidded and crashed into a pew, causing his magnificent marrow to explode. He burst into tears and the vicar, hands raised, looking aghast, rushed to help.

'I'm … umm … ever so sorry,' I said and bent down to help the child.

It was simply bad timing that the girl's mother was already rushing to the rescue. As her knees hit my back, she went right over the top, crashing down and felling the onrushing vicar, whose sprawling demise caused a domino effect among the children, and a shower of tomatoes and freshly laid eggs.

'I didn't mean it,' I said, standing up, rubbing my back, stunned by the carnage I'd caused.

'It's that man again!' cried a lady with blue-rinsed hair and a face that looked like it could chop through logs. 'He's always trouble.'

'Not always,' I said, 'and it was an accident.'

'What have you done to my wife and my little girl?' asked a burly, balding man, striding forward, his face as red as the squashed tomato beneath his foot. As he slid past, arms flailing like a novice ice skater, he demolished the poor vicar, who was just getting back to his feet, his once pristine surplice horribly egged and slimed.

A firm hand grabbed my shoulder. It was shaking with indignation and I was fully expecting painful retribution from an outraged parent, but it turned out to be Mrs Goodfellow's. People were sniggering, trying to look suitably outraged, except for the young werewolves who were howling with laughter.

'I think,' she said, 'it's time to go.'

My cheeks aflame, hanging my head in shame, muttering apologies to anyone who caught my eye, I allowed myself to be frogmarched through the church and evicted into The Shambles.

'I am so sorry,' I said, hoping to calm her anger with a show of penitence, although it really hadn't been my fault. 'I didn't mean any harm. It was just an unfortunate accident.'

'What are you, dear,' she said, looking me right in the eye, 'some kind of Doomsday machine?' She exploded into laughter, leaning against me, her eyes streaming. 'That was the best service I've been to in years, and I don't know about the rest of them, but I feel thoroughly invigorated. Thank you.'

Wiping her eyes, she patted me on the back, as I stood before her, nonplussed and still horrified by what I'd done. From inside came the singing of 'We Plough the Fields and Scatter'. My antics had not held things up for long.

'Anyway,' she said, her hysterics subsiding, 'let's go home and see to the dinner.'

'Great,' I said, feeling immediately better. 'What is it?'

'Nothing special. It's slow roasted belly pork with mashed potatoes, glazed carrots, peas and a nice apple sauce, using some of the windfalls.'

'That sounds delicious, but is that all?' I said, joking.

'No, dear,' she said, seriously. 'I've also made a blackberry and apple pie.'

'I saw it,' I said, wishing dinnertime would hurry up, 'and it looked absolutely marvellous. Let's hope Kathy will be alright with it.'

Mrs Goodfellow shrugged. 'I hope she'll like it.'

'And another thing,' I said, feeling a little sorry for her, 'what will she do when she wakes up and finds no one's home?'

'She'll be fine. I left a note, telling her to help herself to whatever she wanted for breakfast.'

I grimaced, recalling the first time I'd had to make my own breakfast at Hobbes's. Things had not quite gone according to plan and I'd come perilously close to torching the kitchen while trying to make a cup of tea.

'Let's hope she's better at it than you were,' said Hobbes.

I must have leapt a good foot skyward. 'Where did you come from?' I asked on landing.

'From across the road, I've done what I had to at the bank

and was just leaving when I saw you two having a laugh.' He glanced at the clock on the church tower. 'You're out early.'

'Yes,' said Mrs Goodfellow, regaling him with my misadventures as we strolled home.

His guffaw resonated off the church walls like the sound of a great bell. 'How do you manage it?' he asked.

'I only wish I knew.'

'How many did you actually bring down?'

'Only two directly, I think, though a few more came down in the aftermath.'

'It reminds me,' said Hobbes, 'of when Bob Nibblet went to church.'

'Skeleton' Bob Nibblet, the skinniest man in the county, was its most unsuccessful petty criminal and a notorious drinker. The two were not unconnected. I wouldn't have reckoned him a churchgoer.

'Bob was experiencing a run of bad luck,' said Hobbes, 'having been caught red-handed five times in a week. On the sixth evening, he decided to forego poaching and to drown his sorrows. At throwing out time, having taken on board a gallon of Old Bootsplasher Ale, some joker bet him ten pounds that he couldn't vault the car park wall. Eager for easy money, Bob accepted the bet and successfully cleared the wall.'

'Good for him,' I said, as we crossed into Blackdog Street, 'but what's this got to do with church?'

'I was coming to that. Although he got over, he had quite failed to look before he leapt. He landed in a parked car.'

'Don't you mean on it?'

'No, it was parked parallel to the wall and he crashed straight through the driver's window.'

'Was he hurt?'

'He broke his leg. Worse for Bob was that the car belonged to Colonel Squire, the magistrate who'd just fined him one hundred pounds for poaching.'

'That was bad luck.'

'It was, and more so for the colonel, who had just enjoyed a pleasant meal with Mrs Squire. Fortunately, Bob is not the burliest fellow in the world, but it is still not pleasant to have a fully grown man wearing hobnail boots land on your face.'

'I expect not. But what has this got to do with church?'

'I was coming to that.' He paused at the bottom of the steps outside the house. 'Next morning, after a night of being plastered, and having learned that he'd been summonsed, charged with being drunk and disorderly, he realised Colonel Squire's fiery temper would not have been improved by a broken nose and several loose teeth. Therefore, he decided to seek comfort in the church.

'It turned out that a visiting evangelist was leading the service and the vicar, disapproving of the young man's style, had taken refuge in his office.'

'I remember,' said Mrs Goodfellow. 'The evangelist's name was Gordon Cursitt.'

'That's right,' said Hobbes. 'He preached about the healing power of the Lord and, Bob, carried away by the power of his words, struggled to the front of the church, threw aside his crutches and cried "Alleluia!"'

'That's amazing.'

'Gordon Cursitt rushed to tell the vicar of the miracle and the vicar, remorseful for his scepticism, hurried out to see what had happened, but there was no sign of Bob.'

'Where was he?'

'Behind the font, groaning and clutching his leg.'

He chuckled, bounded up the steps and opened the door. I hoped the story was true, though I had to admit I sometimes doubted Hobbes's veracity. The savour of roasting pork drove lesser considerations from my mind as I followed Mrs Goodfellow into the house.

Kathy was sitting at the kitchen table, an empty plate and a glass of water in front of her.

'Good morning,' said Hobbes, as Mrs Goodfellow let Dregs into the garden, 'did you sleep well?'

'Not really. That pesky dog was under my bed. He snores.'

'You should keep the door closed,' said Mrs Goodfellow.

'I did. He must have snuck in when I went to the bathroom.'

'I'm sorry,' said Hobbes. 'You should have pushed him out.'

'He growled.'

'I'm sorry to hear that,' said Hobbes. 'I'll tell him not to do it again.'

'Did you find everything for breakfast?' asked Mrs Goodfellow with a friendly smile, displaying her false teeth.

'Not really. The bread wasn't sliced and you don't appear to have a toaster, I couldn't find the coffee machine and there were no sodas in the ice box.'

'Sorry,' said Hobbes, 'but the lass bakes her own bread and slices it with a bread knife. There's a grill on the cooker and she makes coffee on the hob. Would you like one now?'

'Yes, please. I've only drunk water from the faucet and I can't face the day without my coffee.'

'I'll make you some,' said Mrs Goodfellow. 'Did you find anything to eat?'

'Only a pie,' said Kathy. 'I made do with that.'

'I see,' said Mrs Goodfellow.

'I hope that's alright,' said Kathy.

'I'm sure it is,' said Hobbes. 'If you're hungry, you must eat.'

I couldn't believe she'd guzzled the whole pie, for, unlike Hobbes, I looked forward to my puddings. A slice of that pie would have been the perfect finale to the roast pork and she had deprived me of a real treat. I would have liked to have said something fine, biting and sarcastic, at least, if I'd been able to think of anything, but instead, still trying to be on my best behaviour, I was reduced to a sort of mental spluttering. The whole pie? The old girl was a generous cook and there were always seconds and leftovers and, though Kathy was a large lady (I was still on my best behaviour), I couldn't get my head around it. The whole pie? Succulent with apples and ripe with blackberries? I could have wept and it wasn't because I was obsessed with food, for although I had a healthy appetite, I enjoyed a wide range of interests; anyone fortunate enough to have eaten one of the old girl's pies would have understood my point of view.

Except for Kathy.

'I didn't much like it,' she said. 'It was too fruity.'

'It was a fruit pie,' I said, gritting my teeth.

'Yeah, well,' she said, 'I guess it was at that.'

Hobbes smiled. 'We'd best get out of here and give the lass some space. Shall we all go through to the sitting room?'

'Yes, Daddy.'

I went upstairs, changed out of my suit and into more normal wear, olive chinos and a crisply ironed white shirt. Going back down, I had to squeeze myself in beside Kathy on the sofa. I thought Hobbes looked a little ill at ease on the oak chair, but I approved that he'd got her away from Mrs Goodfellow. I'd have hated the cooking to be disrupted.

'What are we doing this afternoon?' asked Kathy with a smile for Hobbes. 'After luncheon, that is.'

'I really must get back to work.' said Hobbes. 'There was a break in at the bank last night.'

'Wow, I didn't realise how crime-ridden this quaint little town is.'

'Perhaps Andy can look after you? Until I'm free.'

'Do I have to?' I said, wondering about kicking him; I might have had he not been so hard and had I not reminded myself that I was on my best behaviour. 'That is ... umm ... I don't want to interfere with Kathy's plans.'

'I have no plans ... I was just hoping to spend a few hours with my daddy.'

'Unfortunately, I have a job to do, and will probably be busy all afternoon. Andy will show you the sights. Won't you?'

'I guess so,' I said, unable to see why she couldn't go with him. He had, after all, taken me to numerous crime scenes without any problem. Perhaps he thought she would eat the evidence. I smiled, putting on a brave face. 'Actually, I'll be glad to.'

'Thanks,' said Hobbes.

'In the meantime,' I said, 'tell us what happened at the bank.'

'Person or persons unknown drilled into the vault from the cellar of the shop next door.'

'I noticed one of the shops was being renovated,' I said.

'That's the one. The builders weren't at work yesterday, yet witnesses report hearing heavy machinery.'

'So, the builders didn't do it?'

'It would seem not. The perpetrators apparently used an unusually powerful drill that made short work of the old bricks in the cellar and the reinforced concrete walls of the vault. They must have known precisely where they were going.'

'Umm ... does that mean an insider job?'

'It's a possibility, but the buildings down The Shambles are old and it's possible that documents or plans fell into the wrong hands.'

'Did they leave the drill behind? That might give some clues.'

'No, there was nothing,' said Hobbes. 'They evidently had plenty of time to clear up.'

'But wasn't the vault alarmed?' asked Kathy.

He looked puzzled and then smiled. 'I take it that you're asking whether there was an alarm in the vault. Yes, there was. Only it wasn't working, because the wires had been cut by the drill. Unfortunately, it was not a modern alarm, which would have had back up power.'

'Cut to the chase,' said Kathy. 'What was stolen?'

'Bank officials are still checking records, so they don't yet know about everything. However it is clear that Colonel Squire's gold has gone, along with at least two other gold deposits.'

My mind made a connection. 'Was Colonel Squire's gold the same stuff that you retrieved from the gang?'

'It was.'

Another connection popped into my head. 'And don't you have something in there?'

'I did,' said Hobbes. 'That was also stolen.'

'Hey,' said Kathy, 'Inspector Hobbes is back and this time it's personal. I can see why you have to get out there. I'll bet you want to kick some butt.'

'I will do my job in my normal manner.'

'But, how can you just sit here when the bad guys have gotten your property?'

'Because,' said Hobbes, 'I want my dinner.'

'It's important to get your priorities sorted out,' I said, repeating a lesson I'd learned from him and that, one day, I hoped to apply to my life.

She shrugged. 'Well ... OK ... I suppose. But, what if the bad guys get away? It's yours, Daddy. Was it cash? How much was there?'

'I can't remember,' said Hobbes.

'I'm not surprised,' I said. 'Sid reckoned you hadn't looked at it since nineteen t...'

Hobbes's cough interrupted me. He shook his head ever so slightly.

'Dinner's ready!'

Mrs Goodfellow's shrill voice made me jump. I'd never worked out how she moved so silently, and wished she didn't, for my nervous system must have been damaged by all the shocks. Still, it was some consolation to see Kathy's reaction was even more extreme. I'd never before seen such a hefty woman do a vertical take-off.

'Excellent,' said Hobbes. 'Shall we go through?'

Dinner was, of course, superb, the pork succulent and tender, the apple sauce fresh and sharp, the mashed potatoes fluffy, the glazed carrots and peas bursting with sweetness and flavour, and to top it all, there was the crackling, which just exploded into the taste buds and I think even Kathy was impressed, for she ate far more slowly than the previous evening. I put this down to her appreciation of what was before her, although it may have been connected with being full of pie. Even so, she still managed to find room for the apple dumplings Mrs G had somehow managed to rustle up, which made me appreciate the fruit at a new level and almost not regret the pie.

Afterwards, Hobbes sat back with a smile. 'That was delicious, lass, thank you.' He grinned at Kathy. 'Now, perhaps you understand why I didn't want to miss my dinner?'

Kathy nodded. 'Yes, it was pretty good. Thanks a lot, Mrs Goodfellow.'

'And now,' said Hobbes, getting to his feet, 'I've got bank robbers to catch. I hope you two have an enjoyable afternoon.'

He and Dregs departed and Mrs Goodfellow began the washing up.

I smiled at Kathy. 'Is there anything you'd like to do?'

She shrugged, staring at me as if I were a cockroach. 'What is there to do in this one horse town?'

'I could ... umm ... show you the sights?'

'What do you mean? Building sites?'

'No ... umm ... there's the church ... and ... and the park ... and the museum ... and the town. The museum's got some sort of exhibition on, according to *Sorenchester Life*.'

'OK, Mr Caplet, why don't you wow me?'

'I'll do what I can, but you'd better make sure you wear something warm because it's nippy ... cold ... out there.'

'Let's do it.'

She went upstairs to get ready. I waited on the sofa. I wasn't much looking forward to the next few hours.

13

I waited and waited and then waited some more, before Kathy reappeared, wearing a red Puffa jacket that did nothing to hide her bulk, and a pair of tight blue jeans tucked inside cowboy boots. I sincerely hoped she'd never used them for actual riding, as I was quite fond of horses, so long as they kept their distance, for the feeling was not reciprocated. When I was small, a Shetland pony that was supposed to be taking me for a short ride along the beach had bolted and thrown me headlong into the sea. When I'd reached my teens, a larger and meaner specimen had chased me round and round a field, trying to kick me in the head whenever it wasn't trying to bite me. On a third occasion, as I reported on a pet show, a dray horse had used me as a convenient scratching post, crushing me painfully against a stone wall. Still, on balance, I felt I would rather spend the afternoon with a horse than with Kathy, although the two were not entirely dissimilar.

'Let's do it,' she said.

From her expression, she was looking forward to the afternoon with as much enthusiasm as I was, which, for some reason, felt like a snub. Nevertheless, I rose to the challenge, faking a cheerful smile, hoping to generate genuine cheerfulness.

I got up and, as I put on my overcoat, I told her that I liked her jacket. Although a blatant lie, I thought it might smooth the way.

'Thank you, Mr Caplet,' she said.

'My friends call me Andy.'

She paused, just long enough to worry me, before smiling. 'OK, Andy, show me the town.'

I escorted her along Blackdog Street towards the church and, although it would have been nice to have engaged in a scintillating conversation, I couldn't think of anything to say until we were waiting to cross into The Shambles.

'How did you get to Sorenchester?'

'I caught a bus from London Heathrow Airport.'

'So you flew to Britain?' Sometimes I could catch on quickly.

'Of course.'

'How was your flight?'

'Long and uncomfortable.'

'But worth it to see your father?'

'I guess so. I hope so. Are we going to cross this road, or do you plan to stand here freezing our butts off all afternoon?'

'Oh, right … come on.'

We walked towards the entrance to the church. I had more than a few qualms about going back inside.

'This,' I said, 'is the church. It's very old.'

'How old?'

'Umm … I'm not sure … I'd guess at least six hundred years, maybe more. It was around long before Shakespeare.'

'Did Shakespeare come here?' she asked, sounding almost interested.

'No, I was just trying to put it in perspective.'

'OK. It's not very big, is it?'

'This is just the porch. Let's get inside and away from the wind.'

As we entered beneath the Gothic archway, our footsteps echoing on ancient, patterned tiles, I continued, recalling the few facts I could remember: 'Actually, it is quite big for such a small town. You see, hundreds of years ago, Sorenchester became very prosperous on account of the wool trade and the merchants decided to build something that would demonstrate their wealth.'

'What a bunch of show-offs!'

'Well … maybe.'

When we reached the main body of the church, I was impressed that there was no sign of the mess I'd caused. She showed little sign of being interested in the architecture, which many regarded as a first-rate example of English building, appearing equally unimpressed by the towering stone columns, the magnificent wood-vaulted ceiling, the spectacular carved fifteenth century rood screens and the superb stained glass medieval windows.

'It's smelly in here,' she said.

'It is a little,' I acknowledged. 'I've always put it down to generations of unwashed peasants worshipping in here, though it might be because of the damp. I think the roof leaked last winter.'

We walked slowly around until we came to a glass covered recess in a pillar.

'That,' I said, pointing at the gold goblet, 'is the Roman Cup.'

'Oh yes?' she said, suppressing a yawn.

'It's made of pure gold, though it's not actually Roman.'

'Then it's a stupid name.' She perked up. 'Pure gold you say?'

'It's priceless and it's not actually a silly name, because it was donated to the church by Mr Roman, a Romanian refugee. Some believe it was once owned by Vlad Tepes, or, as he is more generally known, Dracula.'

Kathy raised her eyebrows. 'No kidding? If it's so valuable why isn't it kept somewhere safe?'

'Oh, it's quite safe here. That recess is lined with inch-thick toughened steel and the glass at the front is bullet proof. What's more there are all sorts of alarms and CCTV watching it. It was stolen some time ago, but your father and I got it back.'

'You mean Daddy did and you tagged along?'

'No ... it really wasn't like that. It's a long story...'

'Then, save it for the long winter evenings.'

'Alright.' I said, deflated, for it was a good story and I had saved Hobbes and another man from being murdered, not to mention helping solve the crime. Admittedly, things would have turned out very badly for me had Mrs Goodfellow not turned up in the nick of time, but I had, I considered, been quite heroic.

'Let's get out of here,' said Kathy. 'Show me something else.'

Leaving the church, we strolled around town. I pointed out Grossman's Bank, which, like the shop next door, was festooned in police tape. It was guarded by Constable Poll, stamping his feet and blowing onto his long, bony fingers.

'Afternoon, Derek,' I said, assuming an easy familiarity with the lanky cop. 'How you doing?'

'Fine, except that it's a nippy afternoon to be standing guard.'

'That's true. Is Hobbes in there?'

'No, he looked in for a minute with his dog and left with Mr Sharples.'

'Mr Sharples? Oh you mean Sid, the va ... I mean, the director of the bank?'

'That's right,' said Poll with a glance at Kathy.

'Oh ... umm ... This is Kathy. She's staying with us for a few days and I'm showing her around until Hobbes is free. She's his ... umm ... I mean she's new in town. From America.' I hoped he didn't think she was my girlfriend.

Constable Poll smiled. 'You should take a look in the museum. It's got a fantastic new exhibition of Viking gold that was found in a field over towards Hedbury.'

'That' said Kathy, 'sounds like a great idea, and it would get us out of this goddam wind. My ears are frozen.'

'Where are you from?' asked Constable Poll.

'California most recently,' said Kathy. 'I'm not used to this.'

'What a great place,' said Poll. 'I went there on my holidays – my vacation I should say – two years ago.'

'Yeah, it's a blast,' said Kathy grinning, 'though your little town is kinda cute. Andy's just been showing me the church. It's so quaint and I love all the history. You have a pretty neat accent.'

'So do you,' said Constable Poll, grinning back. Then,

standing to attention, he whispered: 'I'll have to stop chatting now. Superintendent Cooper is coming.'

The superintendent, an attractive woman in her late forties, with friendly eyes that belied a steely streak, was approaching. Although we'd only met a couple of times, I'd formed the impression she didn't think much of me.

'Thank you, Constable,' I said, in a loud, unconvincing manner. 'That was most helpful.'

He nodded and we turned away.

'Nice guy for a cop,' said Kathy.

'Yes, Derek's alright. Would you like to see the museum now?'

She shrugged. 'Is it far?'

'No, it's just around the corner.'

'Let's go.'

When we reached Ride Street, although I pointed out the genuine Roman stone arch forming the entrance and the poster showing a golden crown to advertise the Viking hoard exhibition, Kathy ignored them, pushed straight past and joined a long queue.

'Do you come here often?' asked Kathy as we inched forward.

'No, not really. I haven't been in here since your father brought me here on a case. I don't know why, because they've got some really amazing stuff.'

'I'm looking forward to it.'

After about ten minutes, as we advanced another few inches and were next in line to pay, a sudden thought twisted me up inside.

'Kathy,' I whispered, the blood rising to my cheeks, 'do you have any British money on you?'

'What d'you mean, "on me"?'

'Do you have any British money with you? Now?'

'No. Why?'

'Well … umm … the thing is, I haven't either. I forgot. I'm sorry.'

'You really are something else. Jeez!'

'I just didn't think.'

'I can believe that, but, don't worry, I'll get us in.'

'How?'

'Watch and learn, buddy.'

But, just as the young couple in front had paid for their tickets and were heading inside, she groaned, swayed and tottered forward.

'Pardon me,' she said in a feeble voice, 'I'm feeling faint.'

The young man, fortunately a strong young man, caught her as she dropped into his arms and, although his knees sagged, he held firm.

'May I sit down for a moment?' she murmured, exuding fragility.

The young man, with minimal assistance from me, supported her to a bench and the young woman, her face all concern, sat beside her, holding her hand, asking if she was alright. It was clear to me that she wasn't and I was shocked how quickly it had come on.

'Perhaps,' said Kathy, 'I might have a glass of water?'

'I'll fetch you one,' said the woman at the till, hurrying away.

'Shall I fetch Mrs Goodfellow?' I asked, panicking and feeling useless. The old girl always seemed to know exactly what to do in a crisis.

'No,' said Kathy. 'Stay with me, please.'

When the till lady returned with a glass of water, Kathy took it and sipped, before swaying and groaning. For a moment, I thought she was going to pass out.

'Shall I call an ambulance?' asked the till lady, taking the glass back.

'No,' whispered Kathy. 'I'll be alright in a few minutes. I have these turns now and again. It's low blood sugar and comes on when I haven't eaten enough. I've hardly had a bite all day, but I'll be alright in a minute. I always am.'

My mouth gaped. How could she say such a thing?

'Andy, would you sit with me?'

'Yes, of course.'

She took my hand in her soft, pudgy one and gave it a gentle squeeze, leaving me puzzled and slightly alarmed.

'Can we do anything else?' asked the young woman.

'No, but thank you so much for helping me. I'm a little better already. I'm sure I'll be fine in a moment. Please, go and enjoy the museum.'

Kathy smiled bravely and leant forward, head in her hands, as the couple departed, and the till lady returned to her till.

'Right,' said Kathy, glancing around and standing up, 'let's take the tour.'

As we headed towards the first exhibition hall, the till lady called out: 'Excuse me, but you haven't paid yet.'

'We have,' said Kathy. 'Andy had just picked up the tickets when I had my turn.'

'That's not how I remember it,' said the lady.

'Well,' said Kathy, 'you are very busy. Andy, show the lady our tickets.'

'Eh?' I said, wondering whether her brain had been affected.

'They're in your pocket.'

Embarrassed, I went through a pantomime search and was astonished and confused to actually find a pair of museum tickets. I showed them to the till lady.

'He sometimes gets so worried when I have a turn,' said Kathy with a big smile, 'that he forgets what he's just done.'

The till lady smiled, looking at me as at a well-meaning, but hopeless, idiot. 'Sorry,' she said, 'my mistake. Enjoy your visit.'

'I'm sure we will,' said Kathy, beaming.

As we entered the first hall and I realised what had just happened guilt surged through me and I began shaking. I wanted to confess. I wanted to run away.

'Hold it together,' she said. 'Stay cool, or we'll never pull this off.'

'I'll try. I would never have had the nerve to do that. I thought you were really ill.'

'Is it your perceptiveness that Daddy finds so helpful?'

'Yes ... umm ... no,' I said, 'but you can't just go round breaking the law willy nilly. Don't forget your father is a police officer.'

'Who's Willy Nilly?'

'It doesn't matter. But, what about that nice couple who helped you? You stole their tickets.'

'They were already inside, so what's to complain about? No one was hurt.'

'We might have been caught!'

'We weren't, so chill out and enjoy yourself.'

Filled with a strange mixture of admiration for her cool ingenuity, fear we'd yet be found out, wild elation that we'd pulled it off, and guilt, I might have confessed had she not grabbed my arm and hauled me towards the exhibits. She surprised me by wanting to see everything.

We began at the beginning and it was fascinating, even to me, who was ignorant of archaeology and possessed but a sketchy knowledge of history. There were prehistoric stone tools, exquisite Bronze Age brooches, Roman pillars and statues and amazing relics of the Wars of the Roses and the English Civil War. I could have kicked myself for not having spent time there. In fact, the only thing I didn't much like was all the people milling about, looking at what I wanted to look at and getting in the way.

'How weird is this?' said Kathy, grabbing my arm. 'Look!'

She pointed to a black and white photograph of a group of locals that, according to the caption, had been taken following the discovery of a Roman mosaic during renovations to an inn in 1935.

'Sorenchester as it used to be,' I said. 'It hasn't changed all that much, except there weren't many cars back then. It looks better without them, doesn't it?'

'Yeah, I suppose.'

'I think the inn is the Bear with a Sore Head,' I said, 'though it was probably still called the Ram in those days. Hobbes ... your father ... keeps the original bear with the sore head in the attic. It's ... umm ... stuffed of course. It all began with a darts match and ...'

'Yeah, yeah' said Kathy, 'I'm sure it's a very interesting story, but have you seen this guy?'

'The one with the shovel?'

'Doesn't he look like Daddy?'

It was definitely Hobbes.

'Yes,' I admitted, hoping to put her off the scent, 'it does a bit, except for that ridiculous moustache.'

'Shave it off and it could almost be him. It must be a relation of some sort, I guess.'

'I guess,' I said cautiously, afraid she'd realise how old he was and freak out.

'And that guy in the vest, the one leaning against the wall, he looks a bit like Daddy as well. I guess he had family hereabouts.'

I stared in amazement for, although the other man did indeed look a little like Hobbes, he looked a lot more like Featherlight Binks, the landlord of the Feathers. Several ideas tried to get in my head, but I turned them away, not wanting to think about it.

'Actually,' I said, jerking from my daze, 'he once told me he was an orphan and was adopted and raised in the Blacker Mountains. I don't think his family was from around here at all.'

'Oh, well.' She shrugged. 'I guess it's just coincidence.'

'Let's go and see the Viking stuff,' I said.

We entered a twilight world where the only light came from glass cases and stands. The Viking hoard, silver coins, gold arm rings and bracelets, hack silver, precious stones, rusted remnants of weapons, made a marvellous display. What most impressed me was a massive silver goblet engraved with fantastic figures of long ships and warriors and, despite not being gold, it was even more beautiful than the one in the church. I wondered who'd buried it and why he or she had never retrieved it and was amazed it had been in the ground for so long, with generations walking over it, oblivious to the unimaginable wealth beneath their feet. It left me quite melancholic.

We sat on a bench and watched an educational video. One William Shawcroft, a local metal detectorist, had uncovered the hoard in a field by the River Soren. I only realised who it was when a historian, a tall, thin, grey-haired woman, interviewed him. Despite his piping voice and diminutive stature, he came across as authoritative and knowledgeable.

'That's Billy!' I said, 'I know him.'

'The little guy?' asked Kathy.

'Yes, he's a friend of Hobbes ... your father, but I never knew he was into this, though, come to think of it, he did once show me a Roman coin he'd found in Ride Park.'

'Suddenly,' explained the on-screen Billy, 'I had a massive signal on my detector, so I dug down a couple of inches and found a coin. When I cleaned it, I could see it was gold and from the reign of King Athelstan, in the tenth century AD. I went a little deeper and came across the goblet and knew at once I'd discovered something truly amazing.'

The video showed that, before cleaning, the find had looked exactly like something dug up from a muddy field, more like a crushed turnip than something valuable. Then, moving on to the conservation of the articles, it showed the techniques. I was fascinated by how much effort had gone into scraping out the tiny bits of embedded dirt, using porcupine quills and electrical vibrations.

Just before the end, the focus pulled from a bracelet in the process of being cleaned to show the person cleaning it.

I gasped. 'That's Mrs Duckworth!'

'You seem to know a lot of folk in the treasure business,' said Kathy, sounding sceptical. 'Is she a friend of yours, too?'

'No, I've only met her once, but it was last week, just after I'd found her husband's skeleton.'

'Bullshit!' said Kathy. 'Are you some sort of crazed fantasist?'

'No, it's all true. It was when we were camping. I was with Dregs and he found the skull.'

'So you didn't find it. The dog did. If you're gonna impress folk with tall tales, you gotta be consistent.'

'I was with the dog. The police reckoned there'd been an accident, but I don't think so. The man had been buried under rocks and Hobbes thinks he might have been murdered. At least I think that's what he thinks.'

'I've heard enough of your ravings. Let's get out of here.'

'Alright, but I am telling the truth. You should ask your father.'

'I will, too.'

A wall clock showed the time was approaching five o'clock, or, as the museum staff called it, closing time, but she insisted on looking round the gift shop before we left. Although I was nervous, fearing she'd steal something using me as a decoy, all she did was browse a booklet about the hoard. It had been written by Daphne Duckworth, whose photograph was inside.

So that was her name! I liked it: Daphne. I was saddened that I'd never see her again. Not that I could expect anything if I ever did, because I was sure she hadn't thought much of me. Still, getting to know someone over the dry bones of her husband was not ideal and, perhaps, had circumstances been different ...

'Sometimes,' said Kathy, 'I think you're not really with me.'

'I'm sorry,' I said, falling back into reality, 'I was thinking of something.'

'Congratulations. What are you gonna show me now?'

'Well ... umm ... it's getting late, so nothing much will be open now.' Nothing, I thought, except some of the pubs. I didn't half fancy a pint, or two, of lager, but being penniless, that was out of the question. 'We might as well go home. The old girl will make us a cup of tea, or coffee if you prefer.'

She nodded. 'That sounds like a plan.'

We walked out into the street where the lights were already glowing bright and the cold wind was nipping at ears and fingers. I put my hands in my pockets.

'Let's get a move on,' she said, shivering.

We hurried back along Ride Street towards Blackdog Street. A middle-aged woman, carrying a pair of heavy string bags, was a few steps in front when a hooded figure darted from the shadows and shoved her. She fell with a cry, spilling groceries over the pavement. The figure ran away.

'He's got my handbag!'

I picked up a tin as it rolled into the gutter and hurled it, watching as it arced through the evening sky, completely missing the target, but smashing the back windscreen of a parked car. The mugger, running round a bend, went out of sight.

I started after him, as a furious woman got out of the car. She was pretty. She was also familiar.

'What,' she said, holding up the tin, 'did you do that for?'

'Sorry,' I said, biting my bottom lip, 'it was an accident.'

She stared at me and her frown deepened. 'I know you, don't I?'

'Yes, Mrs Duckworth. It's Andy. I found your husband.'

'What are you doing here?'

'I live here. I've just been showing her round the museum.' I pointed at Kathy who was helping the victim retrieve her shopping. 'We saw you on the video. I thought it was very interesting.'

'Great. I'm flattered, but why were you throwing tins of

beans?'

'I was trying to stop a mugger. He's got that poor lady's handbag.'

'Then shouldn't you go after him?'

'Umm ... yes ... I suppose. Sorry about your car. Bye.'

I ran, looking along Goat Street and up Hedbury Road, but it seemed he'd got away. On the point of giving up, I heard an empty drinks can being kicked. It came from the car park on Hedbury Road. A hooded head popped up before ducking back behind the wall.

Stupidly, I ran across the road and vaulted the low wall into the car park.

'Now I've got you,' I said in triumph, intending to prove that I really was packed full of the right stuff. I was going to show Kathy what I was made of and, hopefully and more importantly, I was going to impress Mrs Duckworth: Daphne.

The mugger, the handbag still tucked under his arm, stood up, eyes glinting from the depths of his hood. He was wearing baggy blue jeans and a pair of boots that looked as if they could kick a man in half, but what I most noticed was that he was taller than me.

'Give me the bag, at once,' I said holding out my hand. Despite my bravado, my voice quavered.

'Piss off!' he yelled, his voice harsh.

'Not until you let me have it,' I said, fighting against leg-wobbling fear.

The mugger, a man of few words, pulled out a knife. 'I'll really let you have it unless you back off.'

'Put that down,' I said, filled with a sudden bravery and a sense of elation. 'Just give me the bag, and no one gets hurt.'

'You having a laugh, mate? Get out of here now, or I'll stick you.'

I really did laugh. 'Honestly, it will be so much better for you if you just drop the knife and give me the bag.'

Although I couldn't see his face, his body posture suggested hesitation, or confusion. Taking a hesitant step forward, he waved the knife.

'Sorry,' I said, shaking my head, 'but I did warn you.'

Hobbes, silent as a hunting tiger, leapt from the shadows and rammed a wheelie bin over the mugger's head, jamming it down, pinning his arms to his sides. The knife dropped with a clatter, the handbag dropped with a thud, and the mugger fell to his knees amid an outpouring of swearing and maggots. Dregs, sniffing him, bristled and growled.

'Evening, all,' said Hobbes, leaning on the bin. 'Did you and Kathy have a good afternoon?'

'Umm ... yes ... it wasn't bad,' I said, patting Dregs. 'We went to the museum.'

'I'm pleased to hear it. Now, what did you do to annoy this fellow?'

'Nothing ... he mugged a lady and stole her handbag, so I went after him.'

'That's very public spirited of you, but it might have been dangerous.'

I nodded, still a little weak at the knees. 'I wasn't half glad to see you coming. I thought you'd be hunting the bank robbers.'

'All in good time,' said Hobbes. 'I had to take some rocks for analysis. By the way, where is Kathy?'

'She's just round the corner helping the poor lady that got mugged. Umm ... what rocks?'

'Now is not the time. We'd better check on the ladies. Shift yourself – and quickly.'

'Yeah, but what about him?' I pointed at the bin.

'I'd better bring him along as evidence. Would you mind picking up the handbag? And the knife. It's dangerous to leave them in car parks.'

Grabbing the bin in both arms, turning it over, he carried it towards Ride Lane, with the mugger's legs kicking wildly out the top, the volume of his cursing increasing, and Dregs growling. We found Kathy with her arm around the victim, who, although crying, was unhurt. The lady cheered up immediately as I handed back the bag,

'Thank you,' she said, looking at Hobbes. 'I thought I'd lost it and it would have been awful, because it's got my keys and my credit card and all sorts of stuff.'

'Just doing my job, Mrs Brown,' said Hobbes.

Since I thought I'd done rather well in the circumstances, I was a little miffed to get no credit. Admittedly, I would have been in trouble had Hobbes not showed up in the nick of time, but I had found the mugger and stopped him getting away. Even so, I realised my heroics had been somewhat dimmed by what I'd done to Daphne's car. I looked around to apologise again, but she'd gone. I sighed, though I'd probably not done my chances with her any harm at all. I must merely have hardened her dislike for me.

The lady, thanking Hobbes again, insisting she was fine, picked up her bags and left.

'Good job, Daddy,' said Kathy, smiling proudly. 'Now what are you going to do with this hoodlum?'

'I suppose,' said Hobbes, 'that I should get him cleaned up. It's not very pleasant inside that bin, as his rather incontinent language would suggest.' He glanced at the church clock. 'We'd better get a move on. I wouldn't want us to be late for tea.'

14

When we reached the steps outside the house, Hobbes upended the bin and the mugger, still swearing, slithered onto the pavement, along with a disgusting, putrid stench. Pushing back his hood, dislodging a selection of wriggling maggots and bits of rotten vegetables, he revealed himself as a slim young man with short, blond hair and a narrow face, bursting with acne. He cowered away from Dregs, who was still bristling and growling, before looking up and seeing Hobbes for the first time.

'Please, don't hurt me,' he said, suddenly more like a frightened schoolboy than a hardened criminal: a very dirty, smelly schoolboy, to be sure.

'I have no intention of hurting you,' said Hobbes, 'but accidents can happen. I try to avoid them.'

I was sure, at least I thought I was sure, that he meant it as a mere statement of fact, but I could understand how the mugger might take it the wrong way, especially with Dregs's aggressive posture suggesting a likely cause of an accident.

'Take the dog inside, please, Andy,' said Hobbes.

Dragging him up to the front door, I fumbled for my key. I was still proud Hobbes had trusted me with it, for my parents had never done the same and, until I'd left to find my own way in the world, I'd had to be back home by ten-thirty, which was their bedtime. It had done little for my social life, or my reputation. Opening the door, I shoved Dregs inside, much to his annoyance.

When I turned round the mugger, back on his feet, had adopted a sort of fighting stance. Though Hobbes was smiling, he'd positioned himself where he could protect Kathy from any sudden lunge.

'I warn you,' said the mugger, 'I'm a fifth Dan in Karate and my feet are lethal.'

'Thank you for the warning,' said Hobbes. 'Have you tried washing them with soap and water and applying talc?'

'Are you taking the piss? I don't like it when people take the piss.'

'Nor do I,' said Hobbes, 'and I ask you to mind your language when a lady is present. Now, stop fooling around, or you'll hurt yourself.'

'I'll hurt you.'

'That is not going to happen. Your stance is all wrong and you don't know how to form a fist.'

'I'll show you,' said the mugger, shuffling forward, throwing a few air punches.

'No,' said Hobbes, shaking his head, 'you're doing it all wrong. If you close your hand like this,' he formed a fist that would have cowed a mad bull, 'then you're far less likely to injure yourself.'

The mugger charged in a blur of swinging arms and foul language.

'Stop it,' said Hobbes, ducking and swaying, avoiding or deflecting all the punches.

The mugger's momentum carried him forward until, falling over Hobbes's outstretched leg, he landed full on his face and lay groaning, bleeding from the mouth and the nose.

'I told you to be careful,' said Hobbes, 'and now you really have gone and hurt yourself. That's enough nonsense. I'm going to get you cleaned up and then we're going to have a little chat.'

'Ain't you gonna cuff the creep, take him down the station and book him?' asked Kathy, who'd been watching the encounter with shining eyes.

'I don't think that will be necessary,' said Hobbes. 'He's going to behave now. Aren't you?'

The mugger grunted, and Hobbes, taking this as assent, hauled him back to his feet and handed him a handkerchief.

'Hold this to your nose,' he said and turned to me. 'Would

you mind taking the bin back? I borrowed it from the side of the Firefly.'

For a moment, I was inclined to sulk, thinking that he was exploiting my good nature on such a night. I then reflected that Kathy might consider I'd been exploiting his good nature ever since I'd taken up residence, and, since I was still determined to prove I was an asset, I agreed.

As I pushed the bin back towards the Firefly restaurant, I hoped Mr Yau, the owner, wouldn't spot me. The trouble was that the old man, watching me using chopsticks for the first time, had started to laugh, becoming so helpless that he'd fallen from his stool. Even the pain of a broken wrist had not been sufficient to curb his amusement and, although the incident had occurred five years ago, the mere sight of me still reduced him to giggles; although the Firefly had a great reputation, I went out of my way to avoid it if I could. Just a glimpse of Mr Yau's bald head and wispy beard would set me galloping to safety. I was mighty pleased to complete my mission without being spotted.

I hurried back towards Blackdog Street, my head awash with thoughts and, although Sunday tea drifted there, as did speculation about the mugger's fate, the image of Daphne Duckworth floated highest. It had been a bizarre twist of fate to bring her to Sorenchester and to park just where I would throw a tin of beans through her back windscreen. I really had a way of impressing a woman and I'd sometimes wondered whether I'd been cursed always to be unlucky in love. Had I only been able to throw accurately, I might have been basking in her admiration. It was a fine line between being a hero and someone fit only to return a wheelie bin, and I was always on the wrong side.

When I got home, Kathy was on the sofa, sipping from a mug of steaming coffee. She nodded.

'Where's the mugger?' I asked, hanging up my coat, pleased

to see a pot of tea awaiting my pleasure.

'In the bathroom.'

'Fair enough. He needed a good wash.' I poured myself a drink and sat on the hard chair.

'Does Daddy often bring home freaks off the streets?'

'No, not often.'

'Is that where he found you?'

'No, I came here to interview him when I was a reporter. Umm … do you think I'm a freak?'

'I dunno. Maybe. He sure seems to attract them. There's you and the old woman and that dratted dog.'

'I don't think that's fair,' I said, for although I had noticed how oddballs and weirdoes were drawn to Hobbes, I'd never considered myself as one of them. 'Anyway, you're here, too.'

She nodded and thought for a moment. 'Yeah, I guess you're right.'

As she spoke she looked lost and vulnerable, almost like a little girl, despite her size, and I felt sorry for her; a lonely woman in a strange land, among strange people, trying to build a relationship with a father she'd never met, a father who was as strange as could be.

A shriek from upstairs nearly stopped my heart.

'What was that?' asked Kathy, leaping from the sofa with a grace and fluidity quite at odds with her figure.

'A shriek.'

'But whose? Why?'

Her coffee had spilled down her white blouse and she was pale and big-eyed with fear.

'I'll … umm … go and find out. By the way, where is Hobbes?'

'He went out for some sodas.'

'So, Mrs Goodfellow's alone with that thug?'

'Yes,' said Kathy, clapping a hand to her mouth.

'Oh, the poor guy,' I said, running upstairs.

He was in the bath. Mrs Goodfellow, holding the scruff of his neck, was scrubbing vigorously with a sponge and, although he was trying to protect his dignity, it was hopeless. He cast a despairing look in my direction as the sponge went to work below the waterline. Although I shrugged and shook my head, grimacing, trying to show that I, too, had suffered, his humiliation was temporary and fully deserved, and cleanliness was better than stinking like the Firefly's bin.

I returned to the sitting room to reassure Kathy. 'It's OK, he's fine, but Mrs Goodfellow is sponging him down.'

'Eeuw!'

A few minutes later, the front door swung open and Hobbes returned, a couple of giant plastic cola bottles in his left hand. He took them to the kitchen and returned with Dregs, who was looking a little nervous. Bath time, anybody's bath time, always took him like that, for he was another of the old girl's victims, and had soon learned that resistance was useless. I could understand his concerns, for big black dogs should not smell of lavender and rose water.

However, lavender and rose water was a definite improvement for the mugger, who lurched into the sitting room, wrapped in the flamboyant silk dressing gown that had once belonged to Mr Goodfellow.

'This is Rupert,' said Mrs Goodfellow, following him. 'He would like to say something. Come on Rupert.' Taking his arm, she pulled him into the centre of the room.

There was a stunned, lost expression in his eyes, as if he believed he'd fallen into a surreal nightmare from which he could not wake. He shuffled his feet and stared at the carpet. 'I'm sorry I was bad,' he said, his voice, low and hesitant, sounding well-educated.

'Well done,' said Mrs Goodfellow. 'Now, take a seat next to Kathy and I'll get tea ready. Are you hungry?'

'Yes. Very.'

'Good lad.'

She left us, followed by Dregs, who was not impressed by

Rupert's scent and who was hoping for scraps before supper, although the old girl was always very strict with his mealtimes. Still, he remained an optimistic dog.

When Rupert apologetically shuffled next to Kathy, her expression could not have been more disgusted had Dregs left a deposit there. Rupert sat hunched up, with downcast eyes and trembling hands, with Hobbes looming over him like a potential avalanche.

'Well, Rupert,' he said, quite gently for him, 'I want you to tell me why you assaulted the poor lady and stole her handbag and why you threatened Andy with a knife?'

'I'm ever so sorry,' said Rupert, 'I hope I didn't hurt her, and I would never have used the knife.'

'You were lucky,' said Hobbes, 'that she was shaken up and upset, but uninjured. If she had been, you might have made me angry and you wouldn't like me when I'm angry.'

'He's right,' I said. 'You wouldn't.'

'Thank you, Andy,' said Hobbes, keeping his gaze on the squirming Rupert. 'Why did you do it?'

'I was desperate. My wallet got stolen and I haven't eaten all day. I just wanted to go home.'

'I'm sorry to hear that,' said Hobbes. 'Did you report the stolen wallet to the police?'

'No.'

'I see. Where do you live?'

'A long way from here, in the Blacker Mountains. The nearest town is Blackcastle, but you've probably never heard of it.'

'We ...' I said and stopped, aware of Hobbes's frown.

'We have heard of the place,' he said. 'What brings you to Sorenchester?'

'I had a job to do ... for my father.'

'I see. Aren't you a bit young to be working?'

Rupert blushed. 'I'm eighteen.'

'Old enough, then, but why didn't you ask him for help if

you'd lost your money?'

'I couldn't ... because ... I had no money at all.'

'But,' said Hobbes, 'the lass gave me this.' He held out a very swish-looking smartphone. 'It was in your pocket and it works and it's charged.'

Rupert's voice dropped to a mumble. 'I forgot.'

Hobbes laughed. 'You forgot? I'm afraid I don't believe you.' His voice rose just a little in volume, but several notches in threatening, as he examined the device. 'It appears that you made several calls today. Didn't you?'

'Yeah,' he admitted, looking absolutely miserable.

'So, you didn't forget, did you?'

'No,' said Rupert, staring at the carpet as if he hoped a big hole would open up and swallow him. He sighed.

'Good,' said Hobbes, his bright smile displaying a worrying jawful of teeth, 'now, tell me the truth.'

'I'd rather not.'

'Why doncha kick the punk's bony ass?' said Kathy. 'Then he'll spill the beans.'

'I'm sure there'll be no need for that,' said Hobbes smiling. 'Rupert will cooperate, sooner or later.'

'It's a goddam funny way of policing. Back home, the cops would have busted his ass and thrown him in the slammer.'

'Language, Kathy,' said Hobbes.

'You're a cop?' asked Rupert, looking up, seeing Hobbes's nod and cringing.

'Yes, didn't I say?'

'Am I under arrest?'

'Not yet and maybe not at all, if you answer my questions truthfully and fully.'

'But I can't.'

'Of course you can. What have you got to hide?'

'I'm saying nothing.'

Hobbes shrugged. 'Can you at least tell me how you lost your wallet?'

Rupert nodded. 'I went into a pub for a pint and a bite to eat. After I'd paid, I put my wallet back in my pocket. It wasn't there when I left, so someone must have nicked it.'

'Which pub were you in?'

'One called the Feathers. The landlord's a real big ba ... I mean a real big bloke, like you, but I spoke to the little guy behind the bar.'

'Go on,' said Hobbes.

'I went straight back when I noticed it had gone,' said Rupert, 'and had a look around, but couldn't see it. The little guy kept grinning at me, so I figured he'd got it, but he denied it.'

'I see,' said Hobbes, 'and what did you do?'

'I asked him to turn out his pockets. I did get a bit angry.'

'Then what happened?'

'The big ba ... man charged across the room, picked me up by my neck and trousers and threw me into the street.'

'You got off lightly, my lad,' said Hobbes.

I nodded. Featherlight's temperament might be compared to that of a wild bull and the slightest incident could set him off, which would frequently lead to blood being spilled, though it was a comforting part of his character that he didn't stay angry for long. It was usually, however, long enough for his victim to need a visit to casualty. How he wasn't in prison was a mystery, though he did receive some protection by being a tourist attraction. Some people just seemed to find him fascinating, and a few thought it might be amusing to provoke him, usually not realising their folly until they came round. Still, it's an ill wind that blows no good and Mrs Goodfellow's tooth collection had acquired many of its finest specimens from the Feathers, as well as a few that made me despair for British dentistry.

'Now, tell me,' said Hobbes, 'what did you do last night?'

'I went into the church, hoping for shelter, but a fierce woman with blue hair made me leave when she started locking up. After that, I tried sleeping under a bush in the park, but it was far too cold. That wind!' He shuddered. 'In the end, I just wandered the streets until morning.'

'That can't have been much fun,' said Hobbes.

'It was horrible.'

Rupert looked so miserable that I would have felt sorry for him, had he not pulled a knife on me an hour ago. Thinking about what might have happened, I began shaking and, despite a noble struggle to keep myself together I could easily have gone to pieces, had Mrs Goodfellow not announced that tea was ready.

Hobbes, putting his great paw on Rupert's shoulder, pulled him up and propelled him to the kitchen. Kathy followed, looking utterly perplexed and shaking her head. Making an effort, I shrugged and smiled, trying to indicate that I was completely cool with the situation and that, if she intended staying, she would have to get used to a lot. From experience, this wasn't always easy and there had been occasions early on when I'd come close to running into Blackdog Street, screaming. Since then, I'd learned to cope: mostly. It was worth hanging in there because I'd seen so many things I wouldn't have otherwise. It was true some of them gave me nightmares, but it was great to have a life and to be building up a store of memories.

Another thing that made life worth living was Mrs Goodfellow's Sunday tea. It was only sandwiches and cake, but such sandwiches and such cake! At first Kathy looked a little disappointed, but after Hobbes had embarrassed Rupert by saying grace, she took a bite from a sandwich. A smile spread across her face, for, although it was a simple cheese and chutney sandwich, the cheese was the tangy, nutty, sweet Sorenchester cheese and the bread, like the spicy, mouth-watering, chutney, was home-made and utterly delicious. Rupert kept quiet and stuffed himself. He'd probably told the truth about not having eaten all day.

Mrs Goodfellow opened a bottle of red wine and offered it round. Hobbes, smiling and friendly, kept Rupert's glass topped up. I wondered what he was up to because, while it wasn't unusual for him to treat criminals in an unorthodox manner, he was usually rough, if not brutal, with anyone who'd attacked a woman. Yet, since tipping him out of the bin, he'd shown kindness and understanding towards Rupert. If it was an attempt to impress Kathy it was failing for, whenever her mouth wasn't full, she would glower at Rupert, as if planning a lynching. All I could do was wait and see how things turned out.

After the meal, Hobbes took us back to the sitting room, while Mrs Goodfellow washed up and Dregs hung around, waiting for his supper.

'Did you enjoy your tea?' Hobbes asked, guiding Rupert to the sofa and making sure he didn't spill his wine.

'Yes,' he said, sprawling, making himself comfortable, grinning and emitting a hiccup, 'I was starving, but that was great. I feel fine now.'

'Good,' said Hobbes, topping up his glass. 'It's not at all pleasant to be penniless, without food and shelter, especially now the nights are getting so cool. That's why I'm so surprised you didn't ask for help.'

'I couldn't. My father ...'

'Who is your father?'

Rupert sat up straight. 'Sir Gerald Payne. He's a very important man.'

'That must be *the* Sir Gerald Payne,' said Hobbes. 'I've heard he owns a little land around Blackcastle.'

'A lot of land, actually. Well over a thousand acres and we ... he owns all sorts of property around there.'

'That does sound a lot,' said Hobbes, 'but I don't suppose it gives him a huge income. I mean, the Blacker Mountains are barren and can hardly bring in much cash at the best of times, and they say times are hard there. I don't suppose the rents are

169

very high.'

Rupert grinned. 'That's all true. It is hardly worth our while to rent out the properties.'

'I don't know how he makes ends meet,' said Hobbes, shaking his head sympathetically. 'Unless, of course, he has other income streams? I'll bet he's a shrewd investor.'

'Of course,' said Rupert, his voice dropping to a confidential whisper. 'And the best thing is that we've just reopened the family gold mine.'

'Gosh,' said Hobbes, his eyes wide. 'A gold mine? It's lucky to have one of those to fall back on, just as the price of gold is rising.'

'Luck doesn't come into it,' said Rupert, his smile broad and smug, his words slurred. 'My ancestor Sir Greville Payne discovered the gold and scrimped and saved for years until he could buy the land and open the mine. That's where the family fortune came from.'

'Good for Sir Greville.'

Kathy and I exchanged glances. Hobbes seemed excessively friendly with this young crook.

'But,' he continued, 'if your family has a fortune and a gold mine, and your mobile was working, I don't understand why you couldn't phone for help.'

'He said he'd kill me if I fu ... messed up again.'

'He can hardly blame you for being robbed, can he? More wine?' He refilled Rupert's glass.

'Thanks. You don't know him. My father can be a right bastard.'

'But he wouldn't really kill you, would he?'

'He bloody would ... Well, not literally kill me, but he gets really angry. I say, this is awfully strong wine.'

Hobbes nodded. 'I expect that, when you've done the job, he'll be pleased with you?'

'The thing is,' said Rupert, 'that I haven't done it. I'm going to be in deep sh ... trouble.'

'Maybe not,' said Hobbes. 'Perhaps I can help. After all police officers are here to help the public.'

'What?' said Kathy, looking furious.

Hobbes raised his hand.

'Could you?' asked Rupert, his words increasingly slurred. 'That's very decent of you.'

Hobbes smiled. 'I'm just doing my job. What do you have to do?'

Rupert hiccupped, scratched his head and shifted awkwardly. 'I've got to find where someone lives.'

'Can't you look in the phone book?'

'No, she's just moved here and is ex-directory. My father says she's trouble.'

'Who, exactly, are you looking for?'

'I don't think I should tell anyone.'

'Quite right, you shouldn't tell anyone, but you can tell me.'

'Can I?'

Hobbes nodded.

'OK. I gotta find Daffy Duck.'

'Are you sure?' asked Hobbes, raising an eyebrow.

'No, that's not right. It was something like it.'

'Donald Duck?' I suggested.

'Quiet, Andy' said Hobbes. 'Rupert will get there in a moment.'

'I know. I've got to find Daphne Duckworth.'

'Daphne?' I said, suddenly hot and angry. 'What do you want with her?'

'Shh,' said Hobbes quietly.

I shushed, despite feeling a strange desire to protect her, although I wasn't quite sure from what.

'What,' asked Hobbes, 'are you going to do to the lady?'

'Nothing. I've only got to find out where she lives and what she's doing.'

'Why?'

'I dunno. My father says she's trouble like her old man was, but I don't know what he wants with her. Maybe he just wants to keep an eye on her, but he can be a right bastard sometimes.'

'So,' asked Hobbes, his smile still friendly, though his voice was sharp, 'do you think she might be in danger?'

Rupert shrugged. 'Dunno. He doesn't employ Denny to be nice to people. He's not nice to me.'

'So, you suspect your father might get this Denny to do something unpleasant to Mrs Duckworth.'

'Maybe. I say, my head's spinnin' and I'm feelin' all sleepy.'

His eyes closed and his breathing became deep and regular, interspersed by the occasional snort.

'Well, that was an effort,' said Hobbes.

'What just happened?' asked Kathy, looking at the sleeping Rupert with deep loathing and then at Hobbes with confused admiration.

'I got him to talk. The gentle touch often works with someone who's not too bright and is scared even sillier than he is naturally.'

'It cost you a meal and a bottle of wine,' said Kathy. 'Why didn't you just beat the crap out of him?'

'I am not in the habit of beating people,' said Hobbes. 'Besides, his fear of his father would have stopped him talking until he'd been hurt badly. His brain works too slowly to make sensible decisions in a short time.'

'Mom told me that you once totally demolished a biker gang. She said there were twelve of them and you beat them all unconscious. Is that true?'

'No,' said Hobbes, shaking his head. 'There were fifteen of them.'

'Even better,' said Kathy, with a sudden, proud grin. 'What happened?'

'It was a long time ago. It doesn't matter.'

'I'd still like to know.'

Hobbes sighed. 'The boys were out of their minds on

something and completely out of control. Some of them were armed and all of them were dangerous. When I chanced on the scene, they'd already injured several people. All I did was stop their misbehaviour with the minimum amount of force necessary. It so happened on that particular occasion that the minimum amount was considerable.'

'How did you do it?'

'As quickly and efficiently as I could.'

'Mom said you hit them with a chair.'

'Two chairs, a table and a frozen chicken, if I remember rightly, but it was long ago and best forgotten. What is important now is ensuring the safety of Mrs Daphne Duckworth. I am somewhat concerned.'

I was still feeling protective and worried. 'What d'you think they'll do to her?'

'Nothing,' said Hobbes, 'if I have anything to do with it.'

'And what you gonna do with this creep?' asked Kathy pointing a plump, manicured finger at Rupert.

'That's a good point,' I said. 'He can't sleep here.'

'He appears to be doing just that,' said Hobbes.

'But, where will you sleep? You haven't had time to tidy the attic yet.'

'Anyway,' said Kathy, sounding frightened, 'when he wakes up, won't he steal stuff or murder us all in our beds?'

'There's no fear of that,' said Hobbes. 'I'll get Dregs to keep an eye on him.'

'You're gonna trust a hoodlum to that dumb dog?'

Hobbes nodded. 'He knows his stuff. Right, anyone fancy helping me clean out the attic?' He sprang to his feet.

'Umm … OK, then.' I said.

'I'll give you a hand,' said Kathy.

Hobbes grinned. 'Thank you. Come along then. And quickly.'

15

From my first visit, the attic, lit only by a single, low-powered light bulb, had impressed me with a weird sensation of being in a treasure house, a museum, a junk room and Aladdin's cave all thrown into one. There was a frisson whenever I went up there, for I always imagined I'd discover something exciting. Kathy was still puffing upstairs, as I followed Hobbes up the ladder and past Cuddles the bear, the stuffed guardian of the relics of Hobbes's past. Although he had occasionally talked about Cuddles, claiming my room had once been his, I'd never got him to explain why there was a stuffed elephant's trunk up there, nor why he kept the heaps of old clothes and the various bits of penny-farthings that lined the walls. To my eyes, though most of it was probably junk, there were treasures as well, not least the paintings he'd done, which I found strangely beautiful, if deeply disturbing. In addition, this was where I'd found the fading photographs of Hobbes and Froggy, Kathy's mother. I'd never yet penetrated the darker reaches, where mysterious shapes lay concealed beneath old blankets and rags.

'The lass was right,' he said, 'it is a mess. Where shall we start?'

'Umm ... I don't really know. It depends on what you want to throw out and what you want to keep.'

He scratched his head, sounding like someone sawing wood. 'I suppose if we piled things higher, there'd be enough space for a bed.'

'I suppose so.'

'What the hell is that?' said Kathy, at the top of the ladder, staring wide-eyed into the bear's maw, wrinkling her nose.

'That,' said Hobbes, 'is Cuddles. He won't hurt you, he's stuffed.'

'You gotta get rid of it! All that fluff is coming out of it and it stinks of old socks and who knows what.'

He nodded, a little shamefaced.

She stepped up, looking around with amazement. 'You're not really gonna sleep up here?'

'I'll be fine.'

'But it's cold and it doesn't look like it's been cleaned in a century.'

'I replaced the floor boards not long ago,' he said.

'Jeez! What a mess. Doesn't your housekeeper ever tidy up?'

'This is my space. She leaves it alone, unless I ask.'

'This whole house is your space.'

'Yes, but I like up here as it is. All I need to do is make sufficient floor space for a bed.'

'How you going to get a bed up here?'

'There's one under this.' Kicking aside a spiked German helmet, he pulled back a blanket with a magician's flourish.

The air was suddenly full of mice, spinning and squeaking, and Kathy, with a squeal, covering her head with her hands, turned and ran in a blind panic, straight towards the hatch. Before the last mouse had even landed, Hobbes, diving full length, caught her around the waist with one long arm, but her momentum dragged them both through. There was a scream, a crash, and a groan as, horrified, I rushed to see what had happened, fearing he must have crushed her like an elephant falling on a kitten, albeit a rather overgrown kitten, but he was lying on his back with Kathy cradled to his chest, amid the junk his trailing foot had hooked out.

'Are you alright?' I asked, scrambling down.

Kathy looked up and nodded, her face a mix of relief, shock and amazement.

'Oof!' said Hobbes, opening his eyes.

As I helped her back to her feet, not an easy task, Hobbes sat up with a groan, rubbing his side. Dregs bounded up the stairs followed by Mrs Goodfellow, who, keeping pace, was panting like the dog.

'What happened?' she asked. 'Is anyone hurt?'

'I fell, but Daddy caught me,' said Kathy in a weak voice. She looked down. 'I'm OK, I think. Are you hurt?'

Hobbes pushed himself to his feet, still rubbing his side. 'I reckon I've bust a rib.' Holding onto the balustrade, he grinned. 'Still, mustn't grumble, it could have been worse.'

'We'd better get you to the emergency room,' said Kathy.

'Oh no,' he said, 'I'll be fine after a good night's sleep.'

'But ...' said Kathy and stopped, staring at a photograph that had come down with the mess. Bending, she picked it up and gasped. 'It's ... Mom and you, but ... you look just the same!'

'Hardly,' said Hobbes, taking a glance. 'Look at those trousers! And I wouldn't wear my hair that long these days.'

'I don't mean the clothes, I mean you. You don't really look any different now and this must have been taken in the sixties. I don't get it. How come you haven't grown older?'

'I have grown older, just like everyone.'

'You don't look any older,' she said, staring.

'Put it down to healthy living,' I said.

'And good food,' added Mrs Goodfellow.

'And good genes,' I continued.

'No,' said Kathy, screwing up her face. 'Mom looks like an old lady and you don't.'

'That's because he's not a lady,' I said, helpfully.

She glared.

'I suppose I've just been lucky,' said Hobbes. 'Who's going to help me get a bed ready?'

She shook her head. 'No, I need to know, because there's an even older photograph in the museum and one of the guys in it looks just like you. Andy sort of convinced me it was just a coincidence, but it really was you, wasn't it?'

He shrugged, looking nervous.

'And,' said Kathy, her voice rising in pitch and volume, 'you fall through the goddam hatch and catch me and then get straight back up? You should be dead. What are you?'

'I,' said Hobbes, 'am a police officer.'

'Mom warned me you were a weird kinda guy, but she put that down to you being English. That's not the reason is it? You're not normal. You're not right. And what does that make *me*?'

Detecting the onset of hysteria, I considered slapping her. The trouble was, I wasn't sure it would work. Furthermore, I feared she'd slap me back with interest, and, if she'd inherited only half of Hobbes's power, she'd knock me into the middle of next week. Before I'd made up my mind she stopped talking, turned pale, and swayed. Hobbes, leaping towards her, held her as she collapsed, and grimaced as he took her dead weight.

'Is she alright?' I asked.

'I think she's fainted,' said Hobbes.

He carried Kathy's limp body into his room and laid her gently on the bed.

'Should we get a doctor?' I asked, worried, for it had been a spectacular collapse, and far more convincing than the one at the museum.

'I don't think that will be necessary,' said Mrs Goodfellow, who claimed to have once been a nurse, checking her pulse and looking into her eyes. 'He's right. It is just a faint. It'll be from emotional stress. I'll keep an eye on her, but she'll be alright in a few minutes.' Taking the pillows, she placed them under Kathy's legs.

Hobbes sent me for a moist flannel and applied it to her face.

After a minute, she opened her eyes and gulped. 'What happened?'

'You fainted,' said Hobbes. 'How are you feeling?'

'Bad.'

Mrs Goodfellow checked her pulse again. 'Do you faint often?'

She shook her head and groaned. 'I want to sleep now. Please leave me alone.'

We walked away. Then Mrs Goodfellow turned around, went back in and prised Dregs from under the bed. Hobbes winced as he bent to pick up some of the junk that had fallen through the hatch.

Mrs Goodfellow noticed and gave him her sternest frown. 'Don't even think of trying to clear out that attic now. You'd better rest.'

'But where?' I asked.

'You'd best take Andy's room. Lie down and I'll bring up some of my cordial.'

'Thanks, lass, but where's he going to sleep?'

She thought for a moment. 'I'll call Sydney.'

So it was that an hour or so later, clutching a small overnight bag, I found myself back at the old vampire's house, this time having arrived conventionally.

'Come in,' said Sid, beaming a sharp-toothed smile. 'How the Dickens are you?'

'I'm fine, but Hobbes thinks he's bust a rib.'

As the front door closed behind me, it struck me that I was about to spend the night under a vampire's roof. I felt very brave.

'A bust rib?' said Sid. 'I expect that'll slow him down for a day or two. Come on into the kitchen. Have you eaten? I've got some soup in the fridge if you're hungry.'

'No, thank you.'

'A drink? I usually have a mug of hot milk before I turn in.'

'Can I just have water?'

'I gather,' he said, pouring me a glass, 'that Wilber's long-lost daughter has turned up.'

'Yes,' I said and explained the situation with Kathy while he heated up his milk.

'Who'd have thought it?' he said, with a strange smile. 'I hope, though, that with the excitement of a new daughter, plus an injured rib, he won't forget about solving the robbery. I've had Colonel Squire threatening to sue me unless I retrieve his gold.'

'He can't do that can he?'

'I don't know, young man. We've never before had a successful robbery at the bank. With Wilber on the case, I'm hoping the situation will be resolved soon, before too much harm is done.'

'I hope so,' I said, 'but he may also be distracted by Rupert.' I filled in the details, glossing over the tin of beans incident.

Sid didn't seem surprised.

'Hobbes,' I said, 'is going to help him to do a job for his father, but I don't really understand what he's up to.'

The old vampire looked rather down in the mouth and I wasn't sure how to cheer him up, for I couldn't help wondering whether Kathy's arrival had unhinged Hobbes. She certainly had me worried and I was sure Mrs Goodfellow wasn't happy. Only Dregs, after a suspicious start, seemed pleased to have her in the house. Perhaps the beef wellington had something to do with it.

'The odd thing is,' I continued, 'that I encountered Rupert's father, Sir Gerald, when we were camping. Although it was only for a couple of minutes, I could understand why the lad might be scared of him. He was really arrogant and rude.'

Sid's eyebrows rose. 'I was introduced to Sir Gerald a few months ago at Colonel Squire's Summer Ball. He was a real Payne in the ... well, you get my drift.'

'That's the one,' I said. 'It's a small world.'

Sid nodded. 'Although we only spoke for a few minutes, he tried to persuade me to invest in his gold mine. I wasn't interested. It seemed an unlikely proposition and one the bank should have no part of.'

'Rupert mentioned that his father had just reopened it. It must be nice to have something like that and I suppose it explains why the Payne family evicted all their tenants from the land and why Sir Gerald didn't want us around.'

'He'd certainly want to protect his assets. The price of gold has risen quite substantially this year and looks like going higher, which I suppose is why he feels it worthwhile. I guess he found someone to invest.'

I finished my glass of water and yawned. 'I'm sorry, but all of a sudden, I'm feeling terribly sleepy.'

'You can use Bram's room, young fellow,' said Sid. 'It's all made up.'

Taking my bag, he escorted me upstairs and led me into a bedroom. 'Here you go. You know where the batroom is. Just watch out for the cat. I'll leave you to it. Sleep well.' With a toothy smile, he left.

The bedroom was small, with old football posters on the wall; the bed was by the window. I had just enough energy for a trip to the batroom and to get into my pyjamas before losing control of my mouth, which went into a spasm of deep yawning. I crawled into bed, unfazed by the black satin sheets. They smelt clean and fresh and, having turned out the lamp on the bedside table, I fell asleep as soon as the blankets settled.

So far as I know, I slept through the night and awoke with a start to find the sun streaming into the room. I grasped for memories of dreams, finding them as fragile as the mist that had filled them, but all I could recall were vague, fractured images: Sid clinging to the wall outside, snatching at moths; Sid crawling across the ceiling in pursuit of spiders; Sid's blood red eyes. Although I knew they were merely dreams, they were strangely disturbing. As I tried to bring back more images, the church clock struck nine times.

It seemed I had slept both well and long, and my stomach thought it high time to remind me of breakfast. I wasn't certain Sid would provide one and was wondering whether I'd have to return to Blackdog Street. Yet, before anything, the batroom beckoned. I washed and shaved, checking, despite my better judgement, that there were no puncture marks in my neck.

Satisfied, I dressed and went downstairs, finding Sid in the kitchen, reading the newspaper at the table. A mug of coffee steamed on the table in front of him.

'Good morning,' he said. 'Did you sleep well?'

'Yes.' I nodded. 'Thank you.'

'Excellent, young fellow. Now, would you care to break your fast here?'

'That's very kind.'

'Nonsense. We're old friends now. Blood brothers you might say.'

I wondered what he meant, but a more urgent matter was the question of what to eat. I decided on coffee, and toast and marmalade, finding, to my surprise, that the marmalade was every bit as good as Mrs Goodfellow's. It was less of a surprise to learn she'd actually made it. Sid read his paper as I ate my fill and I was brushing the crumbs from my lips when he spoke again.

'The gold price has gone up.'

'I guess Sir Gerald will be pleased,' I said.

Sid nodded. 'But Colonel Squire won't. The bank will make good what he lost in the robbery, if necessary, but only at the price of gold at the time. The colonel will no doubt be preparing another salvo of sarcasm about his theoretical losses even as we speak. Let's hope Wilber does his stuff quickly.'

'Let's hope so. Of course, he lost something in the robbery as well. I guess it was valuable if he kept it in the vaults.'

'You would think so,' said Sid. 'More coffee?'

'No thanks. It's perked me up considerably.'

'Good,' said Sid, 'because you were looking a little pale.'

'Was I? Well, I'm fine now.' I laughed, thinking it fitting that I should be pale after a night in a vampire's house. Though I felt absolutely safe, I couldn't deny a slight, nagging unease. 'Anyway, I should be getting out now and see what's happening.'

'Ask Wilber to keep me up to date with any developments.'

I nodded, thinking he would, assuming there were any to report. I hoped he wouldn't be wasting too much time with Rupert. In my opinion, he ought to have been protecting Daphne, rather than helping the unpleasant youth spy on her.

Taking my leave, I stepped out into the morning sun, pulling my jacket close against a chill wind, trying to ensure there were as few chinks in my armour as was possible. Denied entry, it expended its fury by whipping up dust and fallen leaves, though there were no trees nearby. I decided not to walk straight back to Blackdog Street, but to make a loop past the museum and, although I pretended I was acting on a whim, deep down, I was hoping to bump into Daphne. I had a vague idea that I could give her a fulsome apology for the can of beans and had a feeble hope that she'd laugh, forgive me and agree to meet me sometime.

I was utterly amazed when that was precisely what did happen. She was walking towards me and agreed to stop and talk. We didn't have long, since she didn't want to be late, explaining that she's just started working at the museum, but, importantly, she agreed to meet me at half-past twelve. Leaving her outside the museum, I walked the rest of the way home in a daze, wondering how to fill the next three hours until our rendezvous at the Black Dog Café.

'Oh, it's you,' said Kathy as I walked in, shutting the door behind me. 'What are you grinning at?'

'I'm just feeling cheerful,' I said. 'It's a beautiful day.'

'Huh! It's goddam freezing. This dump doesn't have central heating.'

'Put a jumper on.'

'A what?' She snapped shut the book she was holding.

'A sweater.'

'I'm wearing two sweaters.'

'Well, how about a brisk walk? That'll warm you up.'

'How about I kick your butt? That'll warm us both up.'

'Is something wrong?'

'Wha'd'ya mean?'

'Well,' I said, 'you're not in a very good mood.'

She hurled the book. It struck me on the ear and smashed a glass vase on the rebound. Although I believed this proved my hypothesis, I didn't hang around to make the point, for she was already reaching for a mug. Rubbing my ear, I fled towards the kitchen, where Mrs Goodfellow was kneeling on the table, scrubbing with a chunk of sandstone.

'What's up with her?' I asked.

'It's lack of sleep, dear. Young Rupert woke in the night and needed the bathroom. He tripped twice on his way upstairs, banged his head on the bathroom door and then fell into the bath. He lay there moaning until I went in and pulled him out. Then he tumbled downstairs. After that, he thought it would be a good time to start a sing-song and wouldn't be quiet.'

'So what happened?'

'Since I reckoned the old fellow needed his rest, I gave Rupert a tap on the chin to shut him up.'

'Did it work?'

She nodded. 'He slept as quiet as a corpse, but woke with a bit of a headache. I think that was from all the wine he'd put away.'

'Where is he now?'

'Out for a walk with the old fellow and Dregs. The old fellow's rib is still a bit sore.'

'I'm not surprised, after catching Kathy like that. There's a lot of her.'

'Shut up!' said Kathy who was at the kitchen door, glowering.

Mrs Goodfellow caught the mug an inch from my nose. 'Calm down,' she said, mildly.

'Make me,' said Kathy, walking into the kitchen, looking mean and dangerous.

'If you want, dear.'

Moving with the speed of a striking falcon, she patted Kathy's neck with an open hand. Kathy's eyes opened in surprise and closed in unconsciousness and Mrs Goodfellow, catching her as she dropped, laid her on the table.

'What have you done?' I asked.

'I've just relaxed her. She'll sit up soon.'

'But how?'

'I could tell you, dear, but then I'd have to kill you.'

I laughed, assuming she was joking. 'Umm … I'll not be in for lunch today. I'm … umm … meeting someone.'

'Oh yes? Anyone special?'

'I'm not sure. I hope so, I think.'

'Good for you, dear. You'll be wanting some pocket money, I expect.'

'Umm …' I said, cursing myself for having once again forgotten my penniless state. 'I hadn't thought of that.'

She rummaged in the pocket of her pinafore, pulled out her purse and handed me a wad of notes. 'Take this, dear.'

'I couldn't possibly,' I said.

I didn't feel good about myself, but I did take it.

Having gone upstairs and changed, I strolled into town, intending to mooch about and see what was going down on the street. I was, in fact, planning to waste time until lunch, but, after an hour or so, somewhat bored, and with money in my pocket, I thought I'd treat myself to a cappuccino and a doughnut at the Café Olé, a hot and happening new coffee shop on Vermin Street, or so the posters led me to believe. On entering, I stood in the doorway, disappointed by the cheap plastic tables and chairs, until the waiter, finishing his obviously-important phone call, showed me, the only customer, to a seat with its very own icy draught. After a brief glance at the menu he'd slapped onto the table in front of me, and a sharp intake of breath at the prices, I got up to leave.

Although I considered myself a man of the world, one well used to verbal abuse, I was shocked by the vileness and vitriol of the waiter's language as I walked out. Trying to ignore him, I marched nonchalantly away, even when he burst out after me, launching barrel-loads of filthy words in my general direction. I couldn't help but think the café's future would be a short one, although, in fairness, Featherlight had successfully used a similar strategy at the Feathers.

He kept on coming and, losing my nerve, I fled ignominiously up Vermin Street towards The Shambles, seeking sanctuary in the church, which was almost empty. I ducked down into a pew just as he burst in, still swearing, and lay flat until I heard him leave. I stretched out, catching my breath, letting my heart rate drop. Someone else walked in and sat down a few rows away. Since I was comfortable and it would have been embarrassing to pop up suddenly like a piece of toast, I stayed put, contemplating the ornate carvings on the ceiling, wondering why some craftsman long ago had carved a cat pursuing a mouse.

'Hello, boss,' a deep, rough, male voice whispered. 'No, I haven't found him. He was in a pub in town yesterday, but no one I've spoken to has seen him since. The little guy in the pub told me he'd found the kid's wallet down the back of a bench and had handed it in at the cop shop.'

My mild curiosity at eavesdropping a stranger's conversation changed to serious interest.

'Yes, boss, I have found where she lives and she's got a job at the museum … No, as I said, no one seems to have seen him and I've already been everywhere I can think of. Sure, boss, I'll keep looking. Should I do anything about her? … Yes, boss.'

I heard the pew creak as he stood up, the heaviness of his feet as he walked away, and sat up to see who it was. Unfortunately, a group of tourists had just come in and blocked most of my view and all I got was a glimpse of a large man with a bald head. He reminded me of someone, but I couldn't work out why. It was frustrating.

I sat for a few minutes, trying to puzzle out what I'd just heard, convinced the man was the one Rupert had mentioned, the one that had made him nervous. After rummaging through the mess in my head, the name Denny came to mind and, I thought, it was just as well he hadn't spotted me eavesdropping, for the vast acreage of his back had suggested massive strength.

What worried me most was the *her* he'd mentioned. Unless I was making a right hash of things, something I was admittedly perfectly capable of, *her* meant Daphne and I had a horrible feeling she was in danger. I'd learned from Hobbes that feelings, or instincts, came from the subconscious and should not be ignored since they were often more reliable than the intellect, especially when the intellect was mine. Sometimes I worried about my brain and wondered if it had a mind of its own.

I stood up, hurried out and looked around, but Denny had long gone. Making my way to the museum, I loitered outside, like a sentry guarding Buckingham Palace, hoping my mere presence might be some protection for her.

After a while, despite stamping my feet and rubbing my hands together, I was getting cold, as well as attracting puzzled glances from passers-by. Realising I was not the usual impecunious Andy, but Andy with a wad of cash in his pocket, I paid the entrance fee and went inside.

16

Having smoothed down my hair, I made a quick reconnaissance. There was no sign of Daphne and, since there were few visitors, none of whom looked a likely threat, I relaxed and took another look at the photo of Hobbes.

Without Kathy to entertain, I took the opportunity for an in-depth examination. I had no doubt it was him, the notion of seeing him in really old pictures no longer striking me as remarkable, but it was his companion who was the real puzzle. If I hadn't known better, I would have sworn it was Featherlight. Several minutes of staring later, I wondered if I knew anything at all, for he did look uncannily like Featherlight, admittedly, minus a couple of chins and belly rolls and sporting a Clark Gable moustache, yet it had to be him. No one else could have looked like that, and, furthermore, he might almost have passed for Hobbes's brother.

The implication took my breath away, as well as the strength from my legs and, had a bench not been within staggering range, I might have collapsed. As it was, I landed heavily and sat gasping and limp. An old lady with fluffy white hair and red glasses asked if I was alright and, although, I nodded, she brought me a glass of water anyway.

'Honestly,' I said, as she tried to make me drink, 'I'm alright. I just need a few moments to recover. I've had a bit of a shock, that's all.'

Huge eyed through thick lenses, she smiled. 'You look awful, but you'll feel better once you've had a sip of water.' She forced the glass towards my lips.

As I opened my mouth to protest, she tilted the glass and cold water gushed in, making me choke and jerk and knock the glass from her hand. The shock of cold water pouring down my neck made me gasp and then choke even more. My eyes streamed and I gurgled, struggling to breathe as I got to my feet. Even in my death throes, the idea that I would go down in history as the man who drowned in Sorenchester Museum struck me as amusing: a silly end for a silly man.

A vivid memory of a long-forgotten incident resurfaced. My little paddleboat had capsized because of the reckless stupidity of older children and I felt the chill of the water, the panic, the fear, as I struggled upwards, only to find myself trapped in blackness beneath the upturned hull. Knowing I couldn't hold my breath any longer, unable to escape, I was going to drown, until a hand grabbed me, dragging me from blackness, and back into the sunlight. I'd choked and spluttered, until my saviour, a large woman with a small, bedraggled dog, thumped my back and set me on the bank.

A thump on my back sent water gushing from my throat like a fountain and knocked me back into the present. I coughed and, as air wheezed into my lungs, I thought I might just live. Wiping my eyes, I turned to face my rescuer. It was Daphne.

'Are you alright?' she asked, her expression a confusion of concern and amusement.

I nodded, still unable to speak.

'I knew a sip of water would make him feel better,' said the old lady, smiling and walking towards the shop.

'She nearly drowned me,' I whispered.

When Daphne laughed, I couldn't help but laugh as well.

'It's nice,' she said, 'to meet a man who lives for excitement. Seriously, though, are you OK, now?'

'Yes ... I think so,' I said, pulling myself together.

'You do look rather wet.'

Since my shirt and trousers were dripping, I took the comment at face value. 'I am a bit,' I admitted. 'I'd better try and dry myself off.'

She smiled. 'You do that. Then come and see me in my office. My door's the one at the end of the corridor.' She pointed past the Roman antiquities.

'The one with "private" on it?'

'That's the one. Would you like a cup of tea … or are you a coffee man?'

'Thank you … umm … I prefer tea.'

'I'll put the kettle on.'

Turning, she walked across the hall and down the corridor.

I watched her go, noticing her navy blue trouser suit was, perhaps, a little too large and didn't really suit her as well as it should. Still, she looked pretty good to me and she'd smelled nice.

'Cor, look at 'im,' said a wizened old man walking past, looking like a goblin, speaking at a volume suggesting his antiquated wife was very deaf, or that he was just very rude and didn't care who heard him, ''e's gone and wet himself.'

I headed for the gents, where I discovered the hand dryer was so positioned that it was nearly, but not quite, impossible to use on trousers. After persevering, getting a contemptuous glance and a completely uncalled-for remark from a fat man who wished merely to dry his hands, I succeeded in making a difference. Looking reasonably presentable, I took a deep breath, made another attempt at controlling my hair and went in search of Daphne's room.

It looked more like a store cupboard than an office, although it had a desk, two chairs, a telephone, a wastepaper bin, a computer and a filing cabinet squeezed into it. She was on the phone, but indicated that I should sit. The window behind her was open, allowing a cool breeze to ripple the papers on the desk.

At last, she put the phone down and smiled. 'I hope you don't mind the window being open, but it was rather stuffy.'

I shook my head.

'How do you take your tea?'

'White, no sugar, please.'

'Me too.' Lurking behind the filing cabinet was a tiny table, supporting a kettle. She filled a couple of mugs and handed one to me.

'Thank you,' I said, taking a sip. It wasn't great, but it was hot and wet and I avoided choking on it. 'Umm ...' I said, 'are you the new curator?'

'I'm afraid not. I'm only the new temporary deputy curator. Why do you ask?'

I told her about Mr Biggs, the previous curator, who, having got himself involved in various nefarious activities, culminating in Hobbes nearly losing his life, had fled to France.

'I had no idea,' she said, 'that this town was such a hot bed of crime. Are the police here as bad as the gruesome twosome we were saddled with in Blackcastle?'

I shook my head. 'No, they're pretty good on the whole – especially Hobbes.'

'Hobbes was the big, ugly copper on top of the getaway van, right?' she said. 'I saw the video.'

I nodded.

'That was impressive, but I don't think I'd like to meet him in a dark alley.'

'You'd have nothing to fear,' I said, 'unless you were seriously up to no good. He's one of the good guys at heart. Mind you, he can be utterly terrifying when it suits him.'

'Do you know him?'

'Very well,' I said, surfing a swell of self-importance. 'He's my friend.'

'Really?'

'Yes. He stopped me getting stabbed yesterday when I went after that mugger. Rupert had just pulled a knife when he scooped him up in a wheelie bin.'

'Rupert? Are you on first name terms with all the local criminals?'

'I only know his name because Hobbes decided to take him home and feed him instead of taking him down the police station.'

'Why?' she asked, looking at me with interest, which I

hoped wasn't all on account of my story.

'I'm not sure. He's like that sometimes. It's maddening, but he usually has a reason, although I'm not always convinced he knows what it is. Still, it usually seems to work out, and it did help him learn that Rupert's father is Sir Gerald Payne and—'

Daphne gasped, her face suddenly pale. 'Sir Gerald? I'd hoped I'd got away from him. What's he up to?'

I wondered if I'd said too much. Then again, maybe I hadn't said enough. I didn't want to alarm her, but perhaps she deserved to know what I knew and, I thought, I owed her some sort of explanation.

'I don't want to alarm you, but ... umm ... Rupert said he came looking for you.'

'No! Is your friend, Hobbes, going to do something about it?'

'I suppose he is, sort of, but, at the moment ... umm ... he appears to be giving him a hand.'

'You mean he's actually helping him?'

She looked scared and angry – and pretty.

'I'm sure he has a good reason.' I said, forcing a confident smile. 'Probably, anyway.'

'But,' she said, 'I came here to get away from the Paynes. They've made my life a misery, even before Hugh died.'

'Hobbes won't let Rupert harm you in any way,' I said. 'You're one of the public and I'm sure he'll want to protect you.'

'I'm not worried about that young idiot, Rupert! He'd be harmless enough without his father. He's the one who scares me, because he's ruthless and vindictive and he's not stupid. What's more he has Denzil to do his dirty work.' She shivered, seeming to shrink into herself.

'Rupert mentioned someone called Denny. Is that him?'

'Yes, Denny hurts people. He once smashed Hugh over the head with a trombone when Hugh remonstrated with him for attacking a brass band.'

'Why didn't the police do something?'

'They tried. Sergeant Beer did, anyway, and Denny nearly killed him. He's not been the same since and he's terrified of Sir Gerald and Denny. Constable Jones is too inexperienced to make a difference.'

'But,' I said, 'how do they get away with it? Can't somebody do something?'

She shook her head and sighed. 'It seems not. Most are too scared to press charges and Sir Gerald knows the ones who aren't and ... well, he has means to persuade them.'

'That's terrible,' I said.

'Yes.' She paused to sip her tea. 'I thought I was getting away from all of that. It seems not.'

'But, why you? What has he got against you?'

She stared at me for a long moment, a frown creasing her forehead. I was struck, and deeply impressed, by how calm she'd become again.

'Sorry, Andy,' she said, eventually. 'I can't tell you. Not yet. Maybe later, when I know you better.'

'If you don't trust me, I understand. I can wait.'

'It's not that. Well, maybe it is that. I *don't* know you yet and after what you said about Hobbes and Rupert, I'm not sure quite what to think.'

As I reached for my cup of tea, I came to a startlingly quick decision and acted on it. Leaping forward, ignoring her gasp and look of alarm, I seized her shoulders and dragged her to the floor. Something missed her by a hair's breadth and hit me on the forehead. White lights and black spots boxed in front of my eyes until the blackness won a knockout.

A woman was speaking to me. I liked the lilt in her voice almost as much as the note of concern. I was on the carpet, lying on my side, my head sore. When I touched it, there was pain and a warm wetness. I groaned.

'Andy?'

There was that woman again. There was something familiar

...

'Do I come here often?' I asked.

'Are you alright?'

'What happened?'

'A brick hit you,' said Daphne. 'Well, half a brick.'

I opened my eyes and pushed myself onto my knees.

'Why?' Everything was hazy and distant, apart from her face. It was pretty, but looked worried.

'Someone chucked it at me, but you headed it into the waste paper bin. Thank you.'

Again I touched my head and glanced at my hand. Although there was some pain and wetness, there was no blood.

'It's tea,' she said. 'You knocked my mug.'

'Ah ... umm.' Although things were starting to make sense, I wasn't sure I was and, when I tried to stand, I needed guidance to reach my chair. 'My head is a bit sore, but I think I'm alright.'

'You were really lucky,' she said as I sat down, 'that it was only a glancing blow. It could have killed you.'

'If I was really lucky, it wouldn't have hit me at all.'

She laughed. 'That's true. Any idea who threw it?'

'Yes,' I said, 'a big bloke ... bald, with a rose tattoo on his arm. I think it was ...'

'Denny,' said Daphne.

'He might have hurt you. Should I call the police?'

She thought for a moment and shook her head. 'No, but I suppose I'd better tell you what's going on, now you're involved. I'll shut the window first.'

As she neared the window, she cried out as a huge, hairy hand, seizing her by the wrist, started to drag her forward, her feet scuffing the floor and kicking wildly. Leaping from my chair, overriding the pain in my head, I grabbed her around the waist, pulling back with all my strength, making her groan. Despite my efforts and her managing to get a grip on the window frame with her free hand, it was no good. A sudden jerk broke my hold and I nearly fell backwards. I dived forward, trying but failing to hold her ankles. She screamed as she was dragged outside and all that was left of her was her left shoe.

Although, following a number of unpleasant incidents, my normal maxim was to look before I leapt, my impulsive vault through the window worked in our favour. Time seemed to move into slow motion. I had a brief vision of Daphne, lying face down in a narrow alley, with a huge, shaven, tattooed man crouching over her. Then my feet, with all my weight behind them, crashed into the side of his head, knocking him down. I landed with a splat onto paving stones, winded and dazed. As I got back to my feet, my heart was pounding and my stomach churning with the thought of what he would do next, certain my intervention would not have improved his behaviour. He began to get up, but she bashed him on the head with the heel of her remaining shoe, leaving him flat on his face and groaning.

'Come on!' she said, grabbing my hand and pulling me after her.

We ran. Denny's lunge barely missed as we hurdled him and, without breaking stride, fled down the alley along the side of the museum and out onto the pavement, where we paused, gasping.

'What now?' I asked.

'Back into the museum.'

We ran inside.

Daphne shouted to the ticket lady: 'Call the police!'

The lady stared, shocked. 'Why?'

'I've been attacked.'

Putting down her magazine, the lady pointed at me. 'Was it him? I saw him lurking outside earlier and thought he looked like he was up to no good.'

'No,' said Daphne. 'Do you think I'd be holding his hand if it was?'

We were still holding hands, which, despite the

circumstances, made me feel on top of the world, until there was a shadow at the door. Denny lurched in and, although his face was smeared with blood, it could not mask the rage in his eyes. Without thinking, I pushed Daphne behind me and faced him, wondering what to do next, for chivalry is all fine and well, but would serve no purpose if I couldn't back it up. As he advanced, cracking his knuckles like rifle shots, I raised my fists in a pathetic gesture of defiance, but I couldn't just stand there, and there was nowhere to run to.

As he took a step towards us, beckoning with both hands, I had an idea. I'd have been the first to admit it wasn't one of my finest, but I had to try something.

'Stop where you are!' I said, using my authoritative voice, the voice that mostly failed on Dregs. 'What do you mean by attacking Mrs Duckworth? If you take one more step towards us, you will force me to make a citizen's arrest.'

Behind me, Daphne gasped. Before me, Denny stopped, shaking his head as if he hadn't heard correctly. Then, a slow, chilling sneer spread across his face and he laughed. The sheer contempt in that laugh aroused something unexpected in me: something dangerous. Adrenalin surged, my heart quickened and my breathing grew more rapid. I had, of course, experienced the fight or flight response many times and had, traditionally, favoured the latter option. This time was different. Rage swept through me, the world changed colour and I saw Denny, red as a devil in hell. Primeval instincts kicking in, I hurled myself at him, with the sole intention of destroying that sneer. Never before had I experienced a feeling of such strength; never before had I felt so coordinated, so whole, so alive, so un-Andy-like. The next few seconds remain vivid in my memory.

Ducking beneath his punch, I swung with all my might, feeling his nose crunch as my left fist struck and, as my right fist thudded onto the point of his jaw, he went over backwards. I fell with him, landing on top, punching, kicking and biting, shrugging off his attempts to grapple until he seized my wrists and tossed me aside. Landing on my back, I slid across the marble floor, but was back on my feet in an instant and landed several swinging punches without reply.

It couldn't go on forever. His massive fist thumped into my solar plexus. I doubled up like a broken deckchair and collapsed, gasping for breath that wouldn't come.

That was the end of my heroics. I was helpless and knew it and expected worse, far worse, to follow. Yet nothing worse did happen and things began to improve considerably. Daphne's arms closed around me and I could feel her warmth and her heart beating, even through my own trembling.

'Are you alright?' she asked, over and over, although I was unable to reply.

I nodded and, at last, air filled my lungs. I sucked it down as the gut pain receded into a dull ache. My knuckles were raw and bleeding. The kiss she gave me as I sat up took my breath away in an entirely different way.

'I'm OK,' I said, looking around fearfully while she helped me stand up. 'What happened? Where did he go?'

'It was strange,' she said, her eyes teary. 'Just as you went down, your big black dog burst in and launched himself at Denny, who ran away.'

'That sounds like Dregs,' I said, knowing it wasn't the first time the brave beast had saved me. 'He's actually Hobbes's dog. That is, he stays at Hobbes's and helps him with his cases.'

As I spoke, I was shocked to realise just how similar my situation was, and wondered whether Hobbes regarded Dregs as just another house guest, or whether he regarded me as just another pet.

'That is one fierce animal,' said Daphne.

'He's a softy, really,' I said, 'though, to be honest, he scared me when he first came along. He was wild and dangerous back then. He isn't now. Not normally.'

Leaning forward, she kissed me again. 'I'm glad he was

fierce then, because Denny looked in the mood for murder.'

'I'm glad, too.'

She smiled. 'And thank you. Most men wouldn't have the guts to fight him and you knocked him down, twice.'

'Well … the first time was a bit of luck.'

'But the second time wasn't. You really went for him.'

'I did, didn't I? I … umm … didn't know what else to do. I'm not normally a fighter.'

She helped me get back to my feet. I was shaking, my knuckles were stiff and sore and my mind seemed to be turbocharged with conflicting emotions. There was pride that I'd fought Denny, though deep down I knew I'd just been desperate, like a cornered rat, and I didn't like the fact that I'd lost control. It took me back to an incident at school, when I'd been nine or ten. Timothy Walsh had grabbed my pencil and run away with it, laughing. Although Timmy was a friend, the pencil had belonged to my sister before the accident and my behaviour regulator had malfunctioned. Instead of treating it as a joke, I'd pursued him, thrown him to the ground, knelt on his arms and raised my fists to pound him. The memory of his face, shocked, scared, and confused remained. Although I'd stopped myself in the nick of time, I'd scared myself as much as him and had always feared unleashing that emotion, the beast within, as Hobbes described it.

A sudden movement in the doorway made my stomach lurch.

'Alright, Andy?' asked Hobbes, peering in.

'More or less,' I said.

'Has someone thrown a rock at you?'

'No, it was a brick and it wasn't thrown at me.'

'Then,' said Hobbes, turning towards Daphne, 'may I deduce that it was aimed at you, Mrs Duckworth?'

Her eyes widened. 'Yes, but how do you know my name?'

'I'm a detective,' he said. 'I take it that the large bleeding man currently being pursued by Dregs is Mr Denzil Barker?'

Daphne nodded. 'Yes. He threw the brick at me, but Andy got me out the way. Then Denny dragged me out the window, but Andy knocked him down. Then he came in here and Andy fought him.'

Hobbes grinned. 'That was extremely well done.'

I blushed. 'It was nothing. Dregs saw him off.' Inside, part of me basked in the praise, while another part wouldn't stop reminding me that I'd just got lucky, that I'd resorted to violence, and that I was a pet, like Dregs, but less useful.

'No,' said Hobbes, 'it's something to be proud of, so don't put yourself down. According to Rupert, Mr Barker is given to bouts of extreme violence and has seriously injured many, including, I regretted to learn, some police officers. To come away from the encounter with a bruise on the head, a wallop in the guts and bloody knuckles is to have acquitted yourself well. I begin to have great hopes for you.'

'Thanks,' I said, embarrassed. 'But what have you done with Rupert? And, if it comes to that, where's Dregs?'

Hobbes shrugged. 'I'm afraid Rupert ran away when I was dealing with a stampede at the Farmers' Market. I expect he'll turn up sometime, probably after getting in trouble.' He put his head to one side as if listening. 'As for Dregs, if I'm not very much mistaken, he's on his way back.'

Daphne was watching him, her expression a strange mix of horror, amazement, and puzzlement. 'You're Inspector Hobbes, aren't you?'

To my surprise, he gave a theatrical bow.

'I am,' he said, grimacing and rubbing his ribs. 'I should have introduced myself.'

'Andy said you were helping Rupert Payne spy on me. Why?'

'It's true that I was trying to help the lad and that he was sent to spy on you, but I wasn't helping him in that. In fact, I strongly discouraged him. I was hoping he'd lead me to Mr Barker, because I want a word with him.'

'I see,' said Daphne, as if she didn't.

With a clicking of toenails and a wagging of tail, Dregs reappeared, a dirty blue rag in his jaws. Having luxuriated in our praise and patting for a few moments, he allowed Hobbes to take it. It was a piece of torn denim.

Hobbes held it up to the light and sniffed. 'That's funny,' he said.

I stopped stroking Dregs's rough, black head. 'What is?'

'This cloth, formerly part of Mr Barker's trousers, has a strange scent, yet it is familiar, if very faint. I can't put my finger on quite why. It'll come.'

'Excuse me,' said the ticket lady, looking rather bored, 'but do you still want me to call the police?'

'No,' said Hobbes. 'I am the police.'

Nodding, she went back to reading her magazine, as if gladiatorial contests between man and monster took place in the museum's foyer every day.

'Inspector,' said Daphne, 'what do you want to talk to Denny Barker about?'

'It's to do with a crime,' said Hobbes, looking thoughtful. 'I would like to rule him into my investigation, but I'm afraid that's all I can say for now.'

She nodded. 'I understand. But can you tell me what brought you here?'

'Of course, Mrs Duckworth. I happened to be approaching the foyer when I saw Mr Barker, who appeared to be in an agitated state, enter the building. Unfortunately, I have a busted rib and can't get around like I usually do, so I sent in the cavalry, in the form of Dregs. He's handy in a brawl, so long as he knows whose side he's on.'

'But,' she continued, 'if you're injured, what were you going to do about Denny?'

'I would have talked to him and tried to dissuade him from doing anything he might have later regretted.'

'No, seriously? He only listens to Sir Gerald.'

'Well, if a little chat didn't work, I would have dissuaded him by other means.' Hobbes smiled.

She frowned. 'But you don't know him. He's really dangerous. Honestly, I've seen him beat up four men at the same time. He might have hurt you badly.'

'He might have, and I suppose he'll have his chance when I find him. Thank you for the warning, but I'll take him as he comes. Are you two alright? It is not pleasant to be attacked.'

'I'm a bit shaky,' said Daphne, 'but I'm alright, apart from scrapes and bruises from when that brute pulled me through the window ... and my trousers will never be quite the same.'

'I'm OK, too,' I said, 'except for a sore head ... and I'm a bit tender.' I patted my stomach and winced. 'I'll get over it, but my hands are very stiff.'

'I'm not surprised,' said Hobbes. 'I'd get some ice on them, if I were you, and the lass will have something to soothe them. Now, Mrs Duckworth, could you show me your office?'

She looked puzzled. 'Yes, I suppose so. This way.'

She led us to the room where he sniffed about for a few moments before picking up a frame of metal bars.

'Last time I was in here,' he said, 'the security grille was on the window.'

'It was until this morning,' said Daphne, retrieving her lost shoe. 'I took it down so that I could open the window and let in a bit of air. It was so stuffy, it smelt like a bear pit.'

'I very much doubt it,' said Hobbes. 'Bear pits have a most peculiar and pungent aroma, but I can quite believe it gets stuffy. However, I would advise keeping the grille in place, at least until I can ensure Mr Barker won't be up to any more mischief.'

'Makes sense,' she agreed.

Lifting the grille, he slotted it into place and held it while she locked it securely with a key from the desk drawer.

'Right,' said Hobbes, 'my work here is done for now. I'd better catch some villains, or Sid will give me an ear bashing.

Good to meet you, Mrs Duckworth. I'll see you at supper time, Andy. The lass is making a pork vindaloo. Goodbye. Come on, Dregs.'

'Right,' said Daphne, as they left, 'are you ready to get some lunch?'

17

The puny, shrouded midday sun only seemed to underline the damp chill and blustery wind as we left the museum. I was still shaking, coming down from my adrenalin high, but Daphne appeared quite cheerful.

'I don't know about you,' she said, 'but I could really do with a stiff one. I don't normally drink at lunchtime, but it's been one hell of a morning. Is there anywhere round here?'

'Sounds like an excellent idea ... umm ... the Black Dog Café does a decent lunch, and it serves wine or bottled beers.'

'I could do with something a little stronger.'

'I know,' I said, inspired by an advert I'd seen in *Sorenchester Life*, 'there's a new place opened on Rampart Street called the Bar Nun and it's said to serve good food. I haven't been there yet, but it's only a two or three minute walk away.'

'Lead me to it.'

As we walked the short distance we talked, and I was comfortable, as if I'd known her for years; I was amazed she was smiling and laughing at my witticisms, some of which were, even to my ears, incredibly naff.

The Bar Nun had been done out to resemble a sort of Hollywood idea of a nunnery. The walls had the look of ancient, rough-hewn stone, the floor tiles appeared medieval, and there were rows of polished wooden refectory tables set along the walls, with dark wooden benches to sit on. Two months previously, it had been an expensive and spectacularly unsuccessful shoe shop, but now it smelt of cooking, beer and paint. Some of the tables were walled off by wooden partitions, like little cells, and offered privacy. I thought we'd choose one of them, but first we headed to the bar, where a pretty young woman wearing a skimpy black habit smiled at us.

'Hello, sir, madam,' she said. 'How can I help you?'

'What would you like?' I asked Daphne, patting the comforting wad in my breast pocket.

She paused for a moment. 'I rather fancy a cocktail.'

'That's a good idea,' I said, as if accustomed to ordering them, and turned to the barmaid. 'Do you do cocktails, miss? Or should I say, sister?'

The girl grimaced. 'Yes, we do the normal ones plus a few specialities of the house.' She pointed to a list on a blackboard above the bar and, while we examined it, served an elderly couple, the only other customers, who wanted milky coffees.

'I think,' said Daphne, when the barmaid turned back to us, 'I'll have a Godchild.'

'Excellent choice,' I said, craning to see what the barmaid put in it: a measure of brandy, something creamy from a rectangular bottle and a small mountain of ice.

The barmaid, placing it on a coaster, looked at me expectantly.

'Right,' I said, with the easy confidence of an ignoramus, 'I rather fancy one of your house specialities. Give me an Ecstasy of Saint Theresa, please. Shaken not stirred.'

'Are you sure, sir?' asked the barmaid.

I nodded and she busied herself with a worrying number of bottles and a shaker. 'Here you are,' she said at last, handing me a glass filled with a clear, innocuous-looking fluid with floating ice, a sliver of lime, and salt crystals round the rim.

'Thank you,' I said. 'Cheers!'

'Cheers,' said Daphne, sipping her drink and smiling.

I took a gulp of mine and instantly regretted it, for it was, quite simply, the nastiest liquid that had ever passed my lips, which was saying something. I shuddered, my tongue went numb and my throat burned, despite the chill of the ice.

'Water! Pleathe!' I said, shocked that I couldn't help but lisp, and found the barmaid had already placed a pint glass of iced water in front of me. Grabbing it, I swilled it down.

'Most customers need water after one of those,' she said

with a merry laugh, quite inappropriate for a nun.

'Thank you,' I said, thinking she might have given me prior warning. 'Do people drink this for pleasure?'

'No, sir. Mostly we have to force them.'

Daphne was reading the menu. 'We'd better get something to eat or we'll end up squiffy. I'll have Chicken Madras. Andy?'

'I do like a curry, but since I'm having one for supper, I'll ... umm ... have a chilli.' I hoped it would be a really spicy one, something that would neutralise the taste of the cocktail. I wished I'd just stuck to lager, which was usually safe.

After ordering, we sat in one of the small cells, towards the back. As a drinker more used to the Feathers and its veneer of filth that nearly masked the squalor beneath, I was delighted to find the table was clean and not at all sticky.

'What a morning!' said Daphne with a shiver. 'I'm so glad you were there. I don't know what might have happened otherwise.'

I smiled and shrugged. 'I'm glad I was there, too.'

'I'm sorry I wasn't very nice when we first met,' she said. 'I had you down as a waster.'

I stared at my drink for a long moment. 'I'm ... umm ... afraid you're not far from the truth. I've tried to kid myself I'm not, but when it comes down to it, I live on Hobbes's charity and the only reason I've got any money for lunch is because Mrs Goodfellow, his housekeeper, is so kind.'

'I thought you were a reporter?'

'Not any more. I did work for the *Bugle*, but I was fired. Since then, I've sort of pretended I've gone freelance, but I haven't actually written anything, except stuff about Hobbes, which I can't do anything with, because ... because he hates publicity. I'm a bit useless really.'

'No,' she said, shaking her head, 'you're not. The way you went for Denny showed what's inside.'

'I couldn't think of anything else to do.'

'Precisely! You followed your instincts and did the right

204

thing. You should trust yourself more often.'

'I don't know when to. I've let myself and others down too often.'

She reached out and put her hand on mine. 'Give yourself a break.'

I nodded. Her hand was warm and soft and smooth and, despite my sore knuckles, I liked its touch. The barmaid placed our cutlery and meals in front of us.

To my eyes, it looked like a terrible curry, a thin, watery, yellow sauce poured over rubbery lumps of boiled out chicken with overcooked rice. Perhaps Mrs Goodfellow had spoiled me, but Daphne ate it without a murmur of complaint. My chilli con carne was edible, if a little bland, and distracted me sufficiently that I took another glug of my cocktail. If anything, it was even nastier second time around. I stared at it, like at a mad dog that I had to get past.

'You're really not enjoying that are you?' said Daphne, finishing her Godchild. 'Why not just give up on it and try something else?'

'Yeth,' I croaked, wondering why I hadn't thought of such a simple solution. 'Would you like another drink?'

'I'll just have a coffee: black, no sugar, please. I'll nip to the ladies while you're getting them.'

I went up to the bar, aware of a man striding briskly past. I was heading back, trying not to spill any coffee, taking sips off the top of my lager, when another man entered. As he walked past, I recognised him as Colonel Squire. I sat back at our table, pleased the lager was diluting the cocktail's lingering aftertaste.

'Ah, there you are, Gerry,' said Colonel Squire, presumably to the first man, who was out of sight, although I could just about hear him. 'Shall I get the drinks in?'

'Good to see you, Toby,' said the first man. 'Make mine a whisky and soda.'

There was something hard and arrogant in his voice and yet

it was oddly familiar. I flicked through my memory and, slightly to my surprise, found a match. It was Sir Gerald Payne, I was almost certain.

Colonel Squire, a tall, neat man in a grey business suit, was carrying two glasses back to his table when Daphne returned. As she sat, I put my finger to my lips and leant over to where I could hear. She looked puzzled, but did as I wanted.

'Bottoms up, Gerry,' said Colonel Squire.

'Cheers, Toby,' said Sir Gerald. 'How goes the hunt for your gold?'

'Not at all well. I keep getting on to old Sharples, but he's hopeless, and the police don't seem to be making any progress whatsoever.'

'What about that big ugly devil who stopped the first attempt?'

'Hobbes? He seems to be a great one for being the action hero, but he doesn't seem to be much good as a detective.'

How little he knew, I thought.

Sir Gerald laughed. 'Well, he can't be any worse than the police around us. We've been lumbered with a matching pair of complete idiots. Anyway, if the worst comes to the worst, you'll get your money back.'

'To an extent, but the price of gold has risen and Sharples says I'll only get the market rate at the time of the robbery. I stand to lose thousands.'

'Just as well you can afford it,' said Sir Gerald with a laugh.

'That's not the point. I intend to make sure I don't lose out at all and I hold Sharples personally responsible. One way or another, I'm going to make him pay. I entrusted him with my gold, he was in charge of security, and he failed. Therefore, he owes me. And it's not just the value of the gold, because some of the coins were quite rare and worth a great deal more than their weight.

'Well, that's enough of my woes. How are things with you, Gerry?'

'They are going very well. It's an ill wind that blows no one any good and the rise in the gold price has meant it is economical to reopen the mine. It's back in production, we've dug up some top-class ore, and have smelted our first ingots. It's the first Payne gold for over one hundred years.'

'Lucky for you,' said Colonel Squire. 'Not many chaps get to inherit their own goldmine.'

'True, but there are not many chaps get to inherit thousands of acres of prime Cotswold farmland as you did.'

'One must count one's blessings I suppose. If my gold isn't recovered, and I'm not hopeful, then at least I'll get plenty of cash, even if it's not nearly as much as it ought to be.'

'I'll tell you what,' said Sir Gerald, 'if you still mean to keep your own gold reserve, I could sell you some ingots from the mine. I know it's not much recompense for those rare coins, but I could mark them with your family crest, and I'm sure I could arrange a most generous discount, since we won't have to go through any brokers.'

'That's very decent of you.'

'Not at all. After all, I partly blame myself for your loss. It was I who persuaded you to put it in Grossman's Bank. I just thought it would be safer there than in your cellar. It *had* a good reputation.'

'Not your fault at all,' said Colonel Squire. 'It was sensible advice and you can't be blamed if the country's going to the dogs. All these robberies in town! We should hang a few more ruffians. That would make them think twice about robbing. And maybe we should start hanging a few bankers as well. Old Sharples should be the first.'

Rage burst up in me and I might have said something had Daphne not been there.

'I tell you what I'll do, Toby,' said Sir Gerald, lowering his voice to a whisper, 'I'll get my man to have a word with Sharples and ensure he gives you what you deserve. He can be most persuasive.'

'Thank you, an excellent suggestion. That'll give the old bloodsucker something to think about. Show him what looking after your customer is all about, eh?'

'That's right.'

'But,' said Colonel Squire, 'first reassure me that he won't go too far and that there will be no way I might be held responsible. People round here respect me as a magistrate and I wouldn't want things to become embarrassing.'

'Don't worry. He knows what he's doing. Besides, even should he happen to go too far, he has no links to you. You'd still be in the clear.'

'What if he's caught?'

'I doubt,' said Sir Gerald, 'that any officer round here could arrest him.'

'What about Hobbes?'

'I'd bet my man against him any day and, even if by some freak chance I'm wrong, then he's loyal and knows to say the right thing. He's been in the family for more years than I care to remember and would do nothing that might cause me trouble. He is an extremely useful chap to have around and I'll make sure he gives Sharples a damn good ... talking to.' Sir Gerald laughed.

I didn't mean to, but I gasped. It just slipped out, because, from what I'd seen, talking wasn't Denny's speciality and I feared for the old vampire's well-being.

'I think someone might be listening,' said Sir Gerald quietly.

I heard him stand up, heard his footsteps approaching and, knowing he'd recognise Daphne, fearing he'd do something, I was paralysed for an instant. Then, before he could see us, inspiration struck. I threw my arms around her, drew her towards me and gave her a passionate kiss on the lips, amazed how easily she participated. I maintained my grip, aware Sir Gerald was looking at us, aware he could not see our faces, so long as we stayed in the clinch.

With a disapproving snort he walked away, but, although

my ploy had worked brilliantly and the danger had passed, I didn't pull away from her, or she from me. The kiss lingered for what might have been several minutes and only ended when, in manoeuvring for breath, I knocked over the remains of my lager.

She was looking at me with a strange expression. I was euphoric, for being kissed by a lovely woman was a rare experience. There had been Violet, of course, but she'd turned out to be a werecat and Daphne was the real thing. Despite barely knowing her, I felt I could be anything: her friend, her lover, her protector. I could even get a job and make something of myself.

'Well,' she said, smiling, 'that was unexpected.' She sipped her coffee.

I nodded, realising I was in an awkward situation. The kiss had been wonderful, but I was wondering whether I needed to tell her my reasons. Although I took a breath and opened my mouth to speak, I asked myself why I should spoil the moment. Deciding to say nothing was, in all honesty, the right decision. The only trouble was that I couldn't think of anything to say instead, so for a moment I must have looked like an idiot, or worse.

'I'll get you another drink,' said Daphne.

'No,' I said, keeping my voice low, 'I'm fine.'

Admittedly my fears of Sir Gerald attacking her in there were probably exaggerated, for the bar had filled up considerably and I was almost certain Colonel Squire would not sanction violence, especially in front of witnesses. He had far too much to lose. Still, I thought it prudent to get out as soon as possible.

She shrugged. 'Well, I ought to be getting back to work soon. It's my first proper week and already I don't know what they must be thinking of me, so … I can't afford to go back late and reeking of alcohol.' She finished her coffee.

'OK,' I said. 'Let's get out of here.'

As we left, I held her hand and whispered in her ear. 'I'm sorry if I was acting a little strangely, but Sir Gerald Payne was sitting behind us and talking about the gold robbery with Colonel Squire. Did you hear any of it?'

She shook her head and I told her what I'd heard.

'It might,' she said, looking serious, 'have become unpleasant, if he'd recognised me.'

'I'll walk with you back to the museum,' I said, as we left the bar, 'but then I really must warn Sid. He's a nice old va ... chap and I wouldn't want him to get hurt.'

'You must,' she said, 'but, please, be careful when you're out. Denny Barker is a really dangerous man and he won't be happy that you've bested him twice. Next time he sees you, there's no knowing what he might do.' She squeezed my hand very gently, for which I was grateful.

I tried to look nonchalant and hoped Hobbes would be around next time I met Denny, although I hadn't much liked Sir Gerald's confidence in his man. Besides, there was always the possibility that I'd be on my own, probably down some dark alley, when next I bumped into him. I almost wished I'd finished my cocktail, for after one of those, anything would be bearable.

The weather hadn't turned any warmer and few people were out and about. There being no sign of Denny or Sir Gerald, I started to relax. We were just passing the end of Blackdog Street when I heard a familiar voice.

'Hi, Andy,' said Kathy, enormous in her red Puffa jacket, smiling as she approached, 'Where are you going to take me this afternoon?'

'Oh,' I said. 'Umm ...'

'Who's this?' asked Kathy.

'Oh ... Right, I should introduce you. Kathy, this is Daphne. Daphne ... this is ... umm ... Kathy.'

Daphne nodded. Kathy did not. I squirmed.

'I'm glad you two have met,' I said, with a feeble smile.

'Kathy is staying with us at the moment and I've been showing her around.'

'I see,' said Daphne.

'Daphne works at the museum,' I said.

'So, shouldn't she be *at work*?' asked Kathy.

'Yes, I probably should,' said Daphne. 'I'll see you around, Andy. Nice to have met you ... Kathy.'

'Ditto.'

'Take care,' I said.

As Daphne turned away, Kathy, heavy with scent, enveloped me in a massive, suffocating bear hug, which was about as welcome as it would have been from a real bear and I was just as powerless. I couldn't understand why she was doing it. She really wasn't my type, if she was anybody's, and her sudden show of affection was as puzzling as it was alarming. Still, part of me felt sorry for her, even though I wished she hadn't just turned up, or, in fact, come into our lives at all.

'Have you seen Daddy?' she asked on releasing me.

'I did before lunch. He'd lost Rupert.'

'I knew he should have slammed that punk in jail. He kept me awake all night.'

'I'm sorry to hear that.'

'And I'm sorry I was a little sharp this morning. I was tired and cold and the coffee hadn't kicked in. I'm not at my best without a strong black one in me.'

'That's alright. I'm not at my best when I'm tired either. Still ... umm ... I don't throw mugs.'

'Well, I didn't hit you, did I?'

'Not with the mug ... but you might have done.'

'Might have wins no prizes. I wouldn't have a cow about it.'

'I won't.'

Smiling, she hugged me again. I tried not to breathe in the scent fumes, which wasn't too difficult as she was squeezing so tightly. All I could do was hope I wouldn't be crushed like an empty beer can and that Daphne couldn't see this unseemly behaviour. When at last she let me go I stepped out of reach.

'Right,' she said, 'since my daddy is nowhere to be found, I'm relying on you to show me a good time. How about it, Big Boy?'

'What?' I said, caught off guard. 'I ... umm ... don't know what to suggest.'

'Well, what d'ya normally do for kicks in this neck of the woods?'

'There's not much to do on a cold afternoon. You've seen the church and the museum.'

'Too true.'

'Well, I sometimes used to go for a drink.'

'Why the heck not? What's the wildest place in town, buddy?'

'Oh ... probably the Feathers. There's usually something happening down the Feathers.'

'Great, let's go.'

'I must warn you it's a bit grotty and the landlord is ... well ... umm ... different, and it can sometimes be dangerous there.'

'It sounds fun.'

We set off, although I wasn't at all sure it was a good idea, but it had been my best shot at short notice and there was no place quite like the Feathers and she had allowed no time for any other suggestions. I just hoped Hobbes would forgive me. She kept squeezing my sore hand, talking and laughing, as if she were the happiest woman in the world. I really did not understand her.

Even the first sight of the Feathers, all peeling paint and grubby windows, didn't dampen her spirits. As we approached the front door it opened, a young man flew out and landed with a splat and a curse on the pavement. Picking himself up, he wiped a smear of blood from his nose and swaggered away as if well satisfied with his experience.

Plucking up courage, I ushered her inside, where Featherlight was resting one of his bellies on the bar, and wiping his hands on his stained and torn vest.

'Caplet,' he said, 'didn't I tell you not to show your ugly face in here again?'

'No, I don't think you did.'

'Well I bloody should've. Who's the lady?'

'This is Kathy.'

'A fine looking bit of skirt. You're a lucky bastard.'

Kathy giggled and patted me heartily on the back. As I stumbled towards the bar, Billy's head appeared.

'Wotcha, Andy. The usual?'

'Please ... and what would you like, Kathy?'

'I'll have a Margarita.'

'Not in here you won't,' said Featherlight, mopping up a puddle of spilled beer with his vest.

'Well, what can a girl drink round here?'

Billy grinned. 'Beer or white wine. I wouldn't trust the spirits.'

'Gimme a beer then, buster.'

'Bitter? A pint?'

'Sure ... whatever.'

Billy poured the drinks, raising his eyebrows when I handed him actual money, but saying nothing to embarrass me. A large gulp of lager, cool and crisp, washed away the cocktail's hideous residue.

Kathy took a hefty swig of her bitter, frowned and shrugged. 'What the heck is this?'

'Hedbury Best Bitter,' said Billy.

'Jeez! What's their worst bitter like? It's warm and it tastes like ... I don't know what the heck it tastes like. Is there something wrong with it?'

I cringed, expecting Featherlight to explode at the slur. Billy reached under the counter for the steel helmet he'd taken to wearing in times of crisis as Featherlight turned to face her.

'She didn't mean it,' I said. 'She's just not used to British beer. She's from America.'

Featherlight's habitual frown had been replaced by a smile, showing off a mouthful of large, insanitary teeth. 'I can tell where she's from, Caplet. You think I'm so daft I can't place an American accent?'

'No ... I was just pointing it out.'

'Well, don't. Sit down, shut up, and drink, while I talk to the young lady.'

Taking my glass to a sticky seat, I sat at an even stickier table as Billy removed his helmet. Featherlight, drawing up a barstool, wiped it with his vest in what was, for him, a gallant gesture.

'Have a seat, miss,' he said, giving a low bow.

She sat as requested and, to give her some credit, without a shudder.

'Can I offer you something different?' asked Featherlight, gesturing at her beer.

Billy's mouth dropped open at this unprecedented offer.

She shook her head. 'No thanks, buddy. I'll get used to it.'

'Well then, Miss Kathy,' said Featherlight, 'what brings an American beauty to my humble establishment?'

'It was Andy's suggestion.'

'Well, I never thought I'd say this, but I'm grateful to him. It's not often we get a genuine American lady in here, but he shouldn't have brought you. This can be a rough place.'

Kathy smiled. 'It looks fine to me and I reckon you're big and tough enough to protect a gal should there be any rough stuff.'

He inclined his head. 'I guess you're right at that. But,' he said, glaring at his customers, 'don't any of you lot think of trying anything.'

There was an outbreak of mumbled denials and much head shaking among the half-dozen or so desperate drinkers.

Featherlight, nodding, turned back to Kathy, still maintaining his disconcerting smile. 'Are you here on holiday?'

'Not exactly. I'm visiting family.'

'Caplet?'

'No, he's just been kind enough to show me around town.'

'Mrs Goodfellow, then?'

'No.'

'Who?'

'Inspector Hobbes is my daddy.'

'Hobbes?' Featherlight raised his hairy eyebrows. 'I didn't think he had it in him.'

'Do you know him?'

'Yes, Miss Kathy. We go way back.'

'I bet you do. You remind me of him a little, except of course, you're much better looking.'

Featherlight's face took on an even ruddier tint than normal and his smile broadened.

I sat, elbows on the table, open-mouthed, for, although I could think of many words to describe him, good-looking was not one that sprang immediately to mind, even in comparison to Hobbes. Like me, Billy was watching, wide-eyed and engrossed by the show. Unlike me, he was not recovering from a toxic cocktail, and the fact that I was enjoying gulping down lager at the Feathers proved just how awful it had been. Still, as my mouth and throat recovered, I was able to concentrate on my kiss with Daphne and felt well-disposed to Featherlight for taking Kathy off my hands, allowing me time to indulge my memory. The trouble was, something kept nagging, a vague, guilty feeling, as if I ought to be doing something urgent. The day's events churned through my head in a random stream until a stray thought snagged my conscience. Knocking back what was left of my drink, I peeled myself off the seat.

'I've just thought of something,' I said. 'I've got to go.'

I ran from the pub to warn Sid.

18

I was legging it towards Grossman's Bank, skilfully weaving between shoppers and charity collectors, hoping I wasn't already too late, when a thought stopped me outside a tea shop. What if Sid was not at the bank? Might he not be at home? Or enjoying lunch somewhere? Or was he somewhere else entirely? After deliberating, panting from the run for a minute or two, I reasoned that I should try his house first, because if he was there, he was likely to be on his own, whereas there would be other people at the bank, not to mention some sort of security. I set off again, just as a little, white-haired old lady stepped out of the tea shop. Tripping over the wheeled basket she was towing, knocking it over, I landed in the gutter. I picked myself up, apologising, retrieved her spilled groceries and listened to a long and bitter lecture, criticising the young people of today. Although at other times I might have been flattered to be considered young, I had a job to do and, turning away with a final word of apology, I ran.

'Stop thief!' she cried.

I was still holding her handbag. Stopping, apologising again, I threw it back and fled.

Reaching Doubtful Street, I stood outside Sid's house, ringing the bell and pounding on the door, without a response. Taking a deep breath, I turned around and headed for the bank at a gentle jog, there being no gallop left in me.

When I was halfway down The Shambles, the bank already in sight, a big hand seized my shoulder and dragged me into an alley, nearly causing my heart to burst from my chest.

'Don't hurt me,' I said, cringing.

Hobbes's deep chuckle gave me instant comfort.

'Oh, it's you. What's up?' I asked.

'We've been told to look for someone fitting your description. The suspect allegedly mugged an old lady before hurling her own handbag at her, striking her a blow on the head.'

'I hit her on the head? Is she alright? I didn't mean it.'

'So it was you. I suspected as much and, no doubt, you'll be pleased to know the lady is fine, apart from being extremely annoyed with the youth of today, by which she means you. Tell me what happened.'

I explained, adding what I'd overheard at lunch and why I'd been in such a hurry.

'It could only happen to you, Andy.' He laughed and paused for a moment, his face screwed up with thought. 'However, your information is revealing. Things are finally starting to make sense.'

'What things?'

'The robbery, the rocks, Hugh Duckworth's death.'

'Not to me they're not. Tell me what rocks?'

'Rocking chairs?'

'No, I mean, what rocks are you talking about?'

'The ones I took from Sir Gerald's mine.'

'I thought you said they were just ordinary ones.'

'They are, which is precisely why they are so important.'

I scratched my head. Conversations with Hobbes didn't always make sense.

'What about Sid?' I asked.

'Don't worry, he can look after himself, but I suppose I should have a word with him.'

'Do you really think he'll be alright?'

'He always has been and I doubt this time will be any different.'

'But what about Denny?'

'I'm sure he'll be alright too, just as long as he keeps out of Sid's way.'

'What? Denny's really strong and he's really mean.'

'You'd be surprised what Sid can do. You're forgetting what he is.'

'He's a nice old man.'

'No, he's not. He's an old vampire, who chooses to be nice. I'm far more worried about Denzil Barker's well-being, and I'd like to give him a word of warning before he does anything else he'll regret.'

'Good,' I said uncertainly, but slightly reassured. 'There's another thing – Sir Gerald was confident Denny could beat you, and don't forget, you are injured.'

He shrugged. 'I hope it won't come down to violence, but if it does, well, who knows?'

Some of my reassurance evaporated, but the jut of his chin suggested he was not to be argued with. 'OK,' I said, 'but could you explain about the rocks?'

'I showed them to a geologist who had them analysed.'

'And what did he discover?'

'*She* confirmed they are perfectly ordinary rocks, just the same as any other in that region of the Blacker Mountains.'

'Well, in that case,' I said, 'it hardly seems worth the effort.'

'On the contrary, it was most illuminating.'

'I don't see why. And what's it all got to do with Hugh Duckworth's death?'

'Mr Duckworth was, I understand, an amateur geologist as well as being a historian. He was planning to publish a booklet on the Blacker Mountains.'

'But what has that got to do with his death?'

'I think,' said Hobbes, 'that it is likely that his research had the potential to reveal a certain inconvenient truth.'

'What truth?'

'That the rocks around Blacker Hollow are quite ordinary.'

'You keep saying that, but it doesn't make any more sense. I don't get it.'

He shook his head. 'I'll leave you to think about it for a while longer. It'll do you good. In the meantime, let's go and tell Sid your news. Come along. And quickly.'

As he strode from the alley, I followed, even more confused

than usual. The rocks completely baffled me, because I could see no significance to them at all. Had they been valuable I might, perhaps, have seen a motive for keeping them secret, even for killing someone, but they weren't.

However I looked at what had happened, it seemed to me that Hugh Duckworth had been murdered and that someone, possibly Hobbes, even though it had taken place outside his jurisdiction, should be investigating. I suspected Denny and it was chilling to know that I'd given him a reason to hold a grudge. Perhaps Daphne also suspected him. She was certainly afraid of him and with good reason. Even so, I didn't know why he'd attacked her after she'd left Blackcastle. I wondered if she had something Sir Gerald wanted. Could it be information? Possibly the inconvenient truth Hobbes had mentioned? Yet, despite my fear of him, I recognised that Denny was the hired help and that he was only doing what he was told to do. It was clear Sir Gerald was behind her problems, although it would be difficult to prove. I really hoped Hobbes would help her and make her well-being his priority, despite the importance of recovering the stolen gold and catching the rest of the gang.

As we crossed The Shambles, heading for the bank, which although still festooned in police tape, was open for business, Hobbes asked about Kathy, reminding me of what was apparently his true priority. 'She was a little dispirited at lunchtime,' he said, 'and I hoped you might bump into her and keep her amused for a while. It's a shame I'm so busy at the moment because I'd like to spend more time getting to know her. By the way, where is she?'

'At the Feathers,' I said, embarrassed. 'She was talking to Featherlight. They appeared to be getting on very well.'

He frowned. 'You left her at the Feathers?'

I nodded. 'I had to find Sid. She'll be alright.'

'I hope so, but it's no place for a lady, especially one on her own.'

'But Featherlight was looking after her. He wouldn't try

anything on, would he?'

'No. In his own peculiar way, Featherlight is an honourable man. I'm just not so sure about some of his customers.'

'He can take care of them.'

Hobbes brightened. 'Of course he can.'

We entered Grossman's Bank, a solid, dark, heavy-barred building that looked as if it had not changed since Queen Victoria was sitting on the throne. My footsteps rang on black and white tiles as we approached a varnished door with a gleaming brass handle. Hobbes knocked and a diminutive, skinny man with pointy elbows, wearing a tight black suit and steel-framed, half-moon glasses, opened the door.

'Good afternoon, Siegfried,' said Hobbes. 'Is Mr Sharples in?'

'Good afternoon, sir,' said Siegfried, with a slight Germanic intonation, giving us a quaint bow. 'He's in his office. Please, go straight through. He's expecting you.'

'Thank you,' said Hobbes, leading me down a gloomy corridor to the enormous, polished, panelled door at the end, a door intended to impress. It bore a brass plaque with the legend: 'Dr Sidney Sharples, manager.' As he knocked, it swung open without a sound.

Sid, immaculate in a navy blue, pinstripe business suit, was behind a vast desk in an old-fashioned and rather grand office, with half a dozen armchairs arranged in a semicircle around a log fire. Rising from his green leather chair, he removed his spectacles and smiled.

'Wilber, Andy, welcome.'

Walking around the desk, he approached with his hand held out. As I shook it, I was again struck by the delicacy and softness of his plump fingers and couldn't see him faring well should Denny ever catch up with him.

'How can I help you? Would you like a cup of tea? Or can I arrange an overdraft?'

'I never say no to a cup of tea,' said Hobbes, sitting in a leather-covered armchair.

'Yes please,' I said, 'tea would be nice.' I wriggled onto the chair next to Hobbes, finding it was surprisingly deep and astonishingly comfortable, and stretched out my hands, warming them at the blaze.

Sid pulled a cord on the wall and Siegfried entered, once again treating us to his bow.

'A pot of tea for three, if you'd be so good,' said Sid.

Siegfried bowed and departed.

Sid sat down with us and I wondered if his smile was a little forced, though I believed his welcome was sincere.

'It's good of you to drop by. It makes a pleasant change from Colonel Squire. I suppose he has a good reason for shouting and threatening, but it doesn't help. Still, I suspect the colonel is all bluster and is mostly harmless, which is more than can be said of his friend, Sir Gerald.

'But, enough of my woes! How are you getting on with the investigation, old boy? Any progress?'

'Some,' said Hobbes, 'and Andy has recently provided me with some interesting points that, combined with the physical evidence, are quite revealing.'

'Well done, young fellow,' said Sid.

I smiled, looking suitably modest, which wasn't difficult as I had no idea what I'd done that was so significant.

'Furthermore,' Hobbes continued, 'Andy informs me that Sir Gerald plans to send his manservant, Mr Denzil Barker, commonly known as Denny, round to talk to you.'

'One more won't make much difference,' said Sid with a shrug.

'Mr Barker,' said Hobbes, 'is not noted so much for his talking as for his extreme acts of violence.'

Sid nodded. 'I see. Any idea when I might expect him?'

'No, except that it's unlikely to be in full public view. Mr Barker, I have been led to believe, favours encounters down dark alleys and on lonely footpaths. He is, according to a young lad I was talking to, particularly handy with a sock filled with sand.'

'Thank you for the warning. How will I recognise him?'

'Tell him, Andy.'

'Oh ... umm ... right. He's a big, brawny man, like Hobbes and just as ug ... umm ... unusually strong, and he has a bald head and a tattoo of a red rose on his right arm.'

'Thank you,' said Sid.

'Besides that,' said Hobbes, grinning, 'Andy is too modest to mention that Mr Barker has a variety of superficial injuries to his face, including a bloodied nose and a split lip that he obtained when Andy knocked him down.'

'Well done that man,' said Sid with approval and some amusement.

'And there's one other thing. Mr Barker may be somewhat lacking in trouser material on his rump following an encounter with Dregs.'

'I get the picture,' said Sid. 'What do you want me to do about it?'

'When you meet him, go as gently as you can,' said Hobbes. 'He's suffered enough for one day.'

'No, he hasn't,' I said, shocked. 'Not nearly enough. He attacked my girlfriend today and he's threatened her in the past and I reckon he killed her husband, but more to the point, he is a big, dangerous bastard.'

'Language, Andy,' said Hobbes, frowning.

'Sorry, but he is,' I continued. 'You need to stay out of his way. I got lucky, but I doubt he'll be careless again. I wouldn't want you to get hurt.'

Sid beamed. 'Thank you for your concern. I really appreciate it, but there's nothing to worry about.'

'Yes, there is. I've met him – I know what he's like.'

'You don't,' said Hobbes, shaking his head. 'You've only seen him when he's working and, for all you know, he might be a friendly fellow in his spare time.'

'No,' I said, feeling, as I sometimes did with Hobbes, that I was in a madhouse. 'He really is dangerous and he's going to hurt Sid. He needs to be stopped.'

'Don't vex yourself about my safety, young fellow,' said Sid. 'I may have slowed down now I'm so advanced in years, but I am still a vampire.'

'What's that got to do with it?'

'Vampires,' said Hobbes, 'are extremely strong, extraordinarily fast and uncannily agile.'

'It's true,' said Sid, complacently.

I shook my head, not understanding how they could be so cool.

'I see you don't believe me,' said Sid. 'I'll show you something. Do you see that glass paperweight on the table in front of you?'

'Yes, of course.'

'Good. Pick it up, if you would.'

'Alright,' I said, more confused than ever, but doing as I was told. It was a pretty thing, made of glittering crystal with a dandelion head entombed. 'Now what?'

'Throw it at me. As hard as you can.'

'I can't do that. It's really heavy. I'd hurt you.'

'Honestly, you won't. Give it a go. I'll be fine.'

'Well, alright, if you're quite sure?'

With a shrug, I pulled my arm back ready to throw and found my hand was empty.

'What do you think of that, then?' asked Sid, strolling back to his chair, bouncing the paperweight in his hand.

'OK,' I admitted, not having even seen him stand up, 'that was fast.' I'd always been impressed by Hobbes's speed, but Sid was something else. I was trembling: not with fear, but awe.

'You should have seen me in my heyday,' he said, his eyes seeming to focus on the distant past.

'I couldn't even see you then,' I said.

The old vampire chuckled. 'Aye, well, maybe I'm still not so slow.'

There was a knock on the door and Siegfried entered, carrying the tea on a silver tray, setting it down and pouring us each a cupful, before departing with a bow. Although I'd never been great at recognising faces, a major handicap for a reporter, I couldn't help thinking I knew him from somewhere. Then I realised how similar he was to Hobbes's tailor. 'He looks like Milord Schmidt.'

Hobbes nodded. 'He's Milord's younger brother.'

'Indeed he is,' said Sid. 'He's been with the bank since before the war and I couldn't do without him.'

Although I'd have guessed Siegfried was in his early forties, I'd come to accept that normal human lifespans didn't apply to everyone in town and it was getting to the stage when I sometimes wondered whether actual humans might be in the minority. Not that it mattered because, somewhat to my surprise, I rather enjoyed living in a town with so many oddballs. As I sipped tea, I mused on my life, luxuriating in the comfort of the chair and recovering from the shock of Sid. At some point, I stopped paying attention to the conversation. I could scarcely believe I'd just described Daphne as my girlfriend and that it had felt perfectly natural, perfectly reasonable, to do so, though I barely knew her. Moreover, there was an even stranger fact. For some reason, I didn't believe I was going to screw things up with her. Something made me feel as if she might put up with me, despite my shortcomings, which were legion.

I hated that she was under threat and kept going back to whatever it was that made her a target. It was obviously something important for Sir Gerald to go to such extraordinary lengths, but why should a wealthy landowner with a working goldmine feel threatened by a widow? There had to be something and I suspected it had to be something connected with the Blacker Mountains and, if Hobbes was to be believed, some ordinary rocks. My brain, not up to sorting out such complex problems, directed me to enjoy my tea.

'Thank you for the chat,' said Hobbes, standing. 'Keep your chin up, because I believe I'm onto something and it's exciting. The only trouble is that it means I'm neglecting poor Kathy. She's come all the way from America to see me and I keep having to tell her I'm busy. I regret it, but it is necessary for the time being. On your feet, Andy.'

I would have been happy to stay there all day, but Sid rose to see us out.

'With any luck' said Hobbes, as I got to my feet, 'I will soon have good news.'

'Excellent, old boy,' said Sid, opening the door. 'I'll make sure to keep Colonel Squire in the dark, though. Goodbye.'

When we left the bank, The Shambles was already showing early symptoms of dusk; the lights were coming on and passing people were even more huddled than earlier.

'There'll be a frost later,' said Hobbes, sniffing and walking away.

'I can believe that,' I said, pulling up my collar and thrusting my hands into my jacket pocket. 'Umm ... can you explain why Sid wants to keep Colonel Squire in the dark? You can't suspect him of stealing his own gold, surely?'

'Stranger things have happened,' said Hobbes, 'but, no, I don't. I took a look at his accounts and, with or without the stolen gold, he's a very wealthy man.'

'Did he show you them? I thought he was a very private individual.'

'He didn't actually *show* me.'

'What do you mean?' I asked, for his expression suggested he'd been up to something. 'You didn't break into his house, did you?'

'I didn't break anything. I did, however, enter it.'

'Doesn't he have security? Alarms and things?'

'He has, and dogs and CCTV. It was fun getting past that lot.'

'Weren't you scared of being caught?'

'No.' He strode on, turning right past the Bear with a Sore Head.

'Why not?'

He shrugged and I could see he wasn't in the mood to say any more.

'Where are we going?' I asked, struggling to keep up.

'To make sure Kathy is alright.'

As we approached the Feathers, a group of men had gathered around a figure lying supine on the pavement outside. Hobbes ran. I followed, a horrible, sick feeling filling my stomach. Although I didn't care for Kathy, I didn't wish her any harm and, besides, I should have been looking after her, even though she seemed quite capable of looking after herself.

It wasn't Kathy. She was inside, yelling. It was Constable Poll.

'See that he's alright,' said Hobbes, pointing at the fallen constable and bursting through the door.

'Umm ... right.' I said to the crowd, 'let me through, I'm an ... umm ... interested party.'

'Wotcha, Andy,' said Billy, who was kneeling at Constable Poll's pointy end. 'You missed all the fun.'

'How is he?' I asked, squeezing between two fat men, who stank of stale beer, sweat, and cigarettes.

'He'll be alright,' said Billy. 'His breathing's fine and he's not bleeding much. I expect he'll come round soon.'

'Did Featherlight hit him?'

'Sort of, but it wasn't his fault and this guy started it.'

'Really?' Derek Poll was the most amiable, peace-loving policeman I'd ever met. 'Why?'

Billy grimaced. 'It started when Featherlight decided to impress the lady with his rat in the trousers trick.'

'He didn't!' I shuddered. 'That's disgusting. Was she impressed?'

'It certainly made an impression on her, if that's what you

mean. To start with, she actually seemed to find it amusing, but it all went pear-shaped when the head came off. Unfortunately, when she screamed, the copper was passing. He rushed in, just as Featherlight was trying to wipe the blood off her face.'

'Not with his vest?'

Billy nodded.

'Ugh! That's horrible.'

'The copper saw her trying to fend him off, jumped to the wrong conclusion, charged at Featherlight, called him a dirty, rotten scoundrel and tried to punch him on the nose.'

'I don't suppose he liked that very much.'

'No, and he looked as if he was going to flatten the copper, but the lady shook her head and he sidestepped instead.'

Constable Poll groaned and twitched.

'In that case,' I asked, 'how did he end up like this?'

'Well,' said Billy, 'he turned to have another go, but stepped in some spilt beer, skidded and fell, head-butting Featherlight's knee on the way down. The copper got to his feet, staggered into the street and passed out. It was a complete accident.'

'Why is Kathy screaming and yelling?'

'Featherlight stepped on her foot.'

I pulled a face; there was an awful lot of him.

'I don't think he did much damage,' said Billy, 'but she can't half make a fuss.'

Constable Poll, groaning again, sat up and rubbed the side of his head. 'What am I doing here? What happened?'

'You had a strop and headbutted the boss's knee,' said Billy. A couple of eyewitnesses confirmed his story.

'Oh, yes,' said Poll, 'it's all coming back.' His pale face took on an angry tinge and he moved as if to stand up. 'What on earth was he doing to poor Kathy? I'll kill him!'

'No, you won't,' said Billy pushing him back. 'Just calm down for a moment.'

'Why should I?'

'There's loads of reasons, mate. Firstly, he was only showing her his conjuring trick.'

Poll blanched again. 'Not the one with the rat in his trousers? He wouldn't!'

'He would,' said Billy, 'although I tried to warn him. The point is, he didn't mean to cause offence and was actually trying to be friendly.'

Poll shook his head. 'Is there something wrong with him?'

'I have often thought so,' said Billy. 'I think, though, he has just taken a bit of a shine to Kathy.'

'I suppose I can't blame him for that,' said Poll, still looking extremely angry, 'but you said there were lots of reasons. Tell me another, or I really will go inside and punch him.'

'Another reason is that he'd flatten you.'

Poll nodded. 'You're probably right.'

'Besides, it doesn't look good if a police officer starts a brawl in a pub over a girl.'

'Yeah. Enough. I'm calm now,' said Constable Poll, getting to his feet, swaying as if still groggy. 'Hi, Andy,' he said, noticing me for the first time, as I helped steady him.

'I'm glad you're OK, Derek,' I said, 'but that's some bump on the head you've got.'

'I'm alright,' he said, 'but you're a fine one to talk about bumps on the head. What *have* you been doing?'

I raised my hand for a tentative touch to the tender spot. 'Someone threw a brick at me.'

'And the other side?'

'Oh yeah, I'd nearly forgotten that one. Someone threw a beer tray at me.'

Poll laughed, heartlessly. 'And your knuckles?'

'I was defending a lady against a brutal attacker and had to resort to my fists.'

'Yeah,' said Poll, 'pull the other one.'

It went quiet inside the Feathers and Hobbes emerged, holding Kathy by the hand. She was crying and his face was flushed and scowling.

'Is she alright?' I asked. 'What's up?'

'I'm taking her home,' said Hobbes. 'We need some time alone.'

They walked away, turning up Vermin Street, out of sight. Featherlight appeared, rubbing his knee and looking grim.

'What's up boss?' asked Billy.

Featherlight scowled. 'Someone is going to be in big trouble.'

That was all he would say.

19

The crowd dispersed and I was left outside with only Derek Poll, who was staring at the point where Kathy had left his vision. Inside, Featherlight roared and one of the fat men burst out and ran down the road. I knew him as a regular customer, a man who knew to keep out the way until Featherlight's rage had run its course. It would not be too long.

'Kathy will be alright, won't she?' asked Poll, his brow furrowed.

'Yes,' I said, 'she'll be safe with Hobbes. He'll take care of her but there's something strange going on.'

'She's beautiful, isn't she?' said Poll, his face reddening.

I'd heard that beauty was in the eye of the beholder, but couldn't help thinking an ophthalmologist would have his work cut out curing any eye that beheld Kathy as beautiful. He seemed to be expecting a positive answer. 'Umm ... I suppose so.' I said.

'Yeah,' said Derek, 'she's some looker and she seems really nice, too.'

Unsure how to react, I nodded, though it was true that sometimes she could be quite pleasant, particularly when she wasn't throwing things at me. Still, she could not compare to Daphne, who I just couldn't imagine throwing anything in anger and, since Hobbes was so busy with Kathy, it seemed Daphne's well-being was going to be down to me again. This thought didn't make me feel heroic at all, but scared, and not scared for myself.

'What time is it?' I asked.

Poll looked at his watch. 'Quarter past five. It's getting dark early.'

'I have to go now,' I said. 'Are you sure you're alright?'

'I'm great,' he said, grinning the soppy grin of a police officer newly in love.

I might have returned a similar grin had I not thought of Denny lurking out there in the gathering dusk. Leaving Poll to his thoughts, I hurried to the museum, strange, conflicting thoughts and emotions struggling for superiority. As I jogged up Vermin Street, I caught myself scanning every shopper, every passer-by, just in case they might be Denny in disguise, but, with no sight of him, the dull ache in my stomach began to recede.

As I reached the end of Vermin Street, a young man, very much like Rupert, alighted from the Pigton bus at the stop outside the church. He was wearing a smart coat and carrying an expensive-looking briefcase and, although I was almost sure it was him, I had doubts because he now looked so prosperous. A big blue van blocked my view and, by the time it had passed, he'd vanished. I dismissed him from my thoughts. Daphne's well-being was my primary concern and, although he was probably still some sort of threat, he was not Sir Gerald or Denny.

Turning left down Rampart Street, passing the Bar Nun, I reached Goat Street and approached the museum, just as the church clock struck five-thirty: closing time. Taking up a strategic position by the door, I waited for her.

It was growing darker and I wondered whether it might be cold enough for snow. So, pulling up my collar, I tucked my hands into my pockets and stamped my feet, watching the last visitors make their way out. Shortly afterwards, some of the museum staff left. She was not among them. Still I waited until, just as the clock struck six, a young man in a duffel coat came out and started to lock the doors.

'Excuse me,' I asked, 'has Daphne Duckworth left?'

'Yeah, she went early.'

'Why?' I asked, my worry level rising.

'I think there was some sort of problem. It might have been to do with her flat.'

'Do you know where she lives?' I asked, with a rising fear.

He turned to face me, suspicion in his eyes. 'Who wants to know?'

'I do. I'm a friend.'

'If you are her friend, why don't you know where she lives?'

'Because she hasn't told me. Not yet, that is.'

'Good friends are you?'

'Yes.'

'Sure you are. I heard she had some trouble today.'

'She did, but I was the one who looked after her. I'm the good guy here and I'm worried.'

'I think I'd better call the police,' said the young man, reaching into his coat pocket and pulling out a mobile.

'Don't bother,' I said, turning away. 'You'll just be wasting their time.'

As I left him, I booted a Coca-Cola can furiously into the gutter, yet I could see his point of view. With all the bumps and bruises on my face, I probably looked a real desperado and he, no doubt, assumed he was doing her a favour.

His assumptions were irrelevant. The point was that I didn't know where to start looking for her and, since she hadn't mentioned any problems with her flat, my fear was growing into stomach-gripping panic. I had a desperate urge to do something, but, since nothing occurred, I ended up walking into Blackdog Street and pacing up and down outside the house, biting my nails and fretting. I considered getting in touch with Hobbes, but, since I had nothing definite to say, it seemed pointless worrying him about what was probably nothing, especially when he had Kathy to deal with and a gold robbery to solve.

Since I could think of nothing sensible to do, other than to wander around town in the hope of spotting her car or stumbling over some other clue, I cursed myself for not asking where she lived. The trouble was that I couldn't shut up a nasty, nagging, negative part of my brain that kept pointing out that, as she hadn't offered to tell me, she might not want me to know. Perhaps I was already expecting far too much of our relationship, if it was a relationship yet. I had past form in that respect. Despite this, and whatever her feelings were for me, if she was in trouble, I was going to help ... if I could.

Glass smashed not far away and a man shouted angrily. Fearing the worst, I sprinted along Blackdog Street and into Pound Street.

It was a false alarm. A van driver, attempting a three-point turn and failing to take account of the ladder jutting from the back of the van, had smashed an antique shop's window, and, judging by the few words from the shop's owner that weren't blasphemous, had also destroyed a rare Georgian mirror. Ordinarily, as a fan of street theatre, I might have stayed to watch. Not this time. I turned away, desperate to find Daphne, and bumped into a dark-cloaked figure.

The impact, like walking into a tree, knocked me backwards.

'Careful, young fellow,' said Sid, grinning to show off his sharp, white teeth and grabbing my arm to keep me upright.

'Thank you,' I said.

'Don't mention it. Now, why are you looking so wild?'

'I need to find a lady ...'

'I see,' said Sid, raising an inquisitive eyebrow.

'... who's in danger. At least, she might be ... I think. Her name is Daphne.'

'I take it,' said Sid, 'that the lady in question is your young lady, and that she's being threatened by Sir Gerald Payne and his wicked henchman.'

'Yes. I think she's probably at home, but I don't know where it is and I don't know who to ask.'

'Would she be Mrs Daphne Duckworth?'

'Yes,' I gasped. 'How did ...?

'A lucky guess. Daphne is not such a common name these days, but we had Mrs Duckworth open an account with us a few days ago.'

'That makes sense.' I said, hope rising. 'She's just moved here. I don't suppose you remember her address?'

'I'm afraid not; we have hundreds of customers.'

'Damn it! Wait, though, could you perhaps look it up?'

'I could, but that would take some time. There are all sorts of locks and timers and alarms to turn off before I can get into my office.'

'Oh, no.' My worry levels were rising again and, forgetting my sore and swollen knuckles, I slammed my clenched fist into my palm in frustration and yelped.

Sid wrapped his cloak around him, frowning, thinking, while my feet performed a stilted dance of frustration.

'There may be a quicker way,' he said. 'I could ask Siegfried. He remembers everything and he'll be at home now.'

'Great! Let's go.'

He hesitated, biting his lip hard enough to produce a pinprick of blood. 'I'll take you, but only if you agree to do exactly what I say.'

'Of course,' I said.

'Alright then, follow me. It's not far.'

He took me down Pound Street and turned left into Sick Hen Lane, allegedly the most ancient part of town, where small, dark houses huddled together, leaning over the cobbled street. After a few steps Sid stopped.

'Shut your eyes, please,' he said.

'What?'

'Please, do as I say. And keep them shut until I tell you to open them. Got it?'

I nodded, closing my eyes, puzzled, but trusting as Sid, grabbing my shoulders, spun me several times until I was disoriented. He nudged me forward and I might have stumbled had he not steadied me.

After a few quick strides, our footsteps echoing as if in a narrow passage, he stopped me and knocked three times on a door. After a short wait, there was a click and a creak and he guided me forward into warm air with a scent of burning logs and spice. A door closed behind us.

'You can open them now,' he said.

I was standing on time-worn flagstones in a narrow, low-ceilinged room, lit only by two small candles on a low table and a log fire blazing in a small, black grate, with three solid-looking oak chairs gathered around it. There was a pair of three-legged wooden stools beneath the heavily curtained window and an old-fashioned clock ticking on the mantelpiece. I would have been fascinated had I not been in such a hurry.

'Good evening, sir, good evening Mr Caplet,' said Siegfried, bowing. 'I am honoured you would choose to visit our humble abode.'

'Ah, Siegfried,' said Sid, returning the bow, 'it is always a pleasure. Are your brothers well?'

'Quite well, sir,' said Siegfried with a glance at the clock. 'It is just past six of the clock, so they return imminently. May I offer you some refreshment?'

'I regret,' said Sid, 'that we cannot stay long. My young friend here requires a little of your expert knowledge. He believes a young lady, one who has recently opened an account with us, may be in great danger. Unfortunately, he does not know her address.'

Siegfried studied me, his blue eyes enormous behind his glasses. 'What is the lady's name, sir?'

'Daphne Duckworth.'

'Ah, yes, I remember the lady. She is a widow, I believe, and hers is a most tragic story.'

'That's her.' I said. 'Do you know where she lives?'

'Please excuse me for one moment,' said Siegfried, closing his eyes. 'Yes, sir, I recall her address.'

'Can you tell me?'

'I should not, sir, since there is her privacy to consider.' He paused for a second. 'However, as it is an emergency, I am prepared to break my rule. She resides in Flat two, number two Spire Street, Sorenchester. Do you know where that is, sir?'

'Umm … yes, I do,' I said, overwhelmed by a tsunami of amazement. Once upon a time, in the bad old days, I'd lived in that same flat, had accidently set fire to it and come horribly close to incinerating myself and the entire block. Since then, the building (so I'd read in the *Bugle*, having never dared go back and talk to my old neighbours) had been repaired, refurbished and gentrified.

'Excellent,' said Sid. 'Thank you, Siegfried, and I bid you a very good evening.'

'Good evening, sirs,' said Siegfried, bowing low.

'Thank you,' I said.

Sid's hand grasped my shoulder. 'Alright, you know the drill. Close your eyes.'

'Of course.'

He spun me round, the door clicked open, and he nudged me forward. The door closed behind us, our footsteps echoed for a few moments and then the cold wind made me shiver. After another spin, I was allowed to open my eyes.

'Sorry I had to do that,' said Sid, 'but Siegfried and his brothers value their privacy. Now you'd better find your young lady.'

'Yes,' I said, 'I will. Thank you so much.'

With a nod of farewell he strode away, his cloak flapping, but despite the urgency, I couldn't help lingering for a few moments, my mind befuddled by the strange and quaint household I'd just visited and, although I looked hard, there was no sign of a house down a passageway. I never did discover where Siegfried and his brothers lived, and was left with an eerie feeling that, briefly, I'd stepped into the fairy realm. Yet, time was not on my side and so, steeling myself for action, I started to run, praying she was safe, hoping my fears were unfounded.

Leaving Sick Hen Lane, turning past the church, I

stampeded down The Shambles, past the offices of the *Sorenchester and District Bugle*, where the lights were still burning as the latest hot news was forged by skilled reporters and editors. I'd never really fitted in there. Sprinting along Up Way and Down Way and crossing Mosse Lane, I turned into Spire Street and slowed down. Although I was sweating and panting, I was alert by the time I reached number 2, a two-storey purpose-built block, dating from the nineteen-seventies, a modern building by Sorenchester standards. The place looked much smarter, more upmarket, than when I'd lived there.

Unable to see Daphne's car in the car park, I swore under my breath, trying to control my fear, my frustration, and to reason clearly. If she wasn't home, she might be almost anywhere and so might Denny. Yet, remembering what I'd done, I considered it quite possible that her car was being repaired. I didn't give up, thinking she might still be home. Never despair, I thought, approaching the block's front entrance.

I was immediately thwarted by an electronic system that restricted entrance to residents and invited guests, an innovation since my day. Undaunted, I pressed the bell marked Flat 2. There was no reply. I pressed again, hoping to hear the intercom crackle into life, but nothing happened. Standing back a few paces, I looked up to see there was a light on in her flat. I tried to convince myself that she was probably fine, that she'd popped out for a minute, or was taking a shower, or listening to loud music on headphones. There were all sorts of reasons why she didn't answer and yet ... and yet I couldn't rid myself of an image of her lying up there injured, or about to be injured: or worse.

A revving engine made me glance over my shoulder to see a gleaming, white Land Rover with tinted windows pulling up in the car park. My adrenalin levels reached critical as I darted behind a holly bush, out of sight, and watched Sir Gerald emerge, carrying a canvas shopping bag that, to judge by the way he was holding it, contained something heavy.

He was joined by Denny, looking particularly mean and dangerous, and something in his expression triggered a memory of a hot day not so long ago when a big bully with tattoos had dunked me in the river. The man I'd believed was the landlord of the Squire's Arms had undoubtedly been Denny and I couldn't believe I'd failed to make the connection long ago. Yet, even as I was beating myself up, I was struck by a thought. Why had he been there? Had it just been a bizarre coincidence? He couldn't have been hunting for Daphne, because she'd still been in Blackcastle. Maybe it had merely been bad luck that I'd bumped into him, for, had the road not been closed in the aftermath of the attempted gold snatch, I would almost certainly have been able to hitch a lift.

As Sir Gerald and Denny headed towards the entrance, I was pleased to see Denny limping, and felt proud to have made the bruises on his ugly face. Yet, I was puzzled by his subservient attitude, for it was quite clear who was the master. Denny pressed Daphne's doorbell, but she was still not answering. Then, looking around in as furtive a fashion as anyone his size could achieve, he reached into his coat, pulled out a crowbar and set to work on the door. After a couple of tortured creaks, it burst open and he stepped back, an unpleasant grin on his face, to allow Sir Gerald inside.

When both had entered, I was left in a quandary: would I be of more use if I rushed in after them? Or would it be better to find a phone box and call Hobbes? Or should I run to the police station and fetch help? It was a sticky situation and there was no time to weigh up the possibilities and be rational. Despite a bowel growling terror gripping me, I came to a decision. I was going to rush to the rescue, although it was more than likely that Denny would simply punch my lights out as soon as I was in range. Yet, I reasoned, I'd been lucky twice before, and I might make a difference, might buy her some time and, if I made enough noise, one of the neighbours would probably call the police. Taking a deep breath, trying to control the fear, I emerged from behind the bush and stepped towards the broken door. I would have liked to have walked with a determined stride, but, the truth was, it took all of my will power to move at all.

I had reached the entrance, vaguely aware of a car pulling into one of the parking bays and a car door slamming, when an unexpected voice called out: 'Hi, Andy.'

It was Daphne. She waved and smiled and turned as if to lock the car.

'Get back in,' I cried, running towards her, 'and drive! We have to get away from here. And quickly.'

'What's up?

'Denny is. We need to go. Now!'

I would have liked to believe it was my authoritative tone that got through to her, but honesty made me suspect it was my look of terror. With a nod, she slid into the driver's seat, started the engine, and reversed out of the parking space as I threw myself into the passenger seat. A glance over my shoulder showed Denny pounding towards us, brandishing the crowbar above his head like a battleaxe.

'Quickly!' I squeaked.

She threaded the car between two others, taking what I considered unnecessary care with Denny catching up so rapidly. As he swung for us, she put her foot down and he missed the back of the car by a cat's whisker. Still he lunged, though the danger seemed over, for we were going faster than him and our exit was just ahead. Just as escape and safety seemed inevitable, a small red car swung across the road, blocking the way out and forcing Daphne to stamp on the brake. I headbutted the windscreen, the impact sufficient to stun and bring pain to my already tender bruises. Since then I have never really questioned the value of seat belts.

Denny's cry of triumph rang in my ears and, as if in slow

motion, I turned to see him raise his crowbar and smash it down on the back windscreen. Daphne ducked as a shower of glass twisted over her. Then, as the window at her side shattered, she threw herself towards me. Denny's massive, tattooed hands reached in, one unbuckling her seatbelt, the other seizing her by the throat. He began to drag her out. Even in my dazed state, there was no way I was going to allow that sort of thing and so, grabbing his right hand, I tried to prise it off her. It had no effect whatsoever. Desperate, I lunged forward and sank my teeth into his little finger. Bellowing in pain and rage, he released her and the next thing I saw was his enormous fist powering towards my face. Shutting my eyes, raising my hands in a pathetic attempt at a block, I awaited pain that never happened.

'Urk!' he said, unexpectedly.

I thought it an odd remark.

Something smashed into the side of the car and, as Daphne flopped back into my arms, trembling as much as I was, I opened my eyes. Hobbes was leaning in at the window.

'It's alright,' I said, 'it's Hobbes.'

'Hobbes?' Her voice was weak and tremulous.

'Are you injured, madam?' he asked.

'No, not really. My throat is sore … and there's glass in my hair, but I'm OK.'

'Andy?'

'I banged my head on the windscreen, but I'll be alright in a moment.'

'Yes,' said Hobbes, 'I saw that. What have I told you about seatbelts?'

'Umm … seatbelts are for wimps?'

'No … well, I may have said it once, but I also said that you should wear one.'

'There was no time … umm … What happened to Denny?'

'Mr Barker is taking a little nap.'

'I see and Sir Gerald? He was here too.'

'I regret he didn't stay to make my acquaintance and made off in the Land Rover.'

'He and Denny broke into the flats,' I said. 'They were looking for Daphne.'

As Hobbes stood up straight, holding his side and smiling, I could feel her relax and only then did I realise I had encircled her in my arms. Since she was snuggling against me, I guessed she didn't mind.

'I suppose,' she said, 'that I should see what damage he's done.'

'Quite right, madam,' said Hobbes, wrenching open the buckled car door for her to get out.

I was very sorry when she broke away but, with a sigh, I got out as well, despite still feeling a little fuzzy round the edges. Denny was lying on his back, eyes closed, a happy smile on his ugly face and with the crowbar bent into a horseshoe around his neck. In addition to the car's shattered rear windscreen and driver's window, there was a dent in the door, about the size of Denny's head, and the inside was sprinkled with glinting diamonds of glass.

'I'd only just picked it up from the garage,' said Daphne, staring and shaking her head. 'I've had it for four years without a single problem and then I decided to come to Sorenchester ...'

'I'm sorry, Mrs Duckworth,' said Hobbes. 'I came as quickly as I could.'

'I'm really glad you did,' I said, 'but why?'

'Sid phoned to say you might need a little help.'

'That was good of him. I should have asked you, but I thought you were busy.'

'I was,' said Hobbes, 'but public safety is important. I'd better check on the flat, now I'm here, but first, I'll move Mr Barker out of the way and then we can put the cars somewhere sensible.'

He dragged Denny onto a patch of grass and left him there,

before parking both cars in marked spaces. Then, with a frown at the shattered door, he led us into the building and upstairs. Daphne's front door had been jemmied open and her sitting room was reminiscent of my old sitting room in that it was a complete mess. Everything that could have been turned over had been turned over. I had to hand it to Denny and Sir Gerald; they were fast. I doubted they'd been inside for more than a minute.

She shrugged. 'I'm just glad I wasn't here. It's only stuff. Everything can be put back or replaced.'

'Stay outside,' said Hobbes, going in, sniffing and examining things, seemingly at random. 'It would appear they were searching for something. Have you any idea what?'

'Not exactly,' said Daphne, 'but I think it may have something to do with Hugh's notes. I'm not sure.'

'Get out!' said Hobbes, turning and running at us. 'And quickly!'

'Eh? What?' I said, as quick on the uptake as ever.

Gathering us up in his great arms, he bundled us down the stairs. We'd just reached the bottom when there was a white flash, a surge of heat, a bang that made my ears ring and a hail storm of debris and dust.

He set us down outside and dusted himself off. Daphne's eyes were wide and frightened.

'What just happened?' she asked.

'A gas explosion. I haven't seen one of those for years.'

'Did they cause it?'

'That,' he said, 'would appear very likely.'

'But why? They might have killed me.'

Hobbes shrugged, and took off his coat, the back of which was smouldering. 'Without evidence or questioning them, I can't know for certain. However, it would be reasonable to speculate they were attempting to get rid of whatever they were looking for. That suggests they didn't find it and that they wanted to destroy it at any cost. I wonder if Mr Duckworth had learned the secret of the rocks?'

Dropping his coat, he stamped on it until it stopped smoking.

Faces were appearing at windows and footsteps were running towards us.

'What about the rocks?' I asked.

'Later,' he said. 'I'd better go back in and make sure everyone is safe. Stay out here, unless I call.'

He ran back up the stairs.

Daphne looked at me and smiled bravely. I put my arms around her, feeling her body shake and kissed her on the cheek. It was wet and her tears somehow made me feel like a hero. We were still hugging when the sirens announced the arrival of the fire brigade and a police car. In moments, firemen were running around, unreeling hoses.

Constable Wilkes approached. 'Are you two hurt?'

I shook my head.

'Good,' said Wilkes. 'Do you know if anyone's inside?'

'Hobbes is.'

'Oh, no, he isn't,' said Hobbes, leading a white-haired couple to safety. They looked oddly familiar, but it took a moment to recognise them as the young newlyweds who'd moved in next door to me about a month before I'd moved out. I hadn't known them, except to nod to, but they'd both had dark hair back then. Only when the woman sneezed and shed some of the whiteness did I realise they were liberally coated in a fine powder, like flour.

Hobbes went back in and returned a few moments later with a furious, dusty, frazzled ginger cat. As soon as he released it, it hissed and ran up a tree. A bunch of firemen rushed into the block, dragging hoses.

Daphne, her face streaked and puffy with tears, pulled away and turned towards Hobbes. 'Is everyone alright?'

'Besides shock and dust, they will be,' he said. 'However, I fear my coat is beyond hope.' Picking it up, he peered through a black-ringed hole about the size of his head in the back. 'I doubt even Milord will be able to do much with this.

'Oh, well, the lass has been on at me to get a new one since the Big Freeze of sixty-three, but I doubt I'll be able to get one like it now.' He shrugged. 'We'll have to find Mrs Duckworth somewhere safe for the night.'

'I'll be alright,' she said. 'I can stay in a hotel. I'll be perfectly safe now you've caught Denny.'

'I'm afraid,' said Hobbes, looking around, 'that Mr Barker may still be a threat.'

20

Denny had gone, and so had Hobbes's car.

'You should have cuffed him,' said Daphne.

'Since he'd struck his head and was unconscious,' said Hobbes shaking his head, 'I could see no reason to cuff him, as I don't condone gratuitous brutality ... or do you mean, why didn't I put him in handcuffs?'

Daphne nodded, looking confused.

'With hindsight, perhaps I should have, but I'm not sure where mine are. I think I had some once.'

'It doesn't matter,' I said, trying to get the situation back under control. 'What does matter is what happens next?'

'That's easy,' he said. 'We will go home and enjoy some supper. The situation will seem clearer on a full stomach and the lass is cooking a vindaloo tonight. Would you care to join us, Mrs Duckworth?'

Her face suggested nervousness and uncertainty.

As she hesitated, I jumped in. 'That's a really good idea. The old girl does the best curries I've ever had, much nicer than anything you'd get in a restaurant. The spices she uses are to die for.'

'I can't just turn up out of the blue. It wouldn't be fair.'

'She'll be delighted to see you,' said Hobbes.

'It's true.' I said.

Although I could tell she was far from convinced, Daphne's resistance crumbled. 'OK. That will be nice. Thank you, Inspector.'

Hobbes, with a nod, went to have a few words with Constable Wilkes and one of the firemen. He returned smiling.

'The fire's out and the gas supply has been made safe until the engineers get here and ensure everything stays that way. It appears that no major structural damage was done, although there'll need to be a proper inspection before anyone can stay in there. I'm afraid, Mrs Duckworth, that your kitchen is wrecked. The fireman says it appears that someone turned the gas on and left an incendiary device. They will investigate further.'

'What's going to happen to the other residents?' asked Daphne. 'They have nothing to do with this. It's not fair.'

'Constable Wilkes has contacted the council, who are sorting out temporary accommodation for those that need it. By the way, the next-door neighbours recognised you, Andy, and suspected you might be the culprit again. I put them right.' He chuckled.

'Why would anyone suspect Andy?'

'It's a long story,' I said, blushing.

'And an embarrassing one,' said Hobbes. 'We can talk about it later, but essentially their suspicions were based on him having previous form. We'd better get a move on. I wouldn't want our suppers to spoil.'

Although we struggled to keep up as Hobbes route marched us back to Blackdog Street, I had sufficient breath to explain how I'd set fire to my flat, and she had enough breath to laugh. For some reason, I was happy with that; it didn't make me feel like a fool, or, rather, no more of a fool than usual.

The church clock was striking half-past six as we entered 13 Blackdog Street to be greeted by a delicious, mouth-wateringly pungent aroma. Mrs Goodfellow had already set the table for the three she was expecting and Kathy was sitting there, picking at a chapatti impatiently. Hobbes introduced Daphne and, following a very quick wash and brush-up, we rearranged the seating. Mrs Goodfellow, having noticed and tutted over the state of my knuckles, applied a strange-smelling yellow ointment that provided instant, tingling relief.

When satisfied I could hold my knife and fork comfortably, she served us, Hobbes said grace and we tucked in to a totally brilliant curry, a perfect combination of flavour and fire, with the most delicious, tender, melting pork and her special rice and chapattis. Daphne, after her first taste, looked delighted and turned to thank the old girl, who had, as usual, vanished.

'You weren't joking.' said Daphne when her plate was clean. 'That really was the best curry I've ever tasted, and I've had a few.'

'Thank you,' I said, accepting the credit with due modesty. 'Mrs Goodfellow is the finest cook in Sorenchester ... and probably in the entire Cotswolds.'

Kathy, who had not said a word since we'd reached home, sniffed loudly. Although at first I assumed she was just being her usual sniffy self and was preparing to defend the old girl's cooking, she stood up before I could say anything, clutched a handful of tissues to her face, and rushed from the kitchen.

'What's up with her?' I asked.

'She's trying to come to terms with herself,' said Hobbes, looking, I thought, a little awkward and quite sad.

'What do you mean?'

'She is acquiring self-knowledge and insight, which can be a painful process. I'll talk to her when she's had chance to compose herself. In the meantime, let's go through to the sitting room and have a cup of tea.'

As we took our seats, I was grateful that he took one of the hard oak chairs, leaving Daphne and me to sit together on the sofa, where her warmth against my leg made the world a better place. Mrs Goodfellow, reappearing with a well-laden tray, beamed gummily and winked at me before taking her leave, for it was Monday evening and time for her Kung Fu class. As often happened, Dregs accompanied her, though he had little to learn about self-defence. Hobbes, having poured the tea, sat back with a sigh and took a great slurp.

'An interesting day,' he said, 'but at least nobody was seriously hurt. Still, losing my car is a nuisance, especially as Billy had only just got it for me. Oh well, I can always get another if I must and, Mrs Duckworth, if it suits you, I'll ask him to fix yours. He's very good.'

'Thank you,' said Daphne, 'I would appreciate that, but it's my flat that worries me most. It's an awful thing to happen just as I was getting it comfortable. What sort of person would do such a thing?'

'Umm ... a bad one?' I suggested.

'That's undoubtedly true,' said Hobbes, 'but it also suggests something more.'

'I don't understand,' I said. 'Wasn't it just nastiness?'

'I wouldn't have thought so,' he said. 'It strikes me that causing a gas explosion and fire is an act of desperation. The risk of being caught was high. It was fortunate you weren't home, Mrs Duckworth. Have you really no idea what they want from you?'

'No ... well yes, I sort of know, but I don't know why. Just after Hugh disappeared, Denny Barker forced his way into my house and demanded his notes. When I told him I didn't have them, he ransacked the place, but didn't find anything. He came back several times, just threatening me at first, but becoming increasingly violent when I denied all knowledge of them. The last time he turned up, I had to go to hospital.'

'Why didn't you tell the police?' I asked, maintaining a superficial calm while I was seething internally, although part of me was ecstatic that I'd managed to hurt Denny, if only a little. It felt like revenge.

'Because,' said Hobbes, 'I suspect that Mrs Duckworth had found out that Sir Gerald and Mr Barker had already rendered the local police impotent by means of bribery and terror.'

'That's right,' she said.

'But,' said Hobbes, 'you do know the whereabouts of Mr Duckworth's notes, do you not?'

She hesitated before nodding.

'Where are they?'

'Under a layer of megalodon teeth in a box in the museum's storeroom.'

'Where did you keep them before?' I asked, impressed and proud that she'd managed to thwart Sir Gerald, while at the same time my loathing for him and Denny was rising.

'In the back garden. I wrapped them in plastic bags to keep them dry and hid them in a big conifer.' She smiled. 'After wrecking the house, Denny took the shed apart and dug up the garden, but I don't think he ever thought of looking upwards and, even if he had, he wouldn't have seen much. The branches were really dense and I don't think he ever suspected.'

'Well done, indeed,' said Hobbes, his chuckle rumbling through the room. 'May I be permitted to examine the notes when we've finished our tea?'

'I'm afraid not,' said Daphne, shaking her head. 'At least, not easily. I don't have a key to the museum yet and even if I had, I haven't been briefed on how to disable the alarms. Security is quite tight. Apparently there was a break in a few months back.'

'There was,' said Hobbes, 'and Andy was of considerable assistance to me in apprehending the perpetrators.'

Although I gave him a glance conveying gratitude, he didn't acknowledge it, so perhaps he was only speaking the truth. Not that it mattered, for she favoured me with a huge smile.

'But,' he continued, 'you wouldn't mind me looking through your husband's notes when we can get to them?'

'No, not at all. I'd love to know what all the trouble has been about. Do you have any ideas?'

'I wouldn't be surprised to find it's all connected to the rocks in the Blacker Mountains.'

'What about them?' I asked.

'I'll tell you when I have confirmed my suspicions,' he said, putting his empty mug back on the tray and standing up. 'Now, I have work to do. I'm not sure when I'll be back, so, if I were you, Mrs Duckworth, I would stay here tonight. You can sleep in Andy's room and Andy can take the sofa. Look after Kathy if she comes down, please.'

'But where will you sleep?' I asked.

'Don't worry about me, I'll be fine. Goodnight.'

He left us alone.

'I don't want to turf you out of your bed,' said Daphne.

'It's alright,' I said, 'you won't have to.'

'Andy!' she said, opening her eyes wide, 'What are you suggesting?'

'Umm ... nothing ... What I ... umm ... meant was that I was turfed out of my room yesterday. I didn't mean to imply that I intend sharing it with you.'

For a moment I was worried I'd offended her. Then, she laughed and I laughed, too. Although I realised she'd been teasing, the mere idea of sharing my bed with her turned me hot and cold in turn.

'Who, exactly, *is* Kathy?' she asked, after a long pause.

'She's Hobbes's daughter,' I said. 'She turned up out of the blue a few days ago and I think she shocked him. He hadn't realised he had a daughter. Why do you ask?'

'I'm just curious. You see, I caught a glimpse of someone, who I now believe was Rupert Payne, hand something to her this morning. I'd quite forgotten with all the excitement, but I remember thinking that something ... shady was going on.'

'That's interesting,' I said, 'because I'm almost sure I saw Rupert getting off the bus this evening. He was looking very smart and prosperous, which was odd as he was sleeping rough yesterday.'

Daphne shrugged. 'Don't forget, his father is in town. The boy probably just got his pocket money.'

'Oh, yes,' I said, 'I hadn't thought of that, though last night he sounded scared of his father and I formed the impression he wouldn't dare approach him for money, because that would mean admitting he'd lost his wallet. I wonder what he was doing with Kathy. Perhaps he got money off her.'

'Who knows? You could ask her.'

'I could,' I said, 'but she can be ... unpredictable. Sometimes she's not too bad and I can tolerate her, but at other times she's awful. She's thrown things at me and been rude to Mrs Goodfellow and she's selfish and ...'

'Don't talk about me behind my back,' said Kathy, entering the sitting room and staring at me through red-rimmed eyes. 'It's not fair.' Running to the front door, she opened it and fled into the night, slamming the door behind her.

'Oh, no ...' I said, ashamed and sorry. 'I didn't mean ...' I turned to Daphne. 'I didn't think she was listening, or I wouldn't have ... I didn't mean to upset her.'

'I know.'

'I'd better go and find her. I feel somehow responsible for her.'

'I'll come too.'

'No, I'd better go alone. Hobbes said you should stay here.'

'I think he meant *we* should stay here, but, if you're going out, I'm going with you. I don't want to be left here on my own.'

Although I had a ton of misgivings, I couldn't dissuade her, and anyway, she had a point. Getting up, we put on our coats and set out.

The heavy clouds had blown away and the moon, ripening towards fullness, lit up a clear sky that still held a faint hint of pink towards the west. A man down the street was scraping ice from his car's windscreen and somewhere in the distance I could hear a gritting lorry. I wasn't at all surprised that Hobbes had been correct about the frost.

'Chilly, isn't it?' I said.

Daphne nodded, pulling up her collar. 'Any idea where she'll be?'

'No, not really. She doesn't know her way around too well. She seemed to like the Feathers, though, so we could try there first.'

We walked through town, hardly seeing anyone, except for some shivering tobacco addicts huddled outside the Barley

Mow in a cloud of smoke. On the way, I tried to prepare Daphne for the full horror of the Feathers, but it was peaceful and almost homely when we arrived. A coal fire was blazing in the fireplace and two old boys were playing darts, while Featherlight slouched against the bar, a mug of beer in one hand, shovelling pork scratchings into his mouth with the other.

'Evening, Caplet,' he said, spraying crumbs. 'And with yet another beauteous lady, I see. Welcome, my lady.'

For a moment I was nonplussed and disconcerted by his affability, but then he'd always managed a certain old-fashioned charm with women in his pub – not that there were many.

'What can I get for you, this cold evening?' he asked.

'Umm … nothing actually … the thing is, I …umm … we want to ask you a question. Is that OK?'

'If that was the question,' said Featherlight with a chuckle, 'then, yes, it was OK.'

'What?'

He sighed. 'Oh forget it. Fire away, Caplet.'

'Right … umm … have you seen Kathy?'

'Of course I have, you dolt,' he said frowning. 'What sort of stupid question is that? You brought her in here yourself.'

'No, have you seen her since then? In the last few minutes?'

'I regret I have not set eyes on the fair Kathy since Hobbes took her away.'

'Thanks.' I looked at Daphne and shrugged.

'Hiya, Andy, what's up?' said Billy, emerging from the cellar, looking dusty and pink in the face.

'We're looking for Kathy.'

'What?' Featherlight roared, the furrows in his forehead deepening. 'Why? What have you done to her? I'll smash your face in.' He took a step towards me, his face taking on a purple tinge.

'Stop,' said Daphne. 'Andy didn't do anything. She overheard something, got the wrong end of the stick and stormed out. We just want to make sure she's alright.'

Featherlight stopped. 'Sorry, my lady. I didn't mean any harm. I'm just worried about her. She's sweet, but she may have problems.'

'What sort of problems?' asked Daphne.

'Well, besides having Hobbes as a father, and hanging around with Caplet, there's the other thing.'

'What other thing?'

Looking around, lowering his voice to a whisper, he leaned towards us, smothering us in beer fumes: 'Drugs.'

'Really?' I said.

'No, not really,' said Featherlight, the purple tinge returning, 'it's the sort of thing I'm always joking about. Sometimes, Caplet, you can be a real clod!'

'Sorry,' I said. 'I didn't know. What sort of drugs?'

'How the hell would I know? Hobbes found out, though.'

'Is that why he was so angry when he came out of the pub?'

'No, it was because of the parlous state of the economy.' He shook his head. 'Of course that's why he was angry, you idiot.'

'Oh, right.' Strangely I didn't feel fear, for he was in a comparatively mellow frame of mind, thanks to Daphne's presence.

'Have you any ideas where she might be now?' she asked.

'Sorry,' said Featherlight, shaking his big head. 'My conversation with her was, alas, too brief. Why don't you ask Hobbes to find her?'

I hesitated. 'I don't think—'

'That is obvious,' said Featherlight.

'No, I don't think I should disturb him. He's really busy and there's no reason to believe she's in danger. I'd just like to find her and make sure. The only thing is, I don't know where to start looking.'

'I've an idea,' said Billy. 'If Hobbes took her drugs away, she might want to score some more.'

'She might,' I agreed, 'but I can't see how that helps.'

'It could,' said Billy.

'How?'

'Well, we had a young guy come in yesterday who I reckon was a small-time dealer. He dropped his wallet and I found it when I was cleaning up. It was stuffed with cash.'

'That was Rupert Payne,' I said, 'but just because he had money doesn't mean he's a drug dealer.'

'Of course not,' said Billy, 'but I know something about dealers. I've met a few in my time and, well, he gave off that vibe. So what I'm trying to say is that if you can find the guy, you might find her as well.'

'It's a possibility,' I said, 'but we have no idea where he might be. I thought I saw him near the church a couple of hours ago, but he could be anywhere by now.'

'We haven't anything else to go on,' said Daphne, 'so we might as well start there. He might still be around, or someone might have seen him.'

'It's worth a try,' I said. 'Let's go.'

Featherlight nodded. 'You do that. We'll keep an eye out for her back here.'

'The way I see it,' I said, as we walked out into the freezing night, 'Rupert can be dangerous, so it might be better if I take you home before looking for him.'

She shook her head. 'You don't get rid of me that easily.'

'I don't want to get rid of you—'

'I'm glad to hear it.'

'—but I'd rather you were somewhere safe.'

'And I'd rather you were somewhere safe, but we ought to find her and we'll be alright together. No more arguments.'

'Oh ... umm ... alright,' I said, unsure that I felt good about this. Then again, it meant she would be with me.

As we walked back along Vermin Street, I was too nervous to talk and Daphne seemed to feel the same way. The streets were almost deserted and the church was in darkness. The church hall's windows, by contrast, glowed bright with electric light, while yells, screams and thuds penetrated the walls.

'That,' I said, 'sounds like Mrs Goodfellow's martial arts class.'

'Isn't she a bit old for that sort of thing?'

'You'd think so, but she's the teacher and enjoys it. Mind you, it's possible it's her marital arts class.'

'You're joking ... aren't you?'

'No, she really does teach marital arts. It started with a printer's error and she didn't want to disappoint people.'

Laughter steamed from her mouth. 'Liar!'

I couldn't blame her, though the story was entirely true.

'We could try there.' I pointed to an alley, which led to Church Fields.

She nodded and hand in hand we walked into it, only a faint glimmer from somewhere ahead to show our way through the darkness. Neither of us spoke, both of us on tiptoe, trying to make as little noise as possible, though I wasn't sure why. When something moved deep within the shadows ahead, Daphne gasped and I pushed her behind me, but it turned out to be nothing more than a fat ginger tom cat, who swaggered past, his insolent eyes radiating indifference to our pounding hearts. Breathing heavily, we continued through the crushing gloom until we were in Church Fields, where the pale light of a single, old-fashioned lamppost revealed a nightmare landscape of ancient gravestones and crumbling tombs.

I could honestly say that I wasn't nervous. I was, in fact, suddenly terrified, reminded of the time, albeit in a different churchyard, when a pair of grave-robbing ghouls had tried to bury me. Back then, Hobbes had dissuaded them with a well swung shovel, but he wasn't with us and neither, fortunately, were the ghouls. I doubted they went there because the medieval bones beneath Church Fields had surely crumbled to dust long ago.

Squeezing Daphne's hand to reassure us, I whispered: 'No one's here. Let's move on.'

'Let's,' she murmured.

We walked away, heading by the back of the church and plunging into total darkness beneath a massive yew tree, a tree Hobbes had once told me pre-dated the church by centuries. A layer of dry needles muffled every sound and all I could hear was our breathing. I began to think we were on a wild goose chase.

Far away, someone screamed.

'Did you hear that?' I asked, hoping she'd say no, hoping I'd imagined it.

'Yes,' she said, getting even closer.

'Do you think it might have been a fox?' I asked, grateful for her presence. I could feel at least one of us was trembling.

'No.'

'Nor do I. I suppose we'd better go and see what's happening. Maybe it's just kids mucking about.'

'On a night like this?' she said. 'Someone's in trouble and it might be Kathy. Come on, I think it came from over there.'

We ran from the tree's cover, and there was just enough light from the moon to make out the broad lawns that were leading us down towards Church Lake. My stomach, already tight with worry, contracted when another scream rang out.

'That didn't sound like a woman,' said Daphne.

There was a yell, a splash and a white flash of disturbed water. As we neared the edge, I saw an arm emerge some way out, followed by a head and another arm. The arms flailed wildly and slid beneath the surface.

'I think someone's fallen in,' I remarked, as perceptive as ever.

'No, he couldn't have. He's too far out.'

She was right again, for when the head reappeared, I realised it was probably ten metres from the bank.

'Perhaps he jumped?' I said doubtfully.

'A long jump, but it doesn't matter. We have to help.'

'Umm … yeah … how?' I asked as we reached lake side, both of us breathing hard, the ground getting soggy.

'Could we throw something?' asked Daphne. 'If we can't, someone will have to wade out to him, unless there are any boats?'

'Not at this time of year. What could we throw?'

'Isn't there a lifebelt around here somewhere?'

'Yes, there is,' I cried, thinking back to a lazy summer afternoon. 'There's one over by the bench. At least, there was in August. Let's get it.'

We turned and ran along the bank where, missing my footing I stumbled in, gasping as extremely cold water filled my shoes, but fortunate it was only ankle deep. I scrambled out, my feet squelching, and we continued towards the bench, finding the lifebelt hanging on a post. As I grabbed it, the man yelled again, a frightened, panicky cry and we hurried back to the water.

'Throw it!' said Daphne as I tried to gauge the distance.

Once, twice, three times I swung, building up a good momentum before hurling it with a cry of encouragement.

It was a good throw again: far too good. There was a thud, a splash, a groan, and silence.

'I think,' said Daphne, 'that you hit him. And shouldn't you have held onto one end of the rope?'

'Damn it,' I stepped into the dark water, 'I'll have to wade.'

It didn't feel quite so shockingly cold as it had done the first time, or, rather, it didn't until it reached my knees. I hoped it wouldn't get much deeper.

'Careful!' said Daphne.

I looked back over my shoulder, nodded and took another step. At least, I intended to. Instead, my feet sank into the ooze and were gripped in its soft, clinging embrace, preventing any movement, other than a wild windmilling of my arms that only ended when I fell, face first. I came up, spluttering and gasping and all I wanted was to be back on solid ground. Had Daphne not been there, I would probably have given up. Instead, I decided to play the hero and swim to the rescue. I soon discovered that my heavy overcoat and tweed jacket had other ideas, restricting all movement in my arms so that it was like trying to swim in a straitjacket. I was barely making any progress and, where a more sensible man might have turned back and stripped off, I continued, floundering and gasping.

'I'm coming,' I yelled between breaths, even though I could no longer see the casualty. 'Where are you?'

'Go away.'

The voice was familiar.

'Rupert?'

'Sod off. You hit me in the face.'

Still, I kept going, although the cold was getting to me, stabbing into muscles that were already crying out for oxygen and finding my gasping lungs weren't up to the task. At last I spotted him. Grasping the life belt, he was kicking for the far shore for all he was worth.

A couple of minutes later, I was in trouble.

'Have you found him yet?' shouted Daphne.

My chest felt as if it was being crushed and all I could manage was a feeble whisper: 'I think I might need help.'

Rupert meanwhile, ignoring, or, to be charitable, ignorant of, my plight, was dragging himself from the lake. Icy water splashed my face and shot up my nose and it struck me how much easier it would be to swim if I took off my coat. Although my hands were too cold to be cooperative, I trod water and, following a brief struggle, undid the buttons. Buoyed by my success, I tried to wriggle from its smothering embrace, only to have it pinion my arms behind my back. The more I struggled, the more it seemed to push me under and the earthy, stagnant flavour of lake water filled my mouth. I raised my face to breathe, the coat over my head and it wasn't long before I realised I was losing the fight. As the dark waters closed over me again, I kicked frantically back to the surface, managing half a breath of air. It wasn't nearly enough and it took all my failing will power not to breathe water as I went down again. Though not prone to panic, I came close in the next few seconds. I really thought this was it, the end of Andy.

Just before despair gripped me, a hand did, seizing my collar, supporting me and keeping my head above water. I flapped like an idiot and tried to grab whoever was there until a sharp slap on my cheek knocked some sense back into me.

'I've got you,' said an authoritative female voice. 'Lie back, relax and let me do the work.'

Still supporting me, she whipped off the overcoat, turned me onto my back and towed me towards the shore.

'Is he alright?' asked Daphne.

'I guess,' said Kathy, 'though why he wanted to undress himself in the middle of a lake beats me. Sometimes he's an idiot.'

'I was trying to rescue Rupert,' I said through chattering teeth.

'That was Rupert?' said Daphne.

'Yes. I thought I'd knocked him out with the life belt.'

'I hope you knocked the punk's teeth out,' said Kathy. 'Can you stand now?'

'Umm ... yeah.'

'So, why don't you?'

I put my feet down and we waded to shore, where Daphne helped us out.

'What happened out there?' she asked. 'I couldn't see you properly and then you started splashing.'

'Tell her on the way home,' said Kathy, 'otherwise we'll freeze our butts off.'

My tale of woe was apparently much funnier in the telling than it had felt at the time, and my chattering teeth only added to the amusement. I wasn't half glad to get back to Blackdog Street. Unfortunately, my front door key was still in my coat pocket and my coat was still in the lake. I stood and shivered while Kathy rang the bell. It seemed a long time before Mrs Goodfellow, still pink from her exertions at Kung Fu, answered the door.

'Have you two been swimming?' she asked. 'You'd better come in at once and warm up. I'll get you some towels and put the kettle on.'

Kathy and Daphne helped me into the light and the warmth and the night was shut out. I enjoyed a wonderful hot bath and a cup of cocoa before being tucked up in my bed. Daphne kissed me on the cheek and the light went out. It had been an eventful day and that last act made all the pain and the fear seem worth it.

21

A knock on the front door catapulted me from bed, instantly awake, alert, fearing that Denny had found us. I stumbled into a pair of trousers and was still fumbling with the buttons as I rushed downstairs.

'Hello,' said Mrs Goodfellow, opening the door, 'can I help you?'

'Good morning,' said a soft voice that seemed strangely familiar and had an accent similar to Daphne's.

Since it was a woman, my fears were partially assuaged and I continued down at a safer pace, ensuring my trousers were properly secured.

'I'm sorry to disturb you, but I wondered if you might know something about my friend.'

'I wonder if I might,' said Mrs G.

'The thing is, that I passed her flat this morning, but there was police tape everywhere. A nice policeman said there'd been a gas explosion, but that no one had been injured and that Inspector Hobbes might help me find her. Do I have the right address?'

'You do,' said Mrs G, 'but, unfortunately, he's out.'

She was talking to a slightly plump, blonde woman with enormous blue eyes, who was wearing a long, pink coat with a pink fur collar, pink trousers and pink shoes. I instantly recognised her as Pinky of Pinky's Tearoom and, although she'd seemed very pleasant back then, I was suspicious.

'What's your friend's name?' asked Mrs Goodfellow.

'It's Duckworth … Daphne Duckworth. Do you know where she might be?'

'Don't tell her,' I said, as I reached the front door.

'Why not, dear?'

'Because, for all we know, she might be working for Sir Gerald.'

Pinky's look of puzzled recognition, twisted into one of anger. 'I would never work for that loathsome man. What's he been doing?'

Although she sounded sincere and I was inclined to believe her, I wasn't yet prepared to take the risk.

'I'm sorry,' I said, 'but we must be careful.'

'You seem familiar. Haven't I seen you somewhere before? Weren't you in Blackcastle?'

I nodded.

'Do you know her?'

'Yes, we're friends.'

'Aren't you the so-called tourist who found Hugh's remains?' Now she was sounding suspicious.

'How do you know about that?'

'She told me. She didn't tell me you were friends though. In fact, I had the impression she didn't much like you.'

'Things have changed since then.'

'Well,' said Mrs Goodfellow, 'you'd better come in, rather than letting all the heat out. Then maybe we can help you.'

Although Pinky still looked suspicious, Mrs G's gummy smile seemed to reassure her. 'Alright.' She stepped inside.

'You'd better get dressed, dear.'

Suddenly embarrassed by my naked torso, I fled upstairs.

When I came back down, washed, shaved and dressed in the neatly pressed clothes that had been laid out for me, Pinky was on the sofa sipping a mug of tea. She looked up and smiled.

'Mrs Goodfellow explained about you and Daphne.'

'Good. I'm Andy Caplet. Andy.'

'And I'm Lillian Pinkerton. Most people call me Pinky. Nice to meet you again.

'After what I've just been told, I can understand why you were wary, but, if you give her a call at work, you'll be able to trust me. We've been friends since she and Hugh moved into Blackcastle.'

'I don't have her number.'

'But you do have one of these.' Putting down her mug and getting to her feet, she went to the telephone table, pulled out the directory and opened it. After running her finger down the page, she picked up the phone and dialled.

'Good morning,' she said. 'Could you put me through to Mrs Duckworth, please?'

After a moment, she handed me the phone.

'Hello?' said Daphne, her voice electronically flattened, 'is anybody there?'

'Yes, it's me ...'

'Andy! How are you today?'

'I'm fine, but ... umm ... do you know Lillian Pinkerton?'

'Pinky? Of course. She's a good friend. Why do you ask? Has something happened?'

'No, nothing's happened. It's just that she's with me now.'

'At the inspector's house? Why?'

'She came to make sure you were alright.'

'That's nice. Can you put her on?'

I handed back the phone and, leaving them to talk, headed to the kitchen in a quest for tea and breakfast, for I was still muzzy headed and would have preferred to go back to bed for an hour or so. The events of the previous night were trying to resurface from the depths of my mind, but I forced them back under. They would have to wait until I was ready.

There was fresh tea in the pot, but I was reduced to making my own breakfast, since Mrs Goodfellow was rushing out, claiming to have a dental appointment. I didn't wish to doubt her but, since all her own teeth, plus countless others, were kept in jam jars, it sounded unlikely. Still, it was none of my business, so, cutting a couple of slices of bread, grilling them until they were nicely brown, plastering them with fresh butter and marmalade, I sat down to eat. Although I regretted the lack of bacon and eggs, I could not really feel hard done by, for the old girl's marmalade was the best. It was a mystery how she did it, for I'd watched her make it and she hadn't appeared to use anything other than oranges and sugar, yet the flavours she produced just tingled the tongue and set the palette on fire.

'Daffy says Inspector Hobbes is with her,' said Pinky, standing in the kitchen doorway.

'Oh ... right. He wanted to take a look at something.'

'Yes, Hugh's notes, so she said. Do you have any idea why?'

She walked over and took a seat, facing me across the table.

'It's apparently something to do with rocks,' I said, after swallowing the last crumbs.

'Rocks?'

'Yes, I think there must be something terribly important about the rocks in the Blacker Mountains.'

'I doubt it,' said Pinky, shaking her head. 'They're just rocks.'

'Umm ... yeah. That seems to be what's significant about them, though I haven't a clue why. I think Hobbes was hinting that there's some sort of connection between them and why Sir Gerald wants Hugh Duckworth's notes destroyed, but it didn't make any sense to me.'

Hearing the front door open and shut, I assumed Mrs Goodfellow had forgotten something, or that Hobbes had returned.

'It might, you know,' said Pinky, looking thoughtful.

'How?'

'Well, I heard Sir Gerald has reopened the old gold mine.'

'He has,' I said. 'So what?'

'So, perhaps the rocks contain gold ore. Does gold come as an ore?'

'I don't know. I thought it came in nuggets. But Hobbes said there was nothing unusual about the samples he took from the mine. He said they were just ordinary rocks, like all the others in the Blacker Mountains, and ordinary rocks don't have gold in them.'

'In which case,' said Pinky, 'how can the Paynes have a gold mine?'

'That's a good point,' I said.

'Inspector Hobbes is the one that was on the telly? The one that chased down the gold thieves, isn't he?'

'That's right.' A thought struck me. 'You don't suppose there's a connection between the rocks and the robbery?'

Pinky shrugged. 'I don't know, but it might explain why Sir Gerald was getting so desperate. I mean, what if his gold mine was a sham?'

'You mean,' I said, 'that it could be a cover? A way of making stolen gold seem legitimate?'

'Maybe. I don't know.'

'It sounds a little far-fetched, doesn't it?'

'Does it? It could explain what's been going on. Hugh was always keen on his geology so what if he'd discovered the mine was a fake? Might that be why Sir Gerald killed him?'

'But *I* didn't kill him,' said a deep drawl from the kitchen door.

Shocked, I leapt to my feet, banging my knees on the table. I rubbed them and stared, open-mouthed, at Sir Gerald.

'Good morning, Pinky,' he said. 'I see you've put on weight. Such a shame. There was a time when you were quite … acceptable.

'And it is regrettable to find you in such low company. Do you know this fool takes his holidays in the Blacker Mountains, and pretends he's up there on his own? As if he could last five minutes!'

'How did you get in?' I asked, ignoring the insults, something I was used to.

He held up a key.

'That's mine! How did you get it?'

'That should be obvious, even to an idiot like you. Quite clearly, it was in the pocket of your coat, which Denzil fished from the lake. By the way, your antics last night were most entertaining and you were lucky Hobbes's daughter rescued you.'

I hung my head, ashamed that until then, I hadn't spared Kathy a single thought or shown any gratitude for what she'd done.

Pinky got to her feet. 'What are you doing here, Gerry?'

'I could ask you the same question, Pinky.'

'She's a guest,' I said, 'and you are not. Give me my key, please, and leave the house.'

'That's not very welcoming. Wouldn't you like to know why I'm here?'

'Why are you here?'

'I'm so glad you want to know. Please, both of you, sit down.'

Pinky sat back down, fear and loathing in her big, blue eyes. Still rubbing my bruised knees, I hobbled towards my chair.

'Take your time,' said Sir Gerald.

'Are you both sitting comfortably?' he asked, when I'd finally planted myself on the seat. 'Then I'll begin. I'm here because I wish to obtain Hugh Duckworth's notes.'

'We don't have them,' I pointed out, confused and afraid that Denny would not be far away.

'I'm aware of that. Mrs Duckworth has them and that uncouth fellow Hobbes is with her.'

'So, what do you want from us?'

'I would like you to pass a message to him.'

'If I were you,' I said, 'I would leave here before you anger him. He can be dangerous and you underestimate him at your peril.'

Sir Gerald smiled. 'I don't underestimate him, or overestimate him. I know his sort. Denzil has, after all, been in my family for years and I expect Hobbes is much like him – strong in the arm, but weak in the head.'

'What do you mean his sort?'

'The Evil Ones. The Mountain Folk,' said Sir Gerald. 'Call them what you will, they're the last of a dying breed that few will miss when they finally die out for good. But, I have to say, Denzil has proved most useful.'

'Evil Ones? Mountain Folk? What are you talking about?'

'The vagrants that used to infest our mountains. Now, kindly stop your blathering. I want you to pass this message to Hobbes.'

'What?'

'Tell him his daughter will come to no harm if he does precisely what I say.'

'What have you done to her?' I said, bouncing back to my feet and taking a step towards him. At least I had the satisfaction of seeing his eyes widen in alarm. He was obviously aware of my violent tendency.

'Calm yourself,' he said, recovering his composure in an instant. 'She's fine. Nothing has happened to her, and I hope nothing will. Tell Hobbes to bring Duckworth's notes to the Squire's Arms at Northsorn at three o'clock this afternoon. Tell him to come alone and that any funny business might have a serious effect on the lady's well-being. Finally, he's not to tell anyone. I have eyes and ears all around the town and, should he try anything stupid, I'll know, and, let's say, there will be consequences.'

'But,' I said, 'what's the point? Hobbes will have read the notes. He'll have worked out what's going on. What's more,' I pointed to Pinky, 'we know.'

'What Hobbes might think he knows is of no consequence without the evidence, and you know nothing, except for wild speculation. Besides, I happen to be friends with the right sort of people, who can ensure nobody will ever believe your malicious attacks on an honourable family. Not that anyone would be likely to believe you anyway. Let's see, we have Pinky, a woman seething with resentment, and you, a failed reporter for a pathetic local rag, a complete incompetent. Oh, no, you'll not be any problem.'

'You may be right,' I said, 'but can you tell me something?'

'Try me.'

'If you didn't kill Hugh Duckworth, who did?'

'Let's just say it was his curiosity. Those mountains are dangerous and anyone who fails to take sufficient care can quickly come to grief.'

'But how did he die?'

'Painfully, but quite quickly. Now, that's enough banter. You're boring me. Tell Hobbes what I said.

'Goodbye, Pinky, darling. It's such a shame to see what time and spite have done to you. I'll let myself out. Nice to have made your acquaintance again, Mr Caplet.'

Tossing me the key, he turned and walked away. The front door opened and shut.

'Are you alright?' I asked.

Pinky was trembling and deathly white. She nodded. 'It's just that I hate him so much.'

'Any particular reason?'

'There are many reasons. Too many. You'd better get that message to the inspector quickly and I hope his daughter's alright. I don't trust Gerry and, if he's here, Denny Barker won't be far away and he really is dangerous.'

'He was hanging around yesterday,' I said, and couldn't stop myself adding: 'We had a couple of encounters and I knocked him down.'

'You did? How?' asked Pinky, sounding a little sceptical.

'Umm … I jumped out of a window onto his head when he was trying to kidnap Daphne and then I knocked him down again.' I showed her my knuckles, which were still raw, though the swelling and soreness had subsided.

Although she nodded and looked impressed, it seemed she didn't quite believe me. I suspected her doubts were nothing compared to mine about my well-being should I ever encounter Denny again and yet, at that moment, my fears for my safety were nothing like my worries for Kathy.

'When you see Hobbes,' said Pinky, 'you'd better warn him

that Sir Gerald is a devious man and it sounds to me as if he's setting a trap.'

'Does it? You might be right, but he'll know what to do. I hope. I'll get my coat ... oh, no, it's still in the lake ... I'll go and find him. He's probably still at the museum.'

'Or you could use the phone,' she said.

'Oh yes. I never think of that.'

We hurried through to the sitting room. I called the museum and, within five minutes, Hobbes, accompanied by a very excited Dregs, burst through the front door. I introduced them both to Pinky, whose evident nervousness at the sight of them was not helped by the ravages of Dregs's tongue, despite my best efforts to keep her dry, or by the heavy, blood-stained, brown paper bag in Hobbes's hand. His feral scent was far stronger than usual and he was twitching, with a wild expression in his dark eyes.

'Welcome to Sorenchester, Miss Pinkerton,' he said and turned to me. 'Spread some papers in the corner and get her out of here ... and quickly. I have a bone to pick.'

Knowing what was coming, I threw a few copies of the *Bugle* onto the carpet, went to grab my coat, remembered where it was, and bundled a bewildered Pinky into the street.

'What's happening?' she asked.

'You don't want to know.'

'I do.'

'Umm ... it's quite warm today, isn't it? I mean compared to yesterday.'

'Don't try to change the subject. What's wrong with him?'

I was unsure how to respond, for I knew that Hobbes, having bought himself a large, raw marrowbone, had undoubtedly already pounced on it, like a leopard onto a tender young antelope, and was crunching it up in his great jaws. Having witnessed the whole process, I found it disgusting and terrifying and made sure to keep out of the way whenever the fit came over him.

'Sorry,' I said at last. 'The thing is, he has his own way of working off stress and it's best to avoid him until it's all over. We should give him half an hour.'

She frowned. 'He's going to crunch up a bone, isn't he?'

'Eh?' I said, confused. 'How would you know?'

'He's one of the Mountain Folk, like Denny Barker, isn't he? I've been there when Gerry threw Denny a bone to entertain his guests.'

'I think I know where you're coming from,' I said, 'because that's what he'll be doing, but Hobbes is one of the good guys. I thought he was unique, until recently.'

'But he looks like Denny and no one else I know eats raw bones. There's something about them, something weird, something dangerous.'

I nodded. 'Hobbes is certainly weird and he might be dangerous sometimes, but he's the best I know. Do you really think he's like Denny?'

'Absolutely.'

'Wow.' I paused, letting the thought sink in. 'Look, do you want to get a coffee or something while we wait?'

'No, I've just had a cup of tea,' said Pinky. 'We could go and see Daphne.'

'She's at work,' I said. 'It's a new job and she hasn't really had a very good start. I think we should give her some peace.'

Instead, we strolled around town for the next half hour or so and I told her everything that had happened to Daphne recently. To my regret, Pinky was far more interested in my accident with the baked bean tin and my near disaster in the lake than with my heroic battles with Denny. She told me a little about herself, claiming she was thirty, though I'd have guessed she was a good few years older than that, that she'd lived in Blackcastle all her life and that she was divorced.

We glimpsed Featherlight riding a bicycle that was far too small for him at the far end of Vermin Street.

'There's another of them!' she said, pointing. 'Until I came here, I really thought Denny was the last of them and now I find two others within a matter of minutes!'

'But, what are they?' I asked.

'The Mountain Folk?'

'Yes.'

We carried on walking and had turned down the Shambles when, stopping to look at a hat shop's window display, she took a deep breath. 'I don't know really. For a long time, I thought they were just a legend … a story to frighten the kids and I really don't know much.'

'You know more than I do.'

'OK, this is what I remember, though I'm not sure how much is true anymore, because most of what I know came from my granddad, who used to work for Sir Digby, Gerry's grandfather. Sometimes, when he'd knocked back a few beers, he'd tell me tales of the Mountain Folk.

'They used to turn up from time to time, though there were never that many of them and they mostly kept themselves to themselves, except at the end of summer when they'd find work with the farmers, taking in the harvest, or in the spring, when they'd help with the shearing. They were hard workers, good with animals and skilled with their hands. Granddad reckoned they built all the drystone walls in the area.'

'They must have been very useful,' I said.

'I suppose they were, but people were suspicious of them. They used to camp under Blacker Knob, which had an evil reputation.'

'People are often suspicious of anything different.' I said. 'I was suspicious of Hobbes once and, even now I'd call him a friend, he can sometimes terrify me, although he's got me out of sticky situations so many times.'

Pinky nodded, a lock of blonde hair falling over her eye. Brushing it aside, she fixed her gaze on a livid pink pixie hat. 'People began to say that they stole things, that they spoiled food, soured milk and swapped their offspring for human babies. What was more, they never attended church and it was rumoured that they were fiends, in league with the Devil. That's why some called them the Evil Ones.'

'Hobbes sometimes goes to church,' I said, feeling weirdly that I should be protecting him and his kind. 'He always goes on Remembrance Sunday. He was in the Great War and won a Victoria Cross.'

I feared I'd said too much, but she didn't appear surprised.

'That just convinces me he's one of them, because Granddad said they lived much longer than other men. When he was young, he sometimes used to work with Denny Barker and he reckoned Denny was the last of them.'

'What happened to the others?'

She shook her head. 'I really don't know. Granddad would always change the subject when I asked. All he'd say was that they'd gone away. It was my impression that something bad had happened and I tried to get some answers from the other old boys. They would never say much, but one suggested I might find something in the Parish records.'

'Did you?'

'I tried, but it turned out that they'd been burned when the old town hall caught fire.'

'When was that?'

'During the Second World War.'

'Was it bombed?'

She laughed. 'No, I don't think Blackcastle was ever of any strategic importance ... or of any sort of importance at all. According to the *Blacker Times* archive from 1941, the cause of the fire was a mystery. It was put down to faulty wiring, though there was some suspicion of arson. That's really all I know about the Mountain Folk. It's not much.'

'Maybe not, but it's interesting. I've often tried to work out what Hobbes is exactly. I can't tell you how much of a shock it was when I first realised he wasn't strictly human. I wonder if he knows anything about them?'

'Ask him.'

'That wouldn't work,' I said, shaking my head. 'He doesn't normally like to talk about the past … his past anyway … and I wouldn't even have found out that he'd won the Victoria Cross if I hadn't been a bit nosy. On the other hand, Mrs Goodfellow likes to talk about him. He adopted her you know?'

Pinky turned from the window to face me. 'Although that seems so wrong, because she looks so much older than him, I can believe it.

'Do you think he's finished his bone yet?'

A glance up Vermin Street to the church clock tower showed the time was approaching midday. 'Probably. Let's go.'

When we got back, Mrs Goodfellow was tidying up the newspapers while Hobbes was upstairs, roaring and singing in the shower. Dregs was barking in the back garden.

'Hello, dear,' said Mrs Goodfellow as we walked in. 'Would your friend like to stay for dinner?'

'Umm … I don't know. I hadn't thought. Umm …Would you?'

'Thank you,' said Pinky, 'but I can't. I have an appointment with my bank at one.'

'Isn't that a bit inconvenient?' I said. 'Why here?'

'I'm thinking of moving here and opening a new café. The thing is, there's not much trade in Blackcastle and Gerry has put the rent up again. I have no intention of filling that bastard's coffers any more.'

'But why here?'

'Because I have a friend here.' She glanced at her watch. 'I'd best be on my way. I'm not quite sure where to go.'

'Which bank?'

'Grossman's. I figured that, since they'd had two robberies, they'd probably tightened up security.'

'We passed it earlier. It's halfway down The Shambles, not far from the hat shop.'

'Thank you,' she said and took her leave.

A few minutes later Hobbes reappeared, looking clean, relatively civilized, and tidy. He was chuckling and grinning.

'What's up?' I asked.

'I have my car back. It was abandoned on Green Way.'

'Good. What are you going to do about Kathy? Shouldn't you be doing something now?'

'All in good time. Firstly though, I'm going to do the crossword and the Sudoku and then it'll be lunchtime. The Butcher of Barnley delivered some of his best pork and leek sausages last night and the lass is making toad in the hole.'

'Last night? Doesn't he always deliver punctually in the afternoons?'

'Normally, but he was delayed.'

'Really? Why?'

'He slipped and sat on the mincer. It meant he got a little behind in his sausage making.'

'Sounds painful.'

'Probably.' He chuckled again.

'Are you joking?'

He winked. 'The point is, I like a good toad in the hole, his sausages are excellent and the lass makes a great batter.' He patted his stomach. 'I'll need a good dinner to set me up for this afternoon.'

'You've still got room after that bone?'

'Of course. Picking a bone just piques my appetite. I'm surprised more people don't try it.'

I couldn't stop myself shuddering, being a little squeamish when it came to raw meat. This, I suspected, dated back to the time when I was a small boy, and Mother had attempted to quick roast a joint of beef she'd only just removed from the freezer. The result had been a crumbling outer layer of charcoal, with cold, bloody meat inside and a core that was still solid. It hadn't stopped her serving it and the sight of bright red mashed potato and the taste of iced blood had made me vomit on the table. I reassured myself, because, with Mrs

Goodfellow in charge, there would be no similar problems. My only slight worry was that Hobbes, in his weirdly euphoric mood, might slip a real toad onto my plate.

Sitting down on the sofa, he reached for the *Bugle* and a pen and started scratching at the crossword. I couldn't believe how relaxed he was. My nerves were jangling and I just wanted to rush out and rescue Kathy, though I didn't understand how Sir Gerald had got his hands on her.

'What are you going to do?' I asked, sitting down beside him. 'And can I help?'

'I intend,' he said, 'to visit the Squire's Arms at the appropriate time and pick her up. I don't want you there, because Sir Gerald requested me to go alone. Hmm ... it's tricky.'

'It could be a trap.'

'I think it's probably apatosaurus.'

'What?' I said.

'Five across: a large plant-eating dinosaur of the Jurassic period ... apatosaurus.' He filled in the squares and frowned.

'Oh, I see. But you ought to take precautions this afternoon.'

He glanced up. 'Ought I? Why?'

'Well, it might be dangerous.'

'I do hope so. Stilton. So, that means two down must be titular.'

Getting up, I left him to his puzzle and paced about the house until Mrs Goodfellow called us through. The toad in the hole was so magnificent, the batter so light and fluffy, the sausages so robust and satisfying, the gravy so aromatic and delicious that it took my mind off poor Kathy and what Sir Gerald and Denny might have in store for Hobbes. But afterwards, a mug of tea in my hand, my nerves returned, for it was my opinion that he was being far too complacent. I decided that, whatever he thought, I would be close at hand. My idea was to stow away in the car boot.

When he went upstairs to put on his boots, I took my

opportunity. I rummaged in his coat pocket for the keys, sneaked outside, opened the car boot, rushed back inside and returned the keys.

'I'm just going out for a walk,' I said casually, as he came downstairs. 'I hope Kathy's alright.'

'Thank you,' he said. 'I'll see you later.'

Hurrying into the street, I climbed into the boot and pulled down the lid, making sure it didn't quite click. It was smelly in there, as if the previous owner had used it for transporting manure and, as it was also uncomfortably cramped, it didn't take much time before I felt I'd already been there too long. I was just beginning to wonder whether I was making a huge mistake when I heard a car pull up nearby.

'Wotcha,' said Billy.

'Afternoon,' said Hobbes. 'Thanks for coming.'

Dregs was sniffing and scrabbling at the boot. It suddenly clicked shut.

'Let's go,' said Hobbes, his voice muffled. 'And quickly.'

Billy's car drove away down Blackdog Street, leaving me a prisoner.

22

Although I'd have been the first to admit to having made some rotten plans in my time, this one was turning out to be a real stinker. Hobbes was gone and I feared he was walking blindly into a trap, and I was going to be as helpful to him as whatever it was that was sticking into my back. There was some comfort in knowing that Billy was taking him and that Dregs would also be there, although, after what he'd done to Denny, his presence might only make matters worse. I hoped Billy would keep out the way. He was far too small to be of any use.

Unable to see anything, other than a fringe of faint light around the top of the boot, I groped around as much as I could, which wasn't much, since I was pinned down. Even so, my hands explored wherever they could reach, hoping to chance on some sort of release mechanism and, despite starting with hope, I was soon entering the realms of despair, especially when my shoulders began to cramp.

Forcing myself to relax, taking long, deep breaths, I tried to think. My first thought was that I was well stuck. The second was that I was stuck in an embarrassing situation. The third was that this was not the time to think useless thoughts. Somehow, I had to find a way to get out and, furthermore, I had to do this sooner rather than later, for it was already getting stuffy in there and I was starting to worry about how well sealed it was and how much oxygen might be left. I tried to imagine what Hobbes would do and came to the simple conclusion that he would not have put himself into such a stupid situation in the first place.

Although everything, other than my own breathing, was muffled, I could still make out sounds from the street, which I assumed meant that passers-by would hear me, should I make sufficient noise. Even so, I had to overcome the massive embarrassment of having to beg for help and of having to explain how I'd got there and I couldn't bring myself to do it for several minutes. Besides, I was in something of a quandary, for screaming would use up my oxygen faster, whereas keeping quiet might just mean I'd die more slowly. In the end I realised I had no choice. I lay as still as a corpse, trying not to breathe more than necessary, until I heard footsteps approaching.

'Help,' I bellowed, banging on the boot lid, 'I'm stuck!'

The only response was heartless laughter and a most unfeeling remark. As the footsteps receded, I ground my teeth and tried to relax.

More footsteps approached and this time, my pleas received no response whatsoever. More footsteps: again nothing. As panic closed in, throwing caution to the winds, I yelled and banged, sweated and gasped.

A crunch and screeching of tortured metal hurt my ears. Then I was blinking in bright sunlight with something dark looming overhead. A vision in pink came into view as my eyes adjusted. Pinky was staring down, looking puzzled.

'What on earth are you doing in there?' she asked.

'Good question,' said a familiar voice.

'Sid?'

'At your service,' said the old vampire who, dressed in a long black cloak and a Homburg hat, was twiddling a crowbar in his fingers.

'Would you mind helping me out? My legs won't move.'

Passing his crowbar to Pinky, he reached in, his surprisingly strong hands grabbed me around the waist, lifted me and sat me on the steps.

'Thank you,' I said. 'I was stuck.'

'Obviously,' said Pinky, 'but why?'

'I was trying to help Hobbes.'

'In a car boot?' Her tone suggested she considered me beyond all hope.

As the feeling returned to my legs as pain, I groaned and

stretched. 'I didn't mean to get locked in. He was going alone and I thought he might need some help. I tried to hide in there, but the lid closed and, then he went off in Billy's car.'

'Billy Shawcroft?' asked Sid.

'Yes. Do you know him?'

'Everyone knows Billy. He's a good man in a crisis.'

'But what can he do? He's so small.'

'There's more to him than you'd think,' said Sid. 'He's a man of no small talent and ability.'

'I suppose he is. Umm ... I thought your sort didn't go out in daylight.'

'Bankers don't normally,' said Sid, 'because they're at work.'

'Oh. I thought you couldn't stand sunlight?'

'It's alright. Too much gives me wrinkles.'

'What's the matter?' asked Pinky, again looking puzzled. 'You're talking as if Mr Sharples were a vampire.'

'Only joking,' I said, 'but what brings you two here?'

'Miss Pinkerton mentioned that Wilber's daughter was in trouble, so I thought I'd offer my services. Alas, it would seem I am too late.'

'I wish we could go after him,' I said, 'because I'm sure he's walking into a trap. It's all Kathy's fault for getting herself kidnapped.'

'Don't blame her,' said Sid. 'She's in danger and he's going because he has no choice. He must help her. That's what he does.'

'I'm sorry. I wasn't really meaning to blame her, but I'm worried. About both of them.'

'Of course you are,' he said, glancing at his watch. 'Look, it's still only quarter to three and we'll probably just about get there in time if we use the Batmobile.'

'The what?' asked Pinky, looking thoroughly bewildered.

'My car,' said Sid. 'That's what Billy calls it on account of it being black and looking like it should have wings.'

'Great!' I said. 'Umm ... where is it?'

'In the Batcave. Before you ask, that's my garage. Follow me.'

He led us along Blackdog Street and into Pound Street at a steady jog. I wondered where we were heading, for there'd been no room for a garage near his house. The mystery was solved when, having crossed the road, he opened an iron gate in the old stone wall and led us into a courtyard surrounded by eleven garages, their doors painted in all colours. The one he approached was the black one, bafflingly numbered 39. He opened it, tugged at a tarpaulin and uncovered a huge, black, gleaming, very old-fashioned, very American car.

'That's lovely,' gasped Pinky, applying a lace handkerchief to her face, which now matched her clothes. 'What is it?'

'That, young lady, is a 1958 Cadillac, Series 62, Extended Deck Sedan. A true classic.'

'Is it? Good, but does it go?'

'Does it go?' asked Sid, chuckling and then looking worried. 'I hope so. I haven't actually used it for some time.'

He squeezed into the driver's seat and a moment later the engine roared. He opened the window as he drove out: 'That's a 365 cubic inch V8 engine, packing 310 horsepower. A marvellous machine. Hop in, there's plenty of room for all of us in the front.'

Exchanging amused, if slightly puzzled glances, Pinky and I got in, sliding along the bench type seat, with me in the middle. It soon became apparent that, despite its mighty-sounding engine, it was a sedate car, comfortable, but totally lacking in zip. It felt slow: frustratingly slow.

'What time is it now?' I asked as we reached the outskirts of Sorenchester.

'Ten to three,' said Pinky. Her watch, I wasn't surprised to see, was pink. 'How long will it take us to get there?'

'About ten minutes,' said Sid.

'Can't we go any faster?'

He shook his head. 'She was designed for long, straight

American highways, not these twisting Cotswold roads.'

Clutching my hands into fists, forcing myself to sit still, I fought against a repeated urge to ask whether we were nearly there yet, a question that had once so exasperated my father that he'd turned the car around and headed straight back home, instead of to the caravan in Wales he'd rented for a week. The disappointment of that day, of that lost week, still resonated, despite the fact that we had stayed there before. The caravan had been cramped, freezing at night, roasting during the day, mildewed and at the very bottom of a marshy field. It had no facilities, other than a tap at the farmhouse, a good ten-minute trudge away, and an old spade for digging holes when nature called, yet I'd loved it because of the mountains rising imperiously behind, the restless sea over the dunes, the little trout stream, and the space and the freedom. Thinking about it helped slacken off my taut nerves.

Even so, it seemed an age before, rounding a sharp bend, we came in sight of the Squire's Arms and the River Soren. There was no sign of Billy's hearse, or of any movement, except for the languid munching of a herd of black and white cows in a meadow on the other side of the road, below an ancient and ridiculously massive church. Sid, slowing to thirty in accordance with the speed signs, was immediately overtaken by a dark-blue van. Ignoring it, he signalled and turned right over the bridge into a lane leading towards Northsorn, with the Squire's Arms on our right. Its car park was empty, and there was a large, handwritten sign saying: 'Sorry, closed due to bereavement'. I presumed, and hoped, it was just to deter visitors.

'Is it three o'clock yet?' I asked.

'Two minutes to,' said Pinky.

'I don't like it.' I said. 'It's too quiet.'

Sid parked by a hedge and we got out into a cool breeze, though the sun was bright.

'Well,' said Pinky, looking around, 'what are we going to do now?'

'Umm ... I don't really know.'

'I think,' said Sid, 'we should stay out of sight.'

'I agree,' I said, 'but then what?'

'How about,' said Pinky, 'finding a place where we're hidden, but from where we can see what's going on? Then we might be able to do something, if there's any trouble.'

Sid pointed downhill. 'There's a footpath running behind the pub. We'll try that, but keep your voices down ... and stay alert. This might be dangerous.'

Having no better suggestion, I went with them, feeling horribly conspicuous until, as we reached the path, there were hedges and bushes to hide behind. The path was sticky with mud, with a collage of human and canine footprints indicating what it was mostly used for. As we tiptoed past a hawthorn tree, glowing bright with red berries, we could see a gate leading towards the back of the Squire's Arms, where the footprints suggested many dog walkers sneaked in for a crafty pint. From there, we could also see one side of the pub, part of the front and most of the car park. As we looked around, wondering if it was the best place, a sudden, stealthy movement ahead made us duck back under the hawthorn's shade.

A diminutive figure in black from boots to hood, slipping through the gate into the pub's backyard, concealed himself behind a stack of gleaming kegs, his arms outstretched.

'That's Billy,' Sid whispered. 'What's he up to?'

'Hiding,' I murmured.

'Shh!' Pinky cautioned. 'Someone's coming.'

It was Hobbes, walking a little stiffly, I thought, through the front entrance of the car park, sporting a new gabardine raincoat and, unusually, with a trilby pulled low over his eyes. He approached the front of the Squire's Arms, stopped, folded his arms across his chest, and said: 'I am here.'

His voice was so hoarse and tense I wouldn't have

recognised it had he not been standing there.

'Very punctual,' said Sir Gerald, sauntering through the open doorway. 'I knew you would be. Your kind has never exhibited any originality.'

'Where's Kathy?' asked Hobbes, barely loud enough for us to hear.

'She's currently enjoying a glass of lager with my son. She apparently prefers it to English ale, which is her loss. Did you know this pub gets an honourable mention in the Good Beer Guide?'

'I'd like to see her,' said Hobbes.

'Of course you would, but first I want Duckworth's notes.'

'How do I know she's alright? I want to see her.'

'This,' said Sir Gerald, 'is my game and we will play it by my rules. You'll see her as soon as I have the notes.'

'How do I know I can trust you?'

'You have my word.'

'That's good enough for me,' said Hobbes.

'It will have to be,' said Sir Gerald.

Reaching into his coat pocket, Hobbes brought out a notebook and held it up.

'And the rest of them,' said Sir Gerald.

He produced three more battered notebooks.

'Good,' said Sir Gerald. 'You can't imagine the trouble I've had getting hold of them.'

'But why do you want them? They're only books, full of scribbles. They looked worthless to me.'

'Because you're a fool! If any geologist saw them, my little game would be up for good.'

'This is not a game,' said Hobbes.

'It's the game of life. There are winners and losers. I am one of the winners. You and your kind are the losers.'

'Games have rules.'

'Oh, rules!' said Sir Gerald with a sneer. 'A man of vision knows when to use them and when to break them.'

'I want to see Kathy.'

'Give me the books.'

'Not till I see her.'

'Very well. If you swear there'll be a fair handover, I'll let you see her.'

'I swear.'

'Good. Put the notebooks down and step away from them.'

Hobbes did as he was told.

'Very well,' said Sir Gerald, looking over his shoulder. 'Denzil, would you care to escort the young lady out here?'

Denny appeared, gripping Kathy by the shoulders. She tried to break away, but his hold was firm.

'Get your paws off me,' she said, squirming.

Suddenly, with a grimace and a cry of pain, she stopped struggling.

'Calm down, please' said Sir Gerald. 'I'd appreciate your cooperation for just a little longer and then you can go home with your father and we'll all be happy.'

Pinky couldn't help snorting. Sid put a finger to her lips.

'Do you expect to get away with this?' asked Hobbes.

'Yes, I do,' said Sir Gerald, smiling.

'Your scheme might have worked for your ancestors, but times have changed.'

'No, they haven't. Not really. You'll still find that a little money, judiciously applied, will sway things the right way, especially when there's a modicum of threat to back it up.

'And now, Inspector, to prevent any unfortunate misunderstandings, I must ask you to move back and to lie face down on the ground with your arms stretched out in front where I can see them.'

Hobbes did as he was told.

'Don't move a muscle,' said Sir Gerald. 'I have you covered.'

As he swaggered towards the notebooks, which were fluttering on the tarmac like autumn leaves, Rupert stepped from behind a bush, aiming a double-barrelled shotgun at

Hobbes, who appeared to be entirely unaware of the danger.

'Look out!' I yelled, 'he's got a gun!'

Ignoring Sid's horrified expression, I ran towards the car park gate. I had no plan, just a desperate urge to do something.

Sir Gerald, glancing over his shoulder, saw me and turned back. 'I said, "Come alone". If you had, no one would have been hurt.' He shook his head and glanced at Rupert and then at Denny. 'Kill them!'

As Rupert stepped towards Hobbes, the shotgun aimed at his back, a powerful engine roared and a dark-blue van, the one that had overtaken us earlier, hurtled along the footpath directly at Sid and Pinky, giving them no chance of escape. I stood aghast, horrified by what I'd done, hearing her scream, seeing her flying backwards, her arms and legs flailing wildly. I stood there, helpless, appalled, paralysed and unable to flee as two burly men, armed with axes, leapt from the van. One of them charged towards me. Over by the pub, Kathy cried out.

Although my brain was frozen, some deep-seated survival instinct threw me to the ground, just avoiding an axe blow that would have split my skull. Kicking out wildly, I caught the man behind the knee, knocking him down, and jumped back to my feet.

Denny was holding Kathy above his head as if he meant to smash her into the ground. For a moment, he hesitated and frowned.

'Do it,' cried Sir Gerald. 'Now!'

Denny nodded. Shifting his grip, he hurled her at the ground, but, as he did, a vast figure, appearing as if from nowhere, moving with feline grace at cheetah speed, dived full length and caught her.

The axeman came at me again and, as the gleaming blade scythed towards my side, I lurched forward, avoiding the sharp edge and receiving a mighty smack in the ribs from the shaft that knocked me headlong into a bush. I sprawled, winded, bruised and groaning, but, despite the pain, I was back on my feet before the axeman regained his balance.

A shot made us both jump and look towards the car park. Rupert had fired into the body of Hobbes, who was lying motionless on the tarmac. I was still frozen in horror when my assailant, with a cruel grin, raised his weapon and this time I seemed to have no chance of surviving, until a high-pitched howl rang out. It distracted him just long enough to allow me to duck out of harm's way, but, tripping over my own feet, I fell and was utterly at his mercy, something I doubted he possessed in any quantity. As I cringed and expected pain, a small, solid, black figure leapt up with a fierce cry and nutted the axeman right between the eyes. He went over backwards like a felled tree and the small, solid, black figure pulled back his hood.

'Wotcha, Andy,' said Billy, rubbing a graze on his forehead and grimacing. 'I reckon that got him a good one. I just wish he didn't have such a thick skull.'

'Thank you,' I said, getting to my feet.

'Are you alright?'

I nodded, though I wasn't really, feeling bruised and shocked and appalled at what had happened to Hobbes, who was sprawled on the tarmac, with Rupert, white-faced, standing over him, staring at the shotgun. I ran towards the gate into the car park and stopped, open-mouthed, doubting my sanity. Another Hobbes, this one hatless, was in the process of kicking the legs from under Denny, who collapsed like a dynamited factory chimney. Kathy, sitting on a bench, was staring, her eyes as wide as my mouth.

I heard the second axeman scream and looked back to see him throw his weapon aside and run, his face cauliflower white, his eyes bulging like a rabbit's.

As I turned back, Sir Gerald pulled a pistol from his pocket.

'He's got a gun, too!' I shouted.

'Oh do shut up!' he said, pointing it at me and pulling the trigger.

A shot cracked, as I was flinging myself to the ground behind the beer kegs. Billy dived in beside me. Another shot showered us with brick dust and I looked up to see a crater in the wall above.

'This is a bit of a mess,' I said between shocked gasps.

'We had a plan,' said Billy, 'and it was all going smoothly until you mucked it up. You weren't supposed to be here.'

'Sorry,' I said, getting to my knees and peering out.

The other Hobbes was talking to Kathy, who was staring at him and nodding, while Denny lay groaning on the floor. Rupert, apparently in shock, had dropped the shotgun and looked like he was crying.

'There are two Hobbeses. I don't understand,' I said.

'I'll tell you later,' said Billy. 'Just keep your head down before you get it shot off.'

Although it was undoubtedly good advice, I felt a compulsion to keep watching.

'Leave the girl alone,' said Sir Gerald.

Hobbes turned to face him.

'I told you to come alone,' said Sir Gerald. 'If you had, and you'd done what I asked, I'd have spared her.'

'I very much doubt it, sir. You couldn't afford to have her as a witness.'

'Maybe I could,' said Sir Gerald with a shrug. 'I'm not a monster. Unfortunately, you've forced my hand and, alas, you will all have to die.'

'What would be the point?' said Hobbes, his voice calm and soothing. 'It's all over now. Too many people have seen what's happened. Why don't you just put the gun down, sir?'

'Do you really imagine,' said Sir Gerald with a harsh laugh, 'that I'm going to give up just like that? I might be in a tight corner, but I'm still in the game.'

'Please, give me the gun,' said Hobbes, taking a step forward, holding out his hand. 'You can't possibly get away with it.'

Sir Gerald raised the gun.

Still Hobbes advanced, his voice quiet and calm: 'Don't be a fool, sir. Put the gun down. Put it down!'

'I'll put you down,' said Sir Gerald.

'I wouldn't do that, Gerry,' said Pinky marching forward, muddied but unbowed, aiming Rupert's shotgun at Sir Gerald.

He turned towards her, his face shocked.

'Today,' said Pinky, her soft, pretty face frozen as hard as ice, 'I get my revenge.'

She pulled the trigger. The retort echoing off the walls made me clutch my ears and duck. Ears ringing, I looked up, puzzled to see Sir Gerald still standing, and apparently unharmed. Frowning, she squeezed the trigger again but she was out of ammo.

'Did you miss me, Pinky?' said Sir Gerald, trying to look composed, though his voice quivered. 'I suppose, when it came down to it, you couldn't bring yourself to do it. You always were weak.'

He raised his pistol.

'Stop!' cried Hobbes.

But before he could intervene, Denny, back on his feet, fury in his eyes, massive fists bunched, clobbered him in the side of the head, making him cartwheel to the ground.

Sir Gerald, with a nasty grin, took aim at the defenceless Pinky, his finger tightening on the trigger. Before he could shoot, there was a blur of movement and Pinky was suddenly lying flat on the tarmac, beneath Sid. His face distorted by rage, Sir Gerald started to adjust his aim, only to find Sid was already back on his feet, diving forward, his arms stretching out his cloak into the semblance of wings. Sid engulfed him and the pistol dropped harmlessly to the ground.

Hobbes, already back up, blood smeared across his face, deflected a bone-breaking clout from Denny with his forearm, ducked beneath the follow up, a wild scything haymaker, and punched him once in the solar plexus. Denny, deflating like a punctured football, crumpled into a foetal position at Hobbes's feet. It was, I thought, the only time I'd ever actually seen Hobbes hit anyone.

'That's enough, Sid,' said Hobbes, glancing over his shoulder. 'You can put him down.'

Sid, though shorter than Sir Gerald by a head, was holding Sir Gerald off the ground by the lapels of his jacket. Yet there was still fight in the man and, as soon as Sid released him, he made a dive for the pistol. Sid, shaking his head, stepped forward and stamped on his hand as it closed around the butt. Sir Gerald screamed and curled into a ball, cradling his mangled fingers as Hobbes ran across, grabbed the pistol and ejected the magazine.

'Have you quite finished yet?' asked the prostrate figure of the first Hobbes, ''cause I want to take this corset off. It's chafing my nipples something rotten.'

'Yes, you can get up now,' said Hobbes, 'and many thanks for your assistance.'

The first Hobbes, the one I'd thought had been shot, got to his knees, removing his hat and revealing himself as Featherlight.

'Give me a hand up,' he said to a bewildered, red-eyed Rupert, 'or I'll tear your bloody head off for shooting me.'

'I'm sorry, sir,' said Rupert extending a shaking hand. 'I didn't mean to. It just went off.'

'Well, no harm done,' said Featherlight, getting to his feet and taking off his coat, beneath which, in place of his habitual grubby vest, he was sporting an extremely tight and uncomfortable-looking whalebone corset. 'Now, you can unlace me. This bloody thing is squeezing my bits into something awful.'

'But I don't understand,' said Rupert. 'I was pointing right in the middle of your back. You should be dead.'

'You'd better thank Billy that I'm not and that you're not on a murder charge,' said Featherlight. 'Now, let me loose, or I really will tear your head off.'

Pinky and Kathy, neither of them apparently hurt, but both looking shocked and confused, stood up. Hobbes gave Kathy a quick hug, before attending to Denny who was groaning where he lay, clutching his stomach and vomiting.

'You're a big man,' said Hobbes, 'but you're in bad shape. For me it's a full time job. Now behave yourself.'

Denny nodded feebly and threw up again.

Hobbes grinned at me. 'I've always wanted to say that. Now is everyone alright?'

'No,' said Pinky, 'I'm all covered in mud!' She pointed an accusing finger at Sid. 'He threw me into a ditch!' She grinned. 'Thank you. You saved my life.'

It turned out that the only ones with any serious hurts were Sir Gerald, whose fingers were sticking out in emetic directions, and Denny, whose capacious stomach was still emptying itself. Hobbes's face, a bloody split beneath his eye, was already starting to bruise. It looked like it would be a good one.

'Well, that's a good result,' he said. 'I suppose I'd better let the superintendent know what's happened and I should call an ambulance for Sir Gerald.' He reached into his pocket for his mobile.

I sidled up to Sid. 'What did you do to that bloke with the axe? He looked absolutely terrified.'

'Nothing much. All I did was look at him.'

'That doesn't sound too bad.'

'It can be, if I do this!'

I wish he hadn't. I had nightmares for weeks.

23

Hobbes rested his feet on the still recumbent Denny and talked to Kathy, holding her hand, while Sid, Pinky and Featherlight disappeared into the pub, leaving Billy and me to keep our eyes on Sir Gerald and Rupert.

'How is it,' I asked, 'that Featherlight and Sir Gerald weren't killed when they were shot? No one can miss at that range: not with a shotgun.'

'There is,' said Billy, 'a perfectly simple explanation.'

'What is it?'

'I'd tampered with the cartridges.'

'Why?'

'Hobbesie had it all planned. One of my jobs was to take care of any firearms. I sneaked into the pub, found the shotgun and removed all the shot and most of the powder from the cartridges.' He showed me a handful of small, grey balls from his pocket.

'That was well done,' I said.

'It would have been,' he continued, 'if I'd realised Sir Gerald had a Walther PPK.'

'A what?'

'His pistol was a Walther PPK, the sort James Bond uses.'

'Really? It was lucky he missed,' I said, pointing towards the bullet crater in the wall.

'Yes,' said Billy, 'that was close, but not as close as the other one.'

He pointed up at my armpit. Just below it, passing right through my jacket and shirt, was a small, neat hole and, although it hadn't touched me, my legs turned to jelly.

'You got lucky,' said Billy, guiding me to a seat, 'but you really shouldn't have been involved. We had the situation under control. Featherlight was the distraction, Hobbes was to take down the villains, and I was to do the guns and the video.'

'I thought I was helping,' I said, ashamed.

'By barging in and putting civilians in the firing line? It's a good job one of them was Mr Sharples or that pink lady would have been killed. Do you have any idea why she tried to shoot Sir Gerald?'

'I don't know,' I said, 'but I don't think she likes him.'

'That explanation had, of course, never occurred to me. Are you feeling any better?'

I nodded and turned to see Hobbes approaching, a handkerchief in his hand, wiping a trickle of blood from his face.

'Andy,' he said, 'your intervention was not at all helpful. You should have stayed in the car boot, safely out of harm's way.'

'I'm sorry. I just saw the gun and panicked ... You knew I was in the boot?'

He nodded. 'Oh well, no major harm was done.' He glanced at Billy. 'Did you get it all?'

'Nearly all. I did miss a few moments when I was looking after Andy, and when Sir Gerald started shooting at us. Still, we should have recorded something on Trilbycam.'

'What,' I asked, 'is Trilbycam?'

'The camera in Featherlight's hat to record the events automatically.'

'That's clever,' I said, 'but ... umm ... tell me, why your arms were outstretched?'

'To ensure a good stereo recording. I've got a mike up each sleeve,'

'So, you're carrying a tape recorder?'

'What century are you living in?' said Billy, shaking his head. 'Everything's digital these days.'

'So, you really did have it all planned,' I said, crestfallen.

It didn't take long for a police car and an ambulance to arrive. Hobbes, the side of his face swelling impressively, went across and explained the situation, pointing out Sir Gerald, who was sitting cross-legged on the tarmac, clutching his fingers and whimpering like a baby, Rupert, who was pale, sweating and incoherent, and, lying stretched out on the bench, the axeman Billy had nutted. The axeman was still out for the count and was, I suspected, going to wake up with a mighty headache. While the casualties were being loaded and driven away, Hobbes perched a dazed-looking Denny on a keg and gave him a stern talking to, a talking to incorporating far more than the standard quantity of finger wagging. By the end, had there been a world record for head hanging and looking contrite, then Denny would have won it by a mile.

'Excellent,' said Hobbes, looking pleased. 'Now it's time to break up our little gathering. I suppose I really should do some paperwork and afterwards I'll go and retrieve the gold.'

'You know where it is?' I said.

'Indeed I do. It's hidden, but I know exactly where.'

'How?'

'Mr Barker is proving very cooperative.'

'Can I come with you? I've always wanted to find treasure.'

'We'll see. Maybe, if you behave yourself and do as you're told. It will require something of a journey. Now Billy, let's get back to Sorenchester … and quickly.'

He walked away, depositing Denny in the police car and collecting Featherlight and Kathy.

'Where's your car?' I asked Billy as he was leaving. 'I didn't see it.'

'Over there,' he pointed across the road, 'behind the village church.'

Realising I'd completely forgotten about the dog, feeling suddenly ashamed, I asked: 'Is Dregs in it?'

'No, Hobbesie took him to guard that nice lady at the museum before we came here.'

'Daphne?' Shocked that I'd hardly given her a thought in all the excitement, my shame rose into the red.

'Come along, Andy,' said Sid as I stood, watching Billy cross the road, 'we really must get Miss Pinkerton home, or she'll catch her death of cold.'

She was shivering, despite being wrapped in Sid's black cloak.

'Good idea,' I said, snapping out of it. 'Where are you staying?'

'I don't know,' she said indistinctly through the staccato clatter of teeth. 'I was hoping to stay with Daphne, but that's obviously out of the question. I suppose I should get a hotel for the night, but I don't know what's available.'

'We can work something out,' said Sid. 'Let's get a move on.'

As we hurried back to the car, leaving two constables to do whatever police constables do at crime scenes after the event, I put my arm round Pinky's shoulder to keep her warm and, though it didn't appear to do her much good, I rather enjoyed the softness of her body, despite her new scent of stagnant ditch mud.

'I've been thinking,' said Sid as we drove away. 'You could stay at my place tonight, Ms Pinkerton. It will save you having to search for a hotel. There's plenty of room.'

'Oh, I couldn't possibly,' said Pinky, in a tone that meant yes, please.

'Excellent. That's settled then. I can make you quite comfortable and I'll be glad of your company. Do you like soup?'

'I love it,' said Pinky, who was obviously a pushover.

The two of them chatted happily all the way back, leaving me confused and completely puzzled by my feelings. Fortunately, I kept my mouth shut, because otherwise I might have said something stupid. I knew I was being silly, but, for some reason, I was getting worked up about her moral welfare and, apparently, my concerns were much greater than hers. The thing was, I really didn't think a young, well, youngish, woman should stay overnight with Sid, a known vampire, and, although I had almost no fear he'd bite her neck and drain her dry, I'd seen far too many films in which vampires exerted an unhealthy fascination on vulnerable women to be entirely at ease. I was worried that, to judge from her smile and conversation, she was relishing the idea.

It wasn't that I was jealous, or perhaps it was, but I shouldn't have been, because I had Daphne, or at least so I hoped. As my thoughts turned to her I began to feel better, for she had a certain something that made me a better man. Pinky had something about her, too, but given the choice, I'd have definitely picked Daphne. At least I thought I would have.

Once back in Sorenchester, Sid parked his monumental vehicle half up on the pavement outside his house.

'I shouldn't really stop here,' he said, 'but Ms Pinkerton ...'

'Pinky, please!' she said.

'... Pinky needs a hot bath as quickly as possible. So, I'll see you soon, Andy. It has been a most interesting afternoon.'

'Alright then,' I said as we got out and my confusing feelings flooded back. 'Bye.'

Turning away, I tried not to mind her delighted giggle as Sid, with a deep bow and a toothy smile, opened the front door and showed her inside.

I headed towards the museum to check on Daphne, to ensure she was coping with Dregs, who could be a handful. It turned out that I had no cause to worry, for I met her outside with Dregs, who was walking to heel like the hero in a Disney film about a very good, heroic dog.

'Hi, Andy,' said Daphne, smiling and stroking his shaggy black head, 'we're just going for a comfort break in the park.'

'Hi,' I said, suffering an unreasonable stab of jealousy. 'How are you?'

'I'm fine. How's the inspector's daughter?'

'She's safe. He had a plan to rescue her and I nearly screwed it up, but it all ended well. Sir Gerald's under arrest, but he was taken to hospital because Sid trod on him. Rupert was taken away, too.'

'I'd love to hear all about it,' she said, 'but later. I'm still at work, but the dog wanted some air. I finish at five-thirty, so I'll see you here in,' she glanced at her watch, 'about forty minutes.'

'Great.' I said. 'I'll take him for his walk.'

Handing me the lead, kissing me on the cheek, she headed back. His tail drooped as she went inside and it was only when we reached Ride Park and he'd chased a rabbit that his spirits revived. As the minutes passed until I could go and meet her, my mind kept churning over the facts and one in particular kept bubbling to the surface. I had come within millimetres of being shot and, although I'd learned that new sensations and new experiences helped prevent one getting stuck in a rut, there was something about bullets that made ruts seem attractive. I might have been wounded, or killed. It would, I reflected, have been just my luck to get killed in action when things were beginning to look promising with Daphne.

Yet the bullets hadn't touched me and the truth was that it had been just my luck to have survived unscathed when things were beginning to look promising with Daphne. I clung to this far more comforting point of view, hoping it was a sign my luck was changing, because, in my opinion, good luck was long overdue. A wave of euphoria broke over me, engulfed me, and deposited me gently back in Ride Park. The case had been solved, the bad men had been thwarted, if my luck held I was going to find gold, and, to top it all, I was meeting Daphne very soon.

I asked an old chap throwing a ball for a yappy miniature poodle, whether he had the time.

'Five twenty-five.'

'Thank you,' I said, fearing I'd be late.

I called Dregs, who was making a point of ignoring the poodle, and attached his lead.

'Come on,' I said, 'let's go and find Daphne.'

On hearing her name, he took off like a greyhound and I only just managed to keep up by taking unfeasibly long strides. Still, the burst of speed worked, for we arrived at the museum just as she emerged. Seeing her, Dregs put on an extra spurt and self-preservation forced me to drop his lead.

Looking up, she smiled. Dregs accelerated, running faster than I'd ever seen him, running straight towards her, despite my calling him back. I was convinced she was going to get flattened.

Instead, avoiding her by a whisker, he leapt at the hooded figure who had just stepped from the shadows behind her. The man screamed as Dregs's sharp white teeth closed on his wrist and the momentum sent him spinning to the ground. A knife skidded into the gutter as the man's hood fell back. It was Rupert Payne.

'Get it off,' he cried, blood spurting from his wrist as Dregs, growling savagely, kept him pinned down. I could have called him off, he might for once have obeyed, but I didn't.

'Drop,' said Daphne in a quiet voice.

Dregs dropped and gazed at her, wagging his tail.

'Good dog.'

'I'm hurt,' said Rupert, in the moments when he wasn't rolling around on the pavement, clutching his arm. 'He bit me. I'm bleeding.'

'Good,' I said with feeling as I ran to Daphne's side. She looked far less shocked than I felt.

'I didn't mean any harm,' Rupert whined. 'I wasn't going to hurt anyone.'

'You had a knife,' I said, 'and you threatened me with one on Sunday.'

'But, I didn't use it, did I? I only pulled it out because I was scared.'

'Were you scared of me?' asked Daphne.

'No, Mrs Duckworth. I only wanted to talk, but, when I saw

the horrible dog coming for me, I panicked and pulled the knife to protect myself. I didn't use it, though, because I didn't want to hurt the inspector's dog after he'd been so kind.'

He groaned. 'My wrist is ever so painful and I'm bleeding. Please, help me.'

He sounded sincere and I nearly believed him, nearly distrusted the evidence of my own eyes. Yet I knew what I'd seen. The knife had been in his hand long before he could possibly have seen Dregs. Daphne stooped, reaching for his arm.

'We'll take care of you,' she said. 'Let's have a look at it.'

As fast as a weasel, he seized her scarf, pulling her down with him, and lunged for the knife. She gasped, trying to break free, but his grip was firm.

Sid had shown me what to do next and I was already in position as Rupert's hand closed around the hilt. I stamped down hard and his wrist snapped with a stomach turning crack. With a scream, he slumped face forward into the road.

'Are you alright?' I asked.

'I'm fine,' said Daphne, pushing herself up. 'Are you?'

I shook my head. The pavement seemed to be rolling, my vision was blurred and her voice reverberated through my skull. I had a vague awareness of people and a voice shouting: 'look at that guy's wrist!' The feel and sound of it overwhelmed me.

'Come on Andy, wake up,' said Constable Poll.

A soft, warm hand stroked my brow.

A hot, wet, stinky tongue licked my face as I opened my eyes. A crowd had gathered to stare.

'What happened?' I asked, sitting up, feeling sick.

'You fainted ...' said Constable Poll.

I would have hung my head in shame had it not already been lolling. Fainting was not manly.

'... and I'm not surprised, because the sight of the lad's wrist

298

made me a bit queasy. It's not pretty, but you did well to disarm him.'

'It was Dregs that stopped him,' I said.

'At first, but I'm sure he was going to stab me,' said Daphne. She turned to Poll. 'Andy was brilliant – again.'

I couldn't hold back a self-satisfied grin as she hugged me, because, although I wished I hadn't hurt Rupert quite so badly, I had been brilliant. Still, I thought I should show some concern. 'How is he?'

'Apart from a very nasty compound fracture of his right wrist,' said Poll, 'dog bites, and serious psychological issues, he's doing fine. Mrs Goodfellow is looking after him until the ambulance arrives.'

'I don't understand,' I said. 'I saw him put into an ambulance about an hour ago. Why isn't he already in hospital?'

'He ran off as soon as they took his father into surgery,' said Poll. 'Superintendent Cooper ordered us to keep a look out for him, because he was believed to be armed and dangerous.'

I was on top of the world by the time the ambulance arrived and the moaning figure of Rupert was carried on board. Constable Poll got in beside the paramedic, although I doubted Rupert was likely to be troublesome for some time. With the ambulance's departure, the crowd dispersed and Mrs Goodfellow approached.

'How about a nice cup of tea?' she said.

'Yes please,' I said. 'Can Daphne come?'

'Of course, dear, and she can stay for supper if she likes.'

Daphne agreed and we walked back to Blackdog Street.

'Look what Mr White, the dentist, gave me.' said Mrs Goodfellow, pulling a brown paper bag from somewhere in her cardigan and opening it with a worrying rattle.

'Lovely,' I said, wondering how Daphne would react to a bag full of human teeth.

All she did was nod gravely and smile politely.

Ten minutes later, we were drinking tea in the kitchen, with Dregs curled up at Daphne's feet. Although an array of warm, enticing, delicious smells arising from the oven made me hungry, I concentrated on not drooling and related the afternoon's events. When I showed the bullet hole beneath my armpit, Daphne paled and squeezed my hand so hard I feared I'd be following Sir Gerald and son to hospital, where the hand and wrist surgeons must have been very busy. Fortunately, she slackened the pressure when I yelped and so the hospital was spared another casualty. Best of all, the way she was looking at me made me feel important and heroic.

We helped Mrs Goodfellow set the table for supper and waited for Hobbes and Kathy to return. A little before six-thirty the front door opened. Dregs's tail wagged once and then he stood up, bristling, growling, standing protectively in front of us and staring at the kitchen door as it opened. In walked Denny.

My heart began to pound and a sick feeling gripped my stomach. Daphne gasped and sat down, as if her legs had given way. Mrs Goodfellow, a steaming wooden spoon in one hand, grabbed Dregs's collar with the other and stepped forward.

'Good evening,' she said. 'Who are you, and what are you doing here?'

Denny, tidier and cleaner than I'd yet seen him, touching his forelock and bowing with an old-fashioned gesture, smiled. 'Good evening, ma'am,' he said and turned towards Daphne and me, repeating the bow. 'Good evening, Mrs Duckworth. Good evening, sir. I'm Denzil Barker. I'm here to apolo ... apolo ... to say sorry for what I done. Mr Hobbes had a long talk with me and taught me that what I been doing was wrong. I am sorry, ma'am, Mrs Duckworth, sir. I didn't want to hurt nobody, but I thought I had to do what the master said. Mr Hobbes says I don't have to do that no more.'

'I am very pleased to hear it,' said Mrs Goodfellow. 'Where is Mr Hobbes? I expect he let you in.'

'Yes, ma'am. He's taking Miss Kathy upstairs, 'cause she's feeling a bit poorly and wants to lie down.'

'Oh, the poor girl,' said Mrs Goodfellow, whose innate kindness overwhelmed her suspicions, 'I'd better go and make sure she's alright.'

'There's no need,' said Hobbes, entering the kitchen and patting Denny on the shoulder. 'She just needs a little time on her own. What's for supper?'

'Sorenchester hotpot,' said Mrs Goodfellow. 'Is Mr Barker going to eat with us?'

Denny nodded. 'I would like that very much, ma'am. I am very starving hungry and I like the smell of what you got cooking. Thank you, muchly.'

'You are welcome, dear' said Mrs Goodfellow. 'There's plenty to go round.'

Still shaking, still very much surprised, still utterly bewildered, I took my seat next to Daphne, whose face showed a weird mixture of fear, suspicion and relief. Denny sat on my other side and Hobbes, at the head as always, said grace. It was a bizarre occasion and, to start with, my nerves were stretched so tightly I was sure they'd snap, until the old girl served us and it was clear she'd excelled herself as usual, when I allowed myself to relax by small degrees. Sometimes I suspected her of witchcraft, for it was clearly impossible for every meal to be better than the previous one, but if I was under a spell, I was in no rush to break it.

Denny, polite and calm, ate in awed silence and when seconds were offered accepted them with alacrity. The same went for thirds and fourths. By the end of supper, I had accepted his presence. He no longer felt like a threat, reminding me instead of an overgrown, over-aged, none too intelligent child. Hobbes had achieved many remarkable feats, but the taming of Denny struck me as one of his most amazing.

Denny volunteered to wash the pots. Hobbes, letting him get on with it, answered Daphne's questions about Nutcase

Nugent, a notorious former resident of Blackcastle, who'd featured in Hugh Duckworth's notes. I went upstairs to relieve myself, and had just finished washing my hands when I overheard Kathy talking on her mobile. She was angry and sounded even more American than usual.

'No,' she said, 'I won't do it. Not now, not ever. This game of yours stops here ... How could you tell me such a pack of lies? ... Baloney, Mom! When have you ever done anything for *my* good? ... Yes, I am going to tell him ... Tonight. He deserves to know ... He's been really kind ... no, he's nothing like you described him ... Well, sure, he is one big, ugly dude, but he's a good man ... I wish he really was my daddy.'

As I headed back downstairs, I wondered how Hobbes would react to suddenly not having a daughter again.

Daphne was helping Denny put things away, while Hobbes, a mug of tea in his hand, was telling them the legend of the Blacker Mountain crocodile that had finally put an end to Nutcase Nugent.

Kathy entered the kitchen, her eyes rimmed with red, breathing heavily, but in control.

'Excuse me for butting in,' she said, 'but I have something important to say. I just wish I didn't have to. I wish everything was different.' Facing Hobbes, she gulped and took a deep breath. 'I'm not your daughter.'

'I know,' said Hobbes with a sad smile. 'I always did. We saved you some supper.'

24

Kathy stood and faced us, tears rolling down her cheeks, her eyes puffy with crying. I could see no nastiness or arrogance in her, just unhappiness and, strangely, dignity. She wiped her face. 'I'd like to explain myself before anything else.'

'Very well,' said Hobbes.

'We'd better leave you to it,' I said, getting up, embarrassed.

'No, Andy, please stay,' she said. 'Mrs Goodfellow, too. All of you stay, if you don't mind. I'm fed up with secrets. I'm sorry Dad … Inspector, but I've only just found out that some of what I told you, some of what I believed, was completely wrong.'

I sat back down.

Denny shrugged his massive shoulders and stood in the corner by the sink, as immobile as a sculpture. Mrs Goodfellow pulled up a chair and joined us at the table.

Kathy stood quite still, except for the rise and fall of her chest as she fought to stay in control, her fists clenched, her face as white as skimmed milk.

'I want to apologise,' she said.

'That's the word I wanted to say,' Denny murmured and resumed his silence.

'I didn't intend to deceive you,' said Kathy. 'I didn't intend to deceive anyone. I really thought I was your daughter. I hope you believe me?'

'We'll see,' said Mrs G, trying to look stern.

'I'll start at the very beginning,' said Kathy.

'A very good place to start,' I responded, before a frown from Hobbes quelled my attempt at lightening the mood.

'I've lived with my mom most of my life and for most of the time it was just the two of us. She told me my daddy hailed from England and that she'd met him when he was on vacation, but he'd gone home before I was born. She said he was a cop and his name was Hobbes.'

Mrs G snorted and shook her head. Hobbes held up his hand to quiet her. 'Go on,' he said.

'I never thought I'd ever meet him, because Mom had no idea where he lived. Anyway, we got by somehow or other, even though we moved about all over the States when I was little. Mostly this was because she kept getting into trouble and running away. For a long time she used drugs and sometimes she was put in jail. At those times, nice folk looked after me and I had a bit of schooling. After I graduated high school, we kind of settled down. I found a job waitressing and Mom got herself clean of drugs.'

'That is good,' said Hobbes. 'I warned her of the risks back in'67, but she was young and foolish then.'

'She's still foolish,' said Kathy, a snap of anger in her voice.

'So,' I asked, 'why did you take drugs yesterday?'

'I didn't knowingly. That punk, Rupert, put something in my soda.'

'Is that why you threw him in the lake?'

'Pardon me, sir,' said Denny. 'Miss Kathy di'n't throw him in. It was me. Master Gerald wanted the young master to feel what failure was like.'

That I'd almost forgotten him testifies to the change Hobbes had already wrought, and made me wonder whether he might always have been quiet and respectful had it not been for the rottenness of the Paynes.

'OK,' I said, trying to compute the new data and staring at Kathy. 'How come you were there?'

'I was getting my head together and I heard a scream.'

'Andy,' said Hobbes, 'interesting as your misunderstandings are, can you please let her continue?'

'A few years ago,' said Kathy, 'Mom persuaded me to use the few dollars I'd saved and go into business.'

'What sort of business?' I asked, unable to envisage her as a businesswoman. She didn't seem the type.

'We opened a shop selling bison products.' She grimaced.

'Bison?'

'Yeah, we called it *Buy Some Bison*. Neat, huh?'

'What did you sell?' I asked, suddenly intrigued.

'Bison leather goods mainly: belts, shoes, coats, trousers, wallets, bags and hats. We also sold fresh and canned bison meat, which is low in fat and cholesterol. The trouble was, when I say sold, I really mean stocked. We never sold too much of anything, but somehow, we kept going for a few years. In the end it became clear, even to Mom, that it was just a matter of time before we went big time bust. It was then she chanced on the video of you on YouTube.'

'So, she still recognised the old fellow,' said Mrs Goodfellow.

Kathy nodded. 'At once and, I tell you, it was one helluva shock for her. I wondered what was wrong and thought she was going to faint, but she showed me and said I was your daughter. Then she took up a bottle of Tequila and drank herself unconscious. She took two days to sober up, which gave me time to think.' She wiped her eyes again. 'I wanted to see my daddy.'

'And get some money off him?' asked Mrs Goodfellow with a disapproving sniff.

With a wry smile, Kathy nodded. 'I'll not pretend that it didn't cross my mind, but I really wanted to meet you ... him. Ever since I was a kid, I suppose I'd always had this crazy idea that one day you ... he would come along and rescue me, but really, I just wanted to see you and talk and find out something about you. I hoped you'd help me understand something about myself. So, I booked a cheap plane ticket to England and found my way here, hoping you'd welcome me and ... and you did. You really did, even though I must have been a shock.'

Hobbes, frowning, nodded.

'At first, I was totally scared of you. Mom had said you were a big guy, but I hadn't realised how big. I put on a front and I hope I didn't offend anyone too much. I guess I might have come across as rude.'

'Perhaps a little,' said Mrs Goodfellow, her face betraying a smile.

'I'm sorry,' said Kathy. 'I soon came to like you, and then when you caught me that time I fell, it was like I'd really come home. I'd dreamt of living in a place like this and leaving all my problems behind but ... but ...'

'You worked out that I wasn't your father,' said Hobbes.

'You couldn't be. You're just too ... different. You're different to everyone, except to Featherlight and Denny. They're just like you.'

'Indeed, they are not!' said Mrs Goodfellow, a look of almost comic indignation on her face.

Hobbes, holding up a hand to quiet her, couldn't hold back a smile.

Kathy wiped her eyes and blew her nose on the tissue Mrs Goodfellow offered her. 'I don't mean you're like them in everything, but seeing the three of you together this afternoon made me certain. I don't know what you are and it doesn't matter, because you're a good man anyway, but you are different. D'you know what I mean?'

'I believe I do,' said Hobbes.

I was impressed. It had taken me far longer to conclude that Hobbes wasn't like the rest of us and I was still amazed at my insight, though it puzzled me why more people hadn't made the jump. Even so, and despite few being as close to him as I was, I often felt I didn't really know him at all. It was difficult enough to understand another human's thoughts, and it was almost impossible to know precisely what was going on in an animal's head. It wasn't that I considered him an animal, except so far as we were all animals. He was a man, but a non-human one, if that made any sense.

'Mr Hobbes is a Mountain Man, jus' like me,' said Denny suddenly, 'and so is Mr Featherlight. I didn't think there was any others like me till I came here. They said our kind was evil. I think I was.'

'But,' said Hobbes, 'you aren't anymore.'

'Whatever you are,' Kathy continued, 'I knew you couldn't be my daddy and, when I called Mom tonight, I finally made her admit it. My real daddy's some guy she met in Pittsburgh long after you'd left her.'

'The old fellow didn't leave her,' said Mrs Goodfellow. 'She left him when his money ran out. She even took his car.'

'I gave it to her,' said Hobbes. 'Her father was ill and she needed it to visit him in Detroit.'

'Her father was killed in Korea in 1952,' said Kathy, 'and granny never remarried. Neither of them ever lived in Detroit. Mom lied.'

'She always did,' said Mrs Goodfellow, smiling at Hobbes, 'only you were too much of a gentleman to acknowledge it. She would have taken your trousers if she'd thought there was money to be made from them.'

A tint of red appeared on Hobbes's cheeks. 'She did take them, which made things awkward. I had to improvise.'

'Was that when you started wearing that awful tarpaulin caftan?' asked Mrs Goodfellow. 'I did wonder.'

Hobbes nodded.

'So,' said Kathy, 'I'm not your daughter, but I didn't mean to trick you. Mom lied, although tonight she said you were the best man she'd ever known. I think that might have been true.'

'I doubt it,' said Hobbes with a sudden grin that was swiftly eclipsed when he saw Kathy's expression of sadness.

'I'm sorry,' she said, 'for everything. I really didn't know. I've packed my bags and I'll find myself a hotel and get out of your lives.'

'There's no need to be hasty,' said Hobbes. 'You're welcome to stay for as long as you want.'

'But there's no room,' she said.

'We can always make room, can't we, lass?'

Mrs Goodfellow nodded. So, to my surprise, did I.

'Thank you.' The relief in Kathy's voice was echoed in her

face.

'That's settled then,' said Hobbes, smiling.

'But, there is one thing,' said Kathy. 'How did you know I wasn't your daughter?'

'I calculated dates and times. I did the math, as you Americans say, and it was impossible.'

'Oh,' I said, surprised, 'I thought it was because you hadn't ... umm.'

'Hadn't what?' asked Hobbes.

'Hadn't ... umm ... hadn't noticed enough similarity.'

'There was that as well,' said Hobbes. 'Although I knew, it appeared to me that you genuinely believed it ...'

Mrs Goodfellow shook her head and chuckled.

'... and,' Hobbes continued, 'I didn't want to let you down. Now you've discovered the truth, I hope we can still be friends?'

Getting up, he embraced her in an immense bear hug.

My eyes moistening, I had to blink until they cleared. Daphne gave my hand a little squeeze.

Hobbes released Kathy, who was displaying a genuine, all-American smile that lit up her face. I could almost see her from PC Poll's point of view.

'Well,' he said, rubbing his hands together, sounding like a carpenter sanding rough wood, 'I'm glad that's all sorted because Denny is going to show me where the stolen gold is. Andy, there'll be room for you, too, but I must warn you, it will be a long night.'

Although a small part of me would have preferred to stay behind with Daphne, I could not turn down the opportunity to go on a treasure hunt, and within a few minutes I was sandwiched in between Featherlight and Denny in the back of Billy's hearse. All I could do was to look out through the windscreen between Hobbes and Billy as the headlights lit up the streets of Sorenchester. Soon we were on the dual carriageway, sided by fields, stark and empty, under a moon that was a little past fullness. The halo around it suggested there'd be a frost later.

'Where are we heading to?' I asked.

'You'll see,' said Hobbes, looking over his shoulder with an infuriating grin. 'Eventually.'

I had to be content with that, and since neither he, nor any of the others seemed in the mood for talking, I tried to relax. It was warm and the drone of the engine and the pulse of the tyres on the road lulled me to sleep.

When I awoke, the car was stationary, the windows misty with condensation, and I was on my own. Bleary-eyed, feeling a little sick and headachy, I climbed out, shivering as I pulled up my collar and tried to get my bearings. The place looked familiar, yet strange under the moonlight, and it took a moment to realise I was back in the Blacker Mountains and that we were parked beside the derelict manor house, where Billy had dropped us off just over a week earlier. It seemed incredible that so much had happened in such a short period, but that was so often the way with Hobbes.

I was annoyed and a little worried that the others had deserted me, until voices from the ruins suggested they were not far away. It was almost as bright as daytime and, as I walked towards the voices, my moon shadow flickered before me over the rocky ground.

'Hello?' I said, with no response.

As I reached the house, I touched its cold, grey, stone wall and called out again, a little louder than before.

'Andy?'

Hobbes's disembodied voice, deep and sepulchral, made me start: 'Did you have a good sleep?'

'Yes ... thanks.'

'Good. Are you going to join us?'

'I would if I knew where you were.'

His hand grabbed my ankle and would have made me jump

into orbit had its grip not been so strong.

'We,' said Hobbes, 'are in the cellars.'

All I could see of him was his hand and his big, yellow teeth, glinting in the moonlight, grinning from the bottom of a steeply sloping shaft. He released me.

'How do I get down?' I asked, my poor heart pounding.

'Just slide down this here coal chute and I'll catch you at the bottom.'

Sitting down, slotting my bottom half into the tight, damp, steep chute, I braced myself for action, but just before I let go I had a thought. The chute was not wide enough for him, or for Denny and definitely not for Featherlight.

'How,' I asked, 'did you get down there?'

'We used the steps.'

As I tried to extricate myself, he gave a tug and, with a little shriek, I slid into the darkness, where, to give him his due, he did catch me and set me down on an uneven floor. There was a stink of mildew and age and, when my eyes had adjusted, I saw I was in a long, low room with a crumbling, dripping, brick ceiling festooned with a crop of what appeared to be small stalactites. Around the chute, everything was mossy, with pale ferns and spiders' webs. In the further reaches I could make out a mess of rusting junk, crumbled rock, and rotting leaves.

'Take care,' said Hobbes, 'it's slippery in places.'

'Where are the others?

'In the wine cellar.'

'So, what's this?'

'The coal cellar.'

'Ah ... that would explain the coal chute.'

'I'll make a detective of you yet,' said Hobbes, leading me to the far end, where half a dozen cracked steps led down into another brick chamber. I could barely see him so, reaching out, I gripped the edge of his jacket.

'There are more steps,' he warned after a few paces across the lumpy floor, 'and they are worn and broken in places. Take care.'

At least twenty steps took us down to an echoing chamber where it was noticeably colder and damper, but where a faint light meant I could make out that we were in a wide space that, to judge by its ceiling, had been hacked from the bedrock. I followed Hobbes, walking briskly as he turned into yet another large chamber, one lined with rotting wine racks. It was a little disappointing as a generous gulp of wine would have fortified me nicely.

At the far end, Featherlight and Billy were holding torches as Denny shoved one of the racks aside.

'This is the door,' he said, putting his shoulder against a section of what I'd taken to be solid brickwork. With a creak it swung open to reveal a small vault.

As Featherlight aimed his torch, my eyes were caught by the pale gleam of metal. Rushing forward impulsively, intending to be first in, I was shocked when Denny shoved me roughly aside. As I fell and sprawled on the cold, wet ground, a rock, bigger than Hobbes's head, crashed down just where I would have been standing.

'Thank you,' I said, getting back to my feet.

'You must always wait. Master Gerald said Mr Duckworth di'n't wait and the rock cracked his bonce, so I had to hide him on Blacker Knob. Master Gerald said it served him right for poking his nose in where it weren't wanted. It's alright to go in now.'

Instead of being first, I was left outside, peering in, looking round Featherlight's back, while Billy opened two solid-looking steel boxes. The first one contained hundreds, maybe thousands of gold coins: the second, gold bars and papers.

Hobbes smiled. 'Well done, Denny. Thank you.'

'Pleased to help, Mr Hobbes.'

'I take it,' I said, peering in, 'that those are Colonel Squire's gold sovereigns?'

'Correct,' said Hobbes.

'And the other box?'

'That's mine.'

'That's a lot of gold,' I said, wide-eyed.

'It was a gift from a lady. I've never been sure what to do with it.'

'For a gift,' said Billy, 'that's not bad. The last one I got was a tie which was too long.'

'Sorry about that,' said Featherlight, 'but it was too tight on me.'

At the very end of the vault, in the corner, lay a small, worm-eaten, wooden chest. Billy opened it. It contained a few pieces of jewellery.

'Denzil,' asked Hobbes, 'do you know anything about this?'

'It was here when I first come down here with Master Gerald. He said it was very old.'

'How did he know?' I asked.

'It was written about in a mouldy old book Master Gerald found in the attic. He said Sir Greville had wrote it, but I don't know Sir Greville.'

'I know about him,' said Hobbes, 'because he was in Roger Jolly's Pirate Miscellany, which claimed that he sailed with Blackbeard, though the Payne family denied it and used their influence and money to suppress the book. Few copies still exist, but I have one. If I were a betting man, I'd wager that box is the last of Sir Greville's ill-gotten treasure.'

'You could well be right,' said Billy, who'd been rummaging through the contents. 'This stuff would appear to date from the late seventeenth century and contains some exquisite examples of Spanish workmanship. We'll have to tell someone.'

'Of course,' said Hobbes.

'But what are we going to do now?' I asked, suddenly aware of the lateness of the hour.

'Load it into the car and return to Sorenchester,' said Hobbes. 'Sid will be delighted to get his gold back. The robbery upset him far more than he lets on and Colonel Squire will no longer have anything to rant about.'

'I'll give you a hand,' I said, squeezing past Featherlight and attempting to pick up one of the metal boxes. I couldn't move it, couldn't even shake the coins.

Featherlight guffawed. 'Put your back into it, Caplet.'

'He'll put his back out if he strains anymore,' said Billy.

It was left to Featherlight and Denny to lift the boxes and to carry them to the hearse. Afterwards, Hobbes removed a few souvenirs from Featherlight's pockets.

'How did they get in there?' asked Featherlight, attempting a look of wide-eyed innocence that suited him as well as lipstick suits a fish.

'I have no idea,' said Hobbes, taking his mobile from his pocket. 'I'd better inform the local boys and then it'll be time to head back.'

As soon as he'd finished speaking to Sergeant Beer we started for home and, although it must have been a long, tiring drive for Billy, I slept most of the way.

I was woken by Featherlight nudging me in the ribs.

'Wake up, Caplet, you lazy git,' he said.

I rubbed my neck and blinked. 'What's happening?'

'We're back.'

We were outside Grossman's Bank, where a tired-looking, but beaming Sid, wrapped in his cloak, his breath steaming in the grey, dawn air, was waiting. I couldn't stop myself from wondering how much of his smile was down to getting his gold back and how much to having spent the night with Pinky. As I yawned and shivered, Hobbes and Denny carried the gold inside, where Siegfried was waiting.

Then we said our goodbyes and went home. I was barely awake enough to drink a cup of tea while Hobbes explained to the others what we'd been up to. Then, to my delight, Daphne kissed me, led me to my own bed and tucked me in. The sheets still retained some warmth from her body as well as a comforting hint of her scent. I slept until lunch time.

Hobbes must have been the only reason that Denny Barker was never arrested or even charged with any crime, and, despite everything he'd done, it felt like justice had been served. Without Sir Gerald's malign influence, he was a friendly, if rather dim, sort of soul, who was eager to please and help out. He stayed with us while Hobbes was tying up the last strings of the case and number 13 Blackdog Street, with Daphne and Kathy still in residence, was consequently very crowded. Despite having to sleep on the sofa, I found it a happy time. The only real problem was that Hobbes and Denny had contrived to sling hammocks in the attic and, most nights, Denny fell out with a frightful crash.

After a week, Kathy, who turned out to be quite likeable, returned to America. We all went to wave her off at the airport with promises to keep in touch, and I knew I was going to miss her. A week after that, Daphne moved back into her flat, which had been restored and was even better than before. I used to go round to see her every evening and we'd meet at lunch times too, when she could make it.

Life in Blackdog Street returned to what passed as normal, except that when I took Dregs for a walk, I had to take Denny as well. He proved no better than Dregs at catching squirrels. Then, one raw morning, just after breakfast, when Denny and Mrs Goodfellow were washing up, Hobbes put down his mug and cleared his throat.

'I'm going away for a while,' he said. 'I'm taking Denny home.'

'OK,' I said. 'How long will you be gone?'

'A while.'

Later that morning, Billy drove them away.

25

With their departure, the house felt empty and quiet. I was often at a loose end and Dregs kept wandering around morosely, as if he'd lost something. Daphne's visits always consoled him, almost as much as they did me and, after a few days, we settled into a sort of routine. Mrs Goodfellow, to my surprise, wasn't as upset by Hobbes's absence as I'd thought she would be.

'It's alright, dear,' she said. 'A week or two in the Blacker Mountains will do him a power of good.'

He didn't return in a week or two.

If possible, her cooking reached new heights, as if she was trying to lure the old fellow back, and the result was that Dregs and I, and frequently Daphne and occasionally Sid and Pinky, were exceedingly well fed. Pinky, who'd hit it off amazingly well with Sid, had taken up permanent residence and her tea room, on the site of the unloved Café Olé, was already doing a brisk trade. We enjoyed some fine times and my feelings for Daphne grew, so that, for some time, she occupied my thoughts most of the day and quite a lot of the night.

Halloween came and went, as did Bonfire night and still there was no sign of Hobbes.

I read in the *Bugle* about Sir Gerald's trial in mid-November when, having pleaded guilty to theft, conspiracy to rob, assault, arson and attempted murder, he received a substantial prison sentence. Young Rupert Payne, having been diagnosed with serious mental health problems, was detained indefinitely in an institution.

As the end of November approached, Daphne and I were spending more and more time together. One evening, after we'd been to the cinema in Pigton, and were enjoying a cuddle on the sofa in her flat, she pulled away and sat up, looking serious.

'Andy,' she said, 'I would like you to stay the night. What d'you think?'

I was so taken by surprise, I was reduced to making fish faces for several seconds, before I heard myself say: 'I think I would like that.'

The following day, I moved in with her. I expected Mrs Goodfellow would be upset when I told her. Instead, her eyes twinkled and she spent a good half hour embarrassing me and poking me in the ribs. It was all very trying, but I forgave her on account of all her past kindness, especially when she invited us to a celebratory supper. It was of course the best meal I'd ever tasted, which was saying a lot, and was washed down with a bottle of Hobbes's best red wine. It made me realise how much I was going to miss her cooking and it said something about my feelings for Daphne that this seemed a fair price to pay.

The next surprising event came the following day when, by chance, I found a job, even if it was only a part-time one. We were at Pinky's Tearoom and I was telling Sid about our last supper, getting so carried away with enthusiasm for the old girl's beef and oyster pie that phrases like 'love in a crust' and 'fresh as an ocean breeze' sprang to my lips.

A young man approached.

'Hi, Andy,' he said. 'Sorry to interrupt you.'

'Oh ... Hi, Phil,' I said, recognising Phil Waring, who'd been my colleague at the *Bugle*, and whose life I'd saved when he was about to become an unwilling blood donor to a wannabe vampire. Since then, our careers had diverged. I was unemployed; he was the editor.

'I couldn't help overhearing you,' he said.

'Sorry.'

'What I mean is this. Can you write about food as well as you talk about it?'

'Umm ...' I began, before catching Daphne's look, 'yes, I expect so. Why?'

'Well,' said Phil, 'the Fatman is retiring and the *Bugle* needs a new food writer. How about it?'

'Great,' I said. 'When do I start?'

'How about next Monday?'

'Why not? I'll see you then.'

December arrived with still no word from Hobbes. On Christmas Eve, I went to see Mrs Goodfellow, taking her a little something bought with my first pay. After fighting off Dregs's friendly exuberance, I was enjoying a cup of tea, while discussing Christmas dinner, to which Daphne and I, Sid and Pinky, Featherlight and Billy had been invited. The old girl was chatting about teeth, while working out how to fit an ostrich-sized turkey into the oven, when Dregs leapt to his feet with a deafening volley of excited barking.

In walked Hobbes, as if he'd never been away.

'Afternoon,' he said, pulling up a chair. 'Is there any tea in the pot?'

Continue Your Unhuman Journey

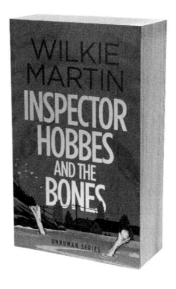

Inspector Hobbes and the Bones
unhuman IV

Wilkie Martin

Start reading here:

go.wilkiemartin.com/hobbes-bones-book2look

Join The Unhuman Readers

FREE ON SIGN UP

Sign up for Wilkie's Readers' List and get a free download copy of *Sorenchester Book Maps,* and see where everything takes place. You can also download a free copy of *Relative Disasters* – his little book of silly verse and *Hobbes's Choice Recipes* by Wilkie as A. C. Caplet.

Be amongst the first to hear about Wilkie's new books, publications and products and for exclusive giveaways.

Join here
go.wilkiemartin.com/join-readers-list

WILKIE MARTIN

Wilkie Martin's first novel *Inspector Hobbes and the Blood*, also published by The Witcherley Book Company, was shortlisted for the Impress Prize for New Writers in 2012 under its original title: *Inspector Hobbes*. As well as novels, Wilkie writes short stories and silly poems, some of which are available on YouTube. Like his characters, he relishes a good curry, which he enjoys cooking. In his spare time, he is a qualified scuba-diving instructor, and a guitar twanger who should be stopped.

Born in Nottingham, he went to school in Sutton Coldfield, studied at the University of Leeds, worked in Cheltenham for 25 years, and now lives in the Cotswolds with his partner of 30 years.

wilkiemartin.com   Wilkie Martin Author Page facebook

A Note From The Author

I want to thank you for reading my book. As a new author, one of my biggest challenges is getting known and finding readers. I'm thrilled you have read it and hope you enjoyed it; if you did I would really appreciate you letting your friends and family know. Even a quick Instagram or Facebook status update or a tweet really can make a difference, or if you want to write a review then that would be fantastic. I'd also love to hear from you, so send me a message and let me know what you thought of the book. Thank you for your time.
Wilkie

Share Inspector Hobbes and the Gold Diggers

go.wilkiemartin.com/hobbes-golddiggers-book2look

Acknowledgements

Once again, I would like to thank the members of Catchword for their support, guidance and encouragement: Liz Carew, Dr Jennifer Cryer, Derek Healy, Richard Hensley, Nick John, Sarah King, Dr Rona Laycock, Jan Petrie and Susannah White.

I would like to thank Ultimate Proof Ltd for copy-editing and for proofreading, and Stuart Bache of Books Covered Ltd for the series covers.

Writers in the Brewery and the members of Gloucestershire Writers' Network have also provided much appreciated support.

Finally, a huge thank you to my family, to Julia, and to The Witcherley Book Company.

Printed in Great Britain
by Amazon

34402435R00189